THE LAST MESSENGER

Jonathan Mark

About the Author

Jonathan Mark is the pen name for Mark Stephenson. After nearly forty years working in finance in the City of London, he retired early to pursue his long-held ambition to write novels. He lives in Essex with his wife Lin. He also spends long periods in Cornwall where the restless seas and wild coast line provide inspiration for many stories, just as they did for Daphne du Maurier.

To kick start his writing career he completed an MA in Crime and Thriller writing at City University London. At the time, this course was the only creative writing MA in the country which focused on commercial crime fiction. The Last Messenger was the novel submitted to complete the MA. It is a story which evolved from a novel collecting dust in his desk drawer for over twenty years. Literary Agents advised that there was no longer a demand for conspiracy thrillers. Therefore, it is with a streak of bloody minded and perhaps misguided optimism that he's brought this book to print himself.

Check out his website at Jonathanmarkwriter.com and follow him on Twitter @jonmark1956.

For Lin:

Thanks for believing in my dream.

THE LAST MESSENGER

Prologue

Kandahar, Afghanistan. August 20th 1998

No one saw the bright light pierce the sky.

He remembered his daughter's smiling face looking back, her veil floating on the evening breeze; the same pink veil her mother had worn on their wedding day. A vision of happiness as she disappeared into the house to prepare for the first night with her husband. He would never forget that last second before his life changed. The last moment before the missile disintegrated his home and destroyed the people he loved.

It took less than five seconds.

The blast threw him off his feet and when the smoke cleared there was nothing left but devastation. His love had turned to hate. He was on his knees clawing at the rubble with his bare hands. Voices around him were shouting but he could not hear. All he could find was a small piece of the wedding veil, embroidered with flowers by his grandmother. A veil to be passed down the generations.

Not anymore.

No longer a symbol of love. In the man's mind, the veil represented his reason to hate America.

It had been a good day. A day of celebration. A proud moment when a father sees his daughter marry. The ceremony had been held late because of the heat, stopping for evening prayer before food was served – lamb with rice and tomatoes. His guests sat at tables laid out in the open, with covers for shade. There was no music because the Taliban forbade it, but nothing would dampen the high spirits of his guests. They fired Kalashnikovs into the sky and peeled oranges for the young groom, making jokes about his prowess in the bedroom. They hoisted him high and fired their guns again.

Collateral damage, the Americans called it, but this man called it murder.

Vienna, Austria. May 15th 2004

I can't hide for ever.

The Schonbrunn Palace gardens is a good place to hand over the truth. I'm standing at the foot of the Gloriette arches, admiring Maria Theresa's symbol of Hapsburg imperial power. I'm here because I want to stand up against the power of the state, lifting my head above the parapet, waiting for it to be shot off. I'm here to provide answers for the falling man. The nameless person plunging to his death from the North Tower. I watch the dusk descending on the palace below and see thousands of people melt into the vast Baroque landscape. I think of the two thousand that died on that day. Why was I not one of them?

Unless I do this, I have no life.

Lost in thought, I don't notice a man approach until I hear his voice. He is speaking English in a heavy German accent.

'Do you know there are thirty-two sculptures in the Great Parterre?'

The question seems out of context because the man's eyes are peering upwards and not taking in the French gardens where the sculptures reside. But this is the question I want to hear. His call sign.

3

'I want to see the Goddess Angerona,' I reply.

'Ah yes. I know…the goddess of anger and fear.'

'Some say the goddess of silence.'

We walk down the hill. The nearest person must be thirty metres away. It feels safe.

'Do you have the recording?' the German man says, gesturing to a carrier bag he is holding with the palace image printed on the paper. I nod and drop a disk into the bag.

The German man is looking around, pensive, as if he expects something to happen. He speaks again, his eyes darting from left to right. 'Why don't you go to the US and give evidence? Why all this secrecy?'

'I have my reasons,' I reply. 'When you hear the contents of the disk, I hope you'll understand.'

But the man doesn't want to listen to the disk. Something is wrong.

Other men come from nowhere. It's over in seconds. A gun digs into my ribs. I'm being frogmarched to the exit. Four of them surround me. I wince with pain as my arm is twisted round my back. It's all been too easy. The German man from the embassy has disappeared. I don't know whether he has got the disk or handed to my captors. At least they know I'm not bluffing.

'Don't say a word,' one of the men shouts with an American accent. East Coast I think. 'If you do, we'll kill you anyway.'

It takes several minutes to reach the road; time to think about options. But there are none. Don't scream, don't struggle, let them take you, most of all do nothing and wait. The familiar voice of the woman I love rings in my head, issuing instructions. I'll do anything for her. Even allow myself to be taken by the CIA. I was naive to expect that Langley would allow my evidence to be heard by the 9/11 Commission. I just had to try.

Reaching the entrance to the gardens, a black BMW 7 series screeches to a halt, the door opening before it stops. Two of the men disappear into the crowded street and the others bundle me into the car. It drives at speed around the Ringstrasse before turning into the cobbled streets of the old city.

The rescue team hit the BMW as they enter a small square. A Fiat Punto jams on its brakes crossing the path of the BMW, too late to avoid a collision; the BMW smashes into the Punto's side door. Another Punto rams the rear wing, pushing the BMW like a sandwich further into the wreckage of the leading car.

'What the fuck!' the driver of the BMW screams, swinging into reverse, the tyres burning smoke onto the cobbles. The car's superior horsepower pushes the Punto until it's wedged fast into a doorway. The cars are not going anywhere. Four men emerge from the Fiats, scarves over their mouths, their AK's firing warning shots into the windows and tyres of the BMW. My captors don't seem ready to return fire. They know they are dealing with professionals. A hand pulls me out of the car.

One of the braver CIA men fires his Glock. The bullet is wide of the mark but bounces off the wall into one of the rescuer's arm. It's only a scratch but I can see the man is angry. As the injured man lifts his gun, one of the others pushes the barrel away.

There are few bystanders about in the square but I'm aware of their screams. It takes no more than two minutes and I'm in another car heading out of Vienna.

Chapter One

London. July 7th 2005

It wasn't the first time Richard Helford had seen fear in a man's eyes in the moments before death. In Iraq, he had been alert to the danger, but he didn't expect to face it on the Piccadilly Line.

A young man had got on at Kings Cross – a bearded West Indian. He'd caught Richard's eye because of the backpack, which took more than its fair share of the limited space. Now they were no more than three or four metres apart. The man looked unsettled, nervous, fidgeting with his pockets even though people were pressed against him. No one else seemed to notice, or perhaps they did notice, but held back. Richard stared, experiencing the same feeling he had when he approached the men in Basra with their broken-down car, alone on an empty dusty road.

It couldn't be.

He tried to tell himself he was being paranoid, but the memory of the suicide bomb wouldn't go away. He tried to shut it out, turning to avoid the man's eyes. As the *Mind the Doors* signal sounded, he leaned forward, bending his neck to avoid the curve of the door. It closed, catching a coat and preventing the train from leaving. The doors slid open again before slamming closed once more. The train seemed to cough as it started moving forward into the darkness.

He saw the blinding flash before he heard the explosion.

An ear-splitting bang lifting the train off the rails. A stream of orange flame came rushing down the side of the carriage, fighting to break free, nowhere to go but up against the roof of the tunnel. The force threw Richard against the ceiling, making him crack his head on a handrail. A gust of hot air littered with glass shards flew through the carriage like a jagged hailstorm, puncturing everything it touched. Then the carriage shuddered and with a violent jolt Richard was flung forward, crashing against the people around him.

Then darkness. Horrible darkness, mixed with smoke and dust and screams. His head spinning, feeling nothing. Choking smoke engulfing him, burning his lungs until he could barely breathe. For a moment, he thought he was back on the streets of Basra, covered in rubble, body parts strewn across a filthy street and a mother with a child standing frozen to the spot.

His eyes opened. Something soft lay on top of him. A woman; her perfume lingering through the acrid smell of smoke and dust. His head was buried in her chest and his hand touched her face.

'Oh shit,' Richard cried, struggling to move. Somehow he managed to pull himself free. As the smoke cleared a little, he could see the woman's charred face covered in blood. The screams were distant, just like those he heard from the woman in Basra; her baby splattered with spots of blood and flesh from the bomber. His ears were ringing and his mouth was dry with the smoke. He blinked, trying to focus, but every time he closed his eyes the horror of Basra invaded his mind. The smell of cordite burning his nostrils, brown smoke spiralling upwards. He no longer knew where he was. Reaching out, he took hold of the woman's arm, trying to help her stand, but it was no longer attached to her body. He dropped the arm, recoiling; his chest tightening with panic. She was dead, he could see that now, the way her head lolled on one side. She must have saved his life by taking the full force of the blast.

7

Everything seemed to move in slow motion. He could hear the driver shouting above the screams, telling people not to panic, that he would get them out. The train's emergency lights barely penetrated the smoke, but somehow Richard managed to crawl forward over the bodies.

'Just stay calm,' Richard shouted an order to himself. Nobody else was listening. His voice sounded muffled. In the blur of smoke, he gasped for air and his throat felt like he'd swallowed splinters of glass. There were dark, hazy shapes in the gloom. A strange smell invaded the carriage. A pungent awful scent of roasting flesh, just like when they burnt the cows on his uncle's farm to avoid foot and mouth disease.

Just like the smell of death in Iraq.

He remembered the body parts strewn everywhere across the street, but most of all he remembered the little girl, a discarded doll, arms twisted in unreal ways, her body mutilated beyond recognition. The memory seemed to blot out the reality of here and now; a disbelief that it was happening again. The past was merging with the present, and still creating a vision of hell.

A man was calling for help, only a few feet from where the bomb had detonated. His voice seemed to rise above the screams. It held a note of familiarity which demanded Richard's attention. It was fortunate that the man was on Richard's side of the carriage because it would have been impossible to get across to him; the train was almost split in two. One of the man's arms had gone and his legs were trapped. Glass and metal protruded from his gut and blood was pumping from his arm. Richard knew a tourniquet was useless as there was no stump to tie it round and the loss of blood was too great. He took off his jacket and tried to stem the flow. It was like pushing a rag up a leaking pipe – no use.

'We'll get you out,' Richard whispered.

The man looked no more than thirty and was Middle Eastern in appearance. A gash in his cheek had folded back the skin and the artery below had severed. Tears mingled with the blood, cleansing the black soot that covered his face. His eyes begged Richard to do something, but there was nothing he could do. He took hold of the man's unharmed hand and felt something in his grip. Leaning closer, he could see his lips moving.

'It's you,' he said.

Richard said nothing, unsure how to respond.

The man's one good arm shook as he tried to raise it nearer to Richard. His lips were quivering as he attempted to speak. Richard leaned closer.

'I'm here…' He coughed and blood seeped from his mouth. 'You...' He paused again, fighting for breath. 'T…Tell Amira I love her and give her this,' he spluttered and more blood pumped from the severed artery in his cheek. 'Sh…She's my wife.'

'Of course I will,' Richard replied, struggling not to look away. He could feel the man's blood on his own cheek and felt repulsed at the pitiful sight of the wrecked body before him.

'What's your name?' Richard knelt forward, once more putting his ear close to the man's lips.

'Masood.'

'Hello, Masood, I'm Richard.'

A flicker of a smile crossed Masood's lips. 'I know,' he said.

'What do you know?'

'You.'

'Me.?'

'It means lucky…My name…lucky.'

Richard smiled back, appalled by his own helplessness. He took hold of Masood's wrist and felt his pulse fade to death.

The driver shouted again. 'I can't raise Line Control, I'll open the emergency door at the front of the train and lower a ladder down so you can get on the track. You'll be able to get out then and walk to Russell Square.'

All Richard could see was the driver in silhouette, issuing instructions.

'You can get out now,' the driver shouted. 'I've lowered the ladder. When you get down, don't touch the track, whatever you do. It may be live.' But Richard wasn't going anywhere.

It seemed like ages before the paramedics arrived. 'You're too late,' he sobbed. They checked for Masood's heartbeat, but finding nothing, quickly moved on. Richard's hand still clutched Masood, whose fingers were locked around the object Richard had promised to take to his wife. Slowly, he prised open the dead man's vice-like grip. It was still too dark to see, but he felt something small and metallic. Without looking, he put it in his pocket and turned away.

'You should go now,' a medic said, taking hold of his arm. Richard instinctively nodded, allowing himself to be guided towards the steps from the carriage down onto the track. Faint lights from Russell Square beckoned in the distance, a blur through the gloom. A smell that made him retch. He could hardly see anything, but a few people walking in front of him guided his way. When he reached the open and blinked at the daylight, London air had never smelt so sweet. Sirens were blaring and lights flashed. A blanket was thrown over his shoulders.

'We need to get you cleaned up,' the man who led him out of the tunnel said. 'You're covered in blood.'

'But none of it's my own,' said Richard. 'Why is none of it mine?'

Chapter Two

London. July 8th 2005

'We need to debrief you,' said Rowena. 'When are you getting discharged?'

Richard looked up from his hospital bed and felt sick. 'Thanks for coming,' he said. 'You must be pretty busy at Vauxhall Cross after the bombing.'

'We are,' she replied. 'Did you see anything that might help us?'

Richard closed his eyes and felt his throat tighten. The memory of the moment before the explosion was trapped in his mind – images of the face he'd tried not to notice. What made it worse was that he'd cheated death for the second time.

'I saw the bomber,' he said quietly.

Rowena looked more surprised than shocked. 'How do you know you saw him?'

'It was him all right. No doubt about it. He was scared shitless. He knew he was going to die and I let him do it.' Richard stared at his shaking hands. He grabbed the sheets and scrunched them together, embarrassed by his own despair. He tried to control his voice, which was breaking with emotion. 'Scared out of his tiny mind…carrying a backpack. A West Indian. I couldn't get to him…I should have shouted.'

Rowena took hold of his hand. 'Listen to me, Richard,' she said in a surprisingly soft voice. 'What good would that have done? It was too late to stop him.'

He turned away from her sympathetic stare. The last thing he wanted was her understanding; a declaration of his own weakness.

'It reminded me of Iraq. The suicide bomb,' he said. 'I sensed something was wrong on that day and didn't act and now this. I don't know what I've done to be caught up in something like this twice.' He stopped and collected himself, taking a glass from the bedside table, gulping some water down to calm his nerves. 'The SAS guy who was blown up, I should have told him to wait in the truck.'

'It wasn't your job to protect him,' she replied coldly. 'He was supposed to save *you*.'

Richard looked at Rowena and then down at his hand that she continued to hold. 'I don't give a shit about whose job it was…that guy…I'll never forget his name – Sergeant Bill Riordan – he had a wife and a kid who now has no father.' He paused and wiped the sweat off his face. 'And now this has happened…all those people dead?'

'Don't beat yourself up over this, Richard. You're in shock and rightly so. You nearly died,' she said, loosening her grip on his hand.

'That's all very well, but you weren't brought back from Iraq in disgrace. Is it any wonder that I think I fucked up by not stopping this guy?'

'You were traumatised by the bomb. That's why we brought you back.'

'That's bullshit, Rowena, and you know it. I was doing okay working on that operation with the Americans.'

Rowena glared at him, looking around to see if anybody was listening. 'That's secret you know. Shut the fuck up,' she said in a low voice, before standing up abruptly and peering out of the window. Anything not to look me in the eye, he thought.

The uneasiness between them dissolved into silence. Richard's mind flashed back to the final days before he left Basra. He'd been working with a CIA guy called Harper who he'd got on with really well, stopping to have a beer after their long days processing detainees. He'd praised Richard's reports on the interrogations of insurgents saying that there was enough detail without the wild west stuff. By that he meant food deprivation, loud music, plenty of disorientation techniques, but never anything really heavy, like water boarding. Then without any warning their friendship changed. Richard saw him once after the bombing and was surprised Harper never asked him how he was. He remembered the coldness between them and when Richard heard he was being sent back to London, Harper refused to see him despite several attempts to say goodbye.

Rowena was the first to say something. 'We think we know who the bomber is,' she said choosing to change the subject.

'Was,' he corrected her, trying to regain some control over the way he felt inside.

'He's called Jermaine Lindsay,' she said, ignoring his interruption. 'MI5 knew about him, but he wasn't under active surveillance. He's only nineteen. How the hell were we to know he'd want to kill himself and twenty-six other poor bastards?'

'Twenty-six! Oh shit, that many.'

'There were three more bombs. More people died.'

Richard swallowed and breathed deeply. His voice softened. 'I'm sorry for being a fucking wreck. I'll be okay. It's just hard to come to terms with what happened.' He paused for a few seconds, wondering if he should tell her. 'You know, I watched one of them die. Middle Eastern, I think…called Masood.'

'An Arab?' Rowena looked mildly interested. 'Did he say anything to you?'

'Nothing of interest,' he lied. 'Look. I'll come in to work tomorrow, we can talk about it then. I'm pretty knackered. I didn't sleep a wink last night and I need to get my head around this shit so I can be of some use to you.'

Rowena leaned forward and touched his arm, the earlier hostility over his time in Iraq had disappeared. She looked concerned.

'Don't worry,' Rowena replied. 'When you're feeling up to it.'

He found himself comparing her sharpness and strong will to the softness and emotional depth of Becky. How things might have been different if he hadn't argued with Becky last night. If only he'd stayed in bed, made love, and missed the train. Instead he left for work early, leaving his girlfriend sleeping, hoping to avoid another confrontation. Rowena was nothing like Becky. Her tailored Jaeger suits reflected her personality. Rowena wasn't the marrying type. She was a classicist, just like himself, but from Oxford whereas he'd come down from Cambridge. Their paths had crossed in the Service because they both spoke Arabic. As he looked at her he realised how much they had in common. Except he'd blown it in Iraq and she was a rising star. Now he was on the Greek desk, an intelligence backwater because they couldn't trust him with the big boys fighting terrorism. They'd chosen him for the job because nobody else wanted it, and besides he could speak Greek just as well as his Arabic. He'd learnt several languages as a child while his father took the family abroad on postings with his bank. Five years in Cairo to learn Arabic and five years in Athens, long enough to master modern Greek, which helped his Classics degree at Cambridge.

'I've got to go,' Rowena said, looking at her watch. 'We'll see you tomorrow. But only if you feel up to it,' she added.

He nodded and tried to smile, but every inch of his body hurt. His face, covered in small cuts made by the flying glass, felt like it had been scraped by sandpaper. The ten stitches in his arm itched like hell and his ears

14

were still ringing from the bang that had almost blown his eardrums.

Alone again, he turned his pillow to face the blank wall, his mind spinning back to the events of the day before. They'd brought him to Royal London Hospital in Whitechapel, insisting he stay overnight for observation. He hated hospitals and last night hadn't altered his opinion. Unable to sleep, those first few minutes after the explosion replayed on a loop in his mind. The sight of Masood, tears in his eyes, gasping his final breath. The smell of the dead woman's perfume lingering on her shattered corpse. The piercing screams and, most of all, the limbs lying loose like discarded cuts of meat on a butcher's floor.

No matter how hard he tried to sleep, Masood's dying face kept interrupting his thoughts and demanding attention. There was something familiar about him even though the bomb had disfigured the Arab's face. Richard had seen plenty of blown-up bodies in Iraq, but somehow these seemed less personal than what he'd seen yesterday. It was the same when he saw Bill Riordan's body; he'd shared a moment of his life with the people lying dead on that train.

In the middle of the night, he'd examined the object Masood had given him. It was a small oval silver frame fringed with emeralds and holding a picture of a saint. It looked like a Christian motif as the halo was prominent, but he had no idea who the saint was. He'd assumed Masood was a Muslim, so why should he hold a picture of a Christian saint? His fingers traced the intricate drawings embossed into the silver, including a shield with three trees, joined in a triangle by a single line. Below the shield, a dragon with many heads stared out with menace. Masood's last words troubled him. He'd said, 'I know,' and when Richard had asked Masood what did he know, he'd replied, 'You.' Could they have met before in Iraq?

He didn't think so. But if they had, why were they on the same train, a train that he so nearly missed. The coincidence would be staggering.

It was less than a year since Basra and only now, triggered by the bomb, could he begin to remember some of the details. Ever since that day, he'd blanked Iraq from his mind, but now it was there in all its excruciating detail, as if the bomb on the train had unlocked a box lost in the recesses of his brain. On the train, he'd imagined the face of the little girl and the mother holding the baby. For the first time, he remembered getting out of the truck, trying to warn Bill. That's why he was blown off his feet; why he saw that hysterical woman with the child, frozen with fear; why he'd been covered in rubble. But the clearer the day in Iraq became, the more he was sure there was something missing from his memory. It would be a small insignificant action that you'd normally not retain, but if he recalled it now, maybe he could work out the connection with Masood.

Something else surprised him. As he lay awake, tossing and turning, trying to make sense of what had happened, he found himself clinging to the most tenuous of threads. He thought about his dead father. It was nearly four years since he'd died and not once had Richard felt sad or shed a tear for his loss. When the job came up in Iraq, he took it to prove something to himself: he was man enough to face his father even in death. When he came back to London in disgrace, he remembered being pleased his father was dead because he wouldn't have to hang his head in shame in front of him. At that moment, listening to the groans of the injured around him in the hospital, he felt a wave of grief. His pillow was wet with tears he couldn't control. He was weeping for the father he never knew. A man who never had time for him, who travelled the world but never kicked a ball in the garden with his son, a man who wasn't there on his graduation and never praised him for doing anything good. But when the bomb went off, they were united by a deadly coincidence.

It was the link to 9/11 which intrigued him. They'd never found his father's body and they weren't even sure he was in the North Tower when the plane hit. When Richard heard the news, he was so indifferent to the circumstances behind the death, he couldn't even be bothered to ask his mother how the FBI had reached that conclusion, except to say that he'd vanished on 9/11.

Lots of people faked their deaths on that terrible day.

The fact they'd both been involved in a major terrorist incident bound them together in Richard's mind. After all the apathy, the violence they'd shared made him wonder whether his father had been killed instantly or suffered the sight of burnt charred bodies, just like he had.

Before yesterday, he hadn't made the connection between his experiences in Iraq and his father's death because he decided suicide bombs were an everyday occurrence in the Middle East and he was just unlucky. But the bomb in London had changed all that. There were so many unanswered questions. Why did Masood recognise him? Rowena had said he was traumatised by the bomb in Iraq but he was sure she was holding something back. Why had Harper refused to speak to him when they'd been so friendly. And now, he knew it was a leap of faith to connect these questions to his father's death. It was a gut feeling, but the more he thought about Iraq, the more he wanted to know exactly what happened to his father. Something in the back of his mind was telling him that, with his father dead, he was now the target? He wrestled with his memory searching for a fragment of truth.

The face of the suicide bomber loomed in his head, eyes staring intently in his direction.

Richard sighed and picked up his mobile phone. His voicemail had twelve messages and seven were from his mother. Becky had called, but was just crying down the telephone without really saying anything.

He called his mother's number. It rang only three times before the phone was picked up.

'That was quick, Mother. It's me. Richard.'

She said nothing. All he could hear was her breathing.

'Mother, it's me. Are you there? Are you all right?'

At last, she spoke. 'Richard, thank God you're safe. I've been sick...you know...worried sick.' Her voice was slurring, as if she been sedated or, more likely, was under the influence of drink.

'I'm okay, Mother. Sorry I didn't call after it happened. I didn't mean to make you worry. I didn't think – I was in shock.'

'They called me last night. How do you think I felt? V...Very s...selfish of you.'

'I'm sorry. Are you sure you're all right?'

She was right. He was a selfish bastard. Selfish to Becky and now selfish to his own mother. The truth was he hadn't wanted to speak to his mother after it happened. She'd never been the sort to smother him and go overboard with kisses and affection. He'd always felt that he was a hindrance, preventing her from following his father around the world.

'I'll come and see you...how about Sunday lunch?' He hesitated a little. 'I need to talk to you about Dad.' There was an uneasy silence. His mother had told him many times that his father was a great man and in her weaker moments, when she'd had too much whisky, that Richard wasn't good enough to wipe his father's boots.

'Why do you want to talk about your father?' She sounded suspicious.

'Don't you see, Mother? I never knew him. He was always away and when he was at home, he had no time for me. Then he goes and dies in a terrorist attack, and I'm spared in a similar situation, in Iraq and now in London. I'm just trying to make sense of it. '

'There doesn't have to be a reason for everything,' his mother said. 'Sometimes things just happen. There is no explanation.'

'That may be so,' said Richard. 'But when I was lying in hospital I suddenly started thinking about him, you know wondering how he died and whether he'd suffered like me. I realised I know nothing about the man. I don't even know what the FBI said which put him in the towers at the time they came down.'

There was silence as if she was thinking what it might lead to. He thought he heard her sigh.

'Of course, we must talk,' she said at last. 'It's strange but I've been thinking about your father a lot recently. I need to tell you something …I'll see you Sunday then. Do you want to bring Becky?'

'No,' he said, rather too strongly. 'This is something I need to discuss with you alone.'

Becky arrived an hour later. She rushed in, flinging her arms around Richard's neck. He winced as she kissed his cut face and lips.

'Darling. You look terrible,' she said with a broad smile so he knew she was joking. 'They wouldn't allow visitors to non-urgent patients yesterday. They said there was too much going on treating the bomb victims. I tried to persuade them but they still wouldn't let me see you.' She hugged him again. 'They said you were alive and okay but that didn't stop me having a sleepless night worrying about you.'

'You look great,' Richard said. It wasn't a lazy remark, she looked wonderful. Her long blonde hair shone under the bright hospital lights. She wore a black Armani trouser suit with the pearls he'd given her draped around her neck, just above the collar of a white silk shirt with ruffled collar. Sexy, not severe like Rowena.

'I'm on my way to work. A bit out of the way, but I had to see how you were.'

'I'm okay,' he said quietly. 'Just a few scratches, I'll be out tomorrow. I'm one of the lucky ones. Nothing to worry about.' But there was everything to worry about. He knew that and he thought she knew it also. 'I'm sorry, Becky,' he continued. 'I'm not myself at the moment. I'm sorry we argued.'

'It's all forgotten,' she replied, kissing his cheek a little more tenderly this time. 'You've been through so much. You might have been killed and then where would I be?' She stood up, releasing her embrace. He sighed, relieved she'd let him go. Being close was comforting, but he resisted the impulse to respond. The bomb had changed his need for security. It was as if a hidden force was closing a door, separating him from his emotions.

'Better off without me,' he replied, a note of sarcasm in his voice. His cheek burned where she'd kissed the scratches on his face.

'Nonsense, darling. I love you.'

She sounded genuine and that made him feel worse. He didn't like confrontation. It was why he'd never argued with his father. For a moment, there was an awkward silence.

She leaned forward onto his bed and took hold of his hands. They felt soft and he wanted to squeeze them, to acknowledge that he appreciated her concern.

'Besides, it was my fault, talking about weddings. I must have driven you crazy,' she said. 'It's just that when he got engaged I thought getting married was the natural next step.'

His eyes were watery; an involuntary action. Deep down he wanted to love her. 'I'm sorry, Becky. I'm in a hopeless mess after this bomb, I need some space...to work things through...to be on my own.'

Becky's eyes widened. She frowned. 'I don't understand...What do you mean, you want to be on your own?'

Richard took a glass of water from beside his bed and didn't stop drinking until it was gone. He placed the glass back carefully, using every available second to delay what he was about to say. At last he spoke; his voice was soft, almost a whisper. 'I never told you what happened in Iraq, did I?'

She looked at him, taken aback by what he was saying. 'No, you didn't, but what's that got to do with us?'

Although he stared, he couldn't look her in the eye. The memories were too overwhelming. He spoke slowly and deliberately. 'I was close to a suicide bomb in Basra...my driver was killed and then they sent me back to London, claiming I was traumatised.'

She gripped his other hand. He could see an expression of horror on her face. 'You poor thing,' she said. 'No wonder you wouldn't talk about it.' Her face became more serious. 'If you love me, you should be able to share something as awful as that.' She stood up and kissed his forehead. 'I often wondered what happened, but know that your job doesn't allow you to talk about these things. I didn't want to press.' She leaned forward onto the bed and looked fixedly into his eyes. 'But I don't understand why you think you wouldn't be in shock over the bomb...I mean, look at you now,' she continued.

'I know. It's just that...' Richard could see how upset she was which made him uneasy. He hesitated, fighting back the tears. 'It's just that...what I saw yesterday reminded me of Iraq...all those bodies.' His voice broke. 'Two times...' he groaned. 'Two times I've cheated death, and my father – you know what happened to him. The FBI say he was killed in 9/11 but I don't know anything about him, because I didn't want to know.' He chuckled to himself, 'You know something, Becky. He was invisible to me in life and now in death, he's vanished into ashes. The bomb made me think about it because when you've been close to death, you wonder what you might have missed. I have to understand exactly what happened to my father. Why he never had time for me.'

Becky thought for a moment and then changed the subject. 'So what's this about disgrace? I mean, you didn't set off the bomb, did you. You didn't kill the driver…'

'The trauma thing was just an excuse. I was back at my desk two days after the bomb. There must have been something else, something I'm not remembering…Everything was fine and then without warning their attitude changed and I was bundled on a plane back to Brize Norton.'

'So why haven't you asked them before? You've been back from Iraq for almost a year.'

'Because I *was* suffering from trauma. I even convinced myself that they were telling the truth, but the London bomb has changed all that.'

'What's changed?' Becky looked shocked and Richard remembered why he wanted to love her.

'When I raised Iraq with my boss this morning, she was deliberately evasive,' he continued. 'But that's not all. In the aftermath of the London bomb, an Arab man named Masood died in my arms…He seemed to know me although I don't recall ever seeing him before.'

'Not even in Iraq?' said Becky.

'You're right, that's a possibility, but I don't remember him.'

'So what does all this mean?' She took hold of his hands and looked straight into his eyes. 'Richard darling, you don't have to go through this on your own. That's what our relationship is for – we're meant to be there for each other.'

Richard hesitated, choosing his words with great care. Before the bomb, he would have procrastinated and said, Of course it doesn't affect our relationship. But now, the door to his emotions had slammed shut and the memory of his father was holding the door closed. Masood was there in his mind's eye, his battered face smiling at him, telling him he needed answers. He tried to focus on her, but his tears were blurring his vision. Not tears for Becky. He cried for the dead people on the train. For Bill. For the woman with the baby in her arms. For Masood.

'You've got to understand; I'd make a crap husband. Look at my family. My dysfunctional dead father and my mother who drinks too much. Hardly a template for harmony.'

'It doesn't matter, honestly, Richard. I love you for yourself, not your family.'

'I know you do, but why didn't I weep for my father when he died in 9/11? I worry I'm incapable of love. It just wouldn't be fair on you.' He hated seeing her unhappy, but he forced himself to continue. 'I'm really sorry, Becky...please forgive me...I'm no good for you right now. I can't give you what you want...It's me, not you. I'm not ready to have kids. I need more time, and I need you to understand this. I need to sort my head out.'

The mention of children flicked a switch, changing Becky's demeanour in a flash; he could see it in her eyes. Her breathing became heavier. She turned her back on him and stared blankly at the wall.

'I wasn't going to tell you this…until I was sure, but what you're saying changes everything,' she said. There was no longer a sense of desperation in her voice and Richard knew why. It was her trump card; one he couldn't ignore.

'You're pregnant?' he said, immediately feeling bad about not wanting kids. He could feel Becky's eyes on him, searching for a sign that he might be happy about the news. The door in his mind had edged open a little. It was almost a relief to say the words. A smile crept onto his lips. 'That's amazing news.'

'Even though you're not ready to have kids?'

Her sarcasm cut him in two. Game, set and match. 'I apologise. I do want kids…just not immediately.'

She turned around and rested her hands on the bed, seizing on the flicker of approval and beamed. 'I never wanted to trap you, Richard,' she said. 'I love you because I know how important it is to you, to be a good father, I mean, to make up for the way your father treated you. But you do want this child…don't you?'

Her words hit him hard because she was right. Too right. 'Yes, I do…But I can't love my own child until I understand what's happening to me. It's something I've got to do on my own. I can't sit back and ignore it…and my father.' He took hold of her hands again. 'I do want the baby, I really do. I just need time to get my head together so I can be a good father. I don't want to stress you, especially now you're pregnant.'

Becky backed off. 'All this is too much for you. The baby hasn't helped.'

'I'm pleased you're having the baby. I really am.'

'Of course you are,' she replied softly. The anger had gone, but he wasn't sure whether it was because she'd accepted that he was a shit or because she really understood where he was coming from. The rational thing would be to stop questioning things and love this woman carrying his child, but the bomb had made him irrational.

Just like his father.

Chapter Three

London. July 9ᵗʰ 2005

The Secret Intelligence Service forgot to be secret when they built their headquarters at Vauxhall Cross. Some called it Legoland and others said it reminded them of an Odeon Cinema. Passing through the air-locked tube, which formed the entrance of MI6, Richard was amused to see armed security guards on edge, checking his pass more thoroughly than usual even though they knew him already by sight. He wondered how they'd react guarding the base in Basra. Although it was Saturday, it felt like a normal day. The Service was in a state of high alert, floundering to come up with intelligence on the London bombers.

By the time he got to his desk, he felt tired despite taking a taxi to avoid travelling on the Tube. There was no sign of Rowena, but a pile of files was sitting on his desk with a list of instructions. He sighed and leaned back in his chair, staring at the grey partitions that fenced him from the others on the floor. Rather than face the files, he called Becky. No matter how much he wanted to put some distance between them, he couldn't just leave her knowing she was carrying his child. He'd tried calling several times, but her phone was switched off. This time it rang, lifting his spirits. He willed her to pick up. When her voice came on the line, he felt relieved.

'Becky, it's me... Please don't hang up,' he pleaded.

'Go away, Richard. You said you want to be on your own so why are you ringing me?' Her voice sounded tired, but also angry.

'I'm back in the office…out of hospital. We should talk…What I said about the baby was shameful…It was a shock.' His words raced off his tongue, worried that she'd put the phone down.

'There's nothing to talk about. You made your position clear. You need time on your own so I'm going to give you that space.'

'But…I want to help…'

'I know you do, Richard, but I've got to be tough on you,' she replied. 'So you can work out what you're missing.'

The phone went dead. He rang her again, but this time there was no answer.

'Shit,' he cursed under his breath, slamming the phone down.

The woman on the train, her head blown away, invaded his mind without warning. It was as if she refused to allow him to do the right thing and marry Becky. Then he thought of Masood, staring through the darkness and smoke, recognising him. He closed his eyes and saw Bill in the moments after the blast, his head separated from his body. Richard wanted to be sick. He gripped the edge of the desk and controlled his breathing, trying to make sense of his feelings. He didn't want a marriage like his parents'. But what sort of parent would turn their back on their child? The horror of that day on the Tube would never leave him until he found some meaning behind it.

He stood up and walked along the row of desks, forgetting, for a moment, the way to the toilets. His colleagues didn't look up, and why should they? They were crouched over their screens, tapping away with furious intent, needing to show they were doing something about the bomb in London. Reaching the toilet, he found a cubicle and leaned over the pan. He retched, but only bile built in his mouth. He needed to empty his brain not his stomach, which was already hurting with hunger. He couldn't remember the last time he'd had a meal.

It took him a few minutes to compose himself. You give into this and your dead, he thought. He went back to his desk, picked up the first file along with Rowena's list of instructions and began to read.

First, he had to prepare a full written statement of his experience. Second, he had to investigate a list of Muslim's who were on the train. At least those that they knew about. Those who weren't injured would have just gone home to their families, thankful to be alive and given the chance to return to being anonymous and unknown to the security services. He decided that his best bet was to look at a full inventory of the injured and in doing so, get a picture of who was on the first carriage. A list of the dead would identify Masood.

He telephoned Special Branch on the secure line.

'Detective Sergeant Temple,' a voice answered. 'Who's this?'

'Richard Helford. Greek desk. I'm on the fringes of the 7/7 investigation. I was in the carriage that exploded on the Piccadilly line. I have some first-hand knowledge.'

'Okay. I'm sorry to hear that, sir. It must have been awful to be there,' said Temple.

Ignoring the comment, Richard cut to the point. 'I'm looking for information on one of the victims. He died in my arms. His name's Masood, Middle Eastern appearance. I'd guess mid-thirties.

'Hang on sir. I'll check.' It took less than a minute before Temple came back on the line. 'There is only one person we haven't identified and I think this could be your man.' said Temple. 'I'll email you some photos of the body taken by Forensics.'

It was Masood. Richard shivered when the ingrained memory of Masood's battered body became reality once more on his computer screen. It took less than an hour to identify Masood. As soon as they put his picture and name into the GCHQ database, it facial recognition software made a match in a matter of seconds even those his face was blackened by burns and disfigured by the blast. Richard's eyes widened, disbelieving what he saw on the screen. A more formal mugshot of Masood peered back at him. He read the text again in case he'd got it wrong.

He hadn't. Masood was a spy.

Masood Al Marami, a former member of the Egyptian General Intelligence Service, known to SIS. He printed off the file, which was marked confidential, meaning he could read it without extra security clearance. It was quite short, less than two pages of A4; the result of a short interview with an MI5 officer when Masood arrived in the UK in December 2003. Apparently, he'd fallen out with Omar Suleiman, the head of GIS, and had left Egypt to come to the UK because his wife, Amira, was British. She had an English mother, who'd conveniently given birth while in London. Her father was Egyptian. MI5 watched him and noticed that he went to St Mark's Coptic Church in Kensington. After a couple of weeks, they stood down the watchers, citing lack of resources, concluding that he wasn't a threat. It was strange that the report didn't go into more detail about why he'd been dismissed. Here was an Egyptian spy swanning around London and MI5 didn't care. 'He wasn't a threat, like Mohammad Atta wasn't a threat. Just like Jermaine Lindsay wasn't a threat,' he muttered to himself as he closed the file. So he was a Christian. Maybe that was why they let the guy off. That would explain the Christian icon.

But Masood recognised him. Richard was certain of it. It was true that he didn't look like a terrorist or a threat. He had such kind eyes. Maybe MI5 crossed him off the list because of his kind eyes and because he was a Christian. The penny dropped without warning. A

Christian; how could he meet a Christian in Iraq? He smiled at his own stupidity. Masood must be somebody he'd met in London, but where? The picture on his screen was very different to the man he'd seen on the train, covered in blood and with face lacerated beyond recognition.

It was time to visit Masood's wife and see what he could find out about who this guy really was.

He called Temple. 'It's Helford again. About Masood. His wife won't have heard anything and I'd like to be responsible for breaking that news as I was with him when he died.'

'That's a good idea. Makes it more personal. You'll need bereavement counsellors to go with you. I can put you in touch with someone in the Met.'

'I'll go on my own. Intelligence reasons,' he lied. 'She'll need to do a formal identification. Just give me the details of where the body is and the number she can call for counselling. I'll tell her the sad news.'

Thirty minutes later, he plucked up the courage and made the call. It took only two rings before she answered.

'Hello.' The voice was quiet, barely louder than a whisper.

'Is that Mrs Al Marami?' he said.

'Yes.'

'My name is Richard Helford. I'd like to talk to you about your husband.'

Silence.

'Are you there, Mrs Al Marami?'

'Yes, I'm here.' Her voice was breaking. 'He's dead, isn't he?'

Expecting to break the news gradually, her abrupt response threw him off guard. He swallowed, clearing his throat and choosing his words with care. 'I'm afraid so,' he replied. 'You might like to know I was with him when he died. He was on the Piccadilly line train at Kings Cross.'

'I know. I...I tried so hard to get through to the helpline, I tried all night. It was always engaged...can you believe that? Nobody would tell me.' She broke off and he could hear her sobbing. At last she spoke again, her voice breaking as she fought to hold back the tears. 'But I knew...oh yes, I knew he was dead.'

'I'm really sorry for your loss,' he said, pausing again as he listened to her crying. He waited for her to collect herself. It seemed like an age until she spoke. 'Thank you,' she said. 'You're very kind.'

'He gave me something for you. Please may I come and see you, today if possible?'

Another pause. He wanted to say something, but stayed quiet.

'Did he die in pain?' she asked.

'Let me come and see you,' he replied. 'I'll tell you everything. He was a good man; I saw that in the minutes that I knew him.'

'I know,' she said. 'Come quickly. Come now. I would like that.' There was urgency in her voice that he couldn't ignore.

A taxi to Dagenham would cost too much and the Victoria line from Vauxhall was too similar to the Piccadilly line to consider taking the Tube so soon after the bomb. He decided to walk across Vauxhall Bridge and pick up the District Line. It wouldn't be easy, but at least the carriages were larger and most of the journey would be over ground. With the traffic quiet on a Saturday, he lingered to admire the view of the Thames as he walked. A light breeze rose from the river, soothing his injured face. He hadn't shaved since before the bomb went off, to avoid opening the cuts on his face, but that fact was contributing to his dishevelled appearance as the wind blew unkempt hair over his eyes. He hoped Masood's wife would not be put off by his appearance.

Reaching the centre of the bridge, he stopped and turned to take in the view. Out of the corner of his eye, he noticed a man halt at exactly the same time and look across the river, about fifty metres behind him. With his nerves still on edge, he moved on until he'd almost completed the crossing and stopped again. The man behind continued walking. Twenty metres separated them. For a brief moment, he considered running, but held back, catching a glimpse of the man in a black tracksuit, trainers and a baseball cap. A young guy, Pakistani probably, feigning indifference, rocking to the beat of whatever was on his iPod, avoiding eye contact as he walked past. To be sure he was not being followed, Richard changed his route to Victoria, checking the man wasn't still on his tail. There was no sign of him but he remained ill at ease. Maybe he was being paranoid, but the memory of Masood recognising him suggested Richard might be right to be concerned.

Victoria station is busy every day of the week. Having a mainline station and a bus station within a few metres of the underground didn't help. As he stepped onto the platform, his hands felt clammy and his breathing exaggerated, as if he'd run a four-minute mile, making him sweat all the more. It was the middle of the day, so the trains were only part full, but he still let two go through before he boarded. When the third train arrived, he clenched his fists, chiding himself for being stupid. 'Get a grip,' he whispered as he climbed onto the train. He'd never been like this after the suicide bomb in Iraq so why now? It wasn't crowded and he found a seat. Slowly his tension began to ease. He sighed, relieved that he'd crossed the first hurdle, but still wondering how he'd cope when the Piccadilly line reopened.

Masood's house was on a long straight road of council housing, built by the government to re-house East Londoners after the First World War. The houses had been built with a front garden and were in rows of identical blocks. As more tenants purchased their houses from the councils, they'd lost their uniformity as gardens were concreted over, and double glazing, fancy doors, pebble dashing and imitation stone cladding were added to give each dwelling a personal stamp. Masood's house was no exception. It had a new white PVC door and a shiny brass knocker. He knocked. Without any delay, he heard bolts go back and a key turning in the lock.

Amira was dressed head to toe in black. She wore a veil that exposed her face but covered her head and neck. He looked at her and smiled, just as he had to Masood. He could only see her face and hands, but that made the experience more intense.

'You'd better come in,' she said, leading him into the lounge. The room was dark with the curtains drawn. A large picture of Masood, draped with a black cloth, hung above a gas fire. Candles burned on the mantelpiece below. There were two armchairs, a matching sofa and pictures of religious scenes from the Bible hanging on the walls. She offered him tea and thanked him for coming. He sat in one of the armchairs.

'I am so sorry about your loss,' he said, repeating what he'd already said on the phone, feeling uneasy in her presence. He looked at her, staring back at him with an unflinching sureness, as though she could see right into his soul.

'Thank you,' she said. Her voice was soft, barely above a whisper. She made the tea and brought it in, laying it down on a small coffee table in front of them. She poured, and for a moment they drank the tea in silence.

'You asked me a question on the phone,' Richard said.

'Yes. I asked whether he died in pain.'

'He tried to make a joke by telling me what his name means,' he replied.

'It means lucky,' she said with a hint of a smile. 'He understands the British sense of irony.'

'He was in great pain and yet he had a sense of humour and the courage to say that he loved you. I admired him for that.'

'Masood used to sit in that chair,' she said after a moment's uneasy silence.

He stood up. 'I'm so sorry. I didn't mean to offend you.'

Amira reached out and took his hand. 'Sit down,' she said. 'I was going to say that I like you sitting in that chair. You've suffered also.'

He sat down again and fumbled in his pocket, pulling out the icon Masood had given him. 'He told me to tell you that he loved you and to give you this.' He handed her the picture and as she took it, their hands touched.

'Thank you,' she said, looking at the picture. 'It's Masood's most prized possession. He took it everywhere. A picture of St Barnabas, very old, perhaps first century AD and very valuable. It's been in Masood's family for generations.' She leaned forward to let him see the icon more closely. 'Did you notice the words?' She pointed to the inscription below the picture. *'Discipulus Christi Evangelium,'* she read. 'That means, Disciple of Christ and Evangelist. There's a story that St Barnabas wrote another gospel, which was suppressed by the Christians. It's regarded as a Muslim gospel but most think it's a forgery.

'Why would Masood think this so precious that he carried it around with him? After all, it undermines your faith as Christians.'

'Masood spoke for truth. That's why he thought it was so precious. Besides, it's very old.'

'But if it is as old as you say it is, then surely it will validate that the Gospel of Barnabas did exist because of the inscription.'

'We thought that but when we ask the experts, they said it proved nothing because Barnabas was known to have worked on Matthew's gospel. Presumably, whoever revered him with that icon wanted to acknowledge the importance of Barnabas in spreading the Gospel.'

'Tell me about the etching on the back of the picture.'

'We never understood what it means. There is a shield with a cross of St George and three oak trees above the cross. A seven-headed beast has its claws wrapped around the shield.'

'So what's that to do with St Barnabas?'

'I wish I knew.'

Amira told Richard about Masood's life and how he'd escaped Cairo to get away from persecution by the Muslims. 'Don't you think it's ironic that he runs away from terrorists only to be blown up here in London where he thought he was safe?'

He knew she was lying. The MI5 report confirmed why he'd left Cairo. Thrown out of the service, it said. He must have hesitated, averting his eyes, displaying his awareness of her deceit. The lie had thrown him off balance and she knew it. He fumbled for a response. 'Yes.' he replied. 'I'm sorry London let Masood down.'

'Is there something else you want to tell me, Richard?' A note of suspicion hung in her voice. 'You don't mind me calling you Richard, do you?'

'N...No,' he said, stuttering, embarrassed at his inept attempt at a lie.

He studied her face and said nothing, biting his lip. The more he stared, the more he was moved by it. There was nothing else to distract him because her clothes covered her almost entirely. She had beautiful hands and her expression no longer appeared to accuse him.

'I need to ask you something,' he said at last. 'Did your husband ever go to Iraq?'

Amira smiled, surprised by his question. 'Why on earth would my husband want to go to Iraq with Saddam Hussein in power?'

'What about after Saddam was removed?'

'No. There was no reason.' Amira sipped her tea and looked at him. 'I can tell you are troubled by what you saw,' she said, and her concern seemed to be real. 'I can't face seeing him. You know it's the tradition for the wives of Orthodox Christians to wash their husband's body before burial, but I don't think I can do that. I couldn't bear to look at his broken body.'

'I'm afraid you'll have to identify him, so you'll have to see his face.'

Her expression changed. It showed sadness rather than fear. 'Of course, I'd forgotten about that.' Despite what she'd said earlier, he was surprised that she did not look scared at the prospect, as if she'd done it before.

'I will be honest,' he replied. 'Identification won't be easy. He must have been in great pain, but he bore it in a courageous way. I felt a great connection to him.'

Amira took his hands again and looked in his eyes.

'Tell me, Richard. Do you think it's possible for a man to be both Christian and Muslim at the same time?'

He was surprised by the question, but everything surprised him about Amira. 'I don't know whether that's possible. I'm sorry to say I don't believe in God.'

'I thought so,' she said. 'Religion has caused so much trouble in the world but that's because they forget that there is only one God. There is not a Muslim God, a Christian God and a Jewish God. There is only one God. Masood understood that.'

He nodded. 'There would be no religious wars if people understood that.'

'Exactly. There are many stories in the Bible that are also in the Koran. Masood was like that. He crossed boundaries.'

35

'He was a good man.'

'Come to the funeral. I would like that,' she said, standing up, indicating that it was time for him to go. 'Goodbye Richard.' She held out her hand in a formal way.

On the train back, he couldn't stop replaying every minute of their meeting over in his mind. An aura of sensuality surrounded Amira, which made him feel uncomfortable. She didn't belong to that house in Dagenham, and her grieving for Masood seemed unreal. If he understood Masood, he'd understand her as well. Why did he leave Cairo in a hurry? What had the Egyptian GIS discovered? Why did he seem to know Richard in those last moments on the train?

Chapter Four

North West Essex. July 10th 2005

It was a relief to leave London behind and look over the Essex countryside. In the distance, Richard could see the house where he'd spent his childhood. It seemed to mingle with the landscape. A perfect Tudor farm, but not somewhere he could call home or remember with any sense of happiness. His father had restored the buildings with a meticulous eye for detail, not that he ever got his hands dirty. How Richard would have loved to have helped his father, but his father delegated everything, including the things that any normal father would do for their son. The farm hands were the only people who showed Richard any affection, teaching him to ride and milk the cows when he was home for the holidays. He never saw his father driving a tractor or working on the roof of the listed timber barn – the work was always done by employees.

He walked up the drive to the house, enjoying the crisp air and views of wheat almost ready for harvest. Bad childhood memories didn't deter thoughts that he might one day bring his son to the farm at lambing time; it never crossed his mind that Becky might have a girl. The more he thought about Becky and the child, the more troubled he was by his own behaviour. It was as if he'd become his father, a ruthless self-centred bastard. He had to slay that demon. He had to understand his father's past.

Mother was waiting at the entrance. She looked embarrassed by her appearance, staring down at the floor rather than straight into his eyes. Her tights were laddered and her beige skirt had a large oval stain suggesting some sort of spillage. Kissing her cheek, he noticed whisky lingering on her breath. It was only two months since he'd seen her last and yet in that short space of time, she'd aged. Her face was pale and her cheeks were drawn in around the cheekbone. She was painfully thin, almost malnourished, loose fitting clothes exaggerating her emaciated figure. He remembered she always used hair dye, but now her hair was turning grey.

'How are you, Mother?' he said.

'Never mind me,' she replied. Her voice sounded anxious. 'It's you they bombed, not me. What about *you*?'

'I'm okay, Mother,' he said, shrugging his shoulders. 'My cuts will heal. At least I didn't die.'

'It must have been awful for you,' she said. 'Do you want to talk about it?'

'No,' he answered abruptly. 'Talking brings it all back. It makes things worse.'

They walked into the house and he followed her into the kitchen. The room was a mess, yesterday's plates piled up in the sink.

'I've got some lamb,' she said. 'Don't know what to do with it. Would you mind putting it in the oven for me?'

'Okay Mother. No problem. Let's stack the dishwasher first and then we'll get started. Have you got rosemary and garlic?'

'You might find some rosemary in the garden but I've no garlic.' There was a bottle of Bells on the side and he watched as she poured herself a generous glass.

'Mother, should you be drinking like that? It's too early.' he said as he began stacking the dishwasher.

His mother scowled. 'Don't lecture me.' She clutched at the bottle, nursing it like a baby. 'I'm under a lot of pressure with the farm, just keeping it going.'

Her reaction annoyed Richard. Bending down stacking dishes, his head hurt; he wondered why he was here when three days ago he'd watched people die. He breathed deeply, trying to stay calm when deep down he wanted to get angry and throw the plates around the kitchen.

'Doesn't the farm manager handle that? What's his name…Joe, isn't it?' he asked sharply.

'Yes. It's Joe. Don't know what I'd do without him,' she replied.

He sighed. 'I know Joe's a great help, but it's been nearly four years since Dad died,' he said, feeling strange using 'Dad' rather than 'Father'. The former seemed to be too familiar and not what his relationship represented. 'Don't you find this house too big and the farm a huge responsibility? Are you sure you can cope?'

'Of course it's too big,' she snapped 'but he wouldn't want me to sell it. Joe does an excellent job.' Richard noticed she was speaking as if his father was still alive. 'Besides, I like doing the wages and discussing the accounts with him,' she continued.

He watched as she paced the room, clenching her fists. 'I'm not saying you should sell it,' Richard pressed, with a reassuring glance in her direction. 'It's just that you don't look well. You're losing weight. Have you been to the doctor?'

'A doctor is the last thing I need,' she retorted angrily.

He changed tack. 'Looks like we should get a good yield from the wheat.'

'Yes,' she agreed.

'But yields of wheat are hardly you, Mother. The trouble is, you always do what Dad would do, but is it what *you* want, now that he's not here anymore?'

'Your father was my life,' she replied quietly, a note of regret in her voice.

'But it's nearly four years since he died. You need to move on,' he replied, exasperated by her willingness to accept the status quo.

He went out into the garden to see if he could find some rosemary. Being outside cooled his frustration. It wasn't her fault; he was sure of that. There were weeds everywhere and the grass looked long. In a corner he found a large straggly rosemary bush that had been left to run wild. He cut some sprigs and went back inside. His mother had gone and so had the bottle. The meat was still in the Waitrose wrapping. He tore it off and screwed the clingfilm into a tight ball, annoyed that they hadn't used lamb from the farm.

After putting the meat into the Aga, he found her in the sitting room; he could see the whisky had been topped up.

'Why didn't you get Joe to give you some lamb from the farm?' he asked.

'I couldn't do that. I become too attached to the lambs after giving them a bottle.'

'A motherly bond., is that it?' he said sarcastically. 'Shame you never gave that to me.'

Her face reddened, clearly hurt by his remarks. Her eyes fought back tears.

'I'm sorry. That was uncalled for,' he said awkwardly. 'I apologise.'

She said nothing and took another swig of whisky. 'Don't apologise. You're right to call me a terrible mother. It's just that...I...I lost your father the moment you were born.' Her voice was breaking and beginning to slur. 'His job in the City became his passion, every minute of the blasted day...travelling all over the world...no interest in family life and being near you...I'm...' She stopped and took another sip. 'I'm sure he loved you...he just couldn't show it...you know what I mean...I suppose...' She stopped again, struggling with her choice of words. 'I resented you because your presence affected how he treated me. That's probably why I was so hard on you.'

Richard stared at his mother and felt sorry for her; trapped by his unthinking egotistical father. She sat on the edge of the sofa, fondling the whisky glass, tense and vulnerable and looked back at him with tired sad eyes. 'So if it's not the farm, what is it that's making you drink?' he said in a softer, more understanding voice.

'I'm sixty-two, for God's sake. My life is over now. I love this farm and now he's gone...' She hesitated. 'That's just the trouble...things have been happening which scared me. Like he's still here.'

Richard's jaw dropped, shocked by what she'd said. 'What are you saying, Mother?'

'I think I'm being watched.' She lifted the glass to her lips, but he stopped her, covering the top with his hands to prevent her drinking.

'No, Mother. I want you to tell me about this.' he said sternly. 'You've had enough whisky for one day.' He gently took the glass and put it on the coffee table out of reach.

'You probably think I'm being ridiculous,' she said.

'No, I don't, not one bit. I want you to tell me everything.'

'I mean, you don't see many Pakistanis round here. It's bound to catch your eye.'

Richard frowned. 'Pakistanis. How do you know?'

'Well, they weren't white for a start, and no turbans so I doubt they were Indian...One of them had a beard like Muslims often have, but I must admit the clothes they were wearing were not what you'd expect.'

Richard seized on the comment. 'A tracksuit and baseball cap? Was that what they were wearing?'

'Yes, that's it,' she said, looking pleased that he was interested.

'But how do you know they're watching you?' he asked.

'There were two of them. Outside the house, sitting in a car. I saw them twice. I told one of our hands to go down

41

and ask them what they were up to. We thought they were after stealing the farm machinery.'

'So what happened?'

'They'd gone.'

'Is that it?' said Richard, disappointed that there was nothing to go on.

'I'm sure they tried to break into the farmhouse. If it wasn't for Joe's sheep dogs barking, they might have succeeded.'

'Did you tell the police?'

'No. Of course not. The police are bloody useless round here. Besides, there's been no crime so they wouldn't be interested.'

Richard stood up and went into the kitchen to check on the lamb. He needed time to think. She followed him and he noticed the bottle had been left in the sitting room.

'So was there anything else?' he said.

'Phone calls, where someone's just listening to your voice…without speaking.'

'How long's this being going on for?'

'Not long. Maybe a month.'

'And the calls…How many?'

'Five or six.'

He stopped and started hunting through the kitchen cupboards. There were some potatoes which would only do for mash.

'I'll peel those,' she said.

'What makes you think this has got anything to do with Dad?' he said, turning to face her.

'I wouldn't normally have made the connection, but there's something else.'

'Go on,' he said, excitement in his voice.

'I received a photograph in the post with no note or indication of who sent it. It was posted from New York. I'll get it for you.'

'Okay…While you're doing that, I'm going to have a look around outside.'

The sun had broken through the clouds, which might have lifted his mood if he hadn't been so worried. He walked towards the farm buildings, glancing from side to side. Nothing seemed out of place. But something strange was going on. He might have dismissed his theory that Masood knew him but with his mother's watcher and the man on the bridge and the certain knowledge that Masood's wife was lying to him, he knew he had to find out more about Masood.

He returned to the house and his mother appeared a few minutes later with a sepia photograph of a man dressed like a shepherd, standing on the top of a mountain with the sea below. A black bushy beard almost covered his face and a thick moustache curling at the edges added to the man's ferocious appearance. He carried a machine gun and was wearing a bandana scarf on his head, dark shirt and knee-length boots worn outside his trousers.

'This is your grandfather, Leonard. I recognised him straight away because your father had a similar photograph, which he kept on the piano in the sitting room. Whoever sent this wanted me to have it. It was addressed to me rather than your father,' she said, scraping the potatoes like her life depended on it. 'Leonard, or Lenny as his friends called him, was the reason why your father rejected you. I used to find him staring at his picture, time and time again, so I knew what his father meant to him. Nobody else would know, so who thought to post the photograph to me?' She stopped and drank a glass of tap water all the way down. Richard gave her an encouraging smile, pleased that she was trying to sober up. 'Whenever I tried to move it, he got very angry.' She stopped and put some water in a pan in readiness for her peeled potatoes. 'You see, he never knew his father. He was killed in the war, in Crete, where the photo was taken. He died before your father was even born. It was as if he resented giving you love that he never got himself. He idolised that picture and the image of the man he thought was a hero. He wanted to emulate Leonard. I think he attributed his own success in life to the man he looked up to who never gave him love.'

'How could he? He was dead,' said Richard.

'Yes, that's true, but it's not the point. Your father thought that leaving you to fend for yourself would bring out a toughness in you; a resilience that he wanted you to have.'

'But why didn't he tell me this? I never knew what happened to Grandfather.'

'I don't know why,' she replied.

'So what happened to Grandfather? You've never talked about it before.'

'I'll make some tea. The joint will be at least another hour.' She put the kettle on and then continued. 'As I was saying, Leonard died before your father was born. He met your grandmother in Alexandria in 1941. It was a whirlwind romance and more than likely your father was conceived on their wedding night because two days later, your grandfather parachuted into Crete never to be seen again. Your grandmother told me, just before she died, that Leonard did great things in Crete, running the resistance movement after the Germans invaded. He was a member of SOE, that's the Special Operations Executive. He's buried in Suda Bay, a Commonwealth War Cemetery in Crete. She must have loved him because she never remarried, but I always wondered why she never visited the grave. I think your father would have struggled to accept a stepfather so perhaps it is just as well.'

She made the tea and they took it back into the sitting room. Putting her mug down, she went over to her writing cabinet and started hunting through the drawers. Finding what she was looking for, she returned to her seat and handed him a small parcel of letters tied with a ribbon. 'These are some letters that belonged to your grandmother,' she continued. 'They include some received from your father. It was strange that he would write these things down, but often they were written from hotel bedrooms when he was away on business. Most people send emails now, but your father preferred to write as your grandmother didn't have the Internet. The last letter was written shortly before he died. What's clear to me is that your father put Leonard on a pedestal. In his mind, he was a hero, but he never knew whether that was really true. He was angry that he never got a medal for his bravery and used to write to the Ministry of Defence about it and spent hours in the National Archives at Kew, trying to unearth his past.'

'Did he find anything?'

'I think he must have done, because one day he came back from Kew looking very excited.'

'But he told you nothing?'

'Nothing at all. He came home, packed his bags and went off to New York. He was always doing that so I just accepted it.'

'How long was that before 9/11?'

She thought for a moment. 'It was in December 2000. I remember because he stayed in New York over Christmas. You came back from university and was livid he wasn't here.'

'I remember,' said Richard, reminding himself of the awful Christmas with just him and his mother staring at an overcooked turkey.

'Your father never had any interest in Christmas, but he was interested in religion, only not Christianity.'

'What do you mean?'

'Well, in the last two years, he became obsessed. Building up a library of books on Islam. I remember him once telling me a story about the way Muslims venerated Mary, mother of Jesus. There is a place in Egypt called…' She hesitated trying to recall the name. 'It begins with B. Bil something…Anyway, there is a Muslim shrine at this place called The Tree of the Virgin where Mary, Joseph and Jesus were reputed to have rested when they fled into Egypt. That was what fascinated him, that Muslims and Christians could worship at the same places.'

Something clicked in Richard's memory. What had Amira said about Masood?

There is not a Muslim God, a Christian God and a Jewish God. There is only one God. Masood understood that.

A shiver ran down his spine. A common thread that linked his father with Masood.

His mother smiled. 'Are you listening to me, Richard? You look as if you've seen a ghost.'

Richard jolted. 'Of course, Mother, I was just reflecting on what you said. Why do you think father's interest in Islam has anything to do with this?'

'When he was home he used to spend a lot of time writing notes while pouring over books, mostly about Islamic history. He even read the Koran. Do you think if…I mean…if that's why I've got Muslims watching the house?'

'I don't know, Mother. It's certainly a theory but it doesn't explain his obsession with Crete and finding out about his father's death.'

His mother sighed and he could see a tear in her eye. 'I know,' she said. 'I wish I had his notebooks which would, I'm sure, explain his thinking, but he took them to New York when he left home for the last time. It's just…' She took another drink of water. 'It's just that I sense this is not over.'

Richard untied the ribbon and began to scan the letters. His father's writing was not relaxed. Without even taking in the words, he could see the frustration on the page. A disillusionment with the world he lived in. One extract caught his attention:

My letters to you are a channel for the way I feel. An opportunity to unload. I know you'll never question me so I'll tell you. I've been let down. I don't want to work in such circumstances. I need a simple life.

Unusually, David Helford still used a fountain pen. It was a gold Mont Blanc, which he took everywhere. He put the letters down. 'Go on, Mother,' he said. 'This is very interesting. I'll have a look at the letters later.'

Telling the story seemed to lift a weight off her mind. Her face became more animated when before she had looked withdrawn and unable to cope. She smiled and he smiled back, pleased she seemed revived by their conversation. 'In his last letter,' she said. 'He confesses about his feelings and how he did not feel any love for you. Totally irrational of course, but I was upset because, for the first time, I felt I'd been unfair to you all these years. That's why I'm such a wreck, what with that and all these other things happening. Of course, I didn't know any of this while he was alive. He didn't write letters to me, only to his mother. I didn't discover it until after her death. All those years were wasted.'

He could see she was finding it upsetting but also liberating. She took another sip of tea and then continued. 'I remember about six months before he died, he came home from yet another trip to New York with cracked ribs and bruising on his face. He said he'd had an accident and fallen down stairs. I didn't believe him. Something happened on that trip which changed him. He became very angry and depressed. One night, he was drinking and I asked him what had happened. You were away at university and we were alone. He refused to talk about it and then after I pushed him further, he shouted at me, hurling abuse and swearing. That was so unlike him.' She stopped and her face became grave as she relived the incident. 'Waving his hands in frustration, he knocked a bottle of whisky over. You can still see the stain.' She pointed at the brown tinge on the carpet. 'Then he sank down onto his knees and was weeping. I had never seen him cry before.' She was crying now and Richard wondered whether he should call a halt.

'Do you want to have a break?' he asked.

She ignored the offer. Her voice was cracking with emotion. 'I couldn't get him to open up and tell me what was troubling him so much.

'After he died, I went through his things and found a letter from Lenny to your grandmother. I think it must have something to do with what upset him so much.'

'Can I see the letter?' said Richard.

'Yes. I kept it. I'll get it for you. It's upstairs.'

While she was gone, he flicked through his father's letters. The general tone surprised him. He seemed disillusioned with his career. At times he ranted about greed in the financial world and how much he despised its materialism.

His mother returned a few minutes later and handed him the letter.

'It's very worn. You can hardly make out the words,' she said. She went over to the desk and produced a large magnifying glass. 'This will help you read it. I've never been able to work it all out myself…Only bits of it.'

Richard laid the letter carefully on his mother's desk and switched on the Anglepoise lamp, manipulating the light for the best possible view of the letter. The paper was wafer thin and torn where it had been folded. The words were written in faded black ink.

'Mother, write this down for me as I read,' he said, sitting at the desk so that he could get as close as possible to the text. Deciphering the words wasn't easy and in some cases it was completely illegible. After nearly half an hour of playing with words, going over sentences repeatedly, a note of sorts began to emerge. 'Now read it back to me, will you, please?' he said, resigned to the fact that not everything was visible so he wouldn't know the whole story.

'Dear Dorothy,' she read. *'If you are reading this, I will have been killed in Crete. I know this because the person that I've entrusted the letter to is under strict instructions only to deliver it to you in the event of my death...'* There was then a long section in the text where it was impossible to read anything. His mother paused before continuing. *'I'm sorry it had to end like this and that we never got to know each other. However, in the brief time we had together, I want you to know that I enjoyed every minute. You are my wife and I bequeath all my personal possessions to you. All my love, Lenny.'*

Richard sighed. 'This is wonderful to have, but so much is missing... You did speak to Grandmother about this, didn't you?'

'Of course I did. She told me that she only received the letter in the post many years later. It was after the war was over. There was a card inside with a note written in Greek and what appeared to be an address. Your grandmother never bothered to get it translated. When she showed it to your father he wrote this down.' She handed Richard another scrap of paper, this time in his father's hand.

'Nikoletta Marides, 252 Eresou Street, Exarchia, Athens.

'Can I keep this?' he asked.

'Yes, of course you can.' She picked up her cup, holding it in both hands, draining the last dregs of the tea. He noticed how her hands were shaking.

'I'll make a fresh cup if you like. That must be cold,' he said.

49

By the time the meal was ready, his mother spoke with a new feeling of optimism. He told her he would get the police to check out her phone.

'Mum. If you see any more of these guys hanging around, you should phone me immediately, doesn't matter what time of day or night it is. And we need to get Joe on board. I'll go and speak to him.'

'You called me Mum,' she said smiling.

'I did. And you know something, it sounds good.'

There was a look of satisfaction in her eyes. 'When you went to Iraq I was worried every day. I thought you went there to prove something, and then you got sent home. I was overjoyed and yet couldn't show it because you were so down.'

'It didn't go well,' he replied. He'd never told her about the suicide bomb in Iraq and didn't want to do now. 'And I don't know why I was sent home. They never told me the truth. But somehow I put someone's nose out of joint.'

She paused while she swallowed some food. 'You know, I can see your father in your blue eyes and your nose, but your hair...' She reached out and touched his hair, pushing some back behind his ear. 'Your father always had short hair, unlike you.'

He laughed. 'It's my Byronic look. Needed to give credibility to my thesis on Byron...'

As they ate, he told her about Becky and how he couldn't go through with the marriage, but said nothing about the baby.

'I don't know whether I'm capable of love,' he said. 'The bomb made me see myself differently and somehow I know that Dad is right in the middle of it all, even my time in Iraq. It's why I'm so screwed up.' He took a mouthful of lamb and some potato and proceeded to chew it slowly. 'The bomb is giving me nightmares and I can't stop thinking about Dad. All his secrets…never saying anything to you…and then the bomb.

'Time is a great healer,' she replied softly. He could feel there was less distance between them than there had been in years. He took hold of her hand and smiled.

The train took longer than usual to get back to Liverpool Street, but he didn't notice as he had become so engrossed in the pile of letters. They were in date order with the most recent letter on top of the pile. He decided to read his father's last letter first. He must have written it on the same day that he last spoke to Mother.

Marriott Hotel World Trade Center
New York City
NY 10048
September 9th, 2001

Dear Mother,

I'm still in New York City and thought I'd write to let you know I'm okay but fed up with my job. The people I work with do not listen. Their greed is inexhaustible and I feel a hypocrite to be part of their organisation.

In my spare time, I'm continuing to make important discoveries about what Father was doing when he died. I've met someone, here in New York, who knew him in Crete and has told me a lot about what a wonderful man he was. But after I dug further into his past I discovered something much more profound. The reasons why my father died are even bigger than the war itself.

If I do one thing before I die, I want my father to be given the recognition he deserves.
Your loving son
David.

Richard looked at the letter date again. A picture was emerging from these letters of a very different man to the one he thought he knew. If this was his father, then he wanted to erase the memory of the man he'd grown to hate. Was hate too harsh a word? His father was an enigma. Someone he didn't understand but wanted to know. His father had only two more days to live after this letter, two days before the planes hit the twin towers and he was never seen again. Richard had once considered staying at the Marriott Hotel himself when he'd visited New York as a student, but couldn't afford it. Smack bang in the middle of the towers, it never had a chance. But his father's body would have turned up if he was in the hotel that day. A disappearance suggested that he would have been in one of the higher floors and was incinerated by aircraft-fuel explosions as the plane hit the tower. That was the most logical explanation and the one that convinced the coroner to declare him dead as a result of the 9/11 attack on America.

Then Richard spotted something.

He didn't notice it the first time he read the letters but the second time he went through more carefully, searching for anything else that might give him a lead to go on. When he pulled one letter out, he tore the envelope by accident. Written inside, as if his father was trying to hide the information, was a sequence of numbers, letters and another name.

HT 674 675 Ikaros Poliakis.

The train pulled into Liverpool Street as the sun set, reflecting a golden light across the glass facades of the City. There were few people around and plenty of taxis on the rank. Nothing unusual for a Sunday evening. The driver, for a change, took him on the quickest route through the deserted city. When they arrived, he felt relieved to be home. His upstairs flat, situated in a tree-lined street, quiet when you considered its proximity to Holloway Road, looked strangely welcoming. An Edwardian terrace with large bay windows and tall ceilings. He felt safe there.

But not safe enough.

It happened before he could react. The taxi had gone and while fumbling for his keys, they hit him hard.

He didn't see them coming. Two of them. The streetlights were poor, hardly penetrating the darkness. He crumpled in a heap onto the pavement as one pushed him while the other grabbed his bag. A professional job, over in seconds. He picked himself up, seeing their backs racing up the road on BMX bikes, carrying his bag and all his father's letters.

'You're a fucking wreck, Helford,' he said out loud, not that anybody was listening. He couldn't be sure, but one of them looked like the Pakistani guy on the bridge, same tracksuit and baseball cap. Maybe the same guys watching his mother? Must have being waiting for him to return. Apart from a newspaper, there was nothing else in the bag except for the letters. A poor haul if they were looking for money, but as he looked down the street where they had already vanished, he knew this wasn't a random mugging.

Chapter Five

Afghanistan, Northern province of Kunduz. July 12th 2005

Klaus Kleiner watched from the open door of a Tiger helicopter as it descended rapidly towards the helipad. He smiled at the sight of the vast German camp that lay five hundred feet below. It had cost Berlin over one hundred million dollars to build, but he considered it worth every cent. A clear sign that German military power was returning.

There was no time to be relieved as they hit the ground. The door opened and soldiers covered him as he ran across the tarmac to the safety of the base. In seconds, the Tiger lifted back into the air and was gone. The short burst of exercise made him feel better; it had been no fun cramming his huge frame into such a small space on the journey from Kabul. He'd chosen to wear desert fatigues and Ray-Ban aviators so, when greeted by the officer in charge, he looked the part, rather than looking like a pompous idiot of a politician who would quickly earn the men's disdain. The gusts from the chopper's blades unleashed his Aryan blond hair and the scarf made him look as if he had been in the desert for months. Like one of Rommel's Africa Korps, he thought.

The officer in charge, Captain Gerhard Langer, was waiting to meet him. He saluted and they shook hands.

'It's a pleasure to welcome you, Herr Minister, on such an important mission,' said Langer, clicking his heels in unison with his salute. Kleiner thought he detected a note of cynicism in his voice and why not? His mission was a waste of time. The Bundeswehr would be a laughing stock in front of the Americans and the British if the proposals to make the army more family friendly ever came to be official policy. It would create a part-time force instead of a ruthless fighting machine. He knew what his report would say before he had even started writing it.

There was another purpose for his visit. Nothing to do with the German government, but if his mission succeeded, he would strike a blow against the enemies of the fatherland and make himself a very rich man; a much better reason to travel all this way to such a horrible country.

Afghanistan, German military base, Kunduz. July 13th 2005

The portable air-conditioning machine woke Kleiner. It vibrated and shook while it fought a losing battle against the rising heat. The noise made it impossible to sleep and with the sunrise penetrating the darkness, adding to his discomfort, he could no longer hold back the day. His eyes blinked against the light as he forced them open. What was he doing in such a shithole? His relationship with Al Qaeda made no sense, unless they could destroy the Jews. They had already let him down once, when they said they were planning an aerial attack on Tel Aviv, but had bombed New York instead. Why could he still trust them?

The truth was Bin Laden owed him. Mohammad Atta and three of his other 9/11 accomplices would have been arrested in Hamburg, long before they flew into the twin towers, had he not used his position in the German Defence Ministry, with access to intelligence reports, to deflect interest in them. He cut the surveillance on students, saying it would save money, but, in reality, it took Atta and his friends off the radar.

In the long hours travelling to Afghanistan, he thought about 9/11 as he had done so many times since that day in 2001. He knew that helping Atta made him guilty, but he didn't care about the dead in the twin towers if it resulted in a war which would ultimately bring about the destruction of Israel. He needed Al Qaeda to help him do it.

Thirty minutes later, he sat opposite Langer watching a worried scowl spread across his face as Kleiner told him about his plans to leave the base.

'You can't be serious?' shouted Langer. 'That's a suicide mission without protection. I can't allow it. I'm responsible for your safety, for fuck's sake.'

Kleiner glared at him. 'Captain Langer. I have a mission to engage with the Taliban. My safety is not an issue, but secrecy is essential. This is a top secret German operation. We haven't even told the Americans and the British. If it succeeds, it will raise the respect for German military prowess and international standing, something we desperately need. I am sharing this with you in confidence, but nobody else on this base should be aware of the operation. My movements should not be reported, not even to your superiors, or to Berlin. Do I make myself clear?'

Langer shuffled in his seat, knowing that he had lost the argument. 'Of course, Minister. I understand, but what happens if you get killed? I'll be blamed for not guaranteeing your safety.'

'I'll leave a note exonerating you,' Kleiner replied, know he had no intention of leaving any notes which might explain what he was about to do.

Hiding in the back of a covered jeep meant that nobody saw Kleiner leave the base. It was normal for the Afghan police to go on a patrol of the villages, so nobody questioned their departure. The meeting point was about ten miles from the base and when they arrived, the policemen needed no encouragement to leave. They'd warned him of the danger. Taliban everywhere, one of them had said as they swung their jeep around and tore off in a cloud of dust. The afternoon sun was still very hot. It was almost silent, except for the sound of the scorching mountain breeze blowing in his face. He was glad of the scarf they had given him and he wrapped it tighter to shield himself from the sun.

The desolate landscape seemed to be moving as he squinted his eyes to adjust for the heat haze blurring the horizon. At first, it was just an object, black and shimmering, but as it got closer, a more defined shape emerged. It moved nearer until the shape became a man. He had a rifle slung over his shoulder. Droplets of sweat ran down Kleiner's back. He drank from his water bottle to calm his nerves and stared at the man as he drew closer, trying to look unconcerned by the Kalashnikov waving in his direction. The water was warm and barely quenched his thirst.

The man with the gun was not Taliban. The close-cut beard, white teeth and clean finger nails set him apart. He wore Ray-Ban shades, not dissimilar to Kleiner's own, and a Rolex, all of which demonstrated status; a man to be reckoned with. A black Toyota Land Cruiser may have been an insurgent's favoured mode of transport, but it didn't make him a terrorist. For all his clean appearance, Kleiner sensed a man consumed by hatred. A man who knew how to inflict fear. This is what made him a terrorist.

Fear.

Kleiner shivered, his muscles tightening. The man's gun dug into his gut while he frisked him with his other hand. The precision of an expert; one false move and Kleiner's dead meat. Their eyes met at what Kleiner assumed would be the end of the search. He saw the man's smirk, moving his face closer until they almost touched.

The final indignity; clammy fingers inside his trousers, cupping the tender skin of his genitals, daring him to protest, while continuing to stare straight into his eyes. Kleiner locked on to the man's glare, doing his best to stay calm, but inside anger seething. Blood rushed through his veins; he clenched his fists until his nails hurt the palms of his hands.

'*Salaam aleikum,*' said Kleiner. Usually, without exception, the *peace be with you* greeting was reciprocated, but this man just continued to stare and said nothing.

Dust covered the windows, as they drove at great speed towards the mountains. The windscreen wipers worked nonstop to clear the smallest area and reveal the hard unforgiving landscape, just enough visibility for his driver to keep on the road. The heat was unrelenting and seemed even more stifling in the vehicle as the air conditioning didn't work. Soon they were climbing, passing camels and overtaking other Jeeps, winding up a mountain.

Without any warning, and about an hour after they had started climbing, they swung off the road and down a track running between two fields. The crops were high on both sides, laden with wheat. As the fields came to an end, they entered a small forest. Without warning the Cruiser screeched to a stop. Kleiner was thrown forward, hitting his head on the head restraints on the front passenger seat.

'Get out. Quick. Get out,' shouted the man in Ray-Bans. His voice sounded strange. He didn't sound like a native. He sounded educated.

He sounded American.

Two other men appeared from nowhere and dragged Kleiner away from the car. They bound his hands and told him to follow. The man with the shades looked on impassively while the other men prodded his ribs with the guns they were carrying, leading the way down a rocky mountain path. The light was fading and at last the heat was subsiding. After about ten minutes, they reached a clearing surrounded by taller rocks. A fire was burning in the centre and looked welcoming. Meat was roasting on a spit and a coffee pot emitted sweet aromas as it bubbled away. At least ten other men sat around with their guns close to hand. The man bellowed instructions to his guards and then disappeared into a cave located just behind the fire.

After several minutes, the man returned and beckoned Kleiner to follow. The cave was lit by several paraffin torches, which threw out flickering flames of shadows across the roof. The floor was covered in rush matting and several elders sat cross-legged on the floor. They were all dressed in a similar manner, wearing a black turban, unruly beard and long off-white tunics, with layers of fabric to ensure easier movement. They are not Taliban, Kleiner decided. That was good. They were Mujahedeen – Soldiers of Allah – veterans from their fight with the Russians.

The man pushed him to the ground. 'Sit,' he shouted, gripping his arm and forcing him down to the floor. Kleiner fell awkwardly, unable to stop himself, as his hands remained tied. A man reached out and pulled Richard off the floor, helping him sit cross legged and face the older men.

Kleiner spoke in English, knowing that they would not speak German. 'I am honoured that you agreed to see me.'

One of them replied. 'Mr Kleiner. Our wise leader wants to hear what you have to say. He is aware of the assistance you have given the jihad in Hamburg. He thanks you for this and begs you to speak to him through me.' The man spoke with an English accent with perfect diction that surprised Kleiner. He must have mixed with the Pakistani elite, he thought, probably educated in an English public school.

'Thank you,' he replied, looking nervously at the guns pointing in his direction. He cleared his throat and began to speak. 'First, let me congratulate you on the success in bombing London. It shows you are winning the Holy War.' He resented sucking up to them, but he was in too deep to backtrack. 'I've come here to tell you that I want your assistance to continue the Nazi fight against the Jews. It's no secret that Nazis continue to live in Germany. I am one of them, forced to hide my true beliefs. Only the forces of Islam are capable of destroying Israel and I am here to help you achieve your goal.'

The man with the public school accent interrupted. 'We do not need Nazi sympathisers to fight our holy war.'

'That may be so,' said Kleiner, adjusting his legs so he could speak more freely on the ground. 'What if evidence emerged that the prophet Muhammad, praise be to him, was accepted by Isa, who the Christians call Jesus, to be the true prophet? What if that revelation originated from Christian and not Muslim texts? If I give you access to the proof, before it is made public, then Al Qaeda will be able to use it against America. If successful it will drive the Americans away from support of Israel.'

'Go on,' snapped the man who'd brought him to the cave. He hadn't removed his shades despite the darkness but Kleiner could see he had his attention. The accent was American; he was sure of it.

'The Christian text I refer to has a direct link to the last book of the Christian Bible – the Book of Revelations. Imagine what the West would make of proof that Jesus Christ deferred to Mohammad as the last messenger of God.'

'Even if you can prove this, it will never cause a war,' sneered the man.

'Maybe not, but your objective is to cause disruption and fear in the West. There are plenty of religious fanatics in America who will do your job for you. They want to cause a war and destroy the Muslim race. A new crusade if you like. The proof will be a direct attack on the fundamental belief of Christians that Jesus is the Son of God.'

'Is this all you have to give us?' shouted the man, barely suppressing his anger. 'Bush used that language. This is nothing new.'

Kleiner could feel the sweat running down his back and his hands were shaking. 'There is a Jewish billionaire who is prepared to pay millions for the proof.' Kleiner paused and looked around the cave to check whether he still had their attention. Some were not listening, presumably because they couldn't understand English, but the American looked directly at him through his dark glasses. 'You may have heard of the Jew. His name is Abel B Multzeimer. He is fanatical about the Book of Revelations and its images of great wars. Although the book appears in the Christian Bible, the author – John of Patmos – is a Jewish prophet who speaks of triumph through war.' Kleiner paused again, shuffling his legs which were getting cramp through sitting cross-legged on the cave floor. 'Multzeimer has interests in the arms trade as well as oil and property and wants the Americans to continue the so called War on Terror, preferably using his arms. He preaches a no tolerance message towards Muslims, even proposing that they should be banned from America. He'll pay $100 million for the proof so he can use it to incite American opinion against Islam.'

'What is this to do with us? He won't be the first non-believer to blaspheme against the holy prophet,' said the American.

'Imagine his annoyance if Al Qaeda got to the scroll first,' Kleiner replied. 'After taking a million dollars as a

61

down payment, I'll give the scroll to you, pretending you stole it from me. In your hands, you can reveal the contents of the scroll with much more impact than a controlled distribution by Multzeimer, designed to press his campaign to be US President.'

The man with the American accent laughed. 'Your plan is ridiculous. How will this incite Christians to convert to Islam?'

'It won't. America is a God-fearing country where television evangelists preach a fire and brimstone view of Christianity just like the Book of Revelations with its prophecies of war and the end of the world.' It was difficult for Kleiner to see the man's expression in the fading light of the fire. What he could see was the Kalashnikov in his hand, his finger twitching on the trigger, pointing directly at Kleiner's chest. He'd never stared down the barrel of a gun before. There would be no wounding. One bullet would blow him apart. His heart raced; it was becoming an effort to speak clearly while his lips trembled. 'Many Americans revere this book.' He hesitated, swallowing hard, determined to say his piece. 'And will be shocked if this new revelation, which proves the supremacy of Islam, actually emanates from the same source. They will be incensed that the text challenges the fundamental belief that Jesus is the Son of God and demand retribution. The Book of Revelations even inspired the 'Battle Hymn of the Republic'. It is ingrained in the American psyche, like a Christian march invoking the Four Horses of the Apocalypse referred to in the book. The first of these signifies war.'

The American held up his hand. 'Stop,' he shouted. 'I need to translate.'

Kleiner stared at the others in the group while they listened to the American as he translated. He was certain that he had their attention. After a few minutes, the

American stopped speaking and waved his hand for Kleiner to continue.

Kleiner cleared his throat and felt a surge of confidence that his story was working. 'What will make the difference is the manner of the delivery of the scroll's message,' he continued. 'When Al Qaeda announce the message to the world, it should be on the back of a major spectacular to rival 9/11.' The American translated some more and Kleiner heard mutterings that suggested they were listening. 'The way to do this is to throw the Book of Revelations back in their faces and imitate the images of retribution described in the text. The impact on such a fanatical Bible bashing nation will be enormous.

'Give me an example,' said the American.

'Chapter nineteen refers to the Destruction of the Pagan Nations. There are many images to take from that book. I quite like the burning lake where sinners are thrown to their deaths.' Kleiner stopped while the translation caught up. He could see the heads of his audience nodding in what appeared to be a sign of approval. 'The association with the Book of Revelations will be devastating. The American people will feel violated by the attack and will demand that the President retaliates, throwing the might of American power into a war that they cannot win and which will ultimately lead to their destruction at the hands of Islam.'

The silence suggested that they were listening and so Kleiner gestured towards his case. 'In there you'll find letters. They're in German,' he said. 'From a German paratrooper, who wrote to his mother during the Battle of Crete in 1941.'

The man removed his sunglasses. 'Did you say Crete?' he asked.

'Yes, I did,' said Kleiner. 'He refers to a discovery on Crete. Something of profound religious significance.'

He noticed a glimmer of interest in the man's eyes. 'Who gave you the letters?'

'A German soldier who was there during the war. He's dead so is no use to you.'

'I'll be the judge of that. What was the German's name?'

'Kohlenz. His name was Captain Wolfgang Kohlenz. He was the German paratrooper's commanding officer.'

The man stared intently at Kleiner and said nothing. The fire continued to cast its tongues across the wall and roof of the cave. Kleiner shivered, noticing the cold despite the fire.

After a long period of silence, the man replaced his Ray-Bans and fiddled with his Rolex while barking out what seemed like instructions in Arabic to two Mujahedeen sat either side of Kleiner. 'Do you know where the document is?' he said.

'It is still on Crete, that much seems certain. I believe I have enough clues to find it there.'

The man nodded at the guards and stood up. An arm pulled Kleiner back and a sack fell over his head. He choked as the rope tightened on his throat. Claustrophobia induced panic. He gasped for breath and felt his legs turn to jelly as two arms on each side pulled him to his feet. They were dragging him, his feet trailing in the rubble. He could hear muffled voices shouting orders. They were no longer speaking English. He shouted protests but they were not listening any more. He was going to die.

Afghanistan. Mountains above Kunduz on the Tajikistan border. July 14th 2005

Mohammed Abdul Alim rose early in time for the first call to prayer. He had wanted to kill the German, but didn't want to attract unwanted attention from the occupying forces. Killing a German minister wouldn't go unnoticed. Besides, he needed Kleiner to lead him to the scroll.

They will have found him by now, shivering like a dog, he thought. He had men watching the kafir patrols on a daily basis. With their knowledge, he knew where to release Kleiner to ensure he would be picked up quickly.

Abdul took his mat outside the cave. He removed his Ray-Bans and Rolex watch, symbols of the Western materialism he despised, but something he'd never let go, however hypocritical it sounded. To remove them cleansed his soul in the face of Allah, praise be upon him.

When he'd finished prayers and rolled up his mat, he put his sunglasses and watch back on and sat cross-legged, facing the sunrise. At times like these, he remembered his beautiful daughter and a tear trickled from the corner of his eye. From under his cloak he took out the small piece of his daughter's wedding veil he'd salvaged from the ruins of his home, holding it up to his cheek, feeling its softness.

'Now is the time,' he whispered to himself. 'After years of searching, it is time to come down from the mountain.'

Of course, he had no time for the plan involving the billionaire Jew, but the idea of the attack based on extracts from the Christian Bible was a masterstroke. The link would be more powerful than yet another bomb. Sheikh Zabor would decide the next move as he always did. But Abdul knew it was not possible to contact him as long as he remained in Afghanistan. How he would have loved to use his satellite phone to contact the Sheikh but he knew only too well that as soon as he'd made contact, the Americans would pick up his signal and send a drone. He'd seen too many of his friends get themselves killed after a phone call.

Chapter Six

London. July 15th 2005

St Mark's looked like a normal Anglican church, as you'd expect in Kensington. Apart from the language, the service appeared similar to what he'd been used to in Christian churches, not that Richard went to church much. Even the music sounded like monks' plainsong, mystical and moving in its simplicity. Amira walked past him following the coffin into the church. He could just see the faint outline of her features, barely visible, but showing enough so that he could tell she knew he was there. A slight tilting of the head, nothing more was needed. He stayed at the back of the church in a haze of thought, not wanting to intrude on the family's grief. Down the aisle, he could see the back of her head, but nothing else. People surrounded her. Friends, relatives, people who mattered, he knew he could never be part of that. But somehow she seemed separate from them. She seemed alone.

The service ended and he waited while the coffin left the church. Outside, people were milling around waiting for the hearse to leave for the cemetery. He turned, expecting that no one would notice him leave. Amira must have seen him go as she appeared out of nowhere. She called his name, not Mr Helford but Richard. The familiarity of the greeting aroused mixed feelings. The pleasure of hearing his name, uttered from her lips, but also a sense of unease that he could not acknowledge her intimacy. He had to remain detached.

'I'm glad you came.' She bowed her head as if in deference to the occasion and her husband's memory. She held out her hand, just as she had done before. Her hand was gloved and her veil continued to shroud her face. Not one inch of her body was on view but that didn't matter.

She was perfect, deprived of outward signs of beauty, stripped to the bare core of her being, she could only communicate to him through her purity of voice and touch. Her face was outlined by the veil, but devoid of expression.

He decided to walk back to the office, his mind lost in a maze of conflicting thoughts. He was angry with himself for being captivated by this woman he hardly knew. It was an infatuation that had nothing to do with why he could not go back to Becky. Amira was a fantasy whereas Becky represented the reality of his life. A fight between normality and danger. The pendulum was swinging towards the latter and he found it hard to resist.

Back at the office, a message sat on his desk telling him to see Rowena. He could hear her voice in the corridor before he entered her office, shouting down the telephone, giving somebody an ear-bashing about the lack of intelligence coming in about the bombings. She slammed the phone down, more in frustration than anger.

She looked up as he knocked on the open door and walked in. 'This is Five's show,' she said. 'But they're really pissed with us for not giving them any leads from our people. GCHQ are getting some noises that this bomb isn't the last. We've got to stop another attack. The public are scared shitless.'

'Having seen what they're capable of, so am I,' he said.

She turned to some papers on her desk. 'You've asked for some information from the Greek National Intelligence Service on Nikoletta Marides?'

'Yes. That's correct.'

'Why?'

'I'm looking into the fascist threat in Greece.' He glared back at Rowena. 'I'm not in Basra now. My job is to keep an eye on Greece, or have you forgotten, Rowena?' His cynical tone betrayed his lack of belief in what he was saying.

Rowena leaned back in her chair and blew up. 'What the fuck are you doing? Nobody gives a shit about Greece. We're under attack by terrorists and you want to know about the fucking fascists in Greece.' She stood up and slammed the door of her office so nobody could hear her. With the door closed, she walked up to him, gripping the armrests of his chair, leaning into his face, looking straight into his eyes. 'Don't bullshit me about this woman. Who is she?' she snapped. 'I'm hearing from our station chief in Athens that Langley asked about her in January 2002. Why on earth would the CIA be interested in an old Greek woman who wouldn't hurt a fly?'

'I've no idea. It's personal. My father knew her.'

Rowena hesitated and her eyes widened, looking surprised by his answer. 'So why are you bullshitting me about fascists?'

'I can tell you why, if you're not too busy.'

'You don't use the Service to look up personal matters. Is that clear?'

'Yes, okay. Sorry, Rowena.'

'Besides, I thought I told you to follow up on the Muslims on the train, and what about that Masood you saw die? Have you found anything?' she shouted, changing the subject.

'My report's in your inbox,' he replied, irritated by her tone. 'I emailed it to you this morning together with my recollections of what happened. There's nothing of interest on the Muslims we've identified as being on the train. None of them are on our watch lists. Masood is more interesting. He's not a Muslim. He's an Egyptian Coptic Christian, known to the Service. A former member of the Egyptian General Intelligence Service, interviewed by MI5 and deemed not to be a security risk. He left GIS in a cloud of acrimony.'

For the first time in their discussion Rowena looked genuinely interested in what he had to say. 'God only knows what all this has to do with the London bombings but I want you to follow up on Masood.' She stood up and walked over to the window where she could see the Thames. 'We need to know why Masood left the GIS. I can't spare anybody else on this, so you'll have to do it.'

That's what he wanted to hear. 'Don't worry, Rowena. I'll find out. I won't let you down,' he replied with a little too much enthusiasm. She no longer seemed interested, returning to the papers on her desk, suggesting that their meeting was over. He turned to leave her office, his hand resting on the door handle, when he hesitated. 'There's something else you should know.'

'What now?' she asked, sounding annoyed that he was still in her office.

'I'm being followed.'

'What did you say?' Rowena shouted, looking up, a bemused expression spreading across her face. 'Why would anyone want to follow you?'

'If I'm so unimportant, why did someone in a high place want me to leave Basra?' Richard replied. 'I was doing a good job there…You said yourself.'

'I thought we'd been into that. You were in shock.'

'Did my work deteriorate after the bomb?' His voice raised as his anger grew. 'Show me the evidence.'

Rowena evaded the question. 'This conversation is over. I can't spend my day bickering with you while we've got terrorists running around London causing mayhem.' Rowena pointed at the door.

Richard turned away, gritting his teeth. He knew he was close to losing his temper. 'I think it's all to do with my father's death in 9/11.'

'Why? The investigators said he was in the North Tower. We looked at all this when we were vetting you for this job.'

'I'm not so sure. I just think Masood may have been following me when the bomb went off.'

'In your dreams,' she laughed. 'No one's interested in you.'

'But he recognised me.'

'That happens all the time. How many times have you seen someone on the Tube you think you might have known at some time in the past?'

'That may be so, but I was mugged last night and all they took were some of my father's letters to his mother. My mother has seen some Pakistanis sniffing around our farm. All these little things seem to stack up into a larger whole. It's something I can't ignore. I need to talk to the Marides woman and see if I can find out why Langley have been asking questions about her. It's a long shot but Masood and Marides may be connected.'

Rowena's face had changed; she looked concerned. 'Mugged. Were you hurt?'

'No, but that's beside the point. I can't let it ride. You've got to tell me why I was made to leave Basra.'

She paced the room, her eyes focused on the floor. He knew it would be unwise to interrupt her chain of thought. After at least two minutes of silence, she swung around to face him.

'Your return from Basra is history, Richard. Let it drop. I'm not going to discuss it.' He watched her face and thought he could see a slight lifting of her eyebrows, suggesting she was holding something back. 'What I can do is allow you to go to Athens,' she said, her voice sounded more sympathetic. 'We're getting a lot of traffic through the Athens's office from the Middle East. The station chief could use some help. You must have spoken to him before – Brian Soper.'

'Yes. I've talked to Brian Soper,' he said.

'It would do you good to get away from London and give you an opportunity to follow up on this Nikoletta

Marides. The bombings were a shock to us all, but you had it harder than most. If you want some counselling, I'll sign off on it.'

He was touched by her concern, something that he'd never seen before. He knew it was the right thing to do. 'Thank you, Rowena. I would like that...to go to Athens, that is. I'll save the counselling sessions for another day.'

'Okay. Help Brian out but talk to the Americans in Athens and find out what interests them about Nikoletta Marides. I'll get on to HR.'

London. July 16th 2005

They'd arranged to meet at the foot of the Millennium Bridge on the South Bank and go to the café at the Tate Modern. Richard wore a dark linen suit and a light blue Oxford button down shirt. Casual, but acceptable to the office and its dress code. His appearance was important, but today he wasn't sure why he was making so much effort to look good. When he arrived at the bridge, he leaned against the wall overlooking the river, admiring the view of St Paul's Cathedral. A breeze blew in his face, ruffling his curly brown hair. While he waited, he ran his hand across his head in a nervous attempt to keep things under control. He couldn't deny he wanted to look his best.

Fifteen minutes passed before she appeared, smiling though the crowd and waving. He wouldn't have recognised her if she hadn't waved; she was different, no longer wearing a long traditional dress and veil. She had evolved from this demure wife in mourning, shrouded in traditional costume, to a confident girl about town in a cerise silk jacket and black skirt. Her hair was jet black, immaculate and straight to below her shoulders. Her eyes sparkled in the sunlight. At her home, he'd seen only her face and hands, which he'd found sensual because what was hidden from view was more alluring. Now, he was looking at the whole woman and saw the real person beneath the subterfuge of the veil.

To say he was pleased to see her again was an understatement. They sat at a table on the piazza outside the gallery and both ordered a salad. He didn't offer to buy any wine because he thought she might not drink.

'Shall we have wine?' she said.

'Well, I got that one wrong.' He smiled. 'I thought you wouldn't want to drink.'

'Copts are allowed to drink like any other Christians, unlike Muslims. It's one of the reasons why it's so difficult to exist side by side in Egypt.'

He ordered a Sauvignon Blanc and continued with small talk, admiring the way the gallery had added another dimension to the South Bank and laughed at how the Millennium Bridge would always be known as the *wobbly bridge* even though the problem had been solved.

When their salad arrived, he said, 'Tell me how you met Masood.'

Amira dropped her head a little and Richard could see pain in her eyes. 'It was a sad time,' she replied. 'He was investigating the car bomb which killed my father, mother and sister.'

Richard didn't know what to say. He could see she wasn't lying even though he'd been taken aback that there was nothing in the file. 'I'm s…sorry,' he stuttered. 'You've had more than your fair share of tragedy, your family and now your husband. It must make you challenge your belief in God.'

'Quite the opposite. It makes me more determined to stand up for my beliefs. It was a religious hatred attack against Copts by Muslim extremists. My family were targeted outside their church. Ten people were killed by the car bomb.'

'So Masood was a policeman?'

'Yes, he was…' She hesitated and looked at him with enquiring eyes. 'Like you, I suppose?'

Richard ignored the question and continued. 'I apologise if this sounds tactless but did you know the real reason why Masood left Cairo?'

The hurt expression on Amira's face said it all. 'I told you. We ran away from persecution.'

Richard felt uneasy about the line he was taking but continued anyway. 'How much do you know about Masood's job?'

Amira's expression had gone from hurt to indignant. 'Why are you asking me all these questions? …Who are you?'

'I work for the government,' said Richard quietly.

'I thought as much.'

He was surprised to see her anger subside. She took a mouthful of salad and he watched her lips crunching through the lettuce, tomato and rocket. He was captivated by every movement, however insignificant.

She took several more mouthfuls of food, chewing slowly. He watched, picking at his own food, transfixed by her beautiful mouth. She seemed to be contemplating what to say. At last she spoke. 'Masood gave me the approval to talk to you when he passed you the icon…He would not give it to anybody he didn't trust.'

'He didn't have any choice in the matter. I was the only one attending to him. He was dying.'

'He did have a choice. He could have left it in his pocket and then the police would have found it on his body and returned it to me. Instead, he chose to give it to you. That's significant.'

'I thought he knew who I was…I mean, I think he recognised me and yet we've never met.'

'I agree. I think he did know you. That's the only reason why he gave you the icon.'

'But you don't know why?'

73

'No. I knew he was in the police but he never really talked about his job. We became close because he opened doors for me when I was trying to find out what was being done to find the bombers who killed my family.'

'And did they find them?'

Amira sighed. 'No, they never did.'

'The thing is, Amira, I believe that Masood had been sacked from the GIS, which is why he was able to come to London.'

Amira looked surprised by what he'd said. 'The Egyptian Intelligence Service...Are you sure? I didn't know he was that kind of policeman.'

'Yes, we are sure, but we don't think it happened while he was in London. We think he was sacked in Cairo.'

Amira nodded. 'This is news to me. I don't know what difference it makes. What's important is why he was dismissed.'

'Exactly.' Richard replied. 'I'd like to know why.' He thought for a moment, certain she'd be upset by whatever he said. 'I don't know how to put this,' he said. 'Would you mind if I asked an impertinent question?'

Amira looked worried, and he was sure she was hiding something. 'If you must,' she said nervously.

'I don't get the impression that you were in love with Masood. Did you think that if you were close to him he might find out who killed your family?'

There were tears in her eyes and the anger had returned. She stood up abruptly. 'How dare you even suggest that I didn't love Masood? I think about him every day and I weep until I can't stop. But I must go on. He's dead and he would want me to be strong.'

'I'm sorry I've upset you...' he said, rising and taking her hand. 'I must have gained the wrong impression.' She snatched her hand away and glared back at him. He could see in her eyes that he'd hit a raw nerve. She checked a text on her mobile, turned away from him and was gone. She didn't even say goodbye.

'I'll get the bill,' said the waitress. Richard knew he couldn't wait while she went back to the desk and retrieved a card reader terminal. Throwing £50 on the table, shouting that she should keep the change, he rushed off in the direction of the Globe Theatre. The embankment was bustling with tourists enjoying the spectacle of the Thames while listening to the many buskers and other street entertainers. He nearly knocked over a mime artist painted from head to toe in silver. The man was standing, as still as a statue, but at the exact moment he ran by, the man's hand started to move and almost hit him. An apologetic smile, a pound in the man's hat and being the butt of the crowd's ridicule was the path of least resistance.

At first, he thought, he'd lost her, but then as the crowds thinned a little, before reaching London Bridge, he saw her again. She was not alone. He stopped in his tracks and ducked into a recess where he could watch without being seen. She was talking in an animated way to three men. They looked Muslim with their traditional long beards, white tunic shirts with flared sleeves and skullcaps. Two were quite young and a third man, clearly the leader, looked to be in his forties. They were pushing her and he could see she was scared. People were walking past, looking concerned, but not intervening, not wanting to get involved. The older one took hold of her arm and began pulling her along the embankment. That was the tipping point. He had to stop it.

He sprinted the twenty metres that separated them and in one clean movement pulled Amira away from them. He took hold of her hand, standing between her and the men. They cursed him in Arabic and then the old man spoke in broken English. 'Leave her. This is not your business.'

'It is my business. In this country we don't allow abuse

of women…I don't know who you are,' he shouted, 'but I can see this woman doesn't want your attention. I'll give you ten seconds to leave or I'm calling the police.' The men did not need persuading. They turned and headed away.

'We don't want trouble,' the older man said.

But one of the younger men had other ideas, shouting abuse at Amira. 'You are a whore and will be punished for your actions.'

Richard felt his blood boil. He launched himself at the man, grabbing his tunic and pushing him up hard against the river wall. The man winced as his back hit the stone and he screamed. 'I never forget a face,' Richard shouted, looking straight into the man's eyes.

The other two men were already some metres ahead of him and when Richard let go, the man who had abused Amira turned and ran. As he left, he shouted again, this time in Arabic.

Richard turned back and looked at Amira. 'What did he say? I speak Arabic but I don't recognise the dialect,' he said. She was standing still, shivering with fear and swaying from side to side, reeling with the shock and clearly deeply affected by what the man had said to her.

'I'm not a whore,' she whispered.

'I know,' said Richard.

'He said I'm a traitor to Egypt for not talking.'

'You better come and tell me what all this is about,' he said.

'Thank you, Richard.' She smiled 'I'm sorry about what I said earlier.'

He took her hand and they walked quickly along the embankment until they reached Borough Market, where they found a stall that was serving tea in the covered area of the market. There were lots of people milling around, drowning the sound of their voices. Richard bought the tea and proceeded to try and fish his tea bag out with the plastic stick they'd supplied him. Amira had black tea.

'Any lemon?' she said, capturing her tea bag.

'You must be joking,' chuckled Richard. He sipped the tea and spluttered. 'Shit. That's boiling hot.' Amira's tea lay steaming on the plastic table in front of them.

'I'd already decided that the tea was too hot by just observing it. Simple really,' she smiled.

Richard laughed again, pleased that she was relaxing after her ordeal. 'Glad I've entertained you, but now you need to tell me who those men were.'

'They knew my husband when he was in Egypt. As soon as they heard he was dead, they flew over and have been following me ever since. They are Muslim and want to force me to convert.' He could see that she was recovering, but was still upset. 'Can you believe that, Richard? My husband has been blown to pieces only a few days ago and they want me to come back with them to Egypt. They call me a whore because I'm not wearing widow clothes. A widow can be ostracised by the local community in Egypt. I'm nothing unless I have a husband.'

'Masood wasn't a Copt, was he?' he said, speaking slowly allowing his words to sink in.

She hesitated. 'No he wasn't…I'm sorry I should have told you earlier.'

'But the funeral?'

'A fake. He'd had a Muslim ceremony. I wanted my friends to remember Masood the way they knew him, as a Copt. He worshipped God and not Jesus or Mohammed. He found the words of the Holy Bible and the Holy Koran equally compelling. The coffin was empty.'

'So I was right about you not loving him.'

'No, you weren't right. It started like that but I did grow to love him. I told you before that he crossed boundaries. The icon proved that. It's been in his family for centuries. A Christian icon belonging to a Muslim

77

family. It shows how closely the major religions relate to one another. He believed it was man's prejudice that drove the religions apart. That's why I grew to love him. He broke down barriers between the religions and he was determined to bring my family's killers to justice. A view not supported by his colleagues.'

'Do those men who attacked you just now know that the funeral was fake?'

'Yes, they did…I had to tell them. They weren't at the funeral you attended…the fake funeral.'

'So they're Sunnis, like your husband?'

'Yes. But they are not Muslim Brotherhood.'

'But Masood was, wasn't he? That's why he got kicked out of the GIS?'

Amira hesitated. 'I didn't know that was the reason.'

'But you knew he worked for the GIS?'

'Yes, I did know. I'm sorry Richard. I shouldn't have lied to you.'

Richard could see she was telling the truth and his tone softened. The fact that Masood was a Muslim changed everything and nothing. A Sunni Muslim in Iraq made perfect sense. Saddam Hussein was a Sunni, so why would Masood not go to Iraq? Placing Masood in Iraq did not make things better, because he had no further recall of Masood in Iraq. Richard covered his eyes and tried to remember. 'It's okay. I forgive you.' He winked to lighten her mood and was pleased when she forced a smile. 'So if these men were friends with Masood, why are they threatening you?' he said.

'They want to know what Masood was up to. They asked who you were.'

Richard tried his tea, taking cautious sips. 'They must be his former colleagues at the GIS. They will be Sunni like Masood but not Muslim Brotherhood. It's his membership of that organisation that was the problem.'

Amira nodded, picking up the paper cup of hot black

tea. She lifted the tea to her lips and took a small mouthful. Richard watched the movement on her lips and immediately thought of Becky, feeling guilty that he could be attracted to this woman in front of him.

'Will the men come back?'

'Probably…But I know nothing. I think they are beginning to believe me.'

'So you don't know why Masood would follow me? He knows I'm not the killer.'

'I think he was working with someone who knew who killed my family.'

'Who?'

'I don't know…That's what these men want to know and there's nothing I can do because I don't know what he was doing any more than they do.'

Chapter Seven

London. July 21ˢᵗ 2005

The British Airways flight into Athens was full. As the plane prepared for its approach, Richard peered down over the city, his mind buzzing with all the possibilities of spending some time here. He could see the Parthenon standing on the hill, presiding over Athens, a city that was reborn after the Olympics, but one year later he knew it was a city in decline.

He closed his eyes as the plane clunked through the noisy routine of lowering its undercarriage. An image of his father came into his mind, not a living memory, but a black and white formal photograph of a man in a suit he remembered seeing on his mother's dressing table. The thought made him angry. He just couldn't build a picture of his real father. The letters were a chink of light in the barrier his father had built up against him. An opening that had come too late and had now been taken away.

As the plane banked once more, straightening up for the runway, he looked out of the window. They were now low enough above the sea to make out men on the decks of fishing boats and hydrofoils winging their way to the islands. *The Isles of Greece,* he said to himself, mouthing the first lines of Byron's poem.

The tyres hit the runway with a bump. Although it was a relief to leave London, he felt guilty that he was running away from Becky while she was carrying his child; from his mother with her mysterious telephone calls; and from Amira standing alone against the Egyptian security service. If anything, his attraction to Amira had drawn him closer to Becky in a perverse way, because he began to appreciate what she really meant to him. He'd sent Becky flowers and was pleased that she'd mellowed a little.

Athens airport looked good, fresh from the modernisation needed for the Olympics. TV screens were everywhere. At first, he didn't look, expecting the usual diet of Greek politics, but then the unmistakable sight of the London Underground filled the screens. The Greek reporters were frantic, as they always were, but it didn't take him long to work out that the bombers had returned. The Service had failed again. Five bombers and they didn't know any of them. At least the terrorists had cocked up this time. The detonators hadn't exploded. One of them had bottled it and left the bomb in a bin. *Thank Christ I'm out of London.* Rowena would be tearing her hair out that terrorists had struck again, thankfully with no loss of life, but still it was very distressing. There was no way he was going to call her to say he'd landed. Instead, he took the taxi to the embassy.

When he arrived, they were busy and didn't have much time for him. The embassy was briefing the press about the bombings and he was in the way. Brian Soper came down the stairs to meet him, looking flustered, sweating despite the air conditioning.

'Have to leave you on your own today,' Brian said, shaking Richard's hand. 'Have you heard the news?'

He nodded. 'Sorry to turn up at a bad time.'

'Bloody terrorists at it again, and we don't have a fucking clue,' he said. 'C's going crazy because we don't have a handle on it. I've got to go to Cyprus tomorrow and see if I can gee them up a bit and get some Intel. GCHQ must be listening in the wrong places.'

Soper didn't look like a spook. More like a colonial, a refugee from the Raj, who still thought we still had an empire. He was in his fifties, dishevelled and past caring. His suit was lightweight and creased and his tie seemed to be an afterthought, tied loosely and hanging at an angle around an unbuttoned collar. Richard caught a faint smell of cologne mixed with whiff of strong Greek cigarettes. A spy should blend in, like a normal member of the embassy staff, Richard thought. Isn't that what the manual said?

'Don't bother coming in tomorrow. Settle in and do the Athens sights. We'll talk on Monday when I'm back from Cyprus,' Soper said, shaking his hand again.

'Okay, I'll do that,' said Richard. 'I don't want to be a nuisance.'

Soper nodded and rushed back upstairs.

His hotel, on the edge of the Plaka district, had views of the Acropolis. He stood in the lobby waiting to be served at reception, looking through huge windows emphasising the hotel's pole position in front of the ancient complex. The sun was beginning to go down and as he peered outwards, the Parthenon's spotlights came on. It looked better illuminated, he decided, because the lights hid its flaws.

As soon as he got to his hotel room, he dialled the number he'd been given for Nikoletta Marides. He almost cheered with excitement when a woman answered.

'Is that Nikoletta Marides?' He spoke in Greek.

'Yes. Who wants to know?'

'Good evening, madam. My name is Richard Helford. I'm British, here in Athens. I understand you knew my grandfather in Crete.'

There was silence which lasted several seconds.

'Are you still there…madam? I would very much like to meet you.' More silence.

'I'm sorry,' she spoke at last. 'Of course, I remember Lenny and I met David years ago, but who are you?'

'I'm his son. My father is dead.'

She coughed and that set her off into a more violent spasm. After a couple of minutes, the coughing subsided and she tried to speak. Her vocal chords sounded as if they'd been rubbed by sandpaper. Her voice was deep and gravelly. 'I'm sorry. I smoke too much and this is a great shock to me. Hearing the name Helford again, and you say he's dead? How?'

'He was killed in New York when the planes hit the twin towers on 9/11.'

Richard was surprised that there was no immediate reaction from the old woman. 'Are you all right, madam?' he said, but still there was no sound. It was as if she didn't know what to say. After several minutes, she spoke. 'That is too terrible for words…' There was another pause. Her breathing became more erratic, she sounded upset. 'I'm sorry…Your family are cursed.'

Richard didn't understand what she was saying but decided not to dwell on the subject of his father's death at the moment. 'You live in Exarchia, I believe, madam. May I meet you in Exarchia Square in Café Exarchia, say about 11 a.m. tomorrow?'

'Yes. I'll be there. I met your grandfather and father, so why not meet another generation of Helfords?'

'I'll be reading a book of Byron's poems so that you can recognise me. I think it's unlikely there will be anybody else reading an English book in Exarchia.'

'I'll know who you are,' she said.

Exarchia Square, Athens. July 22nd 2005

The demonstration had reached a moment when it became a riot. The police needed little prompting as riot helmets were put on, visors pulled down and shields presented to repel the bottles and cans thrown by the students. A car overturned and exploded into flames to a great cheer from the protesters as they swarmed towards the police cordon. Riots were routine in Athens and especially in Exarchia Square. It was more a triangle than a square, covered in trees and loved by anarchists.

He arrived before it started. The people in the Café Exarchia did not appear the least concerned by the commotion on the other side of the square. They looked up as the car burned, before going back to their heated conversations, backgammon, or whatever else occupied them while they supped their daily fix of caffeine. He knew they relished the square's notoriety. It was a place where the sight of graffiti and burning tyres were all too familiar. If you come to Exarchia, you expect trouble, he thought.

Nikoletta hadn't arrived and as the riot escalated, he wondered whether she'd be able push through the crowds. He continued thumbing through his book of Byron's poetry, making sure the cover was visible. Unable to concentrate, he watched the demonstration while others in the café continued to ignore it. The waiter, muttering his disapproval at the students, came over and took his order for a Greek coffee.

When the coffee arrived, she still hadn't come. Twenty more minutes passed before he noticed an old woman out of the corner of his eye. She was stooping, walking with great effort, carrying a large string shopping bag loaded with bulbous tomatoes and two bread loaves. In the other hand, she clutched a book. It looked like a Bible as he could see a gold cross embossed on a leather cover. He stood up, taking hold of her shopping bag and pulling a chair back.

'Madam Marides,' he said, without confirming first that this was the woman he'd arranged to meet. The old woman sank down into the chair as if she was falling into a bed. She wore a burgundy headscarf, which was brightened by gold medallions sewn into the seam and tied tight under her chin. Some grey hair, which had broken loose, was hanging down her wrinkled forehead. The rest of her face was creased, like a gnarled olive tree, from years of exposure to the unforgiving Greek sun.

'Let me get you a coffee while you catch your breath,' he said, glad that she was understanding his Greek. Since he'd taken over the Greek desk his use of the language was mainly confined to reading and watching Greek television. To actually speak it again and be understood pleased him. When the coffee arrived with a glass of water, he stopped talking while she drank some of her coffee, her hands shaking, taking all her effort to stop it spilling. She must be over ninety years old, he thought, and yet there was a sharpness in her eyes which belied her age.

The police were now pushing forward with a line of shields and, from behind that row, tear gas canisters were fired. The rioters immediately backed off while they tied scarves around their faces to avoid the effects. The car flames had receded and thick black smoke repelled the tear gas.

'Fascist bastards,' she said, looking towards the protest. 'They don't remember the Nazis like I do. They don't remember the Military Junta and those that disappeared on November 17th. That Golden Dawn will be the death of Greece.' She lit a cigarette and inhaled deeply. This started another coughing fit, but it eased quickly, as if the smoke was providing some respite to her damaged lungs.

'There's some pills in my bag,' she said, raising her voice so it could be heard above the noise of the protest. 'Hand me one.'

He did as she asked. 'We can go somewhere else,' he said, more concerned at the progress of the riot.

'There is no need,' she said, shrugging her shoulders. 'The gas will never reach us and it looks as if the police have taken control. These things are always happening in Exarchia.' She turned back to him. 'You know, looking at you now, I could have sworn I was looking at Lenny Helford.'

'My grandfather would've been a similar age to me in 1941,' he replied. 'Tell me something, Madam Marides.' He paused to allow her to drink some water and sip her coffee. 'When you met my father, did he tell you how he came to find you?'

'No, he didn't. He seemed agitated when we met, looking around all the time, in a hurry to know what happened to his father.'

'And did you tell him?'

'I never found out how Lenny died. Between 1941, when the Germans came, and the end of the war, I thought he might be hiding in the mountains, but nobody saw him again. When the war cemetery was set up in Suda Bay, his name was inscribed on one of the gravestones. So somebody must have found his remains. Many of the bodies were buried in makeshift graves before they were moved to the cemetery so identification must have been impossible.'

'I suppose they relied on dog collars but what do you think happened to him?'

'The Nazis. They murdered your grandfather, I'm sure of it...I just don't know how but they murdered so many, so why not Lenny? And now your father dies in New York. Like I said, your family is cursed.' Tears were trickling down the old woman's cheeks. She dabbed them away with a paper napkin and, after taking another sip of coffee, she continued. 'You know, I've told people of my memories a thousand times and I still cannot stop crying. It seems like yesterday.'

'Has anybody asked you these questions other than my father?'

'Nobody important. Some of the surviving villagers but…'

'But what?'

'There was an American…said he was a historian researching the battle of Crete. I didn't believe him because he never wrote anything down.'

'When did this happen?'

'About three years ago – 2002. He was very interested in Lenny and asked whether I'd spoken to your father. When I told him that we had met, he seemed relieved it was in the spring of 2001. He said he'd like to talk to him and gave me a number to call if your father ever made contact again.'

'So he didn't know he'd died in 2001, and of course you didn't know either.'

'No. You are right, I didn't know.'

'Do you still have the number?'

'Yes, in my apartment. If you call me, I'll give it to you.'

Richard was puzzled, assuming it was the CIA sniffing around as Rowena had said, their enquiries seemed to be more focused on his father rather than what happened in 1941. He could easily get GCHQ to verify the ownership of the number but surely they would have known about his father being killed in 9/11. None of it made any sense. 'What was it like when the Nazis invaded?' Richard spoke softly, tying to soothe out the bitter memories.

'They were bastards,' she huffed, pulling a face, showing she was disgusted at the images in her mind. 'Their leader was the worst type of human being…a sadistic murderer. His name was Kohlenz. I'm ashamed that he took a shine to me. I was his whore till the end of the war.' Her eyes were hard, the memories still painful. 'I didn't want to be, but it was self-preservation. Give them what they want and you'll survive.' She stared at Richard, grabbing his arm. 'I don't expect you to understand any more than the villagers understood. They called me a dirty collaborator and hounded me, forcing me to leave, treating me like horseshit to be scraped off their boots.'

It was hard for him to imagine this frail old woman being a whore for anybody. Her frank admission surprised him, but his instinct told him that she was telling the truth.

'Tell me what happened,' he said.

Her coughing had started again. Her face was red and puffed up from the effort of breathing. He handed her the glass of water, which she gulped too fast, spluttering the water out of her mouth and down her chin. She picked up the paper napkin and wiped her mouth before spitting mucous into it to clear her lungs. 'He was a great man, your grandfather,' she continued. 'There was so much rivalry among Cretans during the war between fascists and communists. We would fight among ourselves instead of dealing with the real enemy – the Nazis. Your grandfather worked hard to bring the various factions together, but I'm ashamed to say I betrayed him.'

Richard's stomach muscles clenched. He took a deep breath not wanting to be angry with this old woman. 'What happened?' he said abruptly.

'I'm sorry…I can see you're angry,' said Nikoletta. 'And rightly so,' she continued. 'I gave him up to the Germans, to save Ikaros Poliakis.'

Richard ears pricked up when she said the name. The name that his father had written on the inside of an envelope. 'I've heard of that name before,' he said. 'My father wrote it down in a secretive way, as if he didn't want it seen. He wrote *HT674 675 Ikaros Poliakis*. Do you know what that means?'

Nikoletta thought for a moment and then shook her head. 'No, the number means nothing to me,' she replied.

'Where's Ikaros now? Is he still alive?'

'I don't know. I wish I did. I would beg your grandfather's forgiveness if I could see him now.' She hung her head, taking out a dirty rag to wipe her eyes.

'Did you tell the American about Ikaros?'

'No. I did not. I didn't trust him.'

Richard knew he'd have to get Ikaros checked out to see whether he'd died or not. So he dropped that line of questioning. 'So, going back to my grandfather, tell me what happened to make you think you betrayed him?'

The lines on Nikoletta's face became more creased, as if she was ringing out the years of bad memory. 'I did things in the war which make me weep when I think about them now. I thought Ikaros was going to be killed so I betrayed your grandfather so he could be spared.' She looked away from his eyes and back towards the protest, trying to hide her embarrassment at her excuse. 'He was British after all, not that I've got anything against the British, mind you. It's just we needed to protect our own. Ikaros was a Greek and I thought I loved him.'

All the time Nikoletta had been speaking he tried not to notice the book on the table, keeping his eyes fixed on her face but when she stopped his eyes drifted down to towards it. The old woman noticed and pushed it across the table. 'I want you to have this,' she said.

He took it and saw that his earlier suspicions had been correct. It was a Bible, leather bound with pages edged in gold. There were some illustrations in the opening page and a name written in fading blue ink. Callidora Zaminos, it said.

'Who was Callidora?'

'She was a Cretan girl who lived in our village. All the men wanted to marry her as she was very beautiful. When she was ten years old, the family sent her away to the Monastery in Preveli to help the monks with cooking and cleaning. One of the monks educated her. When she came back to the village, the monk used to send her books, which she'd take up the mountains to read while she looked after her goats. I was jealous of Callidora because Ikaros loved her and not me.'

'So where did you get the Bible?'

'I found it quite by chance in one of the caves the resistance used. After Lenny disappeared.' She paused and Richard could see she was back in the cave reliving the past. 'You know I can remember everything in that time as clear as if it happened yesterday, but ask me what I had for dinner last night and I'll be lost for words…Could you get me another coffee?'

Richard ordered the coffee and then turned back to Nikoletta. 'Please go on, Madam Marides, if it's not too tiring for you?'

She coughed and drank some more water. 'I'm all right,' she said. 'There were a lot of discarded things in the cave and when I lifted an old blanket up, this Bible fell out.'

The coffee arrived and Nikoletta took a few sips before drinking the glass of ice-cooled water served up with the expresso. 'There are some cryptic notes in the book which I don't understand.'

'Give me an example,' Richard asked.

She took the Bible back from him and flicked the pages. 'Look at this one that Callidora has underlined. It's from Exodus.' She turned the page and read, *'And Moses wrote down all the words of the Lord. He rose early in the morning and built an altar at the foot of the mountain, and twelve pillars, according to the twelve tribes of Israel.'*

'So – what does that tell me?' said Richard.

'Notice how she has double underlined *foot of the mountain*. She appears to be trying to tell us something, but I have no idea what. There are lots of mountains in Crete. They call them the White Mountains.'

Richard took the Bible back from the old woman and turned a few pages. There were lots of annotations but none of them made any sense. The illustrations were of saints. He thought he recognised St George, but the rest were unclear to him.

'So why is this book so important?'

'I don't know; it was just that your father seemed interested in it.'

'So why didn't you give this Bible to my father when you met him?' asked Richard.

'Good question,' she replied. 'I was going to give it to him but he didn't turn up for a second meeting we'd arranged. He left in a hurry and that was the last I saw of him.'

'But you did tell him about Callidora?' Richard asked.

'Yes, he wanted names of everybody in the village, to trace everybody who might still be alive.'

He could see that the old woman was tiring and that he should not trouble her too much. The riot was subsiding and the police were regaining control. Nikoletta looked back across the square, watching as the students dispersed or were arrested. She finished the last dregs of her coffee. 'I've had my life ruined by the fascists,' she said. 'I don't want to watch Golden Dawn make matters worse. I'm glad that I won't live to see it.' She cleared her throat and began to cough once more. Her face looked troubled as if she might still be holding something back.

'Is there something else you want to tell me?' Richard said.

Nikoletta stopped and closed her eyes as if recalling one more painful memory. With the demonstration still echoing chants around the square and the heat of the sun sucking out what little air remained in the polluted Athens haze, the old woman struggled to breathe. 'You know...Your grandfather wasn't the only person I betrayed,' she said.

'Go on,' said Richard. 'Tell me...I won't judge you.'

Her voice was breaking. 'Ikaros married me after the war, to protect me from the hatred of the people who called me a collaborator. One day, they grabbed me and started cutting off my hair, spitting on me, calling me a whore and a slut. He rescued me. We had to hide in the mountains where nobody would find us.' She stopped talking. Her voice was becoming quieter; he had to lean forward to hear what she was saying above the noise going on in the square. 'He gave up his freedom for me and how did I repay it?' Richard could see how upset she'd become. She sneezed into her rag.

'What did you do?' he asked.

The old woman stared into space; the memory was too much. Her lips began to quiver and she wept. 'I was selfish and couldn't live like that. A hermit in the mountains.' People were beginning to notice her distress, looking up from their coffee. 'I left him after the war and never saw him again...probably dead by now. But if he's alive, he'll be in Crete. If you go there, ask around...someone will know.' Richard steadied her shaking hand as she drank from the glass of water. Her eyes filled with sadness. 'I thought I loved him,' she said. 'To leave him was unforgiveable. I didn't deserve his kindness.' She sighed and shrugged her shoulders. 'I was stupid,' she said.

Nikoletta sat in silence, lost in thought. Even though he stared at her, she seemed oblivious to his presence or the continued commotion in the square. He touched her arm gently and that jolted her back to the real world. 'We must go,' he said. Standing up, she rested her weight on him and he wondered whether she could still walk.

'Pass me my stick,' she said, with apparent impatience.

He handed it over and said. 'I'll call you for that number.'

She nodded.

As they walked slowly away, a man looked up from his newspaper, his eyes following them as they left the square.

Chapter Eight

Crete, Greece. May 20th 1941

It was the best time of the day. A time when, out of breath from her long climb, she heard the first sound of her goats, their bells ringing across the breeze, telling her that they were in good health. At first, she could only hear them, but as she strained her eyes, some looked back through the bushes, feasting on the wild spring harvest of the mountain.

It was a moment she'd never forget.

Without warning a new, hostile sound filled the air. An incessant droning, unnaturally, mechanical, drowning the peace. Callidora had heard bombers before, attacking British ships in Suda Bay, but this was different. It was louder and more ominous. She knew what she was hearing. Today was the day when the Germans would invade her country, just as her brother Nikos had predicted.

And then she saw them, waves after wave of planes in formation, blacking out the sun. These planes were not dropping bombs, but men in their hundreds, changing the sky into a myriad of mushroom shapes, like umbrellas floating to the ground. The men attached were falling helplessly, parachutes swirling in the breeze while they drifted to earth. Nikos had said the invasion would come from the sea, but he was wrong.

It was coming from the air.

She ran towards her village, slipping and stumbling down the path; her long dress only suitable for slow mountain descents. Fear at what danger lay above was taking over. Stopping, she stared again at the lurid sky, scared, but also in awe at the enormity of what she was seeing. Some of the larger planes were towing smaller planes in their wake. As she watched, the smaller planes were released from the tow and began floating to earth. Over in the bay, dive bombers were attacking ships. Screaming death, they were dropping out of the sky at terrifying speeds, like birds of prey swooping on their victims.

Approaching the village, she could see Germans in the sky getting closer. It was relentless and some were falling straight to earth, because bullets had punctured the silk of their parachutes. There were New Zealanders based near the village, she thought, so maybe they were killing the Germans. All around, she could see people coming out of houses, armed with everything they could carry. Pitchforks, scythes, sickles and knives used to cut vegetables. The church bell rang, not to summon to prayer, but to call the people to arms. There was Nikos, leading as he always did, followed by Father Manousos, carrying a rifle. As she ran towards them, she could see Nikos, armed with two large knives and carrying an ancient rifle that belonged to her grandfather. It had been hanging on the wall since she was a small child and never fired in anger. He didn't even use it to shoot birds and now Nikos intended to kill Germans.

Nikos saw her and shouted, 'Quick, Callidora, get inside.' He did not stop, but ran into a field where a German was about to land. She could see the soldier's uniform as her brother raised his rifle. The rifle may have been old, but it still fired and as a cloud of smoke cleared from its barrel, she saw the soldier slump in his harness, clutching his belly, screaming as he continued to fall. He hit the ground and Nikos was on him, snarling with rage, thrusting the knife into the soldier's bleeding body. For a moment, she lost sight of him as the parachute came down on top like a funeral shroud. More soldiers were hitting the ground. One struggled to free his parachute, but Ikaros got to him first, slitting his throat with a long knife. Recovering the German's machine gun, Ikaros fired into the air with some success as more soldiers fell to earth, dead before they hit the ground.

She could not stand the carnage any longer and turned back to the village, finding a barn where she could hide. A great crash shattered any hope that this might be a refuge. Something had hit the barn roof, tiles were breaking and then a loud thud made her jump with fear. She stood up to run, knowing a paratrooper was immediately above her in the hayloft.

She saw the German's legs first, climbing down the ladder. He didn't get far.

Ikaros must have seen the parachute hit the roof. One minute she was on her own and the next, he was by her side, a trail of fire spewing from his gun, hitting the roof, drilling huge splinters of wood as it raked the loft floor. An agonising cry shattered the silence as the firing stopped. The soldier who'd come through the roof toppled head first down the ladder; bullet holes riddled his body.

'Stay down,' Ikaros shouted.

She could see the violence in his eyes as he ran past out of the barn. Shaking, she tried not to look at the soldier, dead at her feet. She moved slowly around him, reaching for the barn door, taking care not to step in the pool of blood that formed a ring round his body. She noticed the soldier's gun lying on the floor and picked it up. It needed two hands to grip it firmly, but she decided to keep it. The door was ajar and for a moment she peered through into the field, nerves jangling with fear, wondering what horrors were out there. Slowly, she pushed the door back. A few weeks ago, she'd have looked at a meadow of wild flowers. Now there was only death. The fighting was moving away from the village as quickly as it had begun. Dead soldiers were everywhere, but there was no sign of the living. The men must have gone into the fields, she thought, determined to push the Germans back.

The smell of death lingered in the air. One of the soldiers was hanging from an olive tree, still attached to his parachute, a vacant stare, his last moments frozen in his eyes. She'd never seen a dead body before today. He was just a boy, she thought, younger than me. Her hands clenched tightly against the cold steel of the gun. Her pace quickened, although she was finding it difficult to move while carrying such a weight. She looked around, turning as she walked, convinced that the danger hadn't passed. It would have been easy to stay hidden until Nikos returned, but the stench of death revolted her; she had to get away.

Then she saw something.

Ever aware of the slightest movement, attuned to the rustling of her goats in the undergrowth, the soldier was easy to spot, his grey combat fatigues standing out against the background of long grass and olive trees. Her gun went off, a nervous reaction to her fear. She fired several rounds and, as the gun recoiled, the bullets went everywhere. The soldier broke cover and charged towards her.

'*Stoppen,*' he screamed, raising his gun but refusing to fire.

She fired again and watched as bullets found their mark. The soldier staggered, but regained his balance, continuing to run towards her. She could see the blood from his wounds streaming from his chest, but he kept going. Terrified, she squeezed the trigger once more. There was no need, the soldier collapsed, falling heavily into the dust. For a moment, she stood motionless, dropping the gun from her shaking hands, staring in disbelief at what she'd done.

Sinking down into the dust, she struggled to breathe as her body began to convulse with terror.

He wouldn't kill me because I'm a woman.

The thought made her weep, but fear overrode her feeling of guilt. Picking up the gun again, she found herself running on the path to the little church of St John. She had no idea why she wanted to go to the church. Maybe she wanted forgiveness, but all she knew was she had to get away from what she'd done. She stumbled up a long trail of steps, painted white to fend off ants and to mark out a path where visitors could pray while crawling up the hillside on their knees completing their personal Calvary. Nearly reaching the top, she sunk to her own knees weeping, crawling the final few steps. At the top, she could see the church looking vulnerable to bombers. She had to save the icons, if only to win forgiveness. 'That's why I've come up here,' she said to herself. 'But God only now made me understand. The icons must not be lost.'

She knew a New Zealand brigade had recognised the weak point and had dug in among the trees that fringed the plain. It looked as if they'd chosen well because in the middle of a field, about a hundred metres away, a crashed glider had ploughed almost headlong into the ground, its fuselage a warped and tangled mess. It seemed to be deserted.

Entering the church, she walked down the aisle and kissed the icons that were on view at the front. Putting the gun down on one of the benches, she made the sign of the cross before lifting them off the wall. There were four icons to take away. The two she had taken were of St John and the Blessed Virgin. The other two were at each side of the altar and were stranger looking and harder to reach. She didn't know whom the icons depicted. Father Manousos considered them to be the more precious. It was the darkest corner of the church, the sunlight providing the faintest illumination through a small window at the side. She extinguished two candles lit in front of these two icons and lifted each one in turn from the wall. They were quite small and would be easy to carry, but her worry was where to hide them where they would be safe from German looting.

A noise caught her attention; a shuffling sound from the back of the church. She turned and peered back towards the entrance. A door opened. She could see something emerging from the shadows.

She noticed the uniform first. A helmet, like all the other dead paratroopers she'd seen. Bending down, she prayed he hadn't seen her. She put the icons on a seat and reached for the gun. She could see him in her sights. Firing would be easy.

But she couldn't kill another man. Not in a church.

'Stop,' she shouted still hidden in the shadows. 'I'll shoot if you come any further.'

'Don't shoot,' the soldier shouted in Greek, putting his hands in the air, while his gun hung loosely by a strap round his neck. She stared at him, conscious that the muzzle of her gun was shaking as she held her finger on the trigger, shivering with fear as his face became clear. He was tall, blond and young, about her age – which was twenty. *Please God. Don't make me kill again.*

'Don't come any closer or I'll fire.' Her finger tightened on the trigger.

'I mean you no harm,' he said again, still in Greek. Slowly, he edged closer to her. She stepped back not wanting to be close enough for him to lunge forward. 'No further,' she screamed.

'Look,' he said, slowly removing the machine gun and placing it on the ground. 'I don't want to hurt you. I'm wounded.' He was holding his arm and losing blood, wincing with pain.

She stepped back again, restoring the distance between them, gun still pointing.

'Those icons,' he said gently, looking across to the bench. 'You're right to take them off the wall and hide them.'

She moved nearer to where she'd put them, blocking the soldier's view.

'Don't touch them,' she screamed. 'They're sacred.'

'Not to be defiled by a German, I suppose,' he replied with a hint of sarcasm. 'I'd love to look closer at them.' He gritted his teeth; she could see the wound was killing him. 'But, you can see I'm bleeding and I don't want to damage them.'

She turned back to him, wondering whether to trust him.

Her voice softened. 'You're bleeding badly,' she said.

'I was in that glider that came down. I'm the only survivor.' He sat down on one of the pews, his face racked with evident pain.

Her natural desire to help a person in trouble fought the voice of her brother. These are invaders, he'd say, scum that should be punished.

'I'm going to take the icons…I'm going,' she stuttered. His hands were held high in the air as she edged passed him, still holding the gun, struggling with its weight. Reaching the door, she grabbed its handle and rushed outside, relieved she'd escaped. She should tell the men. They'll kill him and that will be the end of the matter. The wood where she'd decided to hide the icons ran right up to the church. She knew exactly where to leave them – about two minutes' walk into the wood, a rock fall of what appeared to be heavy, immovable boulders. She knew differently. It had been a hiding place for her since she was small. Somewhere to come when she needed to get away and read the Bible that the monks had given her. A loose rock, no more than six inches wide, had cracked like a chip from the larger piece. When the smaller rock was removed, a large dry hole revealed itself.

When she returned to the church he was standing at the entrance.

He looked up. 'Thank you for not telling your men.'

'How do you know I haven't?' she snapped.

There was no time to answer. A sound had caught his attention. He looked up, the colour draining from his face.

'Stuka,' he shouted grabbing her hand. 'Run.'

The scream of the Stuka was unmistakable. An ear splitting siren rose to a more awful crescendo as it got nearer the ground. Running was easy, but finding somewhere to hide was harder. They reached a group of rocks and crouched down as low as possible, which would have been fine for a ground war. From the air, they were easy targets. The first bombs fell near where the glider had crashed, near the woods that bordered the plain, just beyond where the pilots must have thought the New Zealanders were dug in. Both bombs missed the targets, exploding with enormous ferocity, throwing mounds of earth into the air, igniting scrub. The fire spread and the crashed plane burst into flames. The soldier couldn't contain himself, breaking cover, distraught at the loss of his friends. He was exposed as the Stuka came in again.

This time it took the mantle of fighter, strafing the church with machine gun bursts. At the very last moment, the soldier rolled, the bullets missing him by inches, ploughing up the earth, ricocheting off the rocks. It was a wonder that he'd survived. As the plane pulled away and began climbing, she saw the pilot look down. The engines roared as the aircraft continued to climb and for a second its screeching seemed to go silent as it turned to commence its dive again. The sound was horrifying.

'He's coming for us,' the soldier shouted. There was a small indent in the rocks that he gestured towards. 'We've got to get to that cave. Run now.' He took her hand again

101

and they ran. The Stuka was completing its dive and the bomb was falling. She stumbled and picking herself up, looked in horror, frozen to the spot, as the bomber flew towards them. Bullets riddled the earth, ploughing up the ground, streaking in lines towards them. He dived forward, pulling her down in one movement and smothering her for protection. A bullet tore into his shoulder, passing straight through. With his one good hand, he dragged her towards the cave.

Then the bomb exploded. Bigger than the first two. Two hundred and fifty kilos of high explosive.

It entered the church roof and must have embedded itself in the floor before exploding. The little church never stood a chance. A deafening blast, followed by a whirlwind. It blew the roof into a thousand pieces, scattering debris down the rock face and onto the plain below. They pushed deeper into the rock as a shower of stone rained down on the earth. Her face touched his as he squashed up against her body, his large arms providing a shield from the fallout. For a moment, there was an eerie silence as dust floated across the landscape forming a small cloud until it dispersed a few seconds later. All she could hear was his breathing mingling with her own. The Stuka had gone and the church was no more. He released his grip, allowing her to step out and stare at the devastation. Speechless, she staggered round the ruins, unable to take in the destruction.

'It's a church,' she cursed the sky, waving her fists in defiance. She knelt down weeping. 'God will make you pay,' she moaned. Looking up, she saw the German clutching his shoulder. 'You've been hit again,' she said.

'It's nothing,' he said, trying to put on a brave face.

'You need someone to do something about that arm,' she said, knowing she could not ignore him now. *He saved my life.* Taking out her pocket knife, she removed the petticoat under her dress and cut out a piece large enough for a bandage. 'Give me your arm.'

He approached her and she tied a bandage to stem the flow of blood and then made a sling.

'Thank you,' he said. 'My name is Hans.'

'Why do you speak Greek?' Callidora said.

'That's why I'm here. My mother was Greek and she taught me the language. They picked me, because I could speak Greek. I was in the middle of my Theology degree in Germany when I was called up and now I'm fighting for my life. I'm very grateful to you, but I really need to try and get to my unit before I bleed to death.'

'It will be dark soon. You need to go. My people will kill you if they find you.' Explosions were continuing and planes circled overhead. 'Please don't kill my countrymen,' she pleaded. 'Follow the path behind you. Keep going until you reach the sea and when you do, turn left and that should bring you to the airfield. People will have heard the explosion. They'll be coming to find out what has happened.' She looked over the escarpment and saw some allied soldiers emerging from the cover of the woods. 'Look, you must go.' she said again.

He took hold of her hand. There was sweat dripping from his forehead and blood was now seeping from his shoulder. 'Thank you,' he said, struggling to force a smile. 'I'm sorry for my countrymen. I'm sorry about the church.'

'You are Greek now,' she said. 'You saved my life.'

She looked straight into his eyes. He was more scared than she was and his eyes were kind. 'What's your name?' he said as he walked away in the direction of the woods.

She stared back at him and thought of the soldier she'd killed. Hans had saved her life and the soldier she'd killed had refused to kill a woman. *There must be some good Germans.*

'Callidora,' she called.

He smiled. 'Of course. The gift of beauty. A fitting name for such a beautiful woman.' He turned and walked into the undergrowth and was gone.

For a moment, she stood and looked at the space where he'd been. *He knows what my name means.* That pleased her and she wasn't sure why.

It was a brief respite from the horror. She turned back to face the rubble of the church. Tears ran down her face. The sun had gone down and darkness engulfed her. *Thank God, I've saved the icons.* The moon was almost full and provided some light. She could see the old oak door in silhouette, still standing, closed but fixed to its frame where no stones now stood. She used the door as her guide and opened it moving forward slowly. Just in front of her she could see what was left of the little table with a drawer that held the candles and some matches. She flung herself forward clambering over the pile of rubble. Reaching the table, she scooped out all the candles and the matches. Her feeling of triumph was short lived. The earth began to loosen beneath her feet and collapse around her. She slipped and sat down to stop herself going any further downwards. It was hopeless.

As she looked down, something seemed to reflect back at her and then was gone, as if for a split second it had caught the moonlight. She was kneeling now and moving down the crater. The moon had vanished, perhaps passing behind a cloud, and she could see nothing. Not even her own hands clawing at the earth. Giving up, she tried to clamber back upwards to the door but every time she tried, she slipped down the crater. They would worry about her if she did not return that night, but there was really no way she was going to get back to the village. Retrieving one of the candles from her pocket, she lit it and moved it around in her vision to see if she could find another way out of the crater.

Again something caught her eye. It was like nothing she'd ever seen before. It reflected back her candlelight, appearing to glisten in the moonlight that had reappeared. It was about ten feet from her, so she tried to edge closer, on her stomach this time to reduce movement. Something was drawing her to the object as if her life depended on it.

Chapter Nine

Freiburg, Germany. July 22nd 2005

Although he lived in Berlin, Klaus Kleiner called Freiburg his home. It was where he was born and despite moving around the world, it would always be where he felt most secure. He'd been coming to the old cathedral since boyhood when he used to stare at the devastation of the Allied air raids, watching the men picking through the rubble as they started to rebuild the city.

It had taken him a few days to recover from his ordeal in Afghanistan. Fortunately, he'd persuaded Captain Langer to omit from his report the way he was discovered in remote Afghan terrain fifteen miles from the base. He shivered at the memory of the Muslim American with Ray-Bans, Rolex and a Kalashnikov.

Kleiner did not linger to admire the cathedral's stained glass windows and dark Gothic interior, choosing to head straight for the bell tower where he began climbing the first of the tower's two hundred and sixty-five steps. Half way up, he thought his lungs would burst, but when the discomfort was worth millions of dollars, giving up never crossed his mind.

Near the top, a man took two Euros for the final ascent and a chance to view the city. He slipped him a twenty and waved his government pass, telling him to close the tower until he came down. He continued upwards, passing the cathedral bells before the stairs became narrower and harder to climb, At the top, the reward for his exertions were spread out before him. He could see for miles. Vast swathes of the Black Forest almost surrounded the City.

He could see the Rhine and even France in the distance. He gasped for breath and stared at the perimeter of the tower without absorbing the view.

The man he was looking for stood a few feet from him. Although they'd never met, there was no question that this was who he'd had arranged to meet. Taking photos of the view, pretending to be a tourist, did not fit the man's appearance. He looked out of place in a suit, tie and dark glasses. No one in his right mind would climb the tower dressed like that. They were alone apart from a couple of genuine tourists also taking pictures. The man caught Kleiner's eye and stared without a flicker of acknowledgement. The intensity of the stare unnerved Kleiner; narrow eyes, cold and distant, impervious to fear, forcing him to shift his gaze. Kleiner went up to the tourists and waved his Berlin government pass, telling them to leave. At first they protested, having paid two euros for the privilege, but when he threatened to arrest them, they got the message.

When the tourists had gone he turned back to the man who appeared irritated rather than pleased to see him. 'Why did you bring me up here?' he said sharply.

'I thought you'd like the view,' Kleiner replied, not bothering to hide his sarcasm.

Kleiner noticed the annoyance on the man's face. There was a mutual distaste of each other's company. He suspected that the man was one of Multzeimer's personal bodyguards.

'Tell me, Herr Kleiner, why you would want to sell this document to a Jew?'

Kleiner forced a smile, taken aback by the abrupt question. 'I have no arguments with Israel. This is 2005 not 1939. Hitler is dead.'

The man ignored Kleiner's response and continued. 'Mr Multzeimer wants to see the scroll, but will not pay anything until he gets its authenticity verified.'

'Mr Multzeimer has already seen the letters, which have aroused his interest. I will also give you a photocopy of the scroll and a fragment, which you can use for carbon dating. That should be enough to satisfy him,' Kleiner replied.

'Not good enough. We need to see the original,' the man snapped.

'Well those are my terms. Perhaps Mr Multzeimer will consider that there are others who are interested, not least the Saudi billionaire Sheikh Mohammed Zabor Bin Hitani. He is prepared to pay one hundred million dollars for the document to be made available to the Saudi Wahhabi sect. The most fundamental view of Islam.'

The man grabbed Kleiner and glared, spitting out his words. 'Mr Multzeimer will never allow that to happen. Do you understand?'

Kleiner laughed. 'The Americans will not sanction any attacks on prominent Saudi's like Sheikh Zabor. There is evidence of the Saudi government's involvement with Al Qaeda.'

'It's not evidence, it's fact.'

'Of course I understand.' Kleiner tried to pull away from the man's hold. 'To secure your interest, make sure the first instalment of one million dollars is deposited in the Venezuelan account detailed here, forty-eight hours from now.' Kleiner handed the man an envelope. 'I will advise Mr Multzeimer by email when the photocopy of the document is available, including a fragment for carbon dating. We will then meet in this same location and I will expect a further nine million dollars to have been deposited in the same bank account.'

The man grunted acknowledgement and let go of Kleiner. 'Assuming we are happy with the document, when will we see the original?'

Kleiner laughed. 'That is easy. When I've received my money…I thought you might work that one out yourself.'

He'd touched a nerve. 'Don't fuck with me, you Nazi shit,' the man said, scathingly.

Kleiner struggled to get out his words. 'In the envelope there is a key. It fits a safe deposit box. I will tell you where to find that box when I've received the final instalment.'

'How can we trust you?'

Kleiner shrugged. 'You can't, but you'll know where to find me.'

The man bristled, pushing Kleiner up against the wall. 'If it was up to me, I'd toss you straight over the wall.' His eyes were right in Kleiner's face. 'If you double cross us, I'll kill you. Caput.' He sneered. 'I suppose you understand German.'

Kleiner took two steps backwards towards the stairs. His eyes remained fixed on the bodyguard, uttering a cynical laugh at the attempt to scare him. He moved backwards slowly. Why should he worry about this man when he'd sat in a cave facing the Taliban, not forgetting the Afghan with the American accent? Reaching the exit, Kleiner turned on his heels and disappeared down the stairwell.

The bodyguard lit a cigarette and leaned back on the wall of the tower and waited. After several minutes he took out a pair of binoculars and scanned the ground in front of the cathedral. Picking up Kleiner, he watched as the German hurried across the square.

The bodyguard let out a satisfied grunt. 'You can come out now,' he said.

A woman emerged from behind a tarpaulin which covered scaffolding used by restorers working on the tower.

'Did you get that?' asked the bodyguard.

'Every last word and some incriminating pictures,' said the woman. 'I especially liked the comments about the Americans letting the Saudis get away with links to terrorism. As if we didn't know that already...Do you know, we have evidence that Saudis, linked to the royal family, wired funds to two of the 9/11 hijackers in San Diego?'

'So what's new?'

The woman flicked her hair back over her shoulders, irritated by the bodyguard's flippant comment. She wore black motorbike leathers which contrasted with her blonde hair and pale complexion. 'What's new is that we are going to wipe Sheikh Zabor off the planet and this disgusting Nazi is going to help us do it.'

Chapter Ten

Athens, Greece. July 23rd 2005

Richard's hotel room was small and uninviting, overlooking the narrow streets of the Plaka. It was noisy outside with all the tavernas and shops that never closed whatever the time of day. He put on the TV in his room and found BBC World, thinking he might get an update on the London bombings. He'd seen the pictures the day before of the accidental shooting of Jean Charles de Menezes and now there was another bombing, but this time not in London. It had happened in Sharm al-Sheikh where over eighty people had been killed at hotels. Al Qaeda were again involved and Richard wondered what Amira would make of it when the bombers were once again attacking Egypt.

He needed some clear air to think and as it was Saturday, there was no need to go to the embassy. He decided to walk up to the Acropolis along the wide, pedestrian grand promenade that surrounds the ancient part of Athens. There were many tourists, street entertainers vying for trade and quite a few Greeks enjoying the sunshine, but he was too deep in his thoughts to even notice life around him. He called Nikoletta's number several times as he walked and got no reply. He'd also tried the night before without success. He needed that number to confirm its hotline status through to Langley. If it was CIA, why were they asking about his father? The more he thought about it the more he wondered whether his father had really died in the twin towers. It all seemed too crazy for words. But if he wasn't dead, why would his father fake his own death? There was nothing going on at work and his home life, however humdrum, was no excuse to run away in such dramatic fashion. He thought about his mother and the mysterious calls and the picture of his grandfather sent anonymously from New York. He could wait no longer for the number; he had to go to Nikoletta's flat.

The narrow streets of Exarchia were too far to walk in the intense Athens sunshine. If you did decide to walk, you'd be overcome by the traffic fumes. They'd done a lot to make things better, but in the summer, the streets were still a no go area.

'Are you sure you want to go there?' queried the taxi driver. 'It can be dangerous.'

'Quite sure,' he said.

In the cab, he continued to be lost in thought. Who were those men who attacked Amira? Maybe they were GIS? He didn't buy the story that they wanted to convert her to Islam. There was something else they were after. Information about who Masood was working for? Maybe Masood hadn't been tracking him when the bomb went off. Maybe he'd just imagined that Masood recognised him. All these thoughts swirled around in his mind as he got out of the cab at Eresou Street, close to Exarchia Square, where he had met Nikoletta. The buildings were covered in graffiti, which he tried to read without much success. What he could make out seemed to be anti-fascist and anti-government. It didn't feel dangerous, he thought, while walking down the narrow tree-lined streets to find Nikoletta's apartment. Nobody seemed bothered by his presence. It was quiet, but not somewhere you'd be worried about being mugged. The graffiti was not about crime, it was about defiance of the state. Nikoletta's apartment was above a shop selling second hand books. There was a side entrance and a steep rickety staircase to the first floor. The graffiti had continued inside. The walls leading up to the door were covered in an intricate design of slogans, like a mural, but with the same overall effect as a Jackson Pollack painting. At the top of the stairs, the door was open. The hallway was very dark and the light switch did not work.

'Nikoletta,' he shouted. 'Nikoletta.'

A muffled noise broke the silence. He thought it was coming from the living room.

Slowly, he pushed the door at the end of the hallway. A gloomy eeriness hung over the room. Small beams of sunlight provided some visibility through louvered shutters, which were closed. There was just enough light to take in the scene. A bed in the corner, dirty sheets in a pile, a bookcase, and a musty smell penetrated the room. There was no sign of blood, but there was no Nikoletta either.

Out of the corner of his eye, he saw it coming. The bookcase was moving, toppling towards him. He caught it, but the books kept coming, throwing him off balance as they rained down. Falling, he rolled clear and let the bookcase crash to the ground. Only now could he see his attacker, lunging forward, a knife in his hand. An Arab. Bringing his leg up hard into the man's groin, he stopped him in his tracks, sending the knife skidding across the floor. Instinct had taken over. The man winced with pain and in that split second, while he was disorientated, Richard was on his feet, picking up a dining chair, swinging it towards the Arab's head. He sidestepped, managing to avoid the full force of Richard's attack, but still taking the blow from the chair across his back. Pent up anger flowed through Richard's veins like a torrent, the horror of the bomb unravelling like a spring in his consciousness. This man was on the end of his anger. He wanted to kill him. Out of control, he hit him again until the chair was reduced to firewood. All that was left was one of its legs, gripped in his hand; it was no longer a weapon. He lifted his boot to finish him off. A stupid error. Despite his injuries, the man grabbed Richard's foot and clung on, forcing Richard off balance. He crashed to the floor groaning as his head caught the side of the bookcase. He swung his boot to free himself but still groggy from the assault, his head spinning, the Arab needed no prompting, the attacker rolled over and dashed for the door.

Jumping to his feet, Richard considered going after him but decided against it. He looked around the room. Papers were strewn everywhere. The Arab had been hunting for something, that much was sure, but it seemed he didn't know what to look for. Resisting the urge to start going through the papers, Richard went back into the hall and started to check the other rooms. There was nothing unusual about the kitchen, but then he noticed the bathroom door. Smears of blood were splashed across its surface. Fresh blood and certainly not his own.

His head hurt like hell and there were trickles of blood on his hand where he'd touched his forehead. His eyesight hadn't improved, still blurred as if his eyeballs were out of line with each other. The bruising and stitches from the bomb, which had been slowly healing, started to hurt again. His heart was racing, which didn't help. He was scared, knowing that there was something behind the door that he might not be able to deal with.

Pushing the door ajar was all he needed.

Nikoletta lay on her back, fully clothed in an empty bath, her body twisted awkwardly. Her skin was shrivelled and she was wet, suggesting the bath had been filled at some point. The man must have pushed her head under. Drowning is a great way to make someone talk, he thought, repulsed that anyone could do such a thing to an old woman. Her pulse was faint. Kneeling down, he put his face close to hers, looking for the slightest indication that she was breathing and might live a little longer.

'She's alive,' he said out loud. 'Must call an ambulance.' Talking to himself made things clearer. His brain pounded into his skull making it difficult to think, he couldn't keep any sort of focus. The paramedics couldn't give him a time when they might arrive.

He bellowed at them in Greek, 'It's an emergency. She's dying.' They seemed indifferent to her plight no matter how loudly he shouted. Cutting the call off, he examined her more closely to see whether it would be safe to move her. There were no broken bones, but her eyes were rolling in their sockets. Maybe drugs had been used. Leaning over the bath, he picked her up in his arms and carried her through to the bedroom.

Nikoletta was frail and therefore easy to lift. Laying her down, he tapped her lightly on the cheek. There were definite signs of drugs in her system – her eyeballs were open but glazed over. She looked distant. He shook her a little bit more.

'Nikoletta, can you hear me?'

She let out a louder cry and coughed. Her breathing became faster, wheezing, struggling to move her mouth.

'R...Richard,' she whispered. 'Callid....' Her voiced tailed off.

'I'm here. Nikoletta, do you mean Callidora?' he said.

Her lips were straining. 'I...I didn't tell them,' she stuttered. 'Ara...Arab.' Her eyes were closing.

'I'm so tired...chest so heavy...hurts...terrible pain.' She was gasping for breath, every word an effort. Her voice was barely audible. Her breathing was becoming even shallower.

'Tell them what?' he said. 'Tell me, Nikoletta.' He raised his voice, anxious that he was losing her.

She didn't answer the question. Her face covered in sweat, she let out a long groan. 'My chest. The pain,' she cried, grinding her teeth and rolling her eyes. She was dying, her breathing had stopped.

Richard pushed his hands down onto Nikoletta's lower breastbone, pumping her chest, trying to keep her heart going, but it was impossible. He continued applying CPR, but there was no sign that she would survive. She was slipping away.

Her eyes had closed and he thought she'd gone, but then they flickered open again. Her body was rigid as if an electric shock had been driven through it. A final attempt to stay alive, for just one more second.

'Uma will know,' she cried. There was nothing left. Her face became relaxed and all the trauma and worry of her life drifted away on a cloud. She was dead.

It was never easy to watch someone die, but just like with Masood on the train, he felt a sense of relief, because this woman would no longer cough or be in pain or pay the price of guilt and failure. The mistakes in her life no longer mattered. She was free.

Who is Uma?

For a moment, Richard stared at the frail old woman. She looked at peace, released from the trauma of her memories and the pain of her failing body. There had to be something else in the apartment for him to go on. He moved quickly, scanning the room, hoping he'd find something before the ambulance arrived. He had one advantage over the Arab; he could read Greek. Most of the papers were unpaid bills and the like, except one handwritten letter in rather stilted Greek. In the envelope he found a small photograph. It was a photograph of a woman, which on the back carried some names. One of them was identified by the simple name 'Uma'.

The ink was faded and the paper was cheap and thin, making the words difficult to read. Richard opened one of the shutters to let more light in and began to read.

Professor Uma Kastner
University of Heidelberg
Seminarstrasse 2
69117 Heidelberg
West Germany
20th January 1950

116

'Dear Madam Marides,

Thank you for taking the time to see me and tell me of your experiences in Crete in 1941. Your recollections of Captain Wolfgang Kohlenz are most interesting and also your knowledge of his address in Buenos Aires. I have passed the information you gave me to the relevant authorities in the hope that he may be brought to justice for his crimes. My research, however, is more concerned with what we discussed about a possible religious discovery made at the time of the Nazi occupation. I have evidence that the document relates to the writings of St John of Patmos. You appeared to verify the story but unfortunately do not know where the document can be found.

If you have any further thoughts on this subject, please do not hesitate to contact me. I will be visiting Crete to see whether I can find the missing document. All the background information has proved invaluable in my search for answers. Thank you again for your help.

Sincerely,
Uma Kastner

Given the age of the letter, he felt certain that there must be more letters, but he found nothing. It seemed strange that Nikoletta would remember Uma's name if she hadn't communicated with the professor for over fifty years. He slipped the letter and photograph into his pocket and remembered some of Nikoletta's final words.

'I didn't tell them.'

Didn't tell them what?

The ambulance arrived, but he sent them away again, saying the police would have to deal with the body as he thought the woman had been murdered. When the police arrived thirty minutes later, Richard dreaded the prospect of long police interviews and interminable Greek bureaucracy. Inspector Hector Petronos was, of course, like any Greek, not in a hurry. Why do something today, when tomorrow will do? He seemed rather disinterested in the case, giving off an impression of boredom, that he'd seen it all before.

Petronos did what was necessary and nothing more. He turned up with a forensic team who dusted down a few things and took the body away before the inevitable flies found their way into the hot musty flat which smelt of blocked drains and God knows what else. Richard watched with growing impatience at how long the formalities seemed to be taking, but Petronos ignored him and showed no signs that he didn't have all day. After over an hour, he turned towards Richard, his notebook in hand, playing a part. Richard decided Petronos had watched too many old episodes of *Columbo*.

'Do you know whether she has any next of kin?' asked Petronos.

'Not to my knowledge. I don't think she ever married,' Richard said, preferring not to mention what she'd said about her brief marriage to Ikaros.

'So you think she was murdered?'

'Yes. I'm certain of it,' Richard replied.

Petronos glared at Richard. 'How do you know that?' he snapped. 'It looks like a heart attack to me.'

'Because I interrupted the man who was attacking her. We had a fight but he escaped.'

Petronos smirked, suppressing a smile. 'I'd noticed you've been in the wars.'

'I think it was a drug-induced heart attack...You need to get the pathologist to check for sodium pentothal,' Richard replied, refusing to rise to the bait.

'What did the man look like?'

'He was an Arab, in his thirties, beard, medium build, not as tall as me. He had a small tattoo on his neck.

118

Petronos wrote everything down. 'Do you know what was taken?'

'I've no idea. This is the first time I've been here, so how the hell am I supposed to know?'

Petronos' eyes wandered around the room, settling on the bed. 'Did you find her on the bed?'

'No, she was in the bath, fully clothed. You must have seen that her clothes are damp. I lifted her to the bed because she was still alive.'

'Well that *is* interesting,' Petronos said, looking pleased with himself. 'This doesn't look like a burglary which has gone wrong. It's a deliberate murder.'

'There were lots of papers strewn about. I think they were looking for something,' said Richard.

'Why in God's name should anyone want to kill a little old lady?'

'And why would they drug her in a bath?'

'Exactly. Information…they wanted information…I wonder what they wanted that was worth killing an old lady for.' He was getting more interested in the case. 'Tell me why you'd come to see her.'

'Before I answer that question, Inspector, I should say that I'm a British diplomat.'

This made the inspector perk up a little more. 'So, I have a frail and rather poor old woman meeting an English diplomat. How strange. Then she is murdered for no apparent motive.' Petronos continued to write but faster, reflecting his newfound enthusiasm evident in his face.

He looked at Richard with a fixed gaze. His smirk had turned into a cynical sneer. 'Now tell me what a British diplomat would have to do with an elderly Greek woman who is often seen begging on the streets.' His words were laced with sarcasm.

'She knew my grandfather during the war. I've often wondered how he died. Is that good enough for you?'

'If you want my honest opinion, Mr Helford, I'll tell you,' said Petronos, understating the drama of his pronouncement. 'No. I don't think it is good enough.'

Chapter Eleven

Crete, Greece. May 21st 1941

Machine gun fire woke Kohlenz from his fitful sleep. He'd been walking for most of the night trying to get to his unit and find his men, but exhaustion had got the better of him. Collapsing in the middle of a bamboo thicket was a stroke of luck, giving him good cover while he slept, only for an hour, but at least it was something. Twenty hours earlier, a sudden gust of wind probably saved his life as he floated to earth, blowing him away from his unit, into the safety of the olive grove not easily reached by the enemy. He had watched, helpless as parachutes fell to earth, cut to shreds or in a ball of flames. They said it would be easy, but the first day had been a massacre. 'I'll make the bastards pay,' he said to himself.

A sound.

In the distance he could hear the incessant rattle of machine guns, but this was much closer. He lay still, focusing on the sound of bamboo breaking. Somebody was in the thicket, a few feet from him. He took out his knife, feeling the cold steel under his fingers, preparing to kill. He lunged forward through the bamboo, grabbing the body by the throat, preparing to plunge his knife into its neck. A badge made him stop. An eagle diving towards the earth, above a Swastika; *Fallschirmjager*. He let go and the two men toppled onto the ground.

The face was familiar. 'Hans Tuebingan,' he whispered, conscious that they might be heard by the enemy.

'Sir., Hans panted. 'Yes, it's me. I'm wounded.' The young soldier no longer had the energy to get to his feet, exhausted from his trek and terrified at the sight of blood slowly dripping from his wounds. The makeshift bandage applied by Callidora had stemmed the flow, but only temporarily.

Kohlenz could see that Hans had lost a lot of blood and needed attention. His breathing was irregular. Standing up, he peered out of the thicket. They were not alone. On one side, he could see the enemy, trying to defend the airfield, but he knew sheer force of numbers would soon make that impossible. They were on the edge of a dried-up riverbed, which could only be the Tavronitis. Two gliders had crash-landed just a few feet from him and he could see at least a hundred soldiers preparing to attack the airfield. He looked up at the sound of an aircraft engine approaching. Reinforcements, he thought. The Junkers came into view and with daring accuracy brought the plane to rest on the beach.

Tying a white handkerchief to his gun, Kohlenz stepped into view, hands held high and shouting in German anything he could think of.

'I've a wounded man,' he shouted.

Three miles away, Callidora woke at about the same time as Kohlenz. The sun was finding its place in the sky, burning her eyelids and prising them open. The sound of gunfire in the distance reminded her of what was happening and the memories of the Stuka attack came flooding back. She rolled over in order to get to her feet and saw the box immediately. She scrambled across to it and pulled it out of the earth where it was partly buried. For a moment, she could only stare in awe. Amazed at how perfect it was, untouched by the ravages of age. Using the lining of her dress, she gently cleared the dirt away from the paintings decorating the box. They were beautiful. On one side was a picture of a man, which was unquestionably Jesus. The background was gold leaf, but Jesus' halo was silver, embossed with intricate patterns. He was holding a large book with scripture on it, written in Greek and just large enough to read. Slowly, she read out loud,

'The seeker should not stop until he finds. When he does find he will be disturbed. After being disturbed, he will be astonished. Then he will reign over everything.'

She did not think these words were from the Bible, which seemed strange because on the back of the box was a painting of the Crucifixion. Again, the background was gold. She recognised, the women of Jesus at the foot of the cross. She could see his mother, Mary, weeping and Mary Magdalene stood beside her. On the other side of the cross was St John, the evangelist. There were no thieves crucified with him. Just Jesus, contorted with pain; his body discoloured, even grey, which she knew was meant to depict the final throes of death.

Where did this come from? It must have been below the floor of the church, cocooned in a stone chamber that the bomb had smashed. A miracle, she thought. Buried all this time and then in the heat of battle, it finds its way into the world from deep below the church foundations. She turned the box over in her hands. It was not large and quite light; not made of pine as there were no signs of resin that had leaked onto the surface of the paintings. It looked more like oak. *If it is a painting, why is it on a box and why put it below ground?* She thought about this, looking again at the paintings and, for inspiration, the words on the book Jesus was holding.

'The seeker should not stop until he finds.'

She looked closely and saw some nails that might be removed from the box. At first, she tried pulling with her fingers, but the nails were too deeply embedded into the wood. Then she noticed something unusual. The nails that

123

had been driven into Jesus feet and hands were not painted. They were real and appeared to be made of silver. She took out her knife and gently managed to get the blade under the head of one of the nails. To damage the painting would be a great mistake, but after moving her knife from side to side, it began to loosen. So as not to cause any further harm, she took the loosened nail between her teeth and tried to lift it free. It came out easily. The other two nails were easier to remove than the first and as last nail was freed, she felt the top of the box loosen. Carefully, she separated the painting of Jesus from the box and looked inside. Two cross pieces had been fixed to the inside so that the nails could be attached and the box reinforced. She gasped. Wedged under the two cross pieces, she could see a papyrus scroll tied with a leather cord.

She unwound the cord and opened the scroll. It was quite short and the words were clearly Greek and the ink, although faded, was still clear enough to read.

'I, John of Patmos, who shared with you the Revelations of God, bring you witness to the last word of the God who gave me visions of the end of the world. There is one other prophecy that I was forbidden to write down. It is the prophecy of the little scroll, the scroll that tastes sweet in the mouth and bitter in the stomach, referred to in my book of Revelations but never revealed. Something compelled me to write the words down, against the wishes of the angel who appeared to me in my dreams. I had to write it down in order to release myself from the pain of the great lie, burning a hole into my soul.'

Holding the papyrus in her shaking hands filled her with a sense of disbelief and awe. She couldn't believe her own eyes. Her first thought was to show it to the monks at Preveli. *What would Father Agathangelos think? He'd hail it a miracle.* It was her chance to repay him for the education she'd received as a child while

124

working in the monastery. She'd remembered reading him extracts from the Book of Apocalypse and been terrified by the images of the end of the world. *Could this really be the writings of St John of Patmos?*

But how would she deliver it to him? The Monastery at Preveli was miles away and if the Germans saw it, they'd certainly steal it for themselves. Her first thought was to hide the box with the icons. With great care, she put the scroll back into the box and drove the three nails into place using a small stone as a hammer. With the sun beating down, she could clearly see the way out, scrambling over the rubble of the church. Reaching the top, she looked over the parapet to the steps winding their way up the hillside. Several men were coming up the path. She took the box and returned to where she'd hidden the icons. It was as if her secret hiding place had been waiting for the sacred box all this time. It fitted perfectly and still had room for the icons she'd saved from the church.

Emerging from the wood, she went over to the entrance where the steps ended. Only the last few steps had been damaged by the bomb, such had been its precision. She recognised Nikos leading the group and began to wave.

Nikos waved back. 'Callidora,' he shouted.

'I'm here,' she replied.

'Thank God you're alive.' His face changed in an instant; the joy of seeing her dissolving into despair when he realised the church had been obliterated. 'Oh my God,' he screamed. 'What have they done to our church?'

'Stuka attack. I nearly died,' she said. Her face was black with the soil and her clothes were filthy. Ikaros had come as well and rushed forward to hug her. She couldn't smile. 'I killed a soldier,' she said. Her emotions welled inside, to see her brother again and even Ikaros, to discover they weren't dead, became too much. Tears

125

streaked her face, blackened with dirt. She thought of Hans and wondered whether he'd survived.

Nikos was angry, not with her, but with the Germans. 'How dare they destroy our holy church?' he shouted, waving his fists at the sky. 'We must look for the holy icons.'

'I've saved the icons,' said Callidora proudly. 'That's why I came up here. I've hidden them where the Germans have no chance of finding them.'

'Good,' said Nikos. 'We've got to get back to the village.'

She walked down the hill with Ikaros and Nikos both holding her hands, one on each side. She was relieved neither of them had shown any interest in seeing the icons. Above her, planes continued flying overhead, all of them German. The British Royal Air Force must have abandoned them to their fate, she decided. The fighting may have moved on towards the Maleme airfield, but she was sure the Germans would be back, ready to seek revenge. The final field before they entered the village was full of German bodies, perhaps twenty-five in all. She tried not to look as they walked. It brought back memories of the man she'd killed.

That afternoon, Nikos gathered everyone together where the corpses of the German paratroopers were scattered. 'These men may be our enemy,' he said, 'but they are with God now and it will be for him to judge them, not us. We must dignify them with a proper burial.'

Not everybody wanted to take part, but those who did were used to digging. A single ditch was prepared, big enough to bury all the bodies. Nikos cut down those soldiers left dangling in trees, discovering that one of them was still alive but only just. He hesitated and called Father Manousos over. Callidora watched them kneel down and look at the soldier. They nodded and Nikos raised his gun and fired. A single shot to the head.

Her eyes caught Nikos' as he turned to leave the body. A look of guilt etched across his face.

'He was mortally wounded,' he screamed. 'I had to do it, to put him out of his misery. Father Manousos agreed.'

Of course, he was right, but it didn't matter – she wanted to get away. She turned and headed back up the hill to the ruined church.

There was still plenty of light and the cicadas were in full song as dusk approached. Reaching the summit, she found herself descending the crater once more. 'There is something else. I'm certain,' she said to herself. The memory of the previous night came back. It couldn't have been the box that reflected so much brilliant light in her direction.

A glistening object dazzled as it caught the sun. Kneeling down, she began digging, plunging her fingers into the earth, scraping with her bare hands, clearing a channel until she knew what it was. A chalice, buried in the soil, and a little further down, she found a casket. She couldn't contain her excitement, frantic to lift it free from years of neglect. Not as old as the box she'd found earlier, but still priceless. Seeing the chalice, she knew this was no ordinary metal. She'd seen its like before, at the monastery in Prevelli. It was gold. No question.

But that wasn't the only thing she discovered. She knew now why she'd seen the reflected light. The lid of the chalice was covered in diamonds. She held it upwards, just like a priest might do, allowing the sunrays to enhance its beauty. An animal, possibly a dragon with many heads, was engraved into the base and stem, wrapping itself around the vessel, clinging with its teeth to the rim. She gasped, unable to comprehend how she could be holding an object of such breathtaking beauty.

127

The casket was no less stunning but for different reasons. It opened easily and inside she found another papyrus, about the same length as the scroll she'd seen in the painted box, and also a book. The book, bound in leather, had pages made from papyrus. The words were Greek and it was clearly a religious text. The title was large and striking and the first words immediately recognisable. They were the same as those on the painting:

The seeker should not stop until he finds.

The title took her by surprise, it was a Gospel. Not one by Mathew, Mark, Luke or John:

The Gospel of Thomas.

She turned her attention to the document, also written in Greek, and began to read.

My name is Prochorus. I am a student of John of Patmos. I came to this island to learn from my master, but instead, I watched him die, writhing in agony, his stomach burning with the pain of revelation, his visions of the end of the world haunting him until his last breath.

And now I hold his secret.

His book of Revelations is not the final word. He saw the mighty angel coming down from heaven, wrapped in a cloud with a rainbow over his head; his face was like the sun, and his legs were like pillars of fire. In his hand he held a little scroll.

The angel told him not to write it down. But he did write it down, and now I am the custodian. The man who must honour the angel's wish and keep the prophecy from the world.

It is a secret that you should eat and when you do, it will taste as sweet as honey in the mouth, but bitter in the stomach.

We stood at the entrance to his cave, where visions came to him, where he would write from dawn till dusk everything that God had said. The sun was falling into the sea, throwing a cloak of blazing orange around the little port of Skala that lies beneath us. The dying light picked out the lines of the cave's entrance, making it glisten like a shrine to his memory, as if God had already decided on his beatification. He handed me a wooden box with paintings on both sides. One side showed a crucifixion and the other, a man's face. I've never tired of looking at that face. Every time I look, I sense an all-consuming love, an intensity mixed with sorrow; something I could not explain.

'The prophecy of the little scroll is in this box,' he said. 'Never try to read it. Promise me, you will build a church and bury the box deep into its foundations where it will never be found, unless it is God's will.'

These were the last words he spoke; his pain was too great. I remember him clutching his stomach, bent double in agony. I can see him now, on the edge of that cliff, slowly tipping forward into space. The pull of the earth could no longer be resisted.

He fell into the Devil's darkness.

I wandered for many years with that box, aching to know. I read his book of Revelations over and over, preaching his message to anyone who cared to listen. It describes the existence of the little scroll, but does not hint at the secret it contained.

I built that church and hid the little scroll away from the world.

I never knew.

If you are reading this, maybe you will know.

Callidora gasped. Here was the reason why the scroll was hidden from the world. The secret had been passed into her hands. She must protect it with her life.

Chapter Twelve

Athens, Greece. July 24th 2005

It was mid-afternoon before Petronus let Richard go. He spent the rest of the day wandering around the ancient sites. He had no wish to play the tourist but it was preferable to being stuck in his hotel room staring at the ceiling. At least the stones of ancient Greece would not answer back and he could be anonymous among the huge crowds gathering around the Acropolis. After about an hour of wandering he found himself in the Agora and climbed to the temple of Hephaestus to sit in the garden. It's a Parthenon in miniature, he thought, but better preserved. He was oblivious to the people milling around taking photographs while he tried to make sense of Nikoletta's death. That an Arab was responsible, there was no doubt, and given the uncertain nature of his own departure from Iraq and the possibility that Masood might have been following him, there seemed to be a tenuous connection. What did Nikoletta *not* tell her killer and who was Uma? He needed to talk to someone. He called Becky, but there was no answer. He wanted to apologise and left a message.

'Becky. I'm in Athens. I want to say sorry...' He struggled to find the words. 'It's not that I don't love you. It's just that I can't get married...not now...sorry...call me, please.' He ended the call abruptly, embarrassed by what he was saying.

He continued to stare at the phone, aimlessly scrolling through his contacts over and over again and always stopping at Amira's number. His finger hovered over the green call button for at least a minute before he pressed it.

'Amira?'

'Richard. It's you. Thank God you've called.' Her voice sounded scared.

'Are you okay, Amira?'

'It's just…' Her voice was breaking as if she'd been crying.

'What's the matter? Have those men been back?'

'No…no…nothing like that.' She hesitated and he thought she was lying. Her breathing seemed heavy. He could sense her uneasiness. 'I've found something in Masood's things. There is a reason why Masood was watching you.'

'I'm sure that was just a figment of my imagination,' Richard replied, unconvinced by his own assertion.

'No, it wasn't your imagination.'

'Okay. Maybe you're right. How do you know Masood was watching me?'

'I can't tell you on the phone. We must meet,' she said.

'That could be difficult as I'm in Athens…work related.' He thought for a moment. 'I can't get back to London but I can arrange for a secure line through my work. I'm going to text you a number and a code. Call the number and then key in the code and it will patch through to me on a scrambled line.'

He hung up and texted the details she needed. Fifteen minutes passed and he wondered whether she would actually do it. It was nearly twenty by the time the call connected.

'I was worried, Amira,' he said. 'What took you so long?'

She ignored his question. 'Are you sure this line is secure?' she asked abruptly.

'Yes. My government have the best encrypted lines in the world. Nobody will hear. Believe me.'

Her reticence worried Richard. Something didn't seem right. 'Are you sure you're all right?' he said, anxiously.

She didn't reply. Her silence indicated she didn't want to lie. He was certain there was something wrong. 'Please tell me what's going on, Amira.'

'As I told you, Masood was a Muslim. When he joined the GIS he pretended to be a Copt but they must have found out he was in the Muslim Brotherhood. You were right, that's why he was thrown out of the Service.'

'Okay. Makes sense.'

'He started working for someone else, to understand more about how my family was killed.'

'Who?'

'I'm coming to that…It was fate that you met Masood on that train, but it certainly wasn't fate that you were in the same carriage. He *was* following you.'

It was almost a relief to know his suspicions were right. 'How do you know he was following me?'

'Your name.' she replied. 'Helford. Your name has attracted the attention of Al Qaeda. Masood found this out…I found Masood's notebook.'

'Al Qaeda,' he shouted down the phone. 'Why on earth would they be interested in the Helford name?

'Something your father did which gave them reason to want to kill him.'

'But my father is dead.'

'They think he's alive and that you know where he is…That's why Masood was following you. They thought you might lead them to your father.' Amira paused, allowing the shock to sink in. 'There's something else…I also found a mobile phone with just one number programmed. It has a strange number of digits but I think it's in Afghanistan.'

'It's probably a satellite phone. Give me the number and I'll get our people to track it.'

There was a moment of silence, then she reeled out the number.

'So you didn't call the number?'

'No.'

'Why not?'

'Because I knew already who Masood was talking to...It's in Masood's notebook...He hadn't intended anybody to see it. It was hidden very well.'

'Who was Masood calling then?'

'Mohammed Abdul Alim. He's on the United States Kill List. I know because I checked his name on the Internet.'

Richard didn't know what to say. It sounded too crazy for words. At last, he spoke. 'So let me get this right. Are you telling me that this Abdul Alim guy, wanted by the US government for terrorism, is trying to find my father and kill him? Even though we've got no evidence that he's alive.'

'Yes.'

'Hang on a minute...' Richard knew something in this story didn't stack up. Something clicked in his mind. 'Why on earth would Masood want to work with this guy?'

'He was trying to win his trust,' Amira replied.

'Why?'

'So that he could get close enough to kill him.'

'What? For the bounty on his head?'

'No. He wasn't interested in money. He wanted to kill Abdul to prove his love for me.' Amira was crying now. Although he could only hear her voice, he saw her beautiful face in his mind, tears soaking cheeks. 'I didn't know he loved me so much...He'd risk his own life.'

'Is that why you sounded so distressed when we first spoke?'

'Yes. It was.'

'Why do you want Abdul dead? I know he's a bad guy, but what's he done to harm you?'

Amira was silent for a few seconds. Her breathing was erratic. 'He was responsible for killing my family,' she said. 'Masood has confirmed just that in his diary.'

Richard paused allowing the shock of what Amira was saying to sink in. 'Oh…I see…I'm so sorry, he said at least. 'It must be hard for you knowing Abdul is on the loose and Masood is dead. How are you going to avenge your family's death? It might be wise to drop it and let the Americans find Abdul and either kill him or let him rot in Guantanamo.'

'I will kill him *myself.* Only then will my family be able to rest in peace.'

Although Richard couldn't see Amira, he felt the intensity of her words leaving him in no doubt that she wasn't making idle threats. This surprised him because when they'd spoken face to face, she'd seemed vulnerable. The confidence in her voice, emphasising *myself*, suggested the opposite.

She knew exactly how to kill someone.

After ending the call, he phoned Temple.

'I need you to send a police car to Amira Al Marami at 75 Yellowstone Road Dagenham. Check there is nothing untoward. I'm concerned for her safety.'

'Okay, Richard, I'll get someone on to it straight away.'

'It needs to be low key. If she's there, don't let her know we're watching her. Keep me posted.'

After hanging up, he became aware that he was clutching Callidora's Bible rather too tightly. He flicked through the pages aimlessly and his eyes rested on a quotation from Genesis:

Abraham buried Sarah his wife in the cave of the field of Machpelah before Mamre: the same is Hebron in the land of Canaan. Was she just underlining pieces in the bible that she found uplifting? He had no idea what any of it meant.

Chapter Thirteen

Crete, Greece. June 4th 1941

Callidora had never seen her brother Nikos cry before, not even when the Germans first landed, just two weeks earlier. She could see the despair in his eyes and now his tears made her cry. To see her brother in so much distress was frightening. He'd always been there offering protection but now he looked helpless and unsure what to do. And no wonder, the Allies had left the island. Crete was on her own. She pretended not to notice, but she could read her brother like a book. He may have been crying, but these were tears of anger, anger that their freedom had been taken away in such a brutal fashion and there was nothing he could do about it.

'It's Kandanos,' he shouted, wiping his eyes on his shirt sleeve.

'What about Kandanos?' asked Callidora. 'What's happened?'

'They've burnt it to the ground and killed most of the people who live in the village, including women and children,' he cried.

Callidora made the sign of the cross. 'Oh my God,' she said aloud. Her mother was weeping now and so was her younger brother, Kosmas.

'We must pray for them,' said Nikos. 'Good will always triumph over evil.'

He is trying to be strong, she thought.

They went out into the square and others gathered to hear what Nikos had to say. Father Manousos came to join them.

'I've terrible news,' Nikos said. 'The Germans are committing reprisals against villages that have killed German soldiers. They have burned Kandanos to the ground and executed hundreds.' Callidora watched the

135

crowd as Nikos stopped speaking to allow the news to sink in. Some women knelt down to pray, crossing themselves repeatedly. The men stood defiant, waving their rifles and captured machine guns. One fired a shot into the air.

'What are we going to do?' Ikaros shouted. 'We can't just lie down and die. We must fight them to our last man.'

She knew Ikaros was trying to impress her with his cries of war. He is trying to be a hero, she thought, but he is also stupid. She looked at all the men emulating Ikaros, muttering sounds of defiance, but in her mind, it was an impossible task. How could we fight against the might of the German forces, she wondered? They will be here for a long time and however evil they are; it will be for God to decide who wins. Until he does, we should learn to live with them. How much she wanted to speak and say what she felt, but the men would never allow a woman to voice an opinion, so she stayed quiet and said nothing.

One woman, however, had other ideas. It was Nikoletta, a large but certainly not ugly woman. Buxom was how men would prefer to have described her. Callidora had frequently watched young men ogle her voluptuous figure. She is only three years older than me, she thought, but the men take more notice, respecting her awareness of life and her readiness to stand her ground. Today was no exception.

'I agree with Ikaros. I killed a soldier yesterday and I'm prepared to kill again. They must not break our spirit, just because of Kandanos,' she said.

There were more murmurs of appreciation and Nikoletta smiled with satisfaction. She's acting like one of the men, thought Callidora. That's why they'll listen. *I've killed a soldier and I'm ashamed. Unlike me, she's proud of what she's done.* Callidora clenched her fists as her mind refused to let her forget the horrible sight of the soldier running towards her, his tunic soaked red with blood.

'You're right, Nikoletta,' said Nikos. Callidora was never jealous of the attention she got, but to hear her own brother agreeing with Nikoletta stuck in her throat. She opened her mouth to speak, raising her arm. Nikos looked in her direction, but did not ask her to speak.

'The men may need to flee to the mountains and join the resistance,' he continued. 'It's not just Kandanos. I hear that many villages have had similar attacks. The village of Kakopetro, Floria and Prasses have also suffered with the killings. In Kandanos, those sadistic bastards have put up a notice, saying that they have carried out executions in retaliation for the deaths of twenty-five German soldiers. Nobody in the village of Kandanos deserved to die in this way. It's every man's right to protect his homeland from the invader.'

Yiannis, the little shepherd boy, son of Petros, was running towards them. 'The Germans are coming,' he shouted.

They came in convoy. An open top car with four officers, flanked by five motorbikes with side cars, each mounted with machine guns. Two of the motorbikes led from the front, providing protection for the car, while the remaining three took up the rear. At the back of the convoy were two trucks loaded with soldiers and an unmarked van. All the soldiers were armed to the teeth.

Nikos shouted. 'Stay calm. Don't provoke them.' The villagers stepped back in dismay as the convoy came into the square. The soldiers jumped down from the trucks and formed a cordon within seconds, pointing their machine guns at them. Callidora muttered a prayer to herself and made the sign of the cross. Many women did the same, thinking that they would soon be dead.

And then she saw him. The soldier from the church. Hans. Could he help them? He was heavily bandaged with his shoulder in a sling, sitting in the car at the front. When the leader got out, he got out with him.

The leader began to speak. Callidora studied his face, wanting to try and find some goodness in the man who might hold the key to whether they lived or died. She could find nothing in his favour. He was tall and although he was wearing an officer's cap, she could see his dark hair. His face was chiselled, as if out of rock, with accentuated cheekbones. There was no softness to his face.. His nose was large and straight. His eyes were burning with fury. The man standing next to him was completely different. When they'd first met in the church, she'd not really studied him, except she remembered his wide blue eyes. His features were soft and as he walked around he did not stride with purpose. He was gentle and most of all he looked worried.

'My name is Captain Wolfgang Kohlenz. I am here to tell you that the German army is in control of Crete and we will not tolerate any resistance from the people of this village.' He waited while Hans translated. Callidora could see Hans was still in pain from his wounds as he kept grimacing as he relayed Kohlenz's words back in Greek. 'Resistance will result in immediate death. Many Germans have been killed as they landed on Crete, by your fellow countrymen, stabbing them in their stomachs with pitchforks as their parachutes suspended them in trees and they were helpless to defend themselves. We will not tolerate this barbarity and will punish the perpetrators with death. For every German soldier killed, we will kill ten of your men.'

Hans continued with the translation and she could see the worry etched into his face. She looked at him speaking the words in Greek and, as if their thoughts were wired together, he looked in her direction. For a moment, he hesitated with his translation as their eyes met.

Kohlenz continued. 'Although our enemy has left you to your fate, there are still many enemy soldiers on the island, hiding in the mountains. British, Australian, New Zealanders, it does not matter. If anybody here is found to be providing refuge to these men, they'll be punished by death. Not just one of you will die. We will kill twenty and if there aren't enough men to go round, we will kill the women. Your village will be burnt to the ground if you resist.' Hans translated and she became conscious that his eyes would stray towards her, over and over again as he spoke.

'Finally,' said Kohlenz. 'My men require food. Bring us everything you have.'

Nikos stepped forward. 'But what will our children eat?' Hans translated back to German. Kohlenz launched at him, pulling his Luger out and pushing Nikos to the ground.

'No!' Callidora screamed. She ran forward, throwing herself onto Nikos.

'Kill him and you will kill me,' she shouted.

Hans calmed the situation. He stepped in front of Kohlenz and shouted in German to him. Kohlenz lowered his gun and walked away. The moment seemed to have subsided, but it had not. Old Stephanos was standing on the corner of the crowd.

'Bastard,' he shouted in Greek and swung his stick in the direction of Kohlenz. He was nowhere near him, but that didn't matter. The gun shot broke the silence and old Stephanos toppled forward, face down. Callidora ran to him, pulling Stephanos over so she could see if he was still alive. The bullet had entered his forehead with pinpoint accuracy. She looked at Kohlenz, and she saw him smirk with satisfaction at her evident anger. 'He was an old man,' she wept. 'You are a coward.' Hans had come to her side and she noticed he did not translate. He

139

pulled her away from Stephanos. 'I'm sorry,' he whispered to her in Greek.

She shoved him away and walked back to her family. The food was being loaded onto trucks. Chickens that could be slaughtered and hens for egg laying. The soldier went into the houses and stole bread and eggs and tomatoes. Anything that they could lay their hands on.

Hans caught up with her as she stood and looked dismayed at the quantity of food being taken from them.

'Please stop them taking everything,' she pleaded. 'We'll starve.'

'I'll try,' he said. Then his voice dropped. 'Can I see you? Tonight, at the church, midnight.'

He didn't wait for her reply. She watched him remonstrating with the soldiers, snatching a chicken from one of them and handing it back to an old woman. He was shouting at them to get back on the trucks. He is trying to help, she thought. But he still stood by and watched them murder innocent people. Where was the good in that?

When the Germans had gone, they carried Stephanos into the village church. At least they still had that, a place where they could pray for peace. She preferred the Church of St John on the hillside and that was no more. Could they ever rebuild it, she wondered? Stephanos had one daughter, Helen, who wept as they carried his body into the church. They wrapped him in a white shroud, which was all they had. Some of the men started digging a grave in the churchyard. Life had to go on.

For the rest of the day, Nikos and the other men were locked in discussion over how best to cope with the German threat. Callidora had other thoughts on her mind. The casket and chalice wouldn't fit in the hole where she'd hidden the box and the icons. Instead, before returning to the village, she'd managed to dig a ditch by a tree in the wood. It hadn't been easy as she didn't have a spade or fork. She used a sharp rock found in the ruins of the church to fashion a hole, but when she'd finished she knew straight away it wasn't a good enough hiding place for something so precious and valuable. While the Germans were here the risk in taking them to the monastery was too great. But while she waited for that day, she couldn't leave the treasure here. She needed a better hiding place.

But that wasn't all that worried her. *Should she meet Hans again?* The question haunted her throughout the day. He'd stood by and let Kohlenz kill Stephanos and done nothing. A fraternisation with the enemy would be a risk too far for the village and one they'd punish without mercy. But Hans might help the village, she decided. She was sure he was not as bad as the rest of them. Besides, he was half Greek.

The moon was up when she crept down the stairs and out into the square. Everything seemed so peaceful, as if war had been suspended and hope prevailed. She'd lain in her bed listening for the sounds that would confirm that the family were sleeping. She could hear Nikos snoring and even Kosmas was sleeping soundly.

Finding her way to the church in the partial light of a nearly full moon was easy. She'd been there so many times before. The long trail of white steps stood out in the moonlight. She stopped for a minute and looked upwards. How strange it was to see nothing at the end of the path. No church offering refuge; just rubble and not much else. If he was coming, she thought, he must come from the other side, climbing the escarpment through the woods. It was nearly midnight and she decided that, even if he did not come, she would enjoy sitting in peace, escaping this terrible war for just one small moment in time.

But he was there.

As she reached the top, she manoeuvred around the last few steps that had been destroyed by the bomb. Taking care, she looked down and watched her footing as she stumbled across the stones. Without warning, a hand took hold of her arm. It made her jump, but she relaxed when she heard Hans' voice.

'Thank you for coming. It's dangerous for me, but I had to see you. I feel so ashamed at what my countrymen are doing to your beautiful island,' he said.

She looked up at him, his face only barely picked out in the moonlight. What was she doing, looking this man in the face, the enemy of her people and, most of all, an enemy of her brother? It was a betrayal. She turned to leave, but as she did, she pleaded to his sense of human dignity. It was something that she was sure he had, even if the voice inside her demanded its rejection. 'You have to stop that man, your Captain Kohlenz,' she said with a breaking voice, fighting back the tears. 'You have Greek blood running in your veins. It's your duty to kill him. Look at how he killed the old man. Aren't you ashamed with yourself for not doing anything to stop this murder?' She turned and started back down the steps. He took hold of her arm, not tightly, but enough to make her stop. 'Let go of me,' she cried, pulling herself from his grasp.

He let go. 'If I do kill Captain Kohlenz, it'll do no good,' he said. 'They'll replace him and kill me. They'll blame the Greeks with more terrifying reprisals. Please, don't go,' he begged.

She relented, not wanting any more confrontation, and allowed him to lead her to the back of where the church had once stood, out of sight of the village. He lit a small oil lamp, which he'd brought with him. 'Nobody can see the light from here,' he said.

She saw him wince with the pain of his injuries received on the day they first met. A wave of sympathy for him swept through her head. The voice inside her said she should hate him, but however hard she tried, she could not. She decided to hear him out. Maybe he can help us, she thought.

'I'm going to volunteer to take a small group of men to help rebuild your church, which should never have been destroyed. I'll argue that it will help rebuild relations. If I can get them to agree to that, I'll be able to bring supplies to help your village.'

'What makes you think that the village would agree to your proposal?' she questioned.

'I don't know, but I just want to help. Maybe you could persuade them?'

She stared at him, trying to unravel her feelings. *Was he her enemy or her friend?* The two could not exist side by side. When she'd seen him for the first time in the church, she liked his kind face and now, against all the suffering, she felt no different. Remembering that he was a theology student, she wanted to tell him about the box and the papyrus scroll, but she held back, seeing Nikos' face pleading with her not to collaborate. *He's your enemy. Never forget he invaded your country.*

They parted by shaking hands, which in itself was a sign of reconciliation, whatever way you looked at it. She wanted to see him again and to turn him into a Greek.

Chapter Fourteen

Athens, Syntagma Police Station, Greece. July 25th 2005

'We've found no fingerprints, except your own, Mr Helford. And we've found no evidence that any thing has been taken. We have several leads to follow up after interviews with the locals.' Petronos lit a cigarette and inhaled deeply before blowing a cloud of smoke in Richard's direction. He put his feet up onto his desk, knocking a file onto the floor and making no attempt to pick it up. His office was a mess. There was another chair piled up with paper. 'Move the papers and sit down.' Petronos waited a moment while Richard sat and then continued. 'I wanted to brief you on what we've discovered, just so you know that the Greek police haven't been completely idle.'

'Okay,' said Richard. 'I'm listening.'

'Madam Marides had no enemies that we know of and most people that we've interviewed said she was always arguing with those who would listen, very opposed to the fascists, but nobody would say anything against her. Nothing has been stolen. So it must be to do with what she did in Crete, like you told me. If she was responsible for the death of your grandfather, then I'd expect you'd be pretty angry. The only person I can see with any motive is you, Mr Helford. And we all know you didn't do it.' He paused before adding in a suspicious voice. 'Did *you?*'

It was a loaded question; which Richard didn't rise to. 'Did any of the people you interviewed say that they saw a Muslim in the area?' Richard asked.

Petronos raised his eyebrows, clearly surprised at the question. He flicked through his notebooks to remind himself. 'Nothing at the moment, but I'll follow that up. What makes you think the killer might be a Muslim?'

'Oh, nothing really,' said Richard sarcastically. 'Just that the guy who hit me was of Arab appearance. It's reasonable to suspect that he'd be a Muslim, don't you think?' Richard allowed a small smile to cross his lips.

Petronos went red with embarrassment. 'Of course. I forgot about that.'

Richard looked at his watch. 'Is there anything else to report, Inspector?'

Petronos frowned over his notebook. 'Yes. There is something. I nearly forgot. The autopsy has revealed that she did have sodium pentothal in her blood, exactly as you said.'

'To make her talk?'

'Yes. It's not exactly effective, but for a ninety-year-old woman it would probably be easy, if you could stop her talking rubbish.'

'So that must change the way you're thinking about this case. It's not just an old woman who was going to die anyway, is it?' Richard enquired.

'No, it isn't.' He could see that Petronos had been irritated by the comment. 'Tell me, Mr Helford. Why is a member of the British Foreign Office continuing to be interested in this murder? Why don't you leave it to the Greek police? Why ask about Muslims? I may be a fool, but this smells like terrorist activity. Am I correct?'

Richard ignored the question. 'I told you, Madam Marides knew something about the death of my grandfather and I wanted to find out what she knew.'

'Maybe the killer had already found out,' Petronos replied, stubbing out his cigarette into an overflowing ashtray. 'I've been digging in government files,' he said. 'We policemen have our uses, you know. I've found some papers that might interest you.' He swivelled round on his chair and fished out a box file from the top of a filing cabinet. He took a folder out and handed it to Richard. 'There are many fascists in Greece who collaborated with the Germans during the war. When the Germans went after the war ended, we had a civil war in Greece. Some Germans returned the favour, helping right wing forces against the communists.'

'So. What's your point?'

'It appears that not all the Nazis left Crete. Captain Wolfgang Kohlenz stayed on.'

'So why is that of interest in this case, Inspector Petronos? There were thousands of Germans on the island during the occupation.'

Petronos flicked through the file. 'Kohlenz had some fascist friends in Crete during the Civil War but he also had a lot more enemies. He was responsible for the destruction of villages and the deaths of many Cretans. He should have been executed but the fascists protected him. Nikoletta Marides was accused of collaboration with him in the war and tried to get him arrested to clear her name, but Kohlenz had too many powerful friends forcing Nikoletta to flee the island.'

'So you think there might be a motive, Inspector? After all these years.'

'Except nobody knows what happened to Kohlenz. He disappeared from Crete in 1950 and we assume he was smuggled out to Argentina, where so many Nazis escaped prosecution for war crimes.'

'There is another problem, Inspector.'

'Yes, what's that?'

'Madam Marides' killer was an Arab with, we can only assume, no interest in the Second World War. So how could he be connected to Kohlenz?'

'Kohlenz may have hired the Arab to extract information from Madam Marides.'

Richard nodded. 'I agree, that's possible…The idea that Kohlenz might still be alive is also a possibility…But why didn't he just kill her and walk away? What information is Madam Marides likely to have?'

'So who do you think hired the Arab?' asked Petronos.

'I've no idea, isn't that your job, Inspector?' Richard had his suspicions but it certainly wasn't anything to do with an old Nazi. His number one suspect was Muhammed Abdul Alim or at least one of his cronies. If Amira was right, the Arab was trying to get some information about his father. The fact that Madam Marides was killed was more to do with her age rather than revenge, her system couldn't handle the dose of sodium pentothal. He remembered Nikoletta's words – *I didn't tell him*. Could her attacker have been trying to extract details of where his father was hiding?

Petronos stared back at Richard, picking up Richard's evasive answers. 'I think you know more than you are telling me, Mr Helford.'

Richard shifted in his chair, uneasy about keeping quiet. 'You are right, Inspector. For reasons of national security, I cannot reveal to you what I know, but rest assured I can categorically confirm there is no security threat to Greece.'

Petronos stood up and banged the desk, knocking a pile of files over onto the floor. 'You are a guest in my country. A crime has been committed on Greek soil. You will cooperate.'

Richard leaned forward and started picking up the files. 'I understand, Inspector. Our intelligence services will help you find the Arab and hand him over to you for punishment. I promise justice will prevail in Greece.'

'That's not good enough,' shouted Petronos.

'Look, Inspector, Greece has enough problems without adding terrorism to its list of problems. My country is threatened by terrorism. I should know. I was on one of the trains that blew up in London. If the terrorists know Greece is involved, they'll come after you. You don't want that…do you?'

Petronos sighed taken aback by Richard's outburst. He sat down again and lit a cigarette. 'I didn't know you were directly affected by the London bombings.' He inhaled deeply and stood up. He paced the room. At last he spoke. 'Okay…okay…just bring me Madam Marides' murderer and we'll say no more about it.'

Chapter Fifteen

Dubai, UAE. July 25th 2005

Sheikh Mohammed Zabor Bin Hitani preferred New York to Dubai. New Yorkers were so much more appreciative of his wealth, admiring his collection of Ferraris and luxurious mansions from the Hamptons to Manhattan and from Rhode Island to Miami. In Dubai, wealth was vulgar to the extreme and he took pride in rising to the challenge; his gold-plated Bentley parked in the front of the Burj Al Arab Hotel showing how serious he was about appearances in Dubai. The hotel could have provided a Rolls Royce for his stay but they don't have 8-inch-thick armour plating on the doors and windows strong enough to resist an AK-47 at close range. The car was garaged permanently at the hotel and had been brought out to the front in preparation for the Sheikh's imminent arrival, but would only be used for short journeys to a restaurant or to one of the huge shopping malls. In Dubai, the only means of travel for a billionaire was by helicopter and that was the only way to arrive at this so called seven-star hotel, landing on its helipad perched two hundred and ten metres above sea level, like a bosun's nest sitting at the top of its giant sail-like structure.

Two Bell 429 helicopters approached the hotel, one carried the Sheikh and his favourite fifth wife, Nadia, with three of his most trusted bodyguards. He had dressed for the occasion in full-length Saudi robes and shemagh head scarf. His wife dressed head to toe in black with a niqab veil that covered her face leaving only her eyes on view. The bodyguards were not Arab, they were ex-Navy Seals

149

wearing Armani suits with crisp white shirts and black ties and aviator sun glasses. The other helicopter carried his oldest son, Ahmed, and his Saudi business advisor, the only man he trusted outside his own family, his childhood friend Muhammed Jawad Al Dakir. Two more bodyguards filled the empty seats.

As the Sheikh's helicopter circled only a few feet from the ground, the bodyguards swung the door back and leapt clear of the chopper to cover the Sheikh's exit. The other chopper hung in the air, rocked from side to side by the desert winds, waiting for its chance to land. It was 41 degrees centigrade outside and the Sheikh remembered why his robe made so much sense in the fierce desert sun.

Several of the hotel staff stood to attention but the Sheikh ignored them and went into the lobby. With full head gear and despite the flat soles of his sandals, the billionaire was well over six feet tall; his height reinforcing his commanding presence. The man he really wanted to see greeted him as he entered. He held out his hands and smiled.

'Abdul Alim. Salam Alaikum. It's wonderful to see you.'

The two men embraced warmly with Abdul kissing the Sheikh, first on his hand and then on both cheeks. 'We must go to my suite and talk. We have much to discuss.'

'The Royal Suite is ready, Sheikh Zabor,' said the hotel manager. 'Please follow me.'

The party from the second helicopter had joined them in the lobby. The Sheikh turned to Jawad. 'Take Nadia and Ahmed to the new Ibn Battuta Mall to shop. It has been open for only a few months so should amuse them until I've finished my business. Use the Bentley. I don't want to be disturbed until after dusk.' Jawad bowed and stepped backwards. Nadia and Ahmed moved obediently beside him with heads lowered. The Sheikh ignored the show of respect and walked into the suite. It was the size of the rooms rather than their opulence that appealed; sofas in reds and purples, gold marble pillars with Arabic carpets of the finest quality. None of this interested either of the two men. Abdul would have been happier sitting on rush matting with a goat roasting on an open fire.

'Bring us coffee and then leave us,' he shouted to the hotel manager who was rushing around inspecting the suite, making sure no detail was out of place. 'I don't want to be disturbed on any account. Is that understood?'

'Yes. I understand, your Excellency, Sheikh Zabor,' said the manager, stepping backwards and closing the doors to the suite in one flowing movement. Two of his bodyguards were busily sweeping the room for listening devices. When they had given the all clear the Sheikh waved them away impatiently.

When the two men were alone, they embraced again. 'How was Afghanistan?' asked the Sheikh. 'It's been a long time since we saw you in America.'

Abdul sighed. 'The presence of a foreign force doesn't help,' he said. 'I have to spend most of my time hiding in the mountains. If we didn't have the help from ISI agents in Pakistan, I would've never been able to leave to come and see you. I have a new identity, Doctor Zayan Bashir – the archaeologist. I'm curious why you chose such a profession for me.'

'All in good time, my friend.'

The two men continued to chat informally, asking about each other's health until the coffee arrived. They stopped talking while the waiters attending poured.

When the waiters had gone, the Sheikh's mood changed and Abdul could see that the small talk was over.

'Tell me what you know about the Cretan document,' said the Sheikh.

Abdul related what Kleiner had told him and his proposal to sell it to the Israeli billionaire Abel B Multzeimer.

151

The Sheikh snorted with derision on hearing the name. 'That Jew wants to destroy Islam by provoking the Americans into an all-out war,' he said scathingly. 'We must get to the document first, its propaganda value will be much greater in our hands.'

Abdul nodded. 'That may be so, but how are you so sure of its value to our cause?'

The Sheikh flashed a smile at Abdul. 'The CIA told me that of its importance.'

Abdul's eyes narrowed, not seeing the joke. 'I don't understand,' he replied curtly. 'How could you talk to the CIA? They are our sworn enemies.'

The Sheikh continued to be amused by Abdul's concern. 'Have you ever wondered how you came to be on the CIA Kill List? They never knew about your involvement with 9/11 but out of the blue you became a wanted man, dead or alive.'

'I have. I just assumed they had intelligence about me.'

'You're right. The intelligence came from me.'

Abdul shot the Sheikh a fierce glance. 'What do you mean? You told them?' he snapped.

'Don't be alarmed, my friend. Have you never wondered why an American missile hasn't killed you yet? Not one missile has come even close to you.'

'I wonder about that every day.'

'Of course you do. It's about keeping your friends close and your enemies closer. Didn't some ancient Chinese philosopher say that? I throw them worthless crumbs of information about you to keep them from suspecting me.'

Abdul still struggled to comprehend what the Sheikh was saying.

'Listen, my friend,' said the Sheikh, trying to elaborate. 'The Saudi royal family has a complex relationship with the Americans. They think we are their allies. The buffer against Iran. They think I work for them.' The Sheikh smiled once again. 'You know; I never cease to be amazed how stupid they are. I give them information and they think I'm the acceptable face of Islam.' He gave Abdul a reassuring glance. 'They won't hurt you, my friend, because I've told them you are a major source of intelligence and on no account should they lay a finger on you. The gullible fools accept my word without question.'

Abdul forced a smile but remained uneasy about where all this was leading. 'May Allah forgive me; I still don't understand why the Americans would tell you about the document,' said Abdul, raising his voice – a sign of his growing frustration. He apologised immediately. 'Forgive my impertinence, I'm not questioning your wisdom, your Excellency, I just don't see why the Americans would help you.'

'You are right to be sceptical, my friend…it was a rogue CIA officer who gave me the information and then disappeared, presumed dead in the smoke and dust of the twin towers.'

Abdul couldn't believe what he was hearing. 'The man I told you about? Are you telling me he's a CIA agent? I told you what he said.' His voice was low but vehement.

'Exactly, my good friend. It was the information that you gave me that made me recruit him to our cause. He was sympathetic to the cause of Muslims. He was going to bring us the scroll.

Abdul remembered the man very clearly. He had an obsession that there might be another way to prove the supremacy of Islam – not through jihad, but through the word of God.

That man had told him all about the scroll but nothing about its contents.

He'd learned to love that man, like a brother, until the day that changed everything. The day of all days.

9/11.

153

He remembered their first meeting by chance in the Islamic Cultural Center in New York. It was as if it had been instigated by Allah, praise be upon him.

His name was David Helford.

Never in his life had he become so close to a human being other than his own family. They'd had long conversations about religion and the Holy Koran. His knowledge was astounding. What had fascinated Abdul most of all was the man's interest in the unity of the Holy Bible and the Holy Koran. Their conversations were as clear to him now as if they'd happened yesterday. He remembered the excitement in Helford's eyes when he'd told him about the existence of the scroll in Crete. Evidence that would vindicate Islam as the supreme faith.

'You know that the Archangel Gabriel appeared to Mohammed, praise be upon him, when he had the first revelation,' Helford had said. 'The very same angel that appeared to Mary, Mother of Isa, at the time she heard about the virgin birth.'

'Why does that matter?' Abdul had asked.

'Because it proves that the major religions should be united.' Abdul could see Helford's face in his mind, animated with enthusiasm. 'There is only one God. I'll show you the scroll to prove it,' he said. 'Then you'll believe me.'

He still regretted telling Helford about the plot against America. After hearing about the scroll he was excited and wanted to tell his friend something that would shock. He told him everything he knew, that planes would be high jacked and flown into the twin towers.

Helford's face had changed to ashen grey in an instant. 'Are you sure?' he'd said.

That was the last he'd heard of David Helford.

On that day, when Helford vanished into the dust of the twin towers, his own name appeared on the CIA Kill List. Nowhere was safe, least of all Afghanistan where he spent his life avoiding American drones. He decided that his good friend had betrayed him but now for the first time he knew otherwise.

At first, he mourned the loss of his friend's life, feeling guilty that the man he'd loved for his knowledge of the holy prophet's teaching was brought down by the very people he wanted to help. But nagging doubts crept into his mind. Why would Helford put himself in harm's way, knowing what he knew? Why had Helford not converted to Islam? How had he become a wanted man when before the towers came down he'd done nothing to arouse the interest of the intelligence services?

It now appeared, he'd been wrong all the time. He'd never dreamed that the Sheikh would be the one responsible for his notoriety with the security services.

But nothing he'd found suggested that Helford might be alive.

As the years passed, he'd continued to search, refusing to believe that his friend was dead. He wanted to find the scroll so there would be no more 9/11s. He had intelligence but no clear evidence, like the Americans search for weapons of mass destruction in Iraq. If Helford was alive, he was just as elusive. It was a wild theory with no grounds in truth.

But Allah works in mysterious ways, he thought. The meeting with Kleiner, had aroused his suspicions once more. It was the talk of the Christian text proving the supremacy of Islam that seemed to fit with everything that Helford had told him. The timing was perfect enough to be inspired by God. It must mean that God wanted him to do what Kleiner had suggested.

Helford must be alive.

Abdul looked across to Sheikh Zabor. 'Do you think Helford is still alive?' he said.

'There have been signs before now, not least the evidence that the CIA is looking for Helford again,' said the Sheikh. 'My sources in the CIA say that Helford is not working alone. And now this German has appeared, by the grace of Allah, out of the woodwork, convincing me more than ever that my renegade CIA officer is alive. Find him and we'll find the scroll.'

'And how do you propose to do that?' Abdul asked. 'I've been looking for Helford for four years.' He was surprised by how excited he was that Helford had not betrayed him after all.

'Helford has a son – Richard – who my contacts tell me works for British intelligence. I want you to kidnap his son and threaten to kill him if the father doesn't give us the scroll.'

'And where will I find the son?'

'In Greece, in Athens, looking for his father like the rest of us.'

Abdul stood up and began pacing the room. Of course, he knew all about David Helford's son. He'd been following him, or at least Masood had.

Until he died.

It was the way he'd died which concerned Abdul. By the hand of jihad. A victim of a bomb by his own people. If Allah was guiding him then he was displeased. 'I have two questions,' he said at last.

'I am listening,' said the Sheikh.

'First, what do we do about the Nazi – Kleiner? He believes he knows where the scroll is and Helford does not feature in his plans.'

'Keep an eye on his movements. When we are sure he can't help us, kill him.' The Sheikh cocked his fingers in the shape of a gun and pretended to fire in Abdul's direction. 'And what is your second question?'

'When we find the scroll, what do we do with the contents? How do we announce it to the world?'

The Sheikh thought for a moment and then looked up. 'We need a show, a spectacle, which make the world stand up and notice, in the same way as the September 11th attack.'

Abdul remembered that this is what Kleiner had said. This time it would not be about the number of dead. It needed to have a symbolic significance. When he told the Sheikh, he nodded his approval.

'Find Helford. Find the scroll,' said the Sheikh. 'And Islam will be supreme.'

Chapter Sixteen

Athens, Greece. July 25th 2005

Compared with the carnage of the London bombings, the death of Nikoletta seemed trivial, but Richard still agonised how he would explain it to Rowena. He felt sure that he was on to something big but getting her to accept this was going to be difficult. He decided to talk to Brian first and at 8.15 a.m. he had an excellent opportunity. Brian wanted to see him.

Climbing the stairs to Brian's office, he passed the painting of Byron, dressed in Greek National costume. Pausing for a moment to catch his breath, he looked up at his hero, not having noticed it before but very familiar with the image. He remembered the poet's words written in Callidora's Bible and thought again about his father. Could he still be alive?

'How was Cyprus?' he asked as he sat down in front of Brian. It was the first time he'd been in his office. Papers and files were scattered everywhere. Untidy, just like his dress sense.

'Bloody awful. It's not the Greek islands, is it? The fucking army and the RAF rather spoil things. They've even got the Red Arrows training there; it feels more like Catterick, without the rain.'

'What did you want to see me about?'

Brian leaned back in his chair and sighed. 'You're supposed to be helping me, Richard, making my life easier, and what do I find? The first thing I see on my desk is a message to call Inspector Petronos of the Athens CID about a murder reported by a certain Mr Helford. Does that certain gentleman happen to be a member of the British Diplomatic community, he asks? Of course, Officer, fully paid up member of Her Majesty's Foreign

158

Office. Thank you, says the Inspector. No problem I say. Anytime.'

His sarcasm had the desired effect. Richard flinched at the outburst and if he was honest with himself, knew he deserved it. 'Sorry, Brian. I know it sounds bad, but I can explain.'

'You're damn right you'll explain. What the fuck's going on?'

Richard chose his words carefully. 'I've got something big you need to know about. Rowena knew I was going to meet the Greek woman. It has something to do with my father who was killed in 9/11. It's not that I don't trust you, Brian, but I think Rowena should hear this as well. I would really appreciate if you could set up a call, with you both of course, so I can explain.'

'Why are we wasting our time on this? I'm not interested in what this means for your father or an old Greek woman who is very much dead.'

'But the woman was murdered,' said Richard, annoyed by Brian's flippant remark about Nikoletta. 'Don't you think it strange that Rowena told me to visit this woman and she gets murdered before I can talk to her properly?'

'Okay. I'm listening,' said Brian. 'Convince me we are not wasting our time.'

'This is about Al Qaeda. The Greek woman was murdered by an Arab.'

Brian looked at him with disdain. 'What could you possibly know about Al Qaeda? You are a fucking knobhead from Cambridge who knows sweet FA about anything and a lot about the Greek poets.'

'You forget I went to Iraq.'

'For how long? A few months and then they shipped you back.'

Richard was beginning not to like Brian, but maybe he deserved it. He decided to keep his cool.

'This is worth hearing. Can you set up the call?'

'It better be good, because I'm not getting good vibes about you working for me. That's not the only thing I've been told about you this weekend. I go trotting off to Cyprus to kick some ass out there and what's the first bit of intel I'm given? Not about Osama Bin bloody Laden. Oh no. The first thing I'm told is that a call has been placed to GCHQ from Athens that I knew nothing about. A call from Special Agent Richard Helford, no less. Well that's all right then, I say. No it bloody well isn't.'

'It's all connected,' said Richard.

The call was at 11 a.m. Richard had used the waiting time to prepare what he was going to say. It was going to be a tricky sell and he wanted Rowena to back him.

Brian dialled the number and Rowena came on the line. After some chitchat lasting less than a minute, she cut to the chase.

'So you went to see the old woman – what's her name?' She paused and they could hear paper rustling on her desk. 'Nikoletta Marides, that's it. Brian tells me somebody got there before you. Correct?'

'Yes, I'm afraid so.'

'And killed her, correct?'

'Yes.'

'Do you know why?'

'I don't think it was intentional. She was drugged to make her talk and her heart gave out. She had lung cancer, so I think it just accelerated her death by a few months.'

'Okay. That's a shame,' Rowena replied, the faintest note of concern in her voice. 'So tell me where it leads.'

'The man who killed her was an Arab. I interrupted him.'

'Okay…But that doesn't prove anything sinister except a burglary that went wrong,' said Rowena.

Richard ignored the comment. 'Do you remember the guy who died in my arms when the train was bombed?'

'Masood Al Marami,' she replied impatiently. 'How could I forget?'

'You'll recall I told you that he was once in the Egyptian GIS and was given his marching orders. Five interviewed him and decided he wasn't a risk. His wife reckons that he was following me when the bomb went off.'

'Go on.' Rowena sounded interested.

'She found information in his belongings that suggested he was doing it at the behest of Mohammad Abdul Alim, known as Abdul to his friends, who includes Osama and none other than Ayman Al Zawahiri on his speed dial, Al Qaeda's number two no less.'

'Shit. Did you say Abdul Alim?'

'Yes.'

'The same Abdul Alim who's on the CIA's Kill List.'

'Yes.'

Rowena was incredulous. 'Why in fuck's name would a top man in Al Qaeda be interested in you?'

'I asked myself that question. It's something to do with what happened in Crete during the war that my grandfather was involved with. My father wanted to know the truth before 9/11 cost him his life. I think that's a cover up. I don't think he died in the twin towers.'

Rowena scoffed, 'Since when have Al Qaeda been interested in the fucking Second World War? And as for your father being alive...the FBI say he's dead.'

She was right. It was too ridiculous for words. But he kept going, knowing he had her attention.

'When I got to Nikoletta's apartment, I interrupted the killer. He attacked me and then escaped. I discovered the old woman seriously distressed, laid out in the bath after being drugged. She was fighting for her life. I did my best for her but she was in a bad way.' He paused for effect but out of the corner of his eye he could see Brian waiving his hands for him to continue. 'Just before she died, she told

161

me that *she didn't tell him*. I have no idea what that means. What I am sure about is that the man who attacked me was of Arab descent.'

'So you don't know what that means, I assume?'

'No. I'm afraid not.'

'Second question. The official explanation of your father's death is that he died in 9/11. Why do you think otherwise?'

Richard felt a little happier with this one. 'There is no body. There is a blank in his diary so it's not known for certain that he was in the North Tower when the plane hit. He was in a distressed state of mind shortly before he went to New York.'

'All circumstantial. So what do you think did happen to your father?'

'I believe he's in hiding...on the run somewhere, but I've got no proof. Just a load more circumstantial evidence.'

'Like what?'

'My mother's been getting some strange calls where someone just listens to her voice but says nothing. And there's been some Pakistanis hanging around her house. Also why would an Arab want information from this old woman and why was Masood following me at the time of the bomb?'

Rowena was silent for a minute. Richard opened his mouth to speak, but Brian put a finger up, telling him to keep quiet. After what seemed like an age, she spoke. But it wasn't to them. She was shouting in the background at a speaker on another line. 'Is that you, Calder?'

Brian was mouthing the letters GCHQ.

'I want you to do a search of all the traffic we've picked up and see if Crete comes up,' she said. 'Yes, I did say Crete...Have you got that?'

The conversation with GCHQ ended, Rowena came back on their line. 'I deal in facts and at the moment I can't see anything to support your theory that your father is alive. We also don't know whether Masood's wife is telling the truth about Abdul.'

Richard's jaw dropped. He could feel his emotions were on edge. 'Look, Rowena, we can't ignore Abdul Alim. We've got a lead here which might be useful to the Americans if we can track him down. And another thing…why won't you tell me why I was removed from Iraq?'

Rowena was silent for a minute or so and Richard resisted the temptation to say anything else. At last she spoke. 'Are you finished?'

'Yes, I am,' Richard replied, a note of defiance in his voice.

'I've already answered that question, but – and it's a big but – I think there is enough here to warrant further investigation. Particularly, I want to know why the CIA were interested in this woman – Marides.'

'Yes. Of course, Rowena.'

'We'll get Special Branch to stake out your mother's farm and see who's sniffing around there. Your mother won't know…okay?'

'Thank you. That's great.'

'I'm prepared to let you stay with this for another week. But I want regular reports.'

'Of course. Everything,' he said in a serious tone while trying not to show Brian the smile on his face. '

Brian didn't look amused and Richard knew he shouldn't gloat. He had to work with Brian.

'So much for my intel,' said Brian after the call had been ended. 'No need to look so fucking smug. You'll have to tell me everything you're doing. I want to know when you pick your nose.'

'Okay, Brian. I'm sorry.'

'We need to set up the meeting with the CIA guy. I know him quite well – Jeb Butler.'

'Can we get the Greek police off my back? I've got to see Petronos again.'

'They won't listen to us but they'll bow and scrape for Jeb. We'll ask him.'

Chapter Seventeen

Crete, Greece. June 5th 1941

'I'm not having the Germans rebuild our church and that's final.' Nikos was angry and she never liked to see him annoyed. 'Whatever made you think of such an idea?'

Callidora knew in her heart that Nikos would never agree, but thought she would at least try. 'Do you remember the soldier who was doing the translating? He's half Greek, half German. His mother was Greek,' she said, hoping that, if she mentioned Hans' Greek blood, it would change his mind. 'It was his idea. He's not like the other German's. He wants to help us.'

'I don't care, he's still a German, occupying our soil and killing our people,' said Nikos. 'When this is over, we'll rebuild the church.'

'But…'

'That's enough, Callidora. I don't want to hear anything more said about it.' He didn't wait for her to answer and walked away across the square.

She watched and saw him nod at a man who was sitting at a table in the village kafeneon drinking some coffee. As soon as Nikos had passed, the man stood up. Looking in her direction, he smiled and raised his cap before following Nikos down a narrow passage between two houses. She'd never seen the man before. He was dressed rather like a shepherd, dishevelled, but handsome in the way his black hair was swept back behind his ears. His thick moustache was in need of attention and his boots, worn outside his britches, were dirty and falling to bits, suggesting a life living rough in the mountains. He was a complete contrast to Nikos who would never let his moustache get like that. He would always curl it at the edges, giving an air of authority, but this man didn't have the same level of pride. Maybe, she thought, he had other priorities. She always remembered a smile and just like Hans', she could see one that radiated kindness and warmth.

Ikaros appeared at her side and linked his arm through hers.

'You've noticed our visitor,' he said.

'Yes, who is he?'

'It's best you don't notice him, but never mind that, can I see you tonight?' He flirted with her, winking with a mischievous smile.

He'd misjudged her if he thought he could flirt. She scowled, amazed that he could even think of such things when they were in so much danger. 'Ikaros,' she said. 'We may all die tomorrow. This isn't the time to have fun.'

He looked hurt. 'That's just the point...Don't you see?'

'No, I don't see,' she snapped.

'We've lost the war, but I don't want to lose you,' he said, grasping her hands just like Hans had done, but it wasn't with the same intensity. He looked so pathetic staring back at her with love in his eyes.

'I just don't understand you,' she wailed. 'Yesterday you were killing people and now you want to talk of love.'

Ikaros bowed his head and said nothing. His sad face made her feel sorry for him, but did not make her think of him as a potential husband. She loved him as a brother, just like she loved her real brothers. It wasn't because he was ugly, far from it. He was tall with rugged weather-beaten features, but he'd always been there since she was born, always by her side.

'Who is that man?' she asked, trying to change the subject.

Ikaros looked up, his face reddened with embarrassment of the rejection. 'British agent,' he said. 'A man named Lenny Helford. He's leading the resistance up in the mountains above our village.'

'The Germans will be after him.'

166

Her timing was perfect. A boy ran into the village shouting, 'Germans!'

It was a smaller force this time and, thankfully, there was no sign of Kohlenz, but Hans had come. The usual routine followed with the soldiers in the truck leaping out and training their guns in a circle round the square. Seeing Callidora standing with Ikaros, Hans got off his bike and came to them. He stood to attention in front of her, clicking his heels together while removing his cap. Ignoring Ikaros, he spoke.

'Good morning, madam. It is very nice to see you again on this beautiful day.' He held out his hand and bowed. She wanted to take it, but knew that any sign of friendship towards a German soldier would be frowned upon. So she just stood there, with a blank expression on her face, gazing beyond Hans' shoulder at the mountains behind. She wondered where they'd put the British soldier. There was an uneasy silence between them until she thought of something to say.

'We've not enough food,' she said with a curt expression on her face. 'Your soldiers have taken it. So what's good about it?'

'I know. I'm sorry and we'll see this does not happen again. Have you put forward my suggestion that we help you rebuild your church?'

'We'll rebuild our own church,' she snapped. 'We do not need your help. After all, it was a German bomb that destroyed it.'

He stepped a little closer and this time took hold of her hand. She felt a piece of paper on his palm and gripped it as he let go. 'I'm sorry about that. It was a mistake which is why we want to rebuild it for you,' he said, stepping back. He turned to face the crowd who had come out of their houses to see what the Germans wanted. 'I've come here to warn you that we will be carrying out operations in the hills to root out the resistance forces, including

167

English special agents who we know are operating in this area. Anybody found harbouring the enemy will be shot with consequences for the whole village.'

The expression on Hans' face showed his discomfort, but feeling bad did not make it better. She'd hate him if any more villagers were murdered, but that didn't stop her wanting to see him again. As the soldiers pulled out of the village, she put the note out of sight before Ikaros noticed.

'Bastard,' Ikaros snarled, thrusting his fist upwards in a defiant salute. 'I saw the way he looked at you,' he shouted. 'I felt like hitting him and if the odds were more even, I would've done, but even you, Callidora, are not worth dying for.' He winked again at her and this time Callidora softened. She smiled.

Lenny Helford beamed at Callidora as she stepped through the front door of her family's home. He was sitting at the table, sharing what looked like raki with Nikos and two others. Callidora recognised the two men to be Kostas Voulinakis who had a small farm just outside of the village, and Pavlos Georgakis, who leased fishing boats in Chania. Both men were young and naïve, boasting about how they wanted to kill more Germans.

'Aren't you going to introduce me to our guest?' said Callidora, looking in Lenny's direction and returning the smile. Ever since Father Agathangelos had introduced her to the poetry of Byron, she'd retained a romanticised view of the British and Lenny Helford seemed to personify the image.

Lenny did not wait to be introduced. 'My name's Lenny Helford of the British Army Signals Corp,' he said in Greek; a mixture of the classical and modern language rolled into one. Lenny held out his hand. 'You must be Callidora, I've heard a lot about you.'

She didn't want to acknowledge Lenny's attempt at a handshake, not because she didn't like him, but more because of what the Greek men around her might say if she did.

'I'm helping your brother out against the Germans,'

Nikos glared at Lenny. 'You shouldn't have revealed who you are to Callidora. What if she's captured by the Germans?'

'Callidora will protect me, I'm sure,' said Lenny, winking at Callidora.

Nikos ignored Lenny's comment and returned to the discussion he was having with the men.

'That German soldier was taking quite a risk coming here with hardly any support,' said Kostas. 'We could have killed them all.'

'But we'd have paid the price,' interrupted Callidora.

The men looked up, Pavlos and Kostas seemed annoyed at her intervention but Lenny spoke first. 'You are right to say this, Callidora. They mean what they say and won't shy away from more killings.' He stood up and held out his hand once more. 'May I call you Callidora?'

'Yes, of course,' she said, pleased by his intervention, this time taking Lenny's hand in defiance of the chauvinism of the Greek men. Ikaros shot her a jealous glance and the others looked away in disgust.

'The Germans don't do reprisals by half,' said Lenny. 'They would have killed everyone in the village.'

'Which is exactly why you need to be careful about showing your face,' said Nikos, sounding irritated. 'Someone will tell tales to save their own skin.'

'Of course, I understand,' replied Lenny. 'I'll be leaving by nightfall so you've got nothing to worry about.' He stared once again in her direction. 'Callidora makes a very good point. The resistance movement must be very careful with their targets so that the Germans don't take it out on the villages, as they did in Kandanos.'

When the men seemed to have finished talking, Callidora spoke, telling Nikos that she was going up into the mountains to check on her goats. 'All the noise and explosions will have distressed them,' she said.

Lenny stood up immediately. 'Do you mind if I come with you?' he said. 'I need to broaden my knowledge of the tracks around the mountains and with an expert guide, it'll be easy.'

'It'll be nice to have some company,' she replied.

'I don't want you going in the mountains. It's too dangerous,' Nikos snapped, appearing more frustrated by Lenny every time he spoke. 'The Germans will let you go, but if you're caught with Lenny, they'll kill you.'

'Understood,' replied Lenny. 'I'll make sure she's safe at all times.'

Callidora was reassured by Lenny's support. They set off immediately, anxious that Callidora would be able to reach her goats before nightfall. As they walked, she pointed out herbs and told him what was safe to eat. Reaching the spot where her goats would be near, she felt her spirits rise, a lightness brought on by the fresh mountain air and wonderful views along the coastline. All it took were a few whistles and the goats appeared as if by magic. They seemed to be in good health and not at all distressed.

She liked being with Lenny. He was older than Nikos and less preoccupied with revenge. The war seemed far away, almost impossible to imagine while bathing in the beauty of the mountainside.

'Do you ever worry about being killed?' she said, laying back in the grasses and staring at the cloudless blue sky.

'Of course I think about it,' he replied. 'But I live for the moment because tomorrow may never come.'

'Do you know the poetry of Lord Byron?'

Lenny looked at Callidora and smiled. 'Of course I know Byron, but only in the English.'

'Recite some for me in English,' she said.

He smiled and thought for a moment before speaking.

'The mountains look on Marathon,
And Marathon looks on the sea;
And musing there an hour alone,
I dream'd that Greece might still be free…'

Callidora smiled and said, 'That must be "The Isles of Greece" with the mention of Marathon.'

'Yes. You're right.'

Callidora stared at her goats and sighed. 'Life has to end sometime, just like it will end tonight for one of my goats.'

Lenny frowned. 'One of these lovely creatures has to end on the dinner table?'

'I'm afraid so.'

Callidora walked through the flock and having made her choice, tethered the unfortunate animal. 'She's old and will no longer give birth so it is a good time to end her life.'

They set off once more and she led him along a different route, through a gorge while telling him stories of the caves. By the time they reached the village, they were tired and hungry. He waited for the all clear before re-entering the village, just in case the Germans had come back.

The meal they had that night stretched a long way, but still felt like a feast. She knew that food would become scarce if the Germans continued to loot their supplies, so this meal was special. There was souvlaki, which had to stretch a little further than usual, tomatoes, olives and homemade bread that was still warm from the outside oven. Mother's feta cheese was always superb and supplies had not yet run out. Afterwards, they shared ripe peaches and a plentiful supply of raki. Everybody got

171

quite merry, as if they were trying to forget the horrors of the last few days. Hans' note remained unread in Callidora's pocket, but she couldn't stop feeling the paper, scrunching it in her hands, checking it was still there, that she hadn't dropped it. When they'd finished eating, seeing the men huddled together, she went outside at the back of the house. It would be easy to keep out of sight if she walked between the lemon trees. Convinced no one was watching, her hands shaking, she unravelled the screwed-up note and tried to read it by the moon, which was always brightest when it rose in the evening sky.

A male voice from behind made her jump. 'A love letter by moonlight, what could be more romantic than that?'

She swung round and saw Lenny appear from behind a tree. The ember of his cigarette glowed in the darkness. 'You frightened me,' she snapped. 'It's not that simple.'

He moved closer to her and inhaled deeply holding the smoke before blowing it into the night air. 'What's not simple?' he said.

The urge to tell someone was too great. She knew she couldn't tell her family, but Lenny would help. 'If I tell you, please say nothing to anyone, not even my brother,' she said.

'Of course, you have my word as an English gentleman,' he replied with a flourish and a wink.

Lenny seemed relaxed and not concerned that if he was caught, the Germans would kill him. She turned away and looked down towards the sea. The moon was reflecting off the water and she could see the pinprick lights of some boats in the harbour. She wondered where to start, what to tell him and what to leave out. He came over to her side and followed her gaze. 'The Germans are stocking up. They're in for the long haul,' he said.

Callidora sighed. 'The note is from a German soldier. He wants to meet me.' She turned and looked at him, expecting Lenny to react, but there was no sign of any concern in his face so she continued. 'He's a good man, the one they use to translate. He's half Greek, and doesn't want to have anything to do with this war. He helped me when the church was bombed.'

Lenny's eyes widened. 'What are you meeting him for?'

'Because I want him to help us.'

'Why? What good can one man do? If he's found out, they'll shoot him and then what?'

'I know it's stupid, but there's something else that makes me want to see him.'

'Oh.' Now he looked surprised. 'What's that?'

Callidora hesitated, unsure whether to tell him or not. 'You are an educated man and like Lord Byron you've come to help save our country.'

Lenny smiled. 'I wouldn't put myself in the same league as Lord Byron, but yes I do care for Greece. I've studied the great Greek philosophers and been moved by the tragedies of Euripedes...I do love your country and I can think of worse places to die than the mountains of Crete.'

'It's just that I've found something...and if I tell you, you must guard the secret with your life.'

Lenny put his hand on his heart. 'I promise,' he said firmly. 'On my life.'

Callidora felt a weight lifted from her shoulders. She loved her brothers and the other men in the village but didn't trust them to understand. When Father Agathangelos taught her to read, her way of thinking had changed and Lenny was the only man who could match that. 'When the church was bombed,' she said. 'It formed a great crater that blew up the stone floor, opening up the foundations. I've found an ancient papyrus scroll beneath the floor, something that whoever put it there thought

173

would never see the light of day. If I do nothing more before I die, I want to protect it for the monks at Preveli. They helped me as a child, teaching me to read and write. When they see the scroll, they'll think it's a miracle.' She paused and grabbed Lenny's wrists. 'Whatever happens to me, it must not fall into the hands of the Germans.'

Lenny stared at Callidora. 'It can't be worth dying for. Can it?'

'It's written by St John of Patmos. It's sacred.'

'What? Are you sure?'

'I believe it's authentic, of course it could be a forgery, but I don't think so.'

'So you think it was written by the same person who wrote the Book of Revelations?'

'Yes, you're right.'

'What makes you so sure it's not a forgery?'

Callidora turned away from Lenny's gaze, trying to think why she was sure. 'There is no reason. It's just something inside of me saying it's special. It's holy and God is on my side. '

They sat in silence for a few moments and Callidora wondered whether she should have told him about the chalice and the casket. Not just yet, she decided. At last he spoke. 'So how exactly do you think the soldier can help you?'

'He'll be able to move around the island without being questioned. He's also a Theology student so might be able to assess the scroll's authenticity and value.'

'It's a big risk, trusting a German.'

'I prefer to think about him as a Greek.'

Lenny rested on the perimeter fence and put his head in his hands. He was trying to think so she said nothing. After a few moments of silence, he spoke. 'This is a risky thing to do, Callidora. Nobody will ever trust the soldier. Go and see him, but be careful.' He gripped her hand as if to emphasise the point, fixing his gaze directly on her face. 'However much you like him, he is still the enemy and your family and friends want to kill him. Imagine their distress if you collaborate. Your family will be in disgrace and you'll be tarred a traitor. It doesn't matter if that's unfair. They'll have their revenge on you.' He stopped and paced a few steps deep in thought. 'Maybe we can turn this to our advantage, if he's so disillusioned with the war.'

'How?'

'Could you get him to tell you about German army movements and pass the information on to me? In that way, you'll be a hero.' He paused and looked at her closely. 'But whatever you, do don't fall in love with him.'

'I don't think he wants to be a traitor.'

'Well it's up to you if you want to try.'

As they turned to go back into the room, neither of them noticed that they were not alone. A man emerged from the shadows, his body shaking with anger and his mouth dry with the bitter taste of betrayal.

Chapter Eighteen

Athens, Greece. July 26th 2005

Arriving back at the hotel, Richard retrieved the Bible from the safe and laid it carefully on a desk table in his room. For a moment, he just stared at it in the vague hope that it might reveal its secrets. There was no other choice but to go through the annotations page by page and see if he could establish a pattern. He picked up the book and began to read the writing in the back-fly leaves. It was in Greek so he translated and quickly realised what it was.

In vain – In vain: strike other chords;
Fill high the cup with Samian wine…

I know what this is,' he said out loud, unable to suppress his excitement. 'It's Byron, from his poem "The Isles of Greece".'

Why would she know that? She was a poor Greek peasant girl with little education. How would she know Byron? And why write it down here?

There were two more lines.

Leave battles to the Turkish hordes
And shed the blood of Scio's vine.

He knew the poem word for word and understood it was a hymn to Greek liberty. Maybe she was trying to get inspired by the idea that Greece would be free of the Germans one day.

He sighed, closing the book and putting it down on the table. He stared at it, willing the answer to leap from the pages, running his fingers over the leather cover. As he did, he turned it over in his hand, rubbing it gently, smelling the leather, worn and musty, alive with the secrets of its users over the years. In many ways, he was surprised that Callidora had written on such a wonderful book, but he understood why. This was a working, living document, not something to be admired like a piece of art. Despite its age, it was in good condition. The annotations on the bible were extensive, on almost every page, but very little made any sense. The words from Byron at the back didn't seem to fit with anything and yet he refused to accept that they were irrelevant.

It didn't register with him immediately, but as he ran his finger slowly down the spine, the unevenness of the binding appeared unnatural. He prodded to see how it would fold; it seemed rock solid at the bottom but very soft near the top. Standing up, he found a light to hold the book under, to try and see what it was. There was something stuffed in the spine. It looked like two very small pieces of tightly rolled paper.

He hunted around for something to help him remove the obstruction, finding a pair of tweezers in his toilet bag. Excited, he went back to the book and five minutes later he'd removed the two small bits of paper. He shivered, scared to unroll the paper in case it disintegrated. It was as if the hand of the past was driving him forward. There were two letters, both from Callidora. At first, he couldn't see who the recipient was as the ink was fading, but holding it up to the light, he managed to decipher the name who was the intended recipient of the letters. His heart began to race when he read the words: *Leonard Charles Helford*.

The phone rang. He put the letter down and answered. It was Brian.

'The Greek police have picked up an Arab with a British passport trying to leave the country by road into Albania.'

'How did they find him?'

'With the help of GCHQ, they picked up a mobile call to Afghanistan.'

'Abdul?'

'No. It wasn't him, but at least it proves links to terrorism. He wasn't phoning to make a hotel reservation. That much was clear as soon as we had a fix on him. We just gave the Greek police his coordinates. If you come down to the embassy now, they're sending pictures.'

'I'll be with you in fifteen minutes.'

It took him fourteen minutes to reach the embassy. Although the sun had gone down, the night air was still warm, making running difficult. When he arrived, the security staff gave him disapproving glances, annoyed that he would enter the building in a tracksuit, sweating profusely. As he climbed the stairs, he remembered the letters from Callidora still sitting on the table waiting to be read. After Brian's call he'd left without thinking. He muttered under his breath, cursing his stupidity for leaving them out, praying that they would be safe.

It was nearly 10 p.m. and the embassy was quiet. Brian was on a balcony adjacent to his office smoking a cigarette and staring down at the city. He looked worried.

'You look as if you could do with a shower,' Brian said.

'I ran. Only way to get here quickly,' Richard replied, still panting from the run up the stairs.

Brian stubbed out his cigarette on the balcony floor and walked back into the office, checking his computer, which appeared to be in the middle of a download. 'Think they're coming through now.' He looked at the screen and watched the photo build. It took a long time, but eventually a grainy picture emerged. Clearly it had been blown up, losing its clarity in the process. 'We'll run the analysis with GCHQ. We'll get a fix on our friend here, no mistake,' said Brian.

Richard looked at the picture, staring closely at the image on the screen. 'It's him. Yes. It's definitely him. I remember the tattoo on his neck.' He looked at Brian who seemed lost in thought. The worried look on his face hadn't gone away. 'What's up, Brian? You look as if you've seen a ghost.'

'I'm sorry,' he said looking distracted. That was the first time Brian had shown him any sympathy since he'd arrived in Athens. 'We've picked up the two tracksuited guys who were sniffing around your mother's house. They're lowlifes who think they can win kudos with their mates if they support jihad. But ask them the difference between a Sunni and Shia and they'll give you a blank look.'

'Who are they working for?'

'They don't know. Doing it for the love of Allah.'

'How's Rowena taking all this?'

'You've got her interest, but there's a problem.'

It sounded ominous. Brian lit up another cigarette and walked back on to the balcony. Richard followed.

'What is it?' said Richard.

'It's difficult for me to say this.'

'Go on. I can take it.' He tried to smile but Brian refused not to look serious.

'The CIA know all about your visit to Nikoletta and her death. They called before we could set up a meeting. They want us to back off.'

'What do you mean – back off?' Richard said with growing dismay.

'They want us to stop the operation,' Brian replied.

'Who told them?' Richard snapped.

'Maybe they've got Petronos in their pocket,' Brian speculated.

'I don't understand why they'd do this.' Richard paced the length of the balcony gripping one of the safety rails, trying to keep his emotions in check.

'They think you might compromise their operation to find your father.'

Richard swerved around and glared back at Brian. 'What? My father? Are you telling me the CIA are looking for my father?'

'Well you said yourself you thought he might be alive. Didn't you?'

'What I think doesn't matter.' Richard found himself peering over the balcony looking for answers in the Athens skyline, illuminated by the moon and bright lights of the city. 'They can't do this. You're not going to listen to them, are you?' he asked, turning round to face Brian. Brian didn't reply and went back inside. Richard watched as he poured two glasses of brandy and returned to the balcony, handing him one.

'It's 7 star,' he said.

Richard snatched the glass and gulped down the brandy in one swig, enjoying the warm feeling flushing down into his stomach. 'Why do they care about my father? It must be to do with Abdul. They want him and they don't want the Brits to interfere. My father's not involved.'

'They think otherwise.'

'I don't understand.'

'Your father is wanted by the CIA, dead or alive, for releasing state secrets to the terrorists.'

Richard froze, dumbfounded at what he was hearing, his mouth wide open with shock. His father was many things he didn't know, but he couldn't believe he'd ever make a committed Islamic terrorist. 'But they said he was killed, why change the story now?' he shouted.

'All a smoke screen,' said Brian.

'Shit. Do they know where he is?'

'Not a fucking clue. He's been missing since 9/11 but there was a sighting last year before he dropped out of view once more.

'Do you know where?'

'The CIA won't tell us...fuck the Special Relationship.'

'That's bullshit. Brian. My father may have been a bastard to me but he wasn't a fucking terrorist. The CIA have no right to dictate to us.'

Brian went over to his desk and picked up a mobile phone still in its box. He removed the packaging, inserted a sim card he produced from his jacket pocket, and punched the keypad.

Rowena picked up immediately. 'I've got Richard here on speaker,' Brian said.

'Richard,' she said. 'How are you?' She seemed more conciliatory than before.

'I've told him about the CIA,' said Brian interrupting before Richard could speak.

'I'm not exactly thrilled at what Brian's told me, Rowena,' Richard said, no longer caring about hiding his anger.

'I'm not happy about the CIA pushing us around anymore than you are,' she replied.

'So let me keep on the case.'

'It's out of my control. C's spoken to the CIA Director. He's prepared to go with the Yanks' request officially.'

'Officially?'

'Yes, that means unofficially we can keep going.'

Richard seized on the glimmer of hope Rowena appeared to be offering. 'So what is the US' problem? Are they going after Abdul?'

'Yes, they seem to have got an operation under way and don't want you interfering.'

'Because of my father? They're bullshitting us.'

'We think that as well, which is why this is going off the books.'

'I don't understand.'

'I want you to stay on it. We have a major advantage over the Americans in finding Abdul'

'Oh. What's that?'

'You.'

'*Me*,' Richard exclaimed. 'Why me?'

'The Arabs are also looking for your father. I think they thought Nikoletta knew something and killed her by accident without finding anything out.'

Richard remembered Nikoletta's words – *I didn't tell them* – could it be that she knew where his father was hiding?

'So now there's just you. You'll be the bait to lure Abdul out of hiding.'

'Except I don't know where he is any more than they do,' said Richard.

'That may be so, but we showed a picture of your father to the two guys we picked up watching your mother's house. They've confirmed that's who they were looking out for. So my earlier reservations seem unfounded. Masood was watching you and it's your father that they were looking for.'

Richard's face fell. 'So he is alive,' he said, speaking slowly, the realisation difficult to take in. He should have been happy that his father wasn't dead but all the pent-up fury about his father just made him mad. He was furious because, if it was true, his father had shown no sensitivity to the feelings of his mother, or him for that matter. He hated his father even more than before. The sense of betrayal made him more determined to find answers.

'We think he's alive, or at least the CIA and Al Qaeda think so,' said Brian.

'Wait a minute,' said Richard. 'If my father is a terrorist, why do Al Qaeda want him dead?' His eyes narrowed as a thousand questions flooded his brain. 'And another thing,' he continued, 'if he was working for the CIA, why didn't you know about it?'

'All good questions,' said Rowena. 'I don't have the answers.'

'And I suppose you don't have the answer to why I was moved out of Iraq in a hurry?'

'No…' Richard could hear a hesitation in Rowena's voice.

'No…you don't know? Or no, you're not going to tell me?' Richard replied, exasperated by Rowena's continued refusal to divulge what went on in Iraq.

'I'm not going to answer that question,' said Rowena. 'Do you want to work under the radar on this or not?'

'Yes, never been more certain.'

'You'll be on your own in the field. Brian will be your case officer, but none of this goes through official channels until we get Abdul Alim and find your father. The Yanks will understand then. C will enjoy telling that to the CIA Director,' she said, sounding more upbeat. 'I'm taking a risk here.' Her voice had become sterner. 'If you get caught we'll disown you, say you're operating without permission. There'll be a Top-Secret memorandum on the file, with your signature of acknowledgment, sent to you forbidding any further action in this case.'

'He's got no training in the field,' said Brian. 'It's a big risk.'

'I know,' said Rowena. 'I wouldn't blame you, Richard, if you said no. Normally, I wouldn't even consider you, but I know this is personal. Your father's connection makes you the ideal choice. But it *is* dangerous, you've got to realise that.'

'You're damned right it's dangerous. It's fucking suicide,' said Brian. 'Just suppose Richard finds Abdul by putting himself on the line, we've no idea whether his father will put his head above the parapet. Assuming he doesn't then Abdul will kill Richard without question. Just how do you propose he defends himself?'

'I'll take my chances,' said Richard.

'You won't have any chances to take. Abdul is a cold blooded killer who's carrying a bucket load of hate which drives him on.'

'I don't want you to kill him,' said Rowena. 'Just pinpoint his position and we'll take him out with a drone.'

'I understand the risks, Rowena. But I've got something to prove. I'll do it.'

Richard could see that Brian wasn't pleased.

'Get Abdul and your career will sky rocket,' Rowena continued. 'Fail and you're finished with the Service. I know it sounds harsh but if you bugger this up, you'll be hounded out for working against orders. We'll deny everything, so think about it.'

'I don't need to think. I'll do it.' Richard fixed his gaze on Brian and smiled. Brian pretended to clap and grinned back. He'd won Brian's respect, however grudging it appeared to be.

'Thank you, Richard. Just take care.' She sounded relieved that he'd said yes. 'Get on a plane tomorrow and come back to London. Your new passport will be delivered to your flat. After that you're on your own. I'll leave you and Brian to work out how you'll make contact.'

Rowena cut the call. Despite his bravado, Brian looked surprised that Rowena would even entertain such an idea to make Richard go undercover. 'This won't work. I'm warning you,' said Brian. 'It's a shit idea. Abdul is a professional terrorist. He'll run rings around you.'

'Thanks, Brian, for that vote of confidence,' said Richard, forcing a smile, but inside he knew that Brian was right.

He was scared.

Chapter Nineteen

Crete, Greece. June 6th 1941

Callidora knew it was a risk. Somebody would miss her one day when she went off on her own. She was pleased Lenny had said she should continue to see Hans, but that didn't make it right to betray her brother and everybody else in the village. She wasn't sure why she wanted to ignore what all her senses told her was wrong. It was a rational thing to do, to try and get on with their enemies, but what was rational about war?

There was a noise. Startled, she looked around and listened, forever sensitive to the landscape, just like when she was on the mountain with her goats. She knew every sound, but the sound she could hear wasn't the sound of an animal in the undergrowth. She scolded herself for imagining things, but couldn't stop her nerves jangling. The moon was dim, a small crescent, making it hard to pick up her path and scaring her more than she should have liked. As she moved forward, she heard the sound again. It made her jump. She slipped, putting her hands out to break the fall, just suppressing the urge to cry out. Her hands were grazed and hurt, but in the darkness, she couldn't see any signs of blood. She picked herself up and listened again. There was silence.

Reaching the church, she found the path that would take her to the woods. The tree canopy blotted out the stars and the moon. It was pitch black; so dark she couldn't see her fingers. She edged forward, catching her face as it scraped along low-lying branches. Her heart was pounding until, out of the eerie gloom of the forest, she saw the faintest of lights beckoning her out of the darkness. Hans was sitting on a rock in the clearing, near where she'd hidden the scroll. He looked up and held out a small paraffin lamp to guide her to him.

He smiled. 'I'm grateful that you decided to come. I don't deserve it,' he said, his face casting a shadow across the forest floor.

She resisted returning the smile. The anxiety she'd felt on the way bubbled to the surface. 'They are murdering my people,' she cried. 'And you should bear the blame.'

'I know. You're right of course. I am to blame.' He looked embarrassed, but that just made her angry.

'You're Greek...You've watched your captain put a bullet through my neighbour's head...You did nothing. He was an old man...He was shot without mercy. That's a crime,' she shouted. 'I don't care whether it's war or not.'

Hans hung his head in shame. She could see her point had hit home. 'I'm ashamed to say I've seen Kohlenz do it many times in other villages. He's a murderer,' he whispered. There were tears in his eyes. She looked at him and felt another moment where all the reasons to hate this man vanished into nothing.

'You must stop him, or you'll be just as bad,' she pleaded. She was crying now, seeing the limp corpse of Stephanos in her mind's eye, a pool of blood surrounding his body.

'You said I should kill Kohlenz and I now think you're right...' He hesitated. 'I'm going to desert.' His voice was breaking. 'Yes – they may kill me, but if I have any principles, I can't watch this happen anymore.'

Callidora's jaw dropped. 'You're going to do *what*?'

'I'm going to desert.'

Her instinct was to embrace him, but she held back. 'My brother...the other men will never trust you. They'll think you're a spy.'

'But do you trust me?' he replied. There were signs of desperation in his face.

She wanted to trust him, but the nagging feeling that she was betraying her brother would not go away. 'They will only trust you if you do something to win that trust.'

'Like killing Kohlenz?' he said slowly.

'Yes.' She paused, contemplating her next words. 'There are ways I would trust you without you having to kill Kohlenz.' She lowered her voice, calmer now. Instinct told her she was doing the right thing.

'Anything,' he said, grasping both her hands. 'You trusting me is all I care about.'

She looked at him again. His eyes were wide and insistent, begging her to believe in him. Gently, she freed herself from his hands and walked over to the rock where the icons and scroll were hidden. 'When we met in the church you told me I was right to hide the icons,' she said softly.

'Yes...to hide them from the Nazis. They would see them as plunder, a way to make money, not something holy and precious.'

'Didn't you tell me you were studying Theology?' she continued, locking on to his gaze.

'Yes. You're right. I did say that, but what's that got to do with my desertion?'

'I've found something...in the foundations of the church. It's very special, much more so than the icons.'

Hans' face brightened with evident excitement. 'Tell me, please. I give you my word I'll never tell anyone.'

Callidora stood in front of the rock and removed the cracked piece with great care. One by one she took out the icons, placing them on the ground. Reaching down, she took hold of the box and lifted it free of the hole.

Hans came forward, his mouth open, betraying his eagerness to look. He held up the lamp studying every inch of the painting with his eyes, bright and transfixed.

'It's the most beautiful thing I've ever seen in my whole life,' he said, his face beaming with excitement.

'There's more,' Callidora said, enjoying his enthusiasm. She took out a small knife and removed the nails from the box one by one, laying them on the rock where they would not be lost. Lifting the scroll out of the box, she looked back in Hans' direction, seeing his expression change again.

'Can you read Greek?' she asked, rolling out the scroll.
'Some...let me look.'

Callidora held the lamp while he read the first lines. The look of amazement in his eyes told her she'd made the right decision. 'It's very old. I don't think it's a forgery,' she said.

'John of Patmos,' he replied. 'I can't believe it.' He glanced at Callidora. 'This tells me it's right to help you.'

Callidora smiled for the first time since she'd seen him. 'I'm glad I told you. With your help, I need to take it across Crete to the Monastery at Preveli. The monks will know its true worth.'

'Is that wise?' he asked. 'I mean, the Nazis might raid the monastery.'

She thought for a moment. 'You're right. It'll be safe here for now. Nobody knows about it except us.'

It was true that the man crouching behind the rocks didn't see them look at the scroll, but what he did see was far worse. The woman he wanted to marry was cavorting with a German soldier, complicit in the killing of Stephanos. Shivering with rage he ran back down the hillside. He wouldn't tell Nikos. What had to be done was a question of honour. It was between him and the German.

Chapter Twenty

Athens, Greece. July 26ᵗʰ 2005

It was nearly midnight when Richard left the embassy. He'd spent a couple of hours going through what little information they had on Abdul Alim. He'd arrived in America in October 1998 from Afghanistan and studied at the Center for Islamic Studies at the University of Florida. The pictures they had were of a man who looked westernised. Richard noticed his expensive watch and sunglasses. He seemed to have access to money but there was no record where it had come from. Richard also discussed his options with Brian, who'd agreed to tell the CIA's station chief that the investigation was being stood down at their request. They agreed he'd fly back to London on his own passport, in full view of the CIA, to give them the impression of being sent home. He'd lie low for a couple of days to see if they watched him and then leave again on a new passport with a false identity.

He decided to take the longer route back to his hotel, which took him through the Plaka district. The outdoor restaurants were full and in the bars people sipped cocktails while lounging on sofas put on the street to entice passers-by. The noise of laughter and raucous chatter made Richard feel alone, and the lingering taste of the Metaxa that Brian gave him made him crave a long ice-cold beer. He found himself a comfortable armchair and ordered a large Amstel. His mind raced, only just beginning to grasp the danger he was in. He thought of Becky carrying his child and wondered whether he'd be like his grandfather and get himself killed before he'd seen his son. The thought made him want to cry. There was a real chance Abdul would kill him and he'd never see his child. He called Becky again. Whereas before he'd hesitated to hit the call button on his mobile, this time he found himself growing impatient when she didn't answer straight away. He might never be able to call her again.

He breathed a sigh of relief when he heard her voice.

'Hello,' she said.

'Becky, it's me. Did you get my message?'

'Yes, I did.'

'I just want to say I'm sorry,' he said. 'I wouldn't make a good husband at the moment, but maybe things will change.' He wanted to hold her, let her feel his loneliness.

'You said you were sorry in your message. What's new?' said Becky. 'What are you trying to say, Richard?'

'I'm overseas.'

'Oh,' she replied. 'Where?'

He thought he detected a glimmer of interest. 'I can't say,' he replied. 'It's for work.'

He could almost hear her thoughts. Ten seconds passed before she spoke. 'If we'd got married, Richard, would it have been like this? You never telling me where you're going. Disappearing for weeks on end. Is that what it would've been like?'

'That's exactly my point. I'd be a useless husband.'

'Yes, maybe you would, but I still love you,' she replied.

His lips quivered; fighting to hold back the tears. 'I'm sorry,' he said.

'Bye, Richard, take care,' she spoke softly.

'Don't go,' he whispered.

'What is it, Richard?'

'If I don't see you again. I want you to know I love you and I want you to have our baby. I really do. All that stuff in the hospital was just a reaction to the bomb.'

'I know,' she replied. 'Are you in danger Richard? Why don't you think you might not see me again?'

Richard swallowed. He could hear the distress in her voice. He swallowed but he could no longer hold back the tears. 'I'm sorry,' he sobbed. 'I can't tell you anything.'

He disconnected the call and continued to hold the receiver, listening to the drone of the dialling tone, wondering whether he'd ever see her again, wondering whether Abdul would kill him and wondering about his father. He felt indifferent to the news that his father was alive but he still wanted to see him and hear in his own words why he'd failed as a father.

He was halfway through his beer when he remembered Callidora's letters lying on his hotel bed, waiting to be read. He drank the rest of the beer down in one gulp, slipping 10 Euros into the hands of a waiter as he left the bar, and began trotting towards his hotel.

The hotel lobby was deserted. Stopping, he asked the solitary receptionist whether there'd been any messages. The receptionist looked blank and then, noting his name, handed him an envelope asked whether the new key card was working.

Richard needed no second prompt. He sprinted the stairs, two at a time, reaching the corridor on the third floor in less than a minute. He paused for breath and listened. Apart from the muffled sound of televisions in other rooms, there was no one about. He slowed his pace, moving gingerly along the passage until he reached his door. It was closed, but not quite. A slight push and the door opened a little more.

There was nobody there. The bathroom door was open. Nothing.

But somebody had been in his room. Callidora's letters were missing.

'Shit,' he said out loud, pushing the wardrobe's sliding door to access the hotel safe. 'Shit...shit,' he repeated as he wrestled with the pin number. If he'd only hidden the letters and taken the time to read them. Now he had no idea of their contents. He rejoiced when he saw the Bible was still there, slipping it into the inside zip pocket of his tracksuit. He couldn't risk losing the Bible as well.

Stepping outside, he stared back along the corridor and saw the open fire escape door. Had he surprised the intruder? Maybe he was long gone but he had to find out one way or the other.

He dashed along the corridor, through the fire exit, thundering down the stairs. At the bottom, the door opened onto a side street crammed with parked cars, but with few people about.

Except for a man running.

The pavement was narrow and, when someone stepped into his path, he could only barge past, ignoring the hailstorm of abuse that followed. Reaching the main road that led up to Syntagma Square, he could see the man running along the side of the National Gardens, rattling a gate that was closed at sunset. He'd have to go around.

There must have been one hundred metres between them and Richard knew he could catch him. He ran faster, dodging and weaving around cars blaring their horns as they raced up Vasilissis Amalias.

By the time he reached the Greek Parliament, the gap had closed and Richard could see the man turning the corner. He glanced up to the street name and at that moment realised where he was going.

Vasilissis Sofias. The address of the American embassy. With sight of the American flag, he ducked behind a car and watched as the man turned to cross the road.

The shock that Richard recognised the man he'd been chasing caught him off guard. He didn't see the silver Mercedes van approaching from behind, its back doors opening before the screech of the brakes. As he swung around, two masked men leapt out. An arm gripped him by the neck. He tried to kick out but the other hand smothered his mouth and nose.

Chloroform.

As his legs lifted into the air, he saw the man he'd been following staring back at him.

The face of Mohammed Abdul Alim.

Richard was still conscious when he was hauled into the van and thrown onto its metal floor. He was vaguely aware of the engine firing up, the doors slamming with a deafening clunk before he floated into oblivion. He could see a Greek girl running through the mountains laughing as he gave chase. Her hands beckoned him to come closer, but as he reached out, he could see her smile had turned into a scream.

A scream for help.

Berlin. July 27th[th] 2005

Nine hours later, approximately fifteen hundred miles from Athens, Klaus Kleiner was beginning to wonder whether his career as a junior defence minister in the German government was in tatters. There was nothing unusual about meeting two men and a woman officer from NATO.

But these people were not from NATO.

They'd sold a lie to get them through the door. They were Mossad agents and they had him well and truly over a barrel, dangling by his balls. The photographs strewn across his desk showed him talking to Mohammed Atta, the 9/11 ringleader, in Hamburg. There were also pictures of him in Freiburg meeting Abel Multzeimer's representative and a photograph of the transfer of $1 million into his Venezuelan bank account with a copy of the bank statement showing that funds were received.

'I'm sure Chancellor Schroder will be interested to see these photographs,' said the woman sitting opposite him.

She was clearly the leader of the group, dressed in a black trouser suit, blonde hair cut short so that it barely touched her shoulders. Kleiner never had time for women but found this woman's piercing eyes and severe cheekbones strangely attractive. She reminded him of his domineering governess who use to look after him as a child, never smiling, taking a sadistic pleasure in smacking him when he was disobedient.

The woman spoke German as if it was her native language. 'The Chancellor might also be interested in our evidence that you are a committed Nazi. Someone who has been meeting Muhammed Abdul Alim, a known terrorist on the United States of America Kill List.

'I don't know what you're talking about,' said Kleiner.

The woman smirked, irritated by his answer. 'On July 12th, you visited Afghanistan.'

'Yes, on government business.'

'Don't waste my time, Herr Kleiner. You met someone who was nothing to do with government.' The woman proceeded to toss photographs onto his desk, one after the other. Photographs of him being searched by the American.

'Satellite technology is a wonderful thing, don't you think?'

Kleiner looked at the photos lying on the desk but had no wish to pick them up. He could see the evidence was damning. 'What does this prove? I was about to have a meeting with one of their elders, in search of good relations. It goes on all the time in Afghanistan.'

The woman allowed a smile to creep onto her face. She signalled to one of the other men who placed a small recorder on to the table in front of Kleiner. Leaning forward, the woman flicked the switch.

'Drones are also pretty amazing. This is a recording of your conversation. Clear as a bell from fifteen hundred feet.'

195

Kleiner had to concede the recording was clear, not that it had captured anything useful. However, in the wrong hands and he'd be jailed for the rest of his life.

'The man on your right is Muhammed Abdul Alim travelling under a United States passport by the name of Dr Zayan Bashir.'

'What do you want?' said Kleiner.

'We want you to help us kill Abdul Alim and Sheikh Zabor Bin Hitani.'

Kleiner laughed. 'The idea is absurd. If, as you say, I am a neo-Nazi then why would I want to help the Israeli Secret Service?'

'It is not without precedent. We've used Nazi war criminals in the past. Besides, I think you value your career more than your ideological preferences. Say no and these photographs will be delivered to *Die Welt and Bild*, not to mention the offices of the Chancellor before you have time to piss in your pants.'

Kleiner let out a nervous laugh. 'I don't even know the Sheikh,' he said.

'The Americans are very protective of their Saudi billionaire, so we want you to lure him away from the United States.'

Kleiner shrugged. 'How am I supposed to do that?'

'Through Abdul but also by using a bait he'll find irresistible.'

'What bait?' Kleiner snapped.

The woman swept her blonde hair off her soldiers. 'All in good time…all in good time.'

Kleiner felt sick in the stomach. All his hard work seemed to be brushed away in a stroke of bad luck that the Israelis had decided to follow him. 'And what about the money?' he said.

'Abel Multzeimer works for us. You can keep the money if you help us kill the Sheikh.'

'And what if you don't succeed?'

'We'll ruin your career. It's that simple. Failure is not an option for you.'

'And what about the scroll?'

'We want that as well.' the woman smiled, 'that is assuming you know where to find it.'

Chapter Twenty-One

Crete, Greece. June 22nd 1941

'I don't like the way you look at that German,' said Ikaros, grabbing Callidora's arm.

She tugged herself free, glaring back. 'What's that supposed to mean?' she shouted as she stormed across the square. 'He brought us food...he's trying to help us. Do you want me to throw it back in his face?'

She was worried by his insinuation because, no matter how hard she'd tried to distance herself from Hans and disguise her true feelings, Ikaros had noticed. At least Hans hadn't carried out his plan to desert, which she knew was likely to fail. He'd only just come to the village, armed with a small group of soldiers, handing out biscuits with German labels and some dried fruit and coffee. He'd also given them live chickens, stolen from other villages. She'd told him they couldn't take what didn't belong to them and he'd replied, with a bleak look on his face, that they'd no further need of them, pleading that he was only replacing what they'd already taken.

Callidora turned to face Ikaros. Her headscarf had slipped and her long black hair had escaped, blowing in the hot summer wind that was rushing in from the deserts of Africa. The yellow dust dried her lips. She pushed the hair away from her face and wiped her forehead, roughened by gusts of air laced with grit.

'He's only trying to help,' she said, refusing to get angry, exhausted by the suffering of the last few days.

'What is it with him?' Ikaros bellowed after her. 'He comes every day, while his friends continue to massacre our people. Women and children murdered.'

He was right, but as Father Agathangelos had once said: *You don't counter evil with hate. Only love conquers evil.*

That was her mantra and the reason why she wanted to love Hans.

'Maybe that's why our village has been left alone, because he cares about what's happening,' she replied.

She could see how angry Ikaros was, and who could blame him? 'But they killed Stephanos,' he said, his voice cracking with emotion. Callidora knew Ikaros was right and that she had no answer for him. She turned away and ran across the square towards their house. 'They'll kill more of us if it suits them,' he shouted to Callidora's back. There was no reprieve inside of the house as the innocent eyes of little Kosmas greeted her, which only made matters worse. She felt guilty about Hans, but whatever Ikaros said made her more determined.

She was doing the right thing.

Maybe Lenny will understand, but where is he?

June 23rd 1941

The village seemed strangely quiet without the men. The battle may have been lost by the Allied soldiers in just a few days, but Callidora knew Nikos had no intention of surrendering. He'd led a small band of fighters into the mountains to join the resistance. They were a headstrong bunch, only too pleased to be heroes. She hadn't seen Lenny for over two weeks and wondered whether he was with Nikos up in the mountains. She prayed he would stop them carrying out futile raids on the Germans where, she was certain, there would be only one outcome. The men of the village would end up dead.

Blinking at the sunlight, Callidora gazed at the skies, watching plane after plane land at Maleme. Whatever Nikos tried to do, she was sure that the Germans were going to be unaffected. Why couldn't Nikos understand that the Germans would stop at nothing to avenge the killing of their men? What happened at Kandanos could happen to them.

The threat of violence was never far from Callidora's mind and for a long time she clung on to the hope that Hans was protecting them from a visit from the German firing squads. She longed to see him again and wondered whether he'd be able to give her some vital information about the scroll. Each night at dusk she went back up the hill to the ruined church. Nobody saw her go but there was no sign of Hans. When she was sure he wasn't coming, she retrieved the painted box and looked again at the scroll.

There had been some sort of argument between St John of Patmos and St Paul. That much she understood. Paul had won the argument, but John had recorded that his will was not the will of God. Callidora shivered as she read the startling words of revelation, confused by its meaning, but convinced it was genuine. Who was she to deny the word of God, no matter how unsettling the prophecy made her feel? If Hans read it, he'd understand what it was about. His education in Theology would help, she was sure of it. Just as Father Agathangelos had helped her understand as a child in the Monastery at Preveli, Hans would help her understand the scroll.

He just had to come.

She waited by the church, sitting on the broken stones watching the sun go down. There was no cloudy haze on the horizon, so when the sun finally sank into the sea, it turned the colour of saffron in its dying moments, casting a perfect shimmering sheet of gold across the water. As she looked on with wonder at the power of nature, she remembered the words of Father Agathangelos once more.

No matter what evil man inflicts on the world, Mother Nature reflects the real power of God. It will always triumph.

Darkness had fallen when Hans appeared. He shone a torch at first, so she could see it was him, and then lit a lamp just like he'd done the last time they'd met.

He smiled. 'I'm glad you've come.'

'I've been here every night since I saw you last,' she replied, seeking his approval for her persistence.

He wrapped his arms around her in a warm embrace. 'It's been difficult,' he said, his ashen face appearing worn out from his wounds and the strain he was under. 'I can't stop thinking about it,' he continued, a note of desperation in his voice. 'Horrible disgusting things...I can't repeat. They're happening before my eyes and if I turn away Kohlenz will notice. He even threatened to put me in the firing squad.'

She wanted him to hold her, to rest her head on his chest, but unease forced them apart. She pushed herself away, but as they looked at each other she felt his intense sad gaze boring into her brain, weakening her resistance. Her face began to mirror his sadness. 'Tell me what's going on,' she said. 'What's happened to Chania? What are they doing in the villages?'

Hans looked sick. He winced as she touched his arm. His wounds were still painful. His bandage was filthy, caked in dried blood.

'Chania is a ruin, but the villages...' His voice drifted away.

'What?' she shouted.

'There was a boy...no more than twelve years old, standing in front of a firing squad with his father and grandfather.' He broke off again, sobbing at the thoughts flooding back.

201

'Go on,' she said, moved by his emotions, which she knew were real.

'The grandfather looked too old to lift a gun, let alone kill a soldier. And yet they found him guilty. The father stood tall and proud, singing Cretan songs, pushing his chest in the direction of the guns. The boy was not so defiant – I remember his terrified face – weeping hysterically.' He wiped his eyes on his tunic. 'The soldiers lifted their guns and at that moment, a woman screaming, rushed into the line of fire, trying to save her son.' His voiced cracked. 'Do you know...they never stopped...they just kept firing.'

Callidora felt the anger growing in her stomach. She wept, absorbed by his emotions, seeing he was crying also. The terrifying reality of his story brought them together. She rushed towards him.

For a moment she just held him, allowing his tears to subside and then she spoke.

'So why are they leaving our village untouched from reprisals?'

It was Hans' turn to pull away. He hesitated.

'I told Kohlenz about you and said you were collaborating.'

'You did what?' she said, shocked by what he was saying.

'I did it to help you and your village...and it's working,' he pleaded. 'They're leaving you alone.'

'And what does Kohlenz think I'm going to say?'

Hans looked sheepish, speaking with his eyes averted from her gaze. 'He wants to know about the British soldiers hiding in the mountains.' Hans looked up to her, quizzically, seeing her anger. 'I'm sorry,' he said. 'I was just trying to buy some time.'

Callidora thought for a minute. 'There may be a way to use this to our advantage.'

'How?' said Hans looking interested.

'By feeding Kohlenz false information.' Callidora smiled and she noticed the look of relief on his face.

'But when he finds it's false, he'll destroy the village and probably kill me.'

'Unless we kill him first.' Callidora surprised herself at the way she was thinking. War had changed her. Winning overrode her sense of fair play. She'd fight fire with fire.

A few more minutes passed, while they sat in silence. He took out a clean bandage from his bag and asked her to re-dress his wounds. When that was done, she spoke again.

'I need you to read the whole papyrus I found...I think it's a prophecy of something serious, but I'm confused by its message. I know it's important but I need you to understand it.'

'Of course, I'd like to read it,' he replied. 'What little I've seen tells me it's important. Since you showed it to me, I've been worried about its safety.'

He held her hand as they walked into the wood. As they came up to the clearing where the scroll was hidden, he stopped and turned towards her.

'What can I do to help? You must ask someone to trust me.'

'You could keep us informed about what your troops are doing, so we're ready. That would help us and maybe they'd begin to trust you,' she replied.

He thought for a moment and then spoke. 'It's difficult to get this information out to you...hard to cover my tracks to come and see you like this...but yes, I'll help you.' He took both her hands, staring into her eyes, sincerity etched into his face. 'These last few days, I've realised that it's my Greek blood that calls me. I'm not German any more.'

She moved towards him and kissed him on the cheek. 'It's why I like you so much. You're Greek and I could never love a German,' she said softly.

She could see him smiling with pleasure at what she was saying. 'So what about the papyrus I found?' she said, going over to the rock where the scroll was hidden.

It took her only a few moments to retrieve the scroll. She handed it to him and he sat down on the forest floor and began reading. Every now and again, he looked up and consulted her about a Greek word or phrase. It took him only a few minutes to read it.

At the end, he rolled up the papyrus gently and, tying its leather cord, handed it back.

'The secret is devastating,' he said, his face beaming with excitement. 'It's uncomfortable reading, but very important.'

He took hold of her hands, gripping them firmly. 'I feel privileged to have seen it. It could be the most important find in centuries.' He leaned forward and hugged her. Pulling away, their eyes met, locking their gaze for a few moments. No matter how hard they tried, they could never look away. She knew it was wrong, but as his lips parted, she moved forward to kiss him. She'd kissed Ikaros once, but not like this. She couldn't help herself. A German didn't smell different from a Greek. The uniform of the Third Reich made no difference either. There was something else that drew them together. She couldn't deny it, but kneeling down, her dress damp from the warmth of the night air, a frisson of danger excited her. The fear she'd felt had evaporated, like the riverbanks during a long summer.

But the danger had not gone away. It was real. Her instinct was right.

It took only one bullet to kill him.

They were kneeling when it came. It may have been luck to hit him in the head, but that was where it found its mark. A bullet out of nowhere. It entered his head at the side and came out through his eye socket, missing Callidora by millimetres. His skull shattered, spraying her dress with a shower of blood mixed with brain tissue and bone.

She screamed as he slumped forward, his body limp in her arms. Would the next bullet be for her? She sobbed, terrified, willing it to come. Nobody would hear except the killer. Another bullet drilled into his back. The force of it threw her backwards. It was unnecessary because he was already dead. Unless the bullet was for her. His body had saved her life.

'Oh God, please forgive me,' she wept, as if God had fired the shot.

And then it stopped. There were no breaking twigs or shouts from the undergrowth. There were no more sounds except her own sobs echoing against the trees.

At first she just held him as his blood soaked her shirt, the fabric becoming wet with the red ochre of death. She panted to catch her breath, as the grief and tears flooded out like a torrent. In her own mind her anguish seemed exaggerated. He was just a German, her enemy, but her tears were more than that. Everything she had seen since the invasion filled her with despair and now, as the bullets tore into the man she had just kissed, death became intimate. The church of St John could be rebuilt and Stephanos was already an old man who would have died soon enough. This was different. It tipped her over the edge into a valley of hatred. She knew that the Germans would seek revenge and that could lead to many more deaths. That was why she was crying. She laid him down gently among the leaves of the forest. The lamp was still burning casting her shadow across his corpse, covering him in a last embrace. She picked up the painted box and placed the scroll back where it belonged. There was not a mark of his blood on the document. It was a miracle that it was untouched by the killing, and at that moment she knew that she had something very special in her hands. As she ran back down the hill towards the village, she didn't think about whether Hans' killer was waiting for her, her only thought was how she might hide the scroll. The house was still silent as people slept.

Running up the stairs, she placed the box with the scroll under the bed and ripped her clothes as she tried to remove them more quickly than her hands could unhook the buttons. Pouring water into a bowl, she started washing with increasing desperation, oblivious to the noise she was making, with only one intent, to remove any part of Hans from her body and most of all from her face. There may have been no smell, but she couldn't erase it from her memory. No matter how hard she tried to clean, it would not go away.

'Callidora, what are you doing?'

She turned and saw Nikos staring in disbelief. The sight of her brother brought the tears back. 'I thought you were in the mountains,' she cried.

'We've come back to stop the Nazis burning the village,' said Nikos. 'We came back this evening. I looked for you but none of the women knew where you were.' She rushed forward, throwing her arms around him, her whole body shaking with hysterical sobs. The rest of the house had been awakened by the noise and were peering at her through tired eyes, unable to understand what was going on. Nikos ordered them back to bed and when they were gone, he sat her down on the bed and she began to relate the story in all its detail. When she'd finished, he could hardly contain his anger.

'Please forgive me, Nikos, I'm so sorry,' she wept.

'Do you realise what you've done?' Nikos shouted. 'When they find the body, they'll want revenge and they'll want it ten times over.'

She knew this already, but to hear it from Nikos made it worse. 'I didn't kill him, did I?' she wailed, her lips quivering, trying to defend her position but knowing she was wrong. 'If he'd given us intelligence, it would've helped the resistance. I thought I was doing the right thing. He was on our side and wanted to help.'

Nikos stood up and began pacing the room. 'One of those halfwits killed him,' he said angrily. 'Out of jealousy, at the sight of you sucking up to the Nazis.' He glared at Callidora. 'If we'd only stayed up in the mountains, none of this would've happened...It must be Ikaros.'

'Ikaros would never do anything like that,' she said, but stopped short when she remembered what he'd said when he saw Hans staring at her.

'I'm going over to wake Ikaros and find out if it was him. We need to take the body to the Germans and not wait for them to find it. You'll take us to it tomorrow, Callidora. Is that clear?'

In her bedroom she could not sleep, terrifying images swirling around in her mind. Hans' face kept coming back, laughing in the seconds before his death, excited by the discovery of the scroll. Then the villagers, everyone had the potential to kill a German, everyone a suspect. Nikos said it had to be Ikaros. She refused to believe it was him, but who else was there? It would be an easy task to find a motive for all of them. He was their enemy and whatever the bible said about loving enemies, it didn't apply in a state of war.

And then she thought of the scroll. She needed to hide it. As the faces came in and out of her mind, the scroll found its way into her consciousness. Without thinking, she knew where to hide it, as if some miraculous force had taken control of her reason and told her where to put it. Getting up, she went downstairs to see Nikos returning from seeing Ikaros.

'Does he admit it was him?' she said.

'No, he denies it.'

'Do you believe him?'

'I don't know. This is a disaster. You may have been stupid but whoever did this will destroy this village.'

'I'm going onto the mountain to check on my goats. It's almost dawn and I can't sleep.' He looked up at her and she could see worry etched across his face. 'I'm so sorry, Nikos. Please forgive me,' she said once again. 'I'll be back in a few hours. The body's in the forest behind the church. You'll find it easily.' She went forward and put her arms round his neck, hoping he might respond, just a little, to show he still loved her. But there was nothing. She turned and went back outside into the square. The path up the mountain was easy to find, even in the dark, because she'd walked it so many times. It would take her a couple of hours to reach her destination, but when she did, the scroll would be gone for ever.

Chapter Twenty-Two

Istanbul, Turkey. July 31st 2005

Richard had no idea, how long he'd been asleep. All he felt was an incredible dryness in his mouth. Slowly, he prised open his eyes and stared at the ceiling, trying to focus. The room was white. There were no pictures or furniture apart from the stiff back-breaking bed he was lying on. The mattress was bare, a crumpled sheet barely covering his nakedness.

There was a memory of movement, a vagueness of the passing of time, being offered water and food, which he struggled to hold down. He remembered intense dreams, of floating in space and moving. Always moving. He turned on his side feeling his whole body aching in protest, seized by the pain of lying in an awkward position. Sunlight flooded across his face, making him blink, reviving his senses.

He sat up and wrapped the sheet around himself and tried the door of the room. Not surprised to find it locked, he tried the glass door leading out onto a balcony. It was open. He couldn't believe his luck. There was nobody around. With trepidation, he stepped out into the morning air.

He recognised the view, but that didn't make it any easier to take in. A waterway like no other, a junction where East meets West; where huge lumbering tankers compete with ferries jostling for the little free water available, where fishing boats dodge the waves to catch fish sold on the quay side. All overseen by the places of worship, startling in their scale and breath taking in their simple beauty, a skyline mapped out by domes and minarets.

Istanbul.

A city to sharpen the senses, one of the best he'd ever been in, but a second or two's enjoyment admiring the view was soon swept aside by bewilderment at how he'd come to be here.

Frustrated, he banged the door, shouting and screaming. The key sounded in the lock and Richard was ready to break free.

He needn't have bothered. As the door opened, the sight of the Glock about to shoot his balls off turned escape into a suicide mission. The face he'd seen in the Athens street was covered, but Richard knew it was Abdul. The scarf disguise shielded the Arab's whole face except for his eyes, which were protected by sunglasses.

'I hope you weren't intending to leave us in a hurry,' said Abdul. 'The Turkish police can be unkind when arresting men walking their streets with no clothes on.'

The sarcasm hit the spot. 'I need clothes,' Richard muttered. 'What are we doing in Istanbul?'

Abdul pointed to some clothes on the table. 'Get dressed and we'll talk about it.'

Richard's eyes darted around the room, looking for a way out.

Abdul noticed. 'Before you try anything, I've armed men on the other side of that door who will not hesitate to kill you if you try and escape,' he said.

'You won't kill me,' sneered Richard. 'I'm too important, otherwise why the kidnap? Kidnaps are usually for ransoms.'

'Try me,' Abdul shouted as he left the room. 'I'm not interested in money.'

Richard sank down onto the chair and sighed. The clothing wasn't his own but he put it on anyway. At least it was clean. A white linen smock shirt, sandals and baggy white trousers.

Ten minutes later, Richard sat at a table facing Abdul who had removed the scarf but retained the sunglasses. A beige folder lay on the desk between the two men. He could hear the whirring sound of the ceiling fan spinning in a fruitless attempt to relieve the heat trapped in a windowless room. Two armed henchmen guarded the exit. Even though he could not see his eyes, Richard felt the weight of Abdul's stare, his ragged, weather-beaten skin portraying a hard exterior. Thin lips disclosed gleaming white teeth, not used to smiling. Averting his eyes, Richard noticed damp patches of sweat appearing on his cotton shirt and he wondered whether it was the heat or just the thought that he was facing one of the world's most wanted terrorists who would kill him without question if it suited his needs. He could be dumped in the Bosphorus and nobody would investigate or protest. His mother's pleas would be unheeded because Richard Helford deserted the Service.

Abdul leaned forward. 'You are like your father, you know,' he said. 'I was a great friend of him until he disappeared.'

'My father hasn't disappeared, he's dead,' said Richard, determined not to show that he knew his father might be alive. 'You and your friends killed him.'

'I believe your father is alive,' said Abdul. 'And if I threaten to kill you he'll come out of hiding. Your life spared for the scroll.'

'What scroll?' said Richard, thinking about the cryptic messages in Callidora's Bible.

Abdul reached out and opened the folder. 'I need your help,' he said, taking out two sheets of badly creased paper, which Richard recognised immediately as being the letters he'd found in the Bible's spine.

'My letters,' said Richard.

'Yes,' said Abdul. 'written in Greek...I need you to translate...I believe they'll tell us more about the scroll.'

Richard took the first piece of paper from Abdul and started translating.

June 24th 1941

Dear Mr Helford, please can I call you Lenny? I feel you might be the only friend I have left in my life.

I enjoyed meeting you the other day, but as I write, our village is in mortal danger. The German soldier I told you about, Hans, has been shot dead. I was with him when it happened. My brother Nikos knows that you wanted me to get him to reveal troop movements, but I never got that far. We were in the forest behind the church when a bullet killed him, fired anonymously from the clearing. Nikos is very angry, and as I write, we are preparing ourselves for the visit from the Germans. Their leader, Captain Wolfgang Kohlenz, is a murderer, slaughtering women and children and burning down villages. I am sure that fate awaits us. Sometimes I think it would be a blessed relief to die in Tirata and end all this suffering, but the Cretan spirit prevails and we know it is our destiny to fight on until we fall dead in the dust. Some of the men have taken to the mountains, but I fear for the safety of those who are left. The village needs your help.

You remember that I told you I'd found a papyrus scroll, which I am convinced is a great lost piece of scripture. The last words from John of Patmos, author of the Book of the Apocalypse. I have hidden the document so it can't be found. Hans told me that it should never be given to the German army. They would use it for propaganda.

Please help us. I beg you.

As he read, Richard forgot about the men with the guns holding him captive and concentrated on the words. Their impact reached him in Greek before he passed on the English to Abdul.

Words spoken to his grandfather were now speaking directly to him. Just as Callidora was seeking his grandfather's help, he felt an overwhelming need to take on the mantle and respond to that plea of help. For the first time in his life Richard felt the bond of family ties.

When he finished the translation, he fumbled for words. 'You think my father…if he is alive, that is…you think he knows where this scroll is hidden.'

'Yes. He told me about it before he disappeared, but we need to encourage him to show himself. He needs to know that I will kill *you* if he doesn't.'

Richard was unmoved by the threat to his own life. 'And how do you intend to tell my father when you don't know for certain that he's even alive?'

'You're going to make a little video which we'll send to news agencies.'

Richard forced a laugh. 'I've no idea where my father is and besides, he wasn't a good father to me. He's unlikely to come forward.'

'Father's protect families. It's a God given right.'

Richard shook his head. 'Not this one,' he replied. Inside his head, Richard wanted to be proved wrong. 'Why are we in Istanbul?'

'To evade your friends in MI6, who will be looking for you.'

Richard changed the subject quickly to divert attention away from what MI6 may or may not do. 'If my father was your friend and you wanted to find a historical document, why are you on the US Kill List? My father would not consort with killers like you.'

Abdul flew into a rage, slamming his fist down hard onto the table. 'Nobody calls the Americans terrorists but is it not terrorism to drop a bomb on innocent people?

Richard tried to calm the situation. 'I'm sorry. You must be a man of integrity. That is why my father liked you...but if he was your friend, why kill his son? That seems no way to repay a friendship.'

Abdul's face hardened. Richard could see he had already shut out his emotional outburst. 'We're taking a ship to Heraklion, leaving tomorrow. A trip by plane isn't a good idea. Your friends in MI6 will be looking for you,' said Abdul.

If only that was true, Richard thought. MI6 would not be searching for him. Not now. Not ever. The video would at least alert them to the fact that he was alive.

'Now read me the second letter,' said Abdul.

Chapter Twenty-Three

Crete, Greece. June 23rd 1941

The hiding place Callidora had chosen was a good one, but she knew the casket and chalice, still buried in the wood, should never be separated from the scroll. Reuniting them would not be easy but she had to try. *But what if I don't survive the war?* Somebody needed to know where it was without letting the Germans get to it first. She stopped and took out the Bible the monks had given her when she'd lived at the monastery. At times like these, when she felt so lonely, it became her companion. Father Agathangelos had taught her to understand the beauty of the scripture and taught her to read and write. He'd even shown her a Greek translation of 'The Isles of Greece' while trying to explain what it means to be Greek. He used to say that its author, the English poet Lord Byron, understood the Greek people better than the Greeks themselves. Just like Lenny, she decided. An Englishman who loves Greece would be the ideal person to tell. He'd understand Byron's words. She couldn't remember the whole poem, but the words she wanted seem to fall on the page as she scribbled them into her Bible.

On the way to the cave, she met Yiannis, one of the runners for the resistance, and made him wait while she wrote a letter to Lenny, telling him what had happened to Hans and how she feared reprisals. Yiannis took the letter and promised to see Lenny got it. She emphasised how important it was.

She still had the Bible when she got back in the village, just in time to see the Germans arrive. It was a larger force than before. Callidora counted eight motorbikes with machine guns attached to their side cars. There was no hiding from them. Four lorry loads of soldiers jumped onto the square and began dispersing in a circle. Some trained their guns on the villagers, while the others began to move outwards into the fields. Everywhere she looked, she could see a machine gun pointing in her direction. It must have felt like that to everybody in the village. It would take just a few minutes to kill them, she thought, a short burst of gunfire and just like Kandanos, their village would be declared a *dead zone.*

Unless they fought.

But how could they do that? She was glad the scroll had been hidden. Maybe this could be a bargaining tool, she pondered.

Kohlenz leapt out of the car. Another soldier had been brought in to translate, but he was nothing like Hans in the way he spoke. His Greek was poor and laced with a heavy German accent.

'A German soldier is missing,' Kohlenz shouted, wasting no time with formalities. 'I know he's attracted to this village or at least, should I say, an individual in the village.' The soldier tried to translate, doing more hesitation than actual words. When the Greek's finally came out, Callidora's heart raced and her breathing became more frantic. She started to panic. She could see Kohlenz sweating, his uniform had no place in the searing heat, which made him more agitated. He glared at the hapless soldier, fumbling through the translation, and while waiting for him to finish, waved a bundle of papers in the air in frustration that the message was taking so long. One of the papers blew out of his hand, the wind carrying it across the square. He cursed as one of his soldiers caught and returned it to him. He wanted the crowd to know what they were. At last, the translator found the words.

'These are letters referring to a meeting with a Greek girl and the finding of an important historical document. I want to know who this girl is and where is the document he claims to have found?'

Her heart was pounding. How could Hans have been so stupid? She thought she was going to faint. The rest of the village was silent. Nikos looked in her direction.

'I know that you've killed him and that the village must pay. It's only a matter of time before we find the body. And when we do, we want to know who is responsible for his murder.'

How did he know that Hans had been killed? She couldn't understand why he knew so much. Yes, Hans was missing, but Kohlenz seemed certain of his death. As if someone had tipped him off.

Nikos spoke up. 'We don't know who killed him, but we know where his body is. I'm arranging to bury it. We just want to live in peace. We don't want any more killing.'

Without waiting for the translation, Kohlenz advanced toward Nikos and with one swipe knocked him clean off his feet. As Nikos rolled on the ground, Kohlenz kicked him repeatedly in the stomach.

Callidora could stand it no more. She rushed forward falling on the ground between Nikos and Kohlenz. 'Stop,' she screamed. 'I am the girl you speak of,' she cried. 'I met the soldier, but I swear, I don't know who killed him.'

Kohlenz stopped and turned to walk away. He looked at the translator, although for the first time there was no need to translate. He knew what she was saying without hearing her words in German.

'Take her,' he shouted. Turning towards the crowd, he continued. 'I don't care whether you know who the killer is or not. I'll give you twenty-four hours to come up with the answer. If not, I'll start executing your people. One person every hour.'

He waited for the translator to catch up and for his words to sink in. She could see the soldiers coming. They took hold of both her arms and dragged her, writhing and screaming, towards the truck. She winced when one of them kicked out to stop her struggling. It was only a token resistance, but nothing would make her go quietly, however futile it was to fight. They pulled her on the back of one of the trucks and pinned her down, tying her arms behind her back. She looked out across the square and saw Ikaros running forward, shouting protests, until he was stopped by a cordon of soldiers. Nikos had picked himself up and stood transfixed at the sight of his little sister being taken away. She didn't want him to save her, not this time. Her own stupidity had got them to this point and she would have to get out of it herself. Or die.

She was grateful that they only took her a short distance to Maleme airfield, instead of somewhere further away like Heraklion. On the way, the soldiers laughed at her, muttering lewd comments in German, which she didn't need to understand because the looks on their faces said it all. She glowered back, staring in defiance, never intending to let them know she was scared. Some of the soldiers backed off, blushing a little. Despite their bravado, they were just boys. Hans was different, still as young as they were, but the Greek in him shone through. Maybe that was why he had to die. He was Greek. She told herself that was the reason why she'd kissed him, because he was Greek. None of these boys would ever warrant such attention.

When they arrived, she noticed the men arguing and concluded that they didn't know what to do with her. After a few minutes walking round the airfield, they locked her in a hut. It was more like a storage hanger, made of corrugated iron, which had no windows. As the door was locked behind her, she became aware of the stifling heat.

Her hands were still tied, so she couldn't fan herself to keep cool. There was no air and no water. There was a mattress, but most of the building was packed to the roof with mechanical parts, which she guessed were for the allied planes that were no longer needed, as the Germans now controlled the airfield. It didn't take long before sheer exhaustion caught up with her, the consequences of a sleepless night, the stress and the unbearable heat all compounded her fatigue. She was grateful for the mattress and toppled onto it. Sleep was her only escape.

Awakened by the sound of a key turning in the lock, she blinked open her eyes and for a moment forgot where she was. Two soldiers lifted her off the bed and half dragged her to another hut. She must have been asleep for a couple of hours because she could see the sun was lower in the sky. Inside, she saw Kohlenz again, seated by a desk with the translator by his side. A framed photograph of Hitler had been hastily hung on the wall immediately behind him. He ordered the soldiers to untie her and pointed to the chair in front of his desk where she could sit.

'Nero,' she cried, choking with thirst. The soldier told Kohlenz what she wanted. He poured her a glass of water from a jug that was on his desk and placed it in front of her. Her throat was parched and as dry as sandpaper. It was a wonderful feeling gulping the water down, swilling it round her mouth before swallowing, allowing the dryness to disappear and the soft roof of her mouth to return.

'We've found the body.' Kohlenz said quietly. 'The bullet was from a Greek rifle.'

The translator continued to drive a wedge between them, reducing the immediacy of their conversation.

'That doesn't mean that he was killed by anybody from our village,' she replied.

He ignored the comment and continued, stopping only for the translator to have his say. 'We found a letter in his jacket pocket. A letter which he was in the process of writing to his mother. Shall I read it to you?'

'It doesn't matter if I want it read or not,' she snapped. 'You're going to do what you want anyway. Just as you killed many in the village of Kandanos,' she shouted, spitting out her words in a tirade of disgust.

Kohlenz' face changed in an instant. He stood up and, leaning forward, smacked her hard across the face. The force took her by surprise, knocking her off the chair. She fell awkwardly on to the floor. As she lay there, dazed by his attack, she tasted her blood trickling from her lip. He stepped away from his desk and straddled her, gripping her wrists tightly. She suppressed the urge to scream and just stared into his eyes. 'Shall I read the letter to you?' he shouted.

He stood and pulled her up and forcibly made her sit. He returned to his desk and took out a piece of paper.'

'Your insolence will not be tolerated,' he said.

He started reading.

June 15th 1941
Dear Mother,

It is with a heavy heart that I am writing to you. We've suffered heavy losses as we landed on this island, but the island is ours. Our enemy has been driven out, many evacuating from the shores, while others hide out in the mountains. It is only a matter of time before we have routed them out as well. Great swarms of our soldiers are searching. The Cretan people are ferocious savages who have inflicted heavy losses on our brave paratroopers. They are being punished for their misdeeds. Soldiers fight the wars and civilians must not get involved, otherwise they will pay.

Remember what I told you about the miraculous discovery that I have made. It is an ancient papyrus scroll which may have been written by St John of Patmos, author of the Book of Revelations. I've met a young Greek girl. She is very beautiful and not like her savage compatriots. She knows about the scroll...

The letter was unfinished, so it wasn't signed, but as the soldier translated Callidora became more horrified by the contents. It sounded nothing like Hans and she'd never seen his writing. He was anti-Nazi and yet this was full of propaganda and paid no heed to his Greek roots and his dedication to peace.

'It's a forgery. Hans wouldn't say such things,' she cried.

'Ah,' he snapped, smiling at her error. 'So you're not denying that you met Paratrooper Tuebingen.'

'What's the point, you've already made up your mind.'

'Then you know where the scroll is,' he shouted.

'I don't know what you're talking about. Hans found the scroll not me.' She stared back in defiance, determined not to be intimidated.

'Liar,' he shrieked, slapping her hard across the cheek.

This time, she was almost expecting it and managed to stay seated. Slowly, she lifted her head back to face him, her stinging cheek masked the fear she had inside. Hatred was all she could muster and that gave her strength.

'I don't know what you're talking about,' she repeated, taking her time to spit out the words, her lips quivering in anger.

He turned towards the soldier and she looked at him as well with a face disgusted that he was letting Kohlenz treat her in this appalling manner. 'Leave us, ' he said abruptly.

The soldier left, relieved, glad that he wouldn't have to witness anything more. Kohlenz turned back and, taking a chair, sat down a few inches from her. Communication was now determined by action and facial expression. Everything she needed to know was in his eyes and with the translator gone, she felt vulnerable.

He spoke calmly now and in broken Greek. 'We will destroy your village, killing the men one by one, burning your houses to the ground if I don't find the scroll and the killer of Hans Tuebingen.' It was as if he'd rehearsed the words, as he destroyed village after village throughout the mountains.

'If you do that, God will be your judge and you'll rot in hell,' she spat. He was close enough to catch her spit. It hit his chin, a long trail that dangled, suspended by his stubble, dripping down on to his uniform.

He erupted, leaping out of his chair and grabbing her by the throat. She gasped for air.

'You're choking me,' she whispered, barely able to speak.

He let go of her neck and grabbed her wrists lifting her off the chair and pinning her to the wall of the hut. His face was only an inch from hers. All she could see was evil flowing from his eyes.

'Where is the scroll?' he screamed, this time in German, but she understood, remembering his earlier question which the soldier had translated.

She could feel him hard against her. His breath was revolting which made her hate him even more. She glared back, determined to stand up to him.

'I don't know what you're talking about,' she repeated.

She didn't have time to react, his weight forced her back onto his desk. She could feel him forcing her legs apart and all she could do was close her eyes and wait for it to be over. He was between her legs, one hand pinning her down, while he unbuttoned his trousers. Then he was thrusting, tearing her apart, blood was running down her legs. She tried to fight, kicking her legs out, writhing, but it was no use. She tried to shut it out, but would remember the damp, sticky feeling of his seed mingling with her blood for the rest of her life. It wasn't supposed to happen like this. She wanted to die.

Chapter Twenty-Four

Istanbul, Turkey. July 31st 2005

June 26th 1941

Dear Lenny,
I'm going to kill myself.
No matter how hard I try, there is too much suffering and too much killing. I cannot stand it anymore. You are the only person I can speak to because you are detached from the emotions of family ties. It's hard for me to say this, the very words make me shake with rage and weep with shame.

Kohlenz raped me and I'm terrified I might be pregnant. I don't know for certain as it only happened a few days ago, but something inside tells me that I am to have his child.

There, I've said it. I've never lain down with another man before, so if I'm carrying a child, it must be his. My family would never understand. Whatever I do, I cannot bring disgrace on my family by carrying a German bastard.

If I kill myself, the child will die and that will be the end of it. Even if it turns out that I am not pregnant, it changes nothing. I could never live with the stigma of not being a virgin. Try and help my family through this. Tell them I love them and that I'm sorry.

I want you to have this Bible. It's been my inspiration. The Bible was the signal from God about what I should do with the scroll that I found. It told me to hide it from the world and that is what I've done. It was given to me by Father Agathangelos at the Monastery at Prevelli. He taught me a lot about the unity of faith and how to understand the scriptures. I lived with the monks until I was fifteen. I worked to clean their house. In return, they provided me with food and education. One day when I visited Father, he told me the story of the Seven Sleepers. He said the Bible was from the Monastery at Ephesus, which is dedicated to that story. It is the reason why I hid the scroll.

Seven Christian young men hid in a cave to escape persecution from the Romans. The entrance to the cave was closed and they fell asleep for 309 years. When they woke, they thought that they had been asleep for only a day and were not aware of time passing. Did time really pass? I often wonder how anybody could be taken by such a silly story. Father told me it's known the world over. It's a Christian story, but does not appear in the Bible. It is recorded in apocryphal books and in the Holy Koran. There are monasteries to commemorate the Seven Sleepers. Why is it so popular, I wondered? But now I think I have the answer, I want to escape from my persecutors, to go to sleep and just like them be in a timeless world which, when I awake, will be as if nothing has happened.

What interests me is that the story is both Christian and Muslim. It is the universal struggle of the people to escape persecution and war. We are one race whether we are Muslim or Christian or Jew, whether we are German or Greek or English. The cave is where the secret is to be found.

225

It is the place where time stops and is where I am going. It is where I will go to sleep.

    Take care and don't forget to tell my family I love them.

      Callidora

It was as if Abdul was no longer in the room. Richard read the letter over and over, anger bubbling and churning in his gut, building a little more every time he absorbed the power of her words. What must she have felt to be brutalised by Kohlenz, in such an extreme way, that she'd wanted to kill herself and her baby.

We are one race whether we are Muslim or Christian or Jew.

Abdul, said nothing while Richard mulled over the contents of the letter. Eventually the Arab spoke. 'I can see you are moved by this letter.'

Richard stared at Abdul and channelled the anger he felt at Abdul. 'If you were a true Muslim you would recognise that Callidora's message is a message for all religions. It is a message for peace,' he shouted. 'Why can't you see that?'

Abdul struck Richard across the face. 'How dare you suggest that I'm not moved by the letter.' He took out the piece of the wedding veil he carried with him everywhere and threw it at Richard. 'Go on pick it up…pick it up. Go on. Look at it,' he bellowed. 'That is all that is left of my daughter's wedding veil. An American missile tore her to bits. I had to pick up her severed head out of the rubble of our house,' he screamed. 'Don't talk to me about peace.'

Still reeling from the blow, Richard bent down to pick up the veil. He noticed burn marks across the silk and dried blood staining the exquisite embroidery. His face burned but he could not feel anything but sadness for its owner. How could this grieving father be turned into one

226

of the world's most wanted terrorists? He lowered his voice and said quietly, 'Hatred is not the answer.'

Abdul's expression appeared to soften but only for a second. The need for revenge drove his terrorist instincts, and who could blame him? 'There is only one way,' Abdul whispered. 'The way of Allah. The way of jihad.'

Richard stared at Abdul, trying to read his mind. The veneer of self-righteousness will breakdown, he thought. He does not believe his own rhetoric.

The moment of reconciliation had been lost. Abdul's tone had become more formal, more aggressive. He had a job to do and he wanted it done whatever the cost. 'Your father will have discovered from other sources that the Greek woman committed suicide. This vindicates our reasons for landing in Crete. Take the letters and the Bible and think what this all means. We will sail to Crete tomorrow.'

'How will that help find my father?'

'We believe your father was looking for the scroll when he disappeared. If he's alive then he will have contacts in Crete.'

Nikoletta's words flashed into Richard's mind. *I didn't tell them.* He looked back at Abdul and nodded.

'But why should I help you when you're going to kill me and my father if he isn't already dead.'

Abdul reacted angrily to Richard's response. 'I am not a savage. My anger is the result of the Americans interfering in my country just like the Soviet Union before them, killing and maiming innocent people. Your father understood. But even he betrayed me. I want the scroll and an explanation of why he disappeared and then you can go free.'

They took Richard back to his room and gave him some spiced lamb wrapped in flatbread. He hadn't realised how hungry he was until he'd finished eating. He sank back onto the bed and went through the contents of the letters in his mind. The last section of the second letter intrigued in other ways. Why would Callidora care about that story? *It is the reason why I hid the scroll.* Is it just a metaphor for her own persecution and why she'd committed suicide? Or did the scroll say something which must be left hidden at all costs?

The cave is where the secret is to be found. There were other references to a cave underlined in Callidora's Bible. He picked it up and thumbed through looking for references to caves that she'd annotated. He found one mention underlined, taken from Genesis.

Abraham buried Sarah his wife in the cave of the field of Machpelah before Mamre: the same is Hebron in the land of Canaan.

Abraham breathed his last and died in a ripe old age, an old man and satisfied with life; and he was gathered to his people. Then his sons Isaac and Ishmael buried him in the cave of Machpelah.

Isaac and Ismael. Richard remembered them from his studies at Cambridge. This was the centre of the dispute between Judaism, Christianity and Islam. Who did God ask Abraham to kill and therefore who did he spare? The Koran said it was Ismael and Mohammed was descended from Ismael. The intervention of God to save Ismael would prove that he was the true descendant from Abraham, favoured by God. Muslim scholars had argued that Isaac wasn't even born at the time God asked Abraham to make the ultimate sacrifice. Jesus, being a Jew, was descended from Isaac. Maybe that was what all this was about. The divisions in the religions were built on unsubstantiated argument when it was without dispute that the three great religions all originated from the same source. They all descended from Abraham.

What if they could all be together? It was what Masood wanted. It was what his father wanted.

A man is running towards him, blood pumping from his wounds, his face blackened by scorch marks from the bomb. His shirt torn to shreds revealing a gaping hole in his stomach. Richard stared and the man seemed to transform. His wounds were gone and his hand, which had been blown off, reached out to greet him. Richard couldn't see his face but felt at peace in his presence.

The suicide bomber.

There was something strange about him. He couldn't put a finger on it. The man turned and began to move away. Richard didn't want to let him go but no matter how fast he ran he never seemed to get any closer.

'Who are you?' Richard cried out. The face turned back but this time it was disfigured beyond any recognition.

'Wake up. Wake up. We have a film to make.'

Richard struggled to open his eyes. The barrel of an AK prodded him in the stomach.

'Wake up.'

It was one of Abdul's henchmen but Richard was too focused on the dream to care about the trigger-happy sensitivities of a jihadist. The dream meant something about his time in Iraq. Why he left in a hurry. He tried to picture the suicide bomber but there was nothing but a blackened, mortally wounded face.

Chapter Twenty-Five

Crete, Greece. June 25th 1941

They dumped her at the entrance of the village. Pushing her out of the truck, she rolled in a heap into the dust. The shock of the fall released her from the nightmare. She lay, feeling the heat of the early morning sun warming her back, but only on the outside. Her soul was frozen to the core.

She didn't want to go back. She turned over and let the sun flow onto her face. The previous night spent in the dark windowless hut, lying on a damp mattress, had plunged her deeper into despair. In the brilliant light of morning, the healing power of the sun lifted her shattered spirit, but could not relieve her misery. How could she face her brother Nikos or the rest of her family? She couldn't even face Ikaros, or Pavlos or Kostas. She remembered the village dances when they fought for her attention, competing for her hand in marriage, but would they want her now? Dirty and defiled by a German.

Old man Angelos found her. He'd been out in the fields, collecting vegetables. A man of his age may have gone for help, but not Angelos. She managed a smile to acknowledge his kindness as he lifted her onto his donkey and led her into the village. Seeing the square, and Ikaros running to meet her, made her groan with anguish at the inevitable confrontation with her family. She resigned herself to the lie. They must never know, she thought.

'Callidora's back. Tell Nikos,' Ikaros shouted. Reaching her, she saw him cringe with horror at the sight of her dirty face, bloody lips and listless eyes. 'Are you all right? Callidora. What did they do to you?' he stuttered.

She looked back, saying nothing and not smiling, but wondering what he'd have made of her blood-spattered underwear revealing the loss of her cherished virginity.

Nikos arrived by his side and immediately lifted her off the donkey and carried her towards their home. She felt safe in his arms, but devastated by her own unworthiness. In the house, they laid her on the bed and she looked at them in silence. She heard their voices, but could not discern what they were saying. Her mother took over and shooed them out of the room. She washed her from head to toe and said nothing at the sight of the blood.

Callidora knew her mother's silence spoke a thousand words.

'Nikos must never know,' she said, pleading with her mother. 'Nobody must know.'

Her mother said nothing and went about dressing and preparing her to face the world. There was a look of distrust on her face. Her little girl had been violated. Callidora could see it in her mother's eyes and knew she didn't understand, or perhaps she was in denial refusing to face up to the horror of what had happened to her daughter.

'Some things are best left unsaid,' was all her mother would say and it was all that needed to be said.

A commotion was breaking out in the square. The Germans were back. Callidora didn't want to show her face and see her abuser again. But she could hear him ranting below. She watched as he paced backwards and forwards, staring at the crowd. Was he looking for her?

She got her answer when Kohlenz looked up, pointing at the window where she stood. She heard the jackboots on the stairs and then a kick at the door. She opened the door calmly, prepared for her fate. She had no energy to resist. Two paratroopers dragged her downstairs and pulled her across the square, depositing her in front of the crowd and in clear sight of Kohlenz.

'Paratrooper Hans Tuebingen was murdered.' He paused and paced the area, allowing his words to sink in and for the translator to catch up. 'We know it was a Greek rifle, because we examined the bullet lodged in his brain. It was not fired from a German gun.' He stopped again, a dramatic pause that added to the chilling sense of fear in the air, palpable in every one of the villagers' faces. 'Assassinations of this kind will not be tolerated and will be punished by death.' He spoke loudly and the translator echoed his words in Greek. They sounded worse in German. Understanding meant nothing when the words were uttered from the mouth of Kohlenz. She could see it in his face. No translator could capture the essence of sadistic intent.

He turned to look at her, prostrate on the ground.

'This woman, who I believe you all know, befriended Hans Tuebingen. Together they discovered a valuable manuscript of immense importance. Both of them knew about it and yet she continues to deny that she knows where it is.'

There was silence. They knew what was coming.

'I gave you twenty-four hours to find the culprit. Have any of you got anything to say to me?'

There was more silence.

Kohlenz must have already chosen his target. He signalled to his men and Pavlos Stilakis was pulled from the crowd. He was about the same age as Nikos. She'd never talked to him much, but she liked his wife. She was called Thea. Callidora remembered how she would always praise her husband, say how proud she was to be his wife. Seeing the anguish on her face, she knew that nothing had changed. Screaming, clutching his arm in desperation, Thea did her best, but it was never going to be any use. They pulled Pavlos away, her hand reaching out in despair. They forced him to kneel.

Kohlenz slowly removed his Luger from its holster and for a moment paraded waving it around. He went up to Pavlos' wife and demanded to know where she lived. She was weeping, begging him on her knees, but would not say.

A voice from the crowd spoke up. 'It's this one.' It was Ikaros. Faces looked at him with accusing stares, His finger was slowly raised, pointing over to a house in the corner of the square. It stood alone. Kohlenz barked orders and three soldiers with cans of petrol advanced towards it. They emptied the fuel though the windows and in seconds, it was in flames. She saw people step back, shocked by the inferno, but Kohlenz didn't even look. He turned back to face Pavlos, raising the Luger to his head. She had to stop him, anything to stop the killing. Throwing herself at him, she tried to grab Kohlenz hand.

'Kill me,' Callidora screamed. 'Kill me.' She wanted to die, but he wanted her to suffer. Throwing her aside, he fired at Pavlos, the bullet went through his eye spraying fluid and blood across the earth. Pavlos slumped forward, dead. Screams of shock rippled through the crowd, but none were louder than the screams of the dead man's wife, Thea, who broke out in a series of hysterical sobs. She didn't go and grieve by her husband's body. Instead, she turned her anger towards Kohlenz and ran forward in a violent rage. She must have only got a few feet before he cut her down. The first bullet hit her in the arm, throwing her backwards onto the ground. Undaunted, she picked herself up and kept on running until she reached him. He was unperturbed and grabbed her by the neck, holding her in a tight arm lock. Callidora could only stare in disgust at what she was seeing. But she was not surprised. She'd seen his brutality. Her hatred reached a new level, but she could do nothing. No matter what she did, he would not kill her. Thea flailed and kicked wildly, with no concern for her safety. Callidora thought she saw him hesitate, if only for a second, before, bored with her fighting, he shot her through the heart. He let go of her body as the bullet struck home and Thea fell backwards into the dust. Blood poured out of her. A viscous pool marking the point where she fell.

Callidora sank back onto her knees and wept. She looked for Nikos in the crowd, but there was no sign of him. The death of Thea had an even more dramatic effect on the crowd. They ran forward and the soldiers fired over their heads, stopping them in their tracks.

They're not ready to die yet, she thought. But it was only a matter of time.

Another voice stepped forward. It was Kostas. He ran towards Kohlenz; soldiers held him back, but he kept shouting. 'Please don't kill anybody else,' he said. 'We'll find the killer and bring him to you.' The translator repeated the words for Kohlenz and he nodded.

Kohlenz got back into his car and the driver fired up the ignition. Without warning, Ikaros appeared out of nowhere, jumping on to the vehicle as it moved forward. He wasn't there for long. The car screeched to a stop and soldiers, following on motorbikes, pulled him to the ground. Kohlenz didn't look surprised. He got out of the car and peered down at Ikaros, prostrate on the ground, pinned down by four soldiers. 'Release him,' he said.

Ikaros stood up and approached Kohlenz. The soldiers followed, their guns trained on him. One false move and they'd shoot him dead; Callidora was sure about that, but didn't understand what Ikaros was trying to do. Kohlenz moved out of earshot to hear what Ikaros had to say. She strained her ears but could hear nothing. Out of the corner of her eye, she saw Kostas move forward; a surprised look on his face. She looked back towards the crowd. Faces of despair, eyes darting around with fear and apprehension, but most all she heard their murmurs of suspicion.

Chapter Twenty-Six

Istanbul, Turkey. July 31st 2005

He was taken back to the room where he'd talked to
Abdul. A small camera had been erected on a tripod in the
corner. The bare room would yield none of its secrets in
the video. Abdul nodded and handed Richard a piece of
paper.

'This is what you will read,' he said, pointing to the
chair positioned before the camera.

The green light came on and Richard spoke.

'My name is Richard Helford. I've been taken hostage
by Al Qaeda. I have not been ill-treated but my life will
be taken if you do not comply with their requirements.
You must broadcast this video to your viewers all around
the world. You have twelve hours to comply.'

Abdul played the tape back and was satisfied with the
result. He removed the memory card and handed it to one
of his men, shouting instructions in Arabic before turning
back to Richard.

'So we know the scroll is in the Cave of the Seven
Sleepers,' said Abdul. 'But Crete is a large island with
thousands of caves. In the first letter the Greek girl says
that she lived in the village of Tirata. We should search in
that area.'

'That's true,' said Richard.

'But.' Abdul paused and signalled to one of his
guards. 'We should be able to find the cave with the help
of this…' He gestured towards the door.

A man in a suit came into the room. His smart
appearance was spoiled by sweat dripping from his

forehead. Richard had no idea who he was, but felt there was something familiar about him, like he'd seen him on television. The man took one look at Richard, his face twisting into a mocking smile.

'So you've got him,' the man said in an accented voice. 'There was no need.'

Abdul stared at the man with disdain. 'What do you mean? No need?' he shouted.

'No need to have taken the Helford boy.'

Abdul erupted. He flew at the man and dragged him to his feet. Richard stepped backwards surprised at Abdul's anger. 'This piece of shit is Kleiner,' said Abdul. 'He's a member of the German government. He's also a money-grabbing neo-Nazi. Given the chance, I'd love to put a bullet in his head. Unfortunately, I have to deal with the fact that he might know where the scroll is.'

'I can also give you Helford,' said Kleiner, choking under Abdul's grip. 'Let go of me.'

'What do you mean? Give me Helford?'

'Let me go and I'll tell you,' spluttered Kleiner.

Abdul released his grip and pushed Kleiner away.

Richard stared at Kleiner in disbelief. 'My father?' he said.

Kleiner rubbed his neck and straightened his suit. 'Yes, your father and the scroll as well.'

Abdul was suspicious. 'I've been looking for Helford for over four years. How can I believe what you are saying? How do you know where he is?' he yelled.

'I have my sources. I can give you Helford but there is a condition.'

Abdul drew out his Glock and thrust it into Kleiner's ribs. 'Conditions,' he said, his voice terse. 'You're in no position to make conditions.'

Kleiner was losing the battle to stay in control. His voice was breaking as he struggled to breath. His hands were shaking. 'The condition is made by Helford. He wants to meet Sheikh Zabor.'

Abdul pistol-whipped the German, sending him backwards against the table.

The German groaned, picking himself up. 'Why are you doing this?'

Richard was also wondering what was bothering Abdul. He shot a glance towards him. 'I think you should let him speak.'

Abdul turned towards Richard. 'Your father would never make a deal with a Nazi,' he said.

It was true, Abdul had a point. How did his father know that Kleiner was involved with Abdul in the hunt for the scroll?

'If I give you proof, then will you believe me?' said Kleiner.

'What proof?' said Abdul.

'First, we must go to the cave and you must arrange for the Sheikh to come to Greece, at least as far as Athens.'

'Do you know where the Cave of the Seven Sleepers is?' asked Richard.

'The Greek woman lived in Tirata,' replied Kleiner, relieved that the conversation had changed tack. 'It is a village in the hills above Chania in the west of Crete on its north coast. If she hid the scroll, then it is likely to be within a five-mile radius of that area. Kohlenz the German captain searched the area but found nothing. Presumably they must have looked in every cave. Maybe they were at the right cave but didn't look hard enough.'

'Or maybe they were in the right place, but there was no cave,' said Richard.

'Exactly,' said Kleiner.

'Yes. But the question is, where do we find the right place?'

'Suppose the cave has been subject to a landfall. When they searched, without knowing about the exact location

238

of the Cave of the Seven Sleepers, they'd find nothing,' said Richard.

'Because the entrance was blocked,' said Kleiner. 'I think you're right.'

Abdul sat silently at the table, playing with his Glock. Richard could see he was in deep thought and neither he nor Kleiner wanted to disturb him.

After several minutes, Abdul spoke. 'You haven't answered my question – why would Helford contact you?'

'Helford was trying to find out if Kohlenz was still alive. He came to me in 2000 because I am related to Kohlenz who was my great uncle. Helford wanted to find out whether Kohlenz said anything about the killing of his grandfather, Lenny Helford.'

'And did it prove anything?' said Abdul.

'Nothing at all. I don't know what happened to Kohlenz but the chances are that he is dead by now. After all he will be ninety years old.'

'Go on,' said Abdul in a terse voice.

'I had a phone call from Helford last month. He said he'd seen my face on television at a trade deal that the German government had signed with the Saudis. Sheikh Zabor attended the press conference. One of his companies had a contract to build an office block in Berlin.'

'Why, in the name of Allah, would Helford think that you'd be able to reach the Sheikh?'

'That's just it,' said Kleiner. 'He wanted to keep the contact low key so it would not arouse any suspicions. I'm a junior German defence minister. Nobody notices what I get up to, but my position will open doors. With the association with Germany, after this deal, Sheikh Zabor was bound to take my calls.'

'And there is your association with Kohlenz?' said Richard.

'Yes. But that's not all. There is something else you should see.' Kleiner put his hand into the inside pocket of his suit. Abdul reacted with lightning speed grabbing Kleiner's arm before he could touch his jacket pocket. 'It's not a gun,' Kleiner screamed. 'It's a notebook…Helford's notebook.'

Back in the room where he'd woken up, Richard weighed up his options. If his father was alive, he wanted to see him, but not if it meant risking his own life. Abdul had let him see his father's notebook and Callidora's Bible. The notebook certainly seemed to be in his father's writing, similar to the letters he'd written to his mother. It was a dog-eared with leather binding, his father's initials embossed in gold on the cover. It was small enough to slip into a pocket.

Richard turned the page once more and saw something he'd seen before. This confirmed that the book belonged to his father.

HT 674675 – the number scrawled on the inside of an envelope enclosing his father's letters. What was it? It must be something important. They occupied a whole page of the notebook and had been enhanced with doodles and patterns in biro, as if his father had spent a long time looking at it, trying to find an answer, bored while waiting on the phone, or sitting in a café supping endless cups of coffee, waiting for someone who never came.

Reading on, he could see his father was writing with increased levels of excitement. The nib of his Mont Blanc fountain pen was digging into the paper. There were ink blots and the letters in words became less defined, even illegible, and the spelling more erratic. He was in a hurry. The arguments about Ismael and Isaac were there, echoing Richard's own thoughts as he'd studied Callidora's annotations in the Bible. His father's notes became more and more unstructured, a brain dump – like he didn't have much time.

A quote caught his eye. He read it out loud. 'Recognise what is right in front of you, and that which is hidden from you will be revealed to you. Nothing hidden will fail to be displayed.' In the margin his father had written:

'A quote from the Gospel of St Thomas. This is strange; nobody had found this Gospel until it was discovered in 1945 at Nag Hammadi. Could this be another copy of the same document discovered with the St John of Patmos scroll?? St John was the Bishop of Ephesus before he came to write the Book of Revelations. While he was there he had several encounters with Barnabas. I think the scroll supports the view of Barnabas.'

Richard remembered that the icon that Masood had given him contained a picture of Barnabas. Amira had said that Barnabas had written a Gospel with a different view of Jesus.

Richard's mind was racing with possibilities. He remembered that Callidora had underlined a number of references to Ismael. He found one in Genesis, Chapter 16, which tells the story of Ismael's birth. She had marked verse twelve, which refers to Ismael as being a wild man, his hand against every man and every man's hand against him. In the margin Callidora had written two words in Greek: *No More.* Could that mean that there would be no more conflict between Christians and Muslims?

He went over everything in his mind and identified a problem. My father never saw the scroll, he thought. How could he possibly know all this? He needed access to someone with knowledge of it, who'd seen it. But who is there? Callidora committed suicide and Hans was murdered in 1941. They are the only people who'd seen the scroll and they're dead.

The notebook was an inspiration, but Richard still felt indifferent to the news that his father was alive. He'd shed no tears when the news of his death came through in 2001, so why should he feel differently now? The notebook proved nothing – it was written before 9/11.

The problem was that he could not figure the extent to which Abdul felt betrayed by his father. Would Abdul kill them both?

Chapter Twenty-Seven

Crete, Greece. June 25th 1941

As soon as the Germans had gone, the men rushed forward to put out the fire. A cordon was formed and everybody joined in, even some of the older children. Water was drawn from the well and used to douse the flames. Nobody wanted to deal with the bodies. Putting out the fire was easier. Somebody else would deal with the dead. It was always somebody else. They were never going to save the house, but at least they could stop the fire spreading and hide their fear that it could have been them, shot down in cold blood. Callidora was in no mood to hide from the truth. She stood up and walked over to the corpses of Pavlos and Thea. They were barely ten feet apart, but it seemed a great distance. Thea's hand had splayed outwards as she fell and was reaching towards Pavlos' body. Callidora knelt down and prayed for them as Father Manousos anointed their heads with a blessing. Ikaros appeared by her side.

'We've got to stop them,' he said.

'Of course we do,' said Callidora. She was weary listening to the idle threats and promises. The sarcasm in her voice was plain to hear, but was probably lost on Ikaros. She turned to face him.

'Why did you tell them which was the right house?'

He gave her a shifty, embarrassed stare. 'Because, I know how they are. They're bastards who don't care who they kill. It'd be no use resisting, so I tried to cooperate,' he said. 'That's why I spoke to Kohlenz as he left. I want him to believe that I can help him.'

Callidora looked at him to see if he was telling the truth. She wasn't sure. Maybe she'd lost her faith in men. 'But the people don't trust you. They think you're collaborating.'

Ikaros hesitated and looked uncertain. 'I promised Kohlenz that I'd bring him the scroll, if he stopped the killing. I said I'd persuade you to hand it over.'

'No,' she shouted.

Ikaros looked shocked by the bluntness of her reply. 'Why is it so important, if we can save lives?'

'No. He'll use it for his own ends. He won't stop the killing. It'll do no good.'

'But it's only a few bits of paper. We have nothing left to bargain with.'

'No. They must never know where it is. Even if they kill us all.'

Ikaros was angry. 'If Nikos was here, he'd make you hand it over. Just wait until he gets back.' There were still a few people of the village milling around. She heard a voice in the crowd.

'Collaborator,' it said.

Ignoring the comment, she continued to pray by the bodies of Pavlos and Thea, pretending to be unaffected by the crowd's accusation. Inwardly, her emptiness and alienation was complete because in her heart she knew they were right. The words of Ikaros also made her sick with worry. Was she right to resist handing over the scroll? Would it save some lives? Hans had said it was important and needed careful consideration. Kohlenz would just use it for profit. Should she hand it over for Thea's sake, so she didn't die in vain? She stood in silence as Father prayed.

After a few minutes, she couldn't look down at their mutilated bodies any longer. She spoke. 'Where's Nikos?' Did she really want to know where he was? she asked herself with conflicting emotions. She felt a mixture of betrayal, because he'd gone, and relief that he would never know what had happened to her.

'He's gone into the hills to find the resistance,' said Ikaros. 'So we can hit back.'

'We can't do this,' she shouted at him. 'Don't you see? They'll destroy us and burn the village to the ground, just like they did at Kandanos.' Ikaros looked bemused by her outburst, unable to say the right words.

'We've got to find out who killed the German,' said Ikaros, clumsily trying to change the subject.

His timing was perfect. There was a noise from the other side of the square. Swinging round, Callidora saw Kostas storming towards them followed by a small group of some of the angrier men in the village. She could see in their faces a desire to make somebody pay for what had happened. Kostas was holding a rifle.

'Ikaros, I want a word with you,' he shouted before they reached him.

'I'm listening,' said Ikaros, looking anxious.

'Do you recognise this rifle?'

'No. I don't,' Ikaros replied without hesitation.

'We found it in your shed. It's been fired recently.'

Kostas stepped forward to within a few inches of Ikaros, pushing him, poking his chest, anything to provoke him.

'Did you kill the German?' asked Kostas, adding fuel to the flame of suspicion, sweeping across the square.

'No. I would've been an idiot to do such a thing. Of course I didn't kill the German,' Ikaros snapped.

'I think you did, because you were jealous of Callidora meeting the soldier.'

More people had come out of their houses to see what the noise was about. Callidora could see Kostas beginning to play to the crowd, milking their support. 'We need to give the Germans the guilty person. If we don't, they'll kill us all. We don't want that. Do we?'

245

His rhetoric began to fuel the argument. People were shouting their agreement.

Callidora listened in silence with increasing incredulity that they could even think that Ikaros could be capable of such a thing. She could not let it rest. 'Ikaros did not kill the German.' She wanted to say Hans, but the hatred she had for Kohlenz would not allow it. Hans had become the enemy. 'It's too ridiculous for words,' she shouted back, moving closer to Ikaros in a gesture of support.

'I'm not interested in what a whore thinks,' said Kostas, sneering at Callidora.

There was no Nikos to support her. She flew at Kostas, unable to suppress her rage at the insult. 'How dare you call me a whore after everything my family has done for you.'

Kostas stared, a look of contempt on his face. 'I used to admire you,' he said. 'I dreamt that one day you'd be my wife, but I was jealous of Ikaros because you smiled more at him than me.' He pointed an accusing finger in Ikaros direction. 'It's obvious. Ikaros killed him out of jealousy...Now I see what you are, Callidora.'

'That's not true,' Callidora wept.

'You're a collaborator and so is Ikaros.'

Ikaros ran towards Kostas, swinging his arm, but Nikoletta stepped between the two men. 'I don't often agree with Callidora, but today I do. Ikaros did not do this.' She yelled, moving closer to Kostas; looking him in the eye. A large woman, not to be messed with, and Kostas knew that only too well. 'Are you going to call me a whore, Kostas, just because I support Ikaros?'

Kostas backed off, stuttering in reply. 'N...Nik..oletta,' he stammered. 'Of course not.'

'So why do you insult me?' Callidora wailed. 'My brother is not here and if he was, he would've killed you for saying such a thing.'

246

Despite his nervousness with Nikoletta, Kostas showed no sign of going easy on her. 'You confided with the enemy. You're a collaborator,' he shouted, preferring to look at the gathering crowd, rather than face her directly. 'You have questions to answer. Why will you not give them the scroll you found? Why would they take you away and then release you after spending a whole night in captivity? Tell us what happened, Callidora.'

She could feel the crowd going against her. Their hostility was burning into her soul. These were the people she'd grown up with, her village, and now Kostas' words were cutting her to shreds. Her dignity was in tatters. There was nothing more she could say. Maybe she was a whore. What would they say if she became pregnant with Kohlenz's child? *They'll never listen to me. I have to get out of this village.* She looked towards Ikaros who had remained silent. Why, when he himself was accused, did he not defend her? Perhaps he was guilty of killing Hans, the thought kept on coming back to her. She stood up and walked, stopping only to look at Nikoletta who had defended Ikaros. She was not smiling and had said nothing to support her. She hates me as well, Callidora thought. It was Ikaros she wanted. It had nothing to do with a friendship that might exist between them.

As she walked, the crowd parted to let her through. Nobody smiled. Kosmas broke through the crowd and ran towards her. Seeing him, she bent down and took hold of his hand.

'At least you love me, Kosmas, even if nobody else does.' She looked towards her house, hoping that her mother would come and embrace her, but she remained standing on the step. She could see tears running down her mother's cheeks, but even her own mother said nothing. The reputation of the family was sacrosanct and she had broken it. That was unforgivable. She gave Kosmas a hug and continued to walk out of the village. Kosmas chased, trying to stop her.

'It's what I must do, Kosmas,' she said again to him, when he'd caught up with her once more.

The little boy stood watching as she continued walking. In front of her, she could see her beloved mountains. It was where she would find peace.

Chapter Twenty-Eight

Istanbul, Turkey. August 1st 2005

There would be only one chance to make a run for it.

Richard lay awake all night, going over his plan in his head, wondering whether it could work, questioning whether it was the right move to escape now before he'd seen whether his father was alive or not. Perhaps it was a stupid thing to do, but Abdul was going to kill him anyway. It was only a matter of time. They were leaving before dawn so the streets would be quiet. Abdul wouldn't fire his gun and attract attention. Richard might just be lucky and get away.

The news agencies had circulated his video message so at least Brian and Rowena would know he was alive. The British Ambassador in Athens had also made a statement saying it was a random attack on an individual who had just arrived in Greece on vacation. He reminded the world that the United Kingdom's government never negotiated with terrorists. If he fucked up, they'd leave him to his fate. That much was clear and if his body washed up on a Mediterranean beach, who would care except his mother and, he hoped, Becky? He saw an image of Becky, hands drawn together across her tummy, hiding the smallest of bumps. He could see her tears through the veil. His subconscious mind wanted to believe that Becky loved him.

If Kleiner was right, then his father would come forward without the need to use Richard as bait. He decided he would head for the consulate a short distance away in Beyoglu, but then how would he get in?

Richard pondered all the possibilities and decided he had nothing to lose.

Except his life.

It was just past four in the morning when a silver Mercedes arrived. A hint of dawn twilight spread across the sky. Kleiner went first, crossing the cobbled street towards the car and taking his seat in the front with the driver. A guard followed, making no attempt to conceal his gun, stopping to point it back in Richard's direction.

Abdul prodded him. 'Go,' he whispered.

Richard could hear his heart thumping in his chest. If he grabbed Abdul's gun, he'd have to take out the guard from twenty feet; a high probability he'd miss. Correction. He was certain to miss.

It was suicide. The guard would fire. He wouldn't give a shit if he woke the neighbours.

They reached the ship in less than five minutes. A strong stench of fish filled the air. It looked like a reefer, used to ship food in a giant refrigerator. But it was not too big, nothing like the size of a container ship. The last cargo was being loaded. A whole pallet of fish, confirming Richard's suspicions. They boarded without fuss; Abdul handing over a suitcase, which Richard assumed was full of notes. No passports needed. They had to climb steep steps to get on deck. It was a conventional vessel with huge steel hatches where the crates of fish were being lowered by the ship's own crane. At one end was a bridge tower. Nothing spectacular.

Abdul continued to hold the gun, gesticulating that they should walk towards the ship's prow, taking them further away from the bridge tower. Kleiner was led down below by the guard so there was just him and Abdul walking across the deck. A horn sounded, followed by a deep vibration and a sense of movement in the bowels of the ship as its engines surged into life. The propellers began to plough up the surf and he heard chains rattling on pulleys as the anchor lifted.

He had to go now.

His eyes darted towards the rail; the side facing the open water. A whirring sound of hydraulics as the hatches began to close added to the cacophony of the ship's engines. A noise that distracted Abdul. For a moment he looked to his left, away from Richard. Now was his chance.

He vaulted the rail and stood on the edge, preparing to jump. Abdul reacted, levelling his gun and firing, the noise of the ship drowning the sound of the gunshot. Fear welded Richard to the spot. He was unable to jump. He watched flame rising from the muzzle of the gun, waiting for the bullet to hit home.

But the bullet did not come.

He jumped, hearing the bullet pinging on metal as it ricocheted off the deck. His fear had gone. He called out Becky's name as he fell, as if she was by his side, plummeting into the murky depths of the sea below.

There was no going back.

Chapter Twenty-Nine

Crete, Greece. June 26th 1941

Lenny was uneasy. Attacking the Germans would lead to reprisals against innocent villagers, but Nikos was having none of it.

'If we have to die, we'll take some of them with us,' Nikos said.

They were about four miles from Tirata waiting for something to happen. The twenty-four-hour deadline which marked when another family member would be executed had passed. All they could do was sit and wait. Ammunition was short and their firepower no match for the might of the German army, with their handheld MP40 Schmeisser machine guns. What they did have was an element of surprise and Lenny intended to use that to maximum advantage. First, he'd chosen the point for the ambush with great care. It was where the road went through a narrow ravine, which had plenty of large rocks for cover, and a wood about one hundred feet above the road. The important thing was to cause the damage in the space of a few minutes and then run like hell back up the mountain and disappear into the woods above before the Germans could regroup.

He'd rigged up a crude explosive device, which when detonated would cause the initial confusion. If they could just hit one of the trucks, Lenny hoped it would force Jerry to retreat. That's what he'd told the motley crew of fighters, about fifteen in total, that he'd managed to assemble. There was never any shortage of volunteers and these men were ferocious killers when their freedom had been compromised. They only had three sten guns between them, which they'd recovered from a parachute drop from Cairo. Each machine gun had three spare magazines. If they didn't make every bullet count, they would soon be defeated. Two of the men had Schmeiser guns stolen from dead paratroopers, but limited ammunition. The remainder of the men were poorly armed with knives used to cut down crops and an assortment of ancient rifles and pistols, which were so old he wouldn't have been surprised if they were last fired in anger during the Turkish War of Independence.

'These weapons will be useless against the Germans,' Lenny said to Nikos. 'They're no longer defenceless parachutists falling from the sky. It won't be a chicken shoot, you know. Killing them won't be easy.'

'The weapon is not the gun. It is the Cretan man,' Nikos replied sternly, the tension in his face betraying heroic words. 'A Cretan man alone is more formidable than a mere gun.' Nikos turned and walked away closing down the conversation. Lenny couldn't deny the sentiment no matter how foolhardy, but he'd lost the argument. They were going to attack and there was nothing he could do to stop it. He just had to make sure they were prepared and do his best to minimise the huge risk they were taking. He positioned the men with rifles so they were ready to shoot when the trucks came to a halt. If the soldiers were able to get off the trucks, the chances of hitting a moving target was virtually nil. It was bound to end in chaos.

They'd been waiting for nearly three hours when the signal came. One of his runners was positioned up the mountain and could see for miles. When the boy had sighted them, Lenny knew they'd have about three minutes to prepare themselves. There were always moments of doubt – realising that you might only have three minutes to live, but relieved that the show is finally on. He waved to the men before they hid themselves behind the rocks. Nikos looked engaged and angry, something you needed if you're going to kill people. Lenny felt his throat go dry with anticipation, his heart

253

pumping the adrenalin into his veins. He stroked the trigger to reassure himself he was ready. The guns were old and liable to jam or, conversely, fire unexpectedly, without an effective safety catch. He prayed that wouldn't happen today, but held the gun away from himself, just to be sure – his instinct for self-preservation still intact – while his other hand rested on the detonator.

The convoy took just over two minutes to reach them. Timing was all. The gap between setting the bomb off too early and too late would be seconds. Get it wrong and they'd do no damage at all. Allow for the split second between detonation and the explosion, he told himself. All these things rushed through his mind as the moment got closer. These Germans drove quickly.

Too quickly.

The truck had already passed the bomb when it went off, hitting two of the motorcyclists with their machine gun sidecars. One of the bikes took the full force of the blast, lifting it into the air blowing the bike and sidecar into two bits of twisted metal and throwing the bikers into the gorge below, ripping their limbs apart and killing them in an instant. The other bike, just lost control and plunged at speed into one of the rocks. That wasn't all that went wrong.

There was no sign of Kohlenz.

The best thing to do would be to retreat, but Lenny knew he was wasting his time telling the Cretans what to do. There must have been thirty Germans in the convoy and his gang of fighters wanted blood. He had to stop the soldiers getting off the truck.

It was a bit like firing at rabbits in a fairground as one by one soldiers tried to get out and, with a short burst, he cut them down. Nikos was on the other side training his gun on the surviving motorcyclists, cheering as one of the bikes lost control and span into the ravine. The problem was there were two trucks. Several of the Cretans were in amongst them. He saw Stavros stab one soldier and grab his machine gun. With complete disregard for his safety, he ran at the truck spraying bullets, one hit the petrol tank and the truck exploded. The blast threw Stavros off his feet. He was a dead man unless Lenny could do something.

It was at that moment that he broke cover, loading another magazine into his machine gun. He fixed on the convoy, firing sparingly. There was no time for fear and there was no going back. Stavros was on the floor, still alive. He could see bodies everywhere, but some of the Germans had managed to take cover and were returning fire. Nikos had followed, his gun blazing more indiscriminately but finding its targets. Lenny reached Stavros and started to pull him away. Everything seemed to be in slow motion, trails of gunfire igniting fountains of dust and grit, the smell of cordite. A hail of bullets caught two of his men as they ran towards the soldiers who were pinned down. Somehow the Cretans kept going, refusing to be felled by the machine gun. They were human shields taking the bullets that were meant for him, saving his life but ending their own. They kept going and dived onto the German soldiers and, with their last breath, slit the throats of their invaders. It was time to retreat. Stavros had a wounded arm, but somehow managed to walk. Lenny held his ground but felt exposed. Rolling over, he managed to get behind the burning truck as fire continued to rain in his direction. I'm drawing fire, he thought. That'll let them get out. He killed two soldiers who were trying to give chase.

'Get the fuck out of here,' he shouted to his men. Some of them heeded his order but others pressed on.

'Time for me to go,' he yelled, not because anybody could hear him, but to psyche himself into action. His last magazine was spent. He was aware of the bullets flying in his direction, but all he could do was run and hope for the best. He ran, shouting, 'Please God,' as he zigzagged up the mountain. He reached a rock just in time as a bullet ricocheted, splintering the stone. There was a momentary pause in the firing. He could see Nikos about fifty feet above him.

Time to run again.

The first bullet hit him in the side, just above the hip. He didn't feel any pain, it must have passed straight through. The pain would come later, but his body, only interested in survival, suspended the onset of reality, just like the men who kept running, defying death for one short moment. He stumbled when the second bullet caught his right arm. He had to keep going. Thank God it's not my legs. That thought spurred him on. He found new strength and ran up into the woods. Nikos helped him and they ran until he could run no further. The pain in his side was a stitch of exhaustion, rather than the pain of a gunshot wound. Out of breath, he collapsed into the undergrowth. Nikos tore his shirt and applied a tourniquet to stop the bleeding.

'The bullet in my side is just a scratch,' he panted. His lungs felt like they were going to burst and he could feel his heart pumping harder and harder to make good the loss of blood. 'I've got to slow down,' he gasped. 'Leave me here,' he said. 'Save yourself.'

'I'm not leaving you,' said Nikos. 'I think the Germans have given up. They've lost too many men. But they'll be back. They'll want their revenge. That's for sure.'

They waited and Nikos tried to stem the bleeding in his side. After about thirty minutes, they continued, slowly clambering up the mountain. Nikos knew the mountains well and used the position of the sun to guide their direction of travel. After about an hour, they found the cave.

They'd lost five men and, apart from himself and Stavros, there were three other walking wounded. He was the worst as he was the only one alive who'd actually taken a bullet. Stavros had a severe gash in his leg from shrapnel after the truck's petrol tank exploded.

'We're going to have to get that bullet out of your arm,' said Nikos.

He had no choice but to lose his bullet the hard way, with some spirit and hot tongs burned in the fire. He had to drink himself senseless with raki. It was like firewater, but it dulled the pain and gradually reduced it. Of course, that would come back when they cut his arm to remove the bullet. He consumed half the bottle and waited for the alcohol to take effect. When it had touched its spot, Nikos set to work. Lenny bit on a cloth to stop him grinding his teeth into dust while the other men held him down.

It was nearly nightfall. He'd lain there all day, sometimes falling asleep out of exhaustion, until the pain became too much for his brain to allow sleep of any sort. He looked upwards to the cave roof, watching trickles of water still finding their way out of the rock. He thought of Callidora, still regretting what he'd said to her. Nikos was a good man and had quickly forgiven Lenny for not letting him know what Callidora was up to. 'She's a spirit that's hard to fathom,' Nikos said to him before they'd attacked the Germans. Lenny worried for her life and for all the villagers' lives. The attack had been a partial success because they'd killed a few Germans, but he knew the dead would be easily replaced. Despair fought its way into his consciousness. He could never be as defiant as the Cretans. His head was thumping from the pain of the hangover, which seemed worse than the pain in his arm. Blood was still seeping from the wound onto the bandage, but at least it seemed that the flow had been stemmed and nature would work its magic and his arm would heal.

After what seemed liked hours, Nikos came over to him. 'We have to get to the village and warn them what's going to happen,' he said. 'The runners are telling me that the Germans sent over a hundred troops to clean up the mess and retrieve the bodies of the dead. They took away our dead people as well.'

Lenny looked at Nikos, grimacing with the pain. Kohlenz, he decided, would be in no mood to procrastinate now they'd killed at least twelve of his men.

'Tomorrow, they'll hit us by force,' said Nikos.

'Why did we attack them? If we knew how they'd react?' Lenny said, indignant that more lives would be lost.

'The only way to be free is to be a thorn in their side, to show they cannot break our spirit whatever they do. It is the only way the Germans will listen,' said Nikos.

'They won't listen,' sighed Lenny.

'But we will die proud,' said Nikos.

'Proud and foolish,' said Lenny. 'When do we leave?'

'We've got to go now,' Nikos said. 'We'll take you down the mountain and hide you in another cave. You can't stay in the village, but Nikoletta will look after you.'

Chapter Thirty

Istanbul, Turkey. August 1st 2005

He almost lost consciousness as he hit the water. There was no time to prepare for the impact, keeping his arms crossed to his chest, legs tightly together and straight. None of that. Oblivious to the danger, he let the water rush over and consume him into its litter-strewn oily blackness, made worse by the churning wash of the ship as it left the quay. Swirling currents sucked him down even deeper. Instinct was all he had left and mercifully that hadn't deserted him.

He started to fight. Arms thrashed the water and his legs kicked, desperate to halt his descent. Saltwater choked his mouth, making him gag. His lungs burst in a frantic effort to avoid death. He was kicking harder now, reaching with his arms for the surface. Faint flickers of the harbour lights twinkled above him, willing him to break through, willing him to stay alive.

At last he gulped in the air, coughing and spluttering, bobbing on the surface as the sea current thrust him to the quayside. The ship was already moving away and nobody was looking. His arms were aching as he fought to stay afloat. For several more minutes he edged along the quay, fighting the currents sloshing him onto the wall, trying not to swallow any more water, avoiding small slicks of oil, left festering from leaking shipping. A ladder was all he needed. Seeing one made his spirits lift, but against his exhaustion, it was almost no contest. Grabbing the bottom rung, he tried to pull himself nearer, but the current ripped him away, forcing him to let go. A second try and this time he hung on, letting the sea bash relentlessly against the metal rungs of the ladder. He began to climb.

Exhaustion took hold. The final steps up the ladder and onto the quay were difficult to negotiate while his legs shook like jelly. Reaching the top, he collapsed onto the pavement and tried to calm down, taking deep gulps of air. Traffic was beginning to build and people ignored him, despite his wet clothes. He'd lost his passport and had no money, so relying on a taxi to take him to the British Consulate was out of the question. Picking himself back up onto his feet, he crossed the road and tried to get his bearings. He realised he had no idea where the consulate was and when he tried to ask somebody, they shook their heads and hurried away. They think I'm mad, he decided. He started climbing the steep hill that rose away from the port, following the narrow streets. As he got higher, he caught a glimpse of Santa Sophia across the water. The streets became more familiar. He'd been here before, with Becky, last year on a romantic break. It was just after he'd returned from Iraq. Becky booked a long weekend as a surprise but as they walked the sights, he knew it was too soon. Becky had to stop him staring at every Muslim he saw, convinced that they were all wearing suicide vests. Maybe Rowena was right about him being traumatised. For the next three days they hadn't left the hotel. A big hotel – very British – like the Grande Bretagne in Athens. The name escaped him but he kept walking from memory. It was only when he stood in front of the hotel that he remembered the name of the Pera Palace. The consulate would be near and he could ask the hotel for directions.

The doorman blocked his path but Richard was too quick, bursting into the hotel lobby and rushing towards the receptionists.

'I'm the missing Englishman kidnapped in Athens,' he shouted. 'It was on the news.'

Extra security arrived and grabbed him by both arms, preparing to throw him back onto the street. It was the concierge who recognised him. He shouted instructions in Turkish and then came over to Richard. He spoke in English, apologising for his situation. 'The British Consulate will deal with this. I'll call them and they'll confirm your identity,' he said.

At last, they found him a room. He stripped off his wet clothes and got under the shower, enjoying washing off the salt water and taking full advantage of the hotel's herbal soaps and shampoo. He put on the dressing gown and called room service to launder his clothes. After the maid had gone, he collapsed onto the bed feeling his eyes getting heavy and knowing that Abdul was on his way to Crete.

It would be easy now to track the boat and pick Abdul up.

But only if he told Brian.

He had to let Abdul run unhindered until he found Richard's father and the scroll. Richard continued to fight off sleep and forced himself to piece together all the strands of what he knew now. One thing came to mind. He remembered he hadn't spoken to Uma Kastner. Nikoletta had told him she would know something, but was she still alive? The letter was dated 1950 so she'd be at least eighty years old by now. There was no way she'd still be working for the University of Heidelberg. He'd left the letter and photograph in his hotel room, which Brian would have recovered. It was a long shot but maybe the university would know where she lived.

Even though he'd memorised the number Brian had given him, he wondered whether the number was wrong, breathing a sigh of relief when Brian finally answered.

Brian sounded pleased to hear his voice, disguising the fact with his annoying words of reprimand for getting caught so quickly.

'You wanted me to be bait,' said Richard. 'And that's what you got. It only took them an hour to find me.'

'So where's Abdul now?'

'He's on a boat sailing towards Crete. It's a small cargo vessel carrying fish and your favourite terrorist. It's called the *Istanbul Star*.'

'We can track the boat on satellite and pick him up when he lands.'

'No,' said Richard, firmly. 'We must let this run its course.'

'Bagging Abdul is pretty big,' said Brian.

'But what about everything else? What about the scroll and the fact that my father might still be alive?'

For a moment, Brian didn't respond. Fighting his instinct not to leave a rookie like me to get on with it – thought Richard.

At last, Brian spoke. 'Okay, Richard. I'll agree to hold off but we mustn't let Abdul slip through the net. How long before they reach Crete?'

'I don't know,' said Richard. 'I'd guess it'll take three days at least – while we wait I need you to do something for me.

'What?' Brian asked abruptly. He sounded annoyed.

'I'm sorry, Brian, for being such a pain but I need a new passport, money and credit cards, oh…and a new phone. I've lost everything.'

'What the fuck have you been doing?' Brian shouted.

'Best you don't know. Remember I'm off the radar…But I do want you to do some digging for me.'

'Okay, I'm listening,' said Brian. 'This better be good. I have my own job to do, you know.'

'That photograph you found with my things and the letter from a Professor Uma Kastner from the University of Heidleberg. She'll be in her eighties. I need you to find her. We need to find out what she knows.'

'Why?'

Richard was getting impatient but breathed deeply, realising that he needed to tread carefully with Brian and not play the cocky little upstart. 'Nikoletta said she'd know something. I found the letter and photograph in her apartment.'

Brian grumbled about the request but agreed to do what Richard asked.

Richard hung up and thought about Becky and his mother. They would have seen his face on the news; they'd be worried. Fortunately, he could remember their numbers. He punched out Becky's number, looking at his watch, which mercifully had continued to tell the right time

'Becky, it's me,' he said.

Becky shrieked when she heard his voice. 'Richard, thank God,' she said, her voice breaking with joy. 'Oh my God you're safe. When I saw that video I was terrified someone might hurt you…your mother was on the phone to me, really frantic.'

'I'm okay. I've been freed. I just wanted you and Mother to know that and to say I'm thinking about you…Thinking about our child growing in your tummy.'

Becky let out a nervous laugh. 'That's nice to know, but where are you?' Her voice was softer now.

'I'm afraid I can't tell you, but we'll work this out, Becky. I promise…Just tell Mother I'm okay.'

'I will,' Becky replied 'And Richard…'

'What?'

'I love you…Look after yourself. When are you coming home?'

'I'm sorry, I don't know,' he replied. 'I love you too.'

He could feel her tears because his own eyes began to weep.

The silence on the other end of the line said all that needed to be said. The fog in his brain was lifting. Only his father had the answers. Everything that had happened would mean nothing if he had no one to love or to love him. His life would be worthless. There would be no reason to stay alive.

After putting the phone down, Richard sat without moving for several minutes, jumping out of a trance when the hotel reception rang to say that his bill had been settled by Mr Simpson. He had no idea who Mr Simpson might be but he was certain Brian would be behind the call. His new passport wouldn't arrive until tomorrow so he'd have to stay in Istanbul for another day. The hotel offered him a security guard outside his room but he declined. Intel like that would travel fast in this city and reach one of the many Al Qaeda sleeper cells, who will have received instructions to kill him. He need to keep a low profile if he wanted to stay alive.

Richard must have fallen asleep, because when he looked at his watch, it was nearly midday.

'Shit,' he said to himself, feeling his body ache with the buffeting he'd received from the waves bashing him onto the quay as he tried to reach the ladders and safety. Pangs of hunger made him want to eat, even though it was the last thing he cared about. After ordering a burger and fries from room service, he flopped back onto the bed and tried to work out what to do next. One thing was certain; he needed to get to Crete before Abdul arrived and took the scroll. He began to worry whether he'd done the right thing by escaping, putting his father in more danger. Impatience began to drive his mind. He paced the room, frustrated that he'd have to wait for his passport to arrive.

He looked out of the window, but could only see the car park. There was no view of the Golden Horn. He studied the black and white pictures of famous people that adorned the walls of his bedroom. Agatha Christie, Ernest Hemmingway and Greta Garbo had been to the hotel in its heyday, but it was trapped in time when Istanbul had moved on. When room service arrived, he was glad of the chance to do something to take his mind off the waiting. The burger was rubbery, but it was food. He chewed the meat slowly, looking at his watch for the umpteenth time. The famous espionage quote invaded his brain.

Spying is waiting.

Chapter Thirty-One

Crete, Greece. June 27th 1941

Since leaving the village, Callidora wanted to be with her goats but knew that would be the first place they looked. The mountains embraced her like a guardian angel, providing the solitude she needed and the place of safety to think. She lived on herbs and wild fruit, drinking water from the many streams that flowed from the melted mountain snow. In a couple of months, it would have been harder to find somewhere to drink, but now there was plenty. She used her skills at snaring wild rabbits to good effect, roasting the result on a fire she lit at dusk. When the sun was at its highest, she sheltered in rock crevasses, spending time with her Bible, looking for answers, wanting to combat the evil that had afflicted her island. At times, she would feel a new sense of optimism, but then on the second night, she woke filled with despair, haunted by the leering stare of Kohlenz. She prayed that she would not be with child.

Maybe it was God's punishment for killing the soldier without mercy. Of course, it was too early to tell but something inside told her it was true. She was carrying the bastard child of a German. It was now three days since it happened and there were no outward signs that she might be pregnant. In a few more days she'd be certain, but her instinct made her prepare for the worst.

At least the scroll was safe. She wondered whether it should remain hidden for ever. Whoever hid it under the foundations of the church had not wanted it found.

She understood why.

The prophecy was too terrifying to contemplate. That was why she had to die and if she could spare her family the shame of her rape then all well and good. But the real reason was to take the secret with her which was worth more than her mere insignificant life. It was the reason why Hans had been murdered. It was God's will.

There was still one more thing she had to do. The chalice and casket needed to be hidden with the scroll. It would take her a day to walk back to the ruined church, lying low and keeping clear of German patrols.

June 28th 1941

She wondered whether the Germans would be guarding the wood where they found Hans' body. After everything that had happened, the darkness came as a relief. Before the invasion, the night had scared her, but now it wrapped its cloak around and sheltered her from the cruelty of the day. Since leaving she'd walked for many hours to reach this spot. Her legs were tired and the emotions she'd been through sapped any strength she had left. When she rested, tears kept flowing down her cheeks, compounding her thirst and sadness. Her inner strength came from the thought that the chalice and casket had to be saved. Her own life no longer mattered because she no longer cared to live. Approaching the wood from the other side, instead of taking her more normal route up the steps to the church, had made the journey longer, but also safer.

She could hear voices. German voices. Her worries were justified. A path provided some guidance in the darkness and as she moved through the undergrowth the voices got louder. The soldiers had used the crater where the church had been to dig-in. She could see a large machine gun, trained on the village, established near the last steps where the church entrance had been. A sacrilege to be in such a holy place, ready to wage war. She watched

267

them from the wood. There were four men at the post; they were laughing and drinking, unconcerned that they were horribly exposed to an attack.

Slowly, she began to edge her way back into the forest, pleased that there were no more soldiers on patrol. Her method for finding the tree was straight forward but, in the pitch black of the night, nothing seemed familiar.

The fact she found the tree was miraculous, as if a greater force had provided guidance. She just walked straight to it and couldn't believe her luck. Sinking to her knees, she began tearing at the earth with her hands, like a dog digging a hole with its paws. The treasure was buried about two feet under and the soil was loose from when she'd dug the hole in the first place. Lifting the objects out, she placed them in her sack and began to move. The darkness disorientated her and the voices were louder, just a few feet separated them. She'd walked the wrong way.

It was a white owl that saved her. It squawked and took off disturbed by the soldiers, who shone torches into the air to catch its climb. She froze. They were less than three feet away and had they not been distracted their beam would have picked her out. She held her breath, praying that the distraction would make them change direction.

God had come back to her side. The soldiers gave up their patrol and walked back to their machine gun position.

June 29th 1941

She continued to walk all night, fighting off a desperate need to sleep, only feeling safe when she reached the gorge. The sun was rising when she collapsed, unable to walk another step. She dragged herself across the earth and sheltered from the strengthening sun under a rock overhang.

A familiar smell dragged her out of sleep. Not pleasant and she wanted to resist it. An earthy, animal smell. One she seemed to recognise. The soft fur rubbing across her face provided another clue. This time her eyes opened and the playful face of one of her herd staring down at her made her smile. A goat carrying milk. With no receptacle to capture it, she pulled herself under the animal and took the teats between her lips, squeezing gently until the rich creamy taste nourished her parched mouth. Replenished, she took the casket and chalice into the cave and then returned to her Bible, reading it voraciously, devouring its wisdom one last time. Sometimes she would stop and underline entries and write notes, lost in thought.

As day turned into night, it was time to leave and find Yiannis to give him the letter and Bible. It was easier to find him at night because she knew where he would sleep. He looked after goats and many times they'd shared a cave with their animals, sheltering from a storm. It took about an hour to reach him and, just as she'd guessed, he sat by the fire, roasting meat and preparing some tomatoes.

He was pleased to see her and they embraced. Yiannis lived most of the year on the mountains and knew the trails even better than she did. He'd become a runner between the various resistance cells taking messages that couldn't be passed on by radio.

'Did you deliver the last letter I gave you to the British soldier?' she asked.

'I gave it to Nikoletta, who said she'd give it to him.' Yiannis replied.

Callidora looked at him with annoyance. 'Why? I told you to give it to him and *only* him.'

Yiannis looked concerned. 'Nobody told you?' he replied.

'Nobody told me what?'

Yiannis paused, even his eyes looked sad. 'The Englishman was badly wounded. I don't know whether he's still alive. I gave the letter to Nikoletta because she knew where he was, but she didn't know whether he'd survived.'

Callidora groaned. 'Oh my God. He can't be dead,' she almost prayed, looking up to the roof of the cave. 'I must go to him...' Her eyes filled with tears. 'Did Nikoletta tell you where he's hiding?'

Yiannis looked upset, hurt that he hadn't done what he'd been asked. 'I'm sorry, Callidora,' he said sheepishly. 'I did ask, but she wouldn't say...in case I got taken by the Germans.'

She hesitated and wiped her eyes, worried that Lenny might be dead, but knowing it would not change a thing. She had to die and if Lenny never knew where she'd hidden the scroll then it was clear God wanted the secret to remain hidden.

'Take this letter anyway. I'll keep the Bible just in case.'

Chapter Thirty-Two

The Aegean Sea, Greece. August 3rd 2005

Abdul clutched the rail and began to retch. The hot dry sirocco wind, blowing from North Africa, had hit the ship head on as they emerged out of the Dardanelles. It pitched and rocked as it battled through the waves and Abdul's gut seemed to want to go the opposite way to the vessel. The Turkish captain had told him that the Aegean is often like a mill pond, but today had not been one of those days.

'Tomorrow it might change,' the captain said. 'Or maybe not. A wind like this can blow itself out in a few hours or go on for days. Nobody knows what it will choose to do.'

'But the helicopter…it must be able to land on the ship,' said Abdul.

'We must pray to Allah,' said the captain. 'And the winds will be calm.'

But the wind was not listening. Shocked by a sudden wave, the boat rolled, throwing Abdul forward. He tried to regain his balance but toppled into the captain. The seaman seemed unconcerned, smiling to himself as he grabbed the Arab's hands and made him grip the gunwale. Abdul cursed out loud, even more annoyed by the choice of transport. The whole point of sailing on this ship was to avoid detection and now satellites would be tracking their every move. No one was to blame but himself for allowing Helford to escape. From such close range, he would never miss.

Unless he intended to miss.

271

His hand had faltered as he squeezed the trigger. A deliberate act to keep his friend's son alive. He cursed himself for showing weakness but he wanted to believe that David Helford was still his friend, that there had been no betrayal, that Sheikh Zabor was the only reason he'd been placed on the Kill List.

The longer they sailed the more optimistic he got that they were not being tracked after all. Maybe Helford's son had decided to keep quiet because he needed to find his father without interference.

As did Abdul. David Helford had a lot of questions to answer.

With the boat still swaying from side to side, he staggered down the stairs to Kleiner's cabin. He found the German prostrated on his bunk, looking greener than Abdul felt.

'I want to know how you think you can bring me Helford,' said Abdul.

Kleiner turned over. 'I'm too sick to talk.'

Abdul's face contorted with anger. He hurled himself at Kleiner, pulling him off the bunk. The German fell in a heap on the floor.

'Sick, are you?' bellowed Abdul, kicking Kleiner in the groin. 'Now you've good reason to be sick.' Kleiner lay in a foetal position groaning. His face was gaunt with the effects of seasickness and the pain of Abdul's boot added to his discomfort.

'What do you want?' Kleiner moaned.

'I've only just started,' Abdul sneered. 'I'll be throwing you over the side of this ship if you don't tell me where Helford is.'

'I don't know.'

Abdul was taking no more negative answers. He bent down and grabbed Kleiner under each arm dragging him up to his feet before manhandling the German up the stairs and back on to the deck. Abdul drew his gun and prodded

Kleiner to walk. He pushed him hard against the first rail they reached and lent into his body, forcing the gun into Kleiner's spine. Still holding the gun, Abdul bear hugged the German lifting his legs into the air, tipping him head first over the side. It would have been easy to let go, but clung on as Kleiner thrashed about with his arms, suspended over the sea raging below.

'Where is Helford?' Abdul shouted. 'If you don't talk I'll let you go.'

The blood was rushing into Kleiner's brain. Bile and sick filled his mouth. His head felt like a dead weight pressing against his skull. He screamed again as Abdul let his grip loosen for a split second so that Kleiner fell a few inches further over the side.

'I'll talk. I'll talk,' Kleiner cried. 'Just let me go.'

Abdul pulled the German back over the rail and threw him onto the deck. 'If you don't talk. I'll kill you.'

Kleiner rolled over, crawling to his knees, opening his mouth to speak. 'What do you want to know?' he spluttered.

'How do you contact Helford to let him know that the meeting with Sheikh Zabor has been agreed?'

'He said he knew where we'd be…at the Cave of the Seven Sleepers. He said he'd know if the Sheikh had not come…I swear it's the truth…'

Abdul's eyes narrowed. 'There is a problem with what you say.'

'W…What…I don't understand,' replied Kleiner.

'The Cave of the Seven Sleepers is on Ephesus, not Crete.'

'So why would the Greek woman refer to it?'

Abdul could see the fear in Kleiner's eyes. He was inclined to believe he was telling the truth. 'It is a metaphor. I think there is a cave, it is just not really called by that name.'

273

'You've got to believe me...I would tell you where he is if I knew. All I know is he must be somewhere on Crete.'

A sudden silence had descended on the ship. Without warning the wind had dropped, calming the sea. The boat was no longer swaying. Abdul breathed a sigh of relief and turned to face Kleiner. 'The Sheikh is going to land on this boat in fifteen minutes by helicopter. The ship will dock shortly afterwards on the Cretan island of Gavdos off the south coast near Hora Sphakion and from there you'll take us to the so-called Cave of the Seven Sleepers.'

The fighter jet came out of nowhere. First a deep rumble of thunder and then a crescendo of high-pitched deafening noise. Abdul knew an F15 only too well. He'd seen them in Afghanistan. Low flying over the sea, approaching at five hundred miles per hour. He thought it was going to attack.

With only seconds to react, he dived under one of the lifeboats and waited for the missiles.

But there were no missiles. In a second, the jet had flown over the boat, so close it seemed it might hit the radio mast, before swooping upwards towards the horizon. The noise continued even though Abdul could no longer see it. Kleiner was still kneeling, panting for breath. 'They're on to us,' he muttered.

The captain came running towards them. 'In the name of Allah, what was that about?'

Abdul also wondered what was going on. Something was up. But whoever it was had lost the element of surprise. And why not do something – fire some missiles, sink the ship? End it here and now. He ignored the captain and stared across the shimmering waters of the Libyan Sea. They had moved out of the Aegean and were now sailing along the island's southern coast. He could see the mountains of Crete rising into wisps of cloud that punctuated the deep blue sky.

It was that moment of silence that made him realise.

Like the moment before the missile destroyed his house in Afghanistan. The F15 was going to shoot down the Sheikh's helicopter.

Abdul screamed at the Captain. 'Give me your radio,' he shouted. 'What frequency is the helicopter on?' It was already too late. The distinctive thudding noise of the chopper's rotors shattered the silence. He scoured the sky for the F15. There was nothing. He knew the missile could be fired from twenty miles away.

No jet in sight did not mean there was no danger.

In desperation, he bellowed into the radio. 'Get out now. Abort the landing. Under attack.' There was no reply. He strained his eyes towards the noise of the engine. The Sheikh's Bell helicopter was in full view and getting closer. The roar of the engine growing louder.

He watched in horror as the chopper veered sharply to the left. Abdul looked to his right and saw the streak of the Sidewinder at the same time that the pilot tried to take evasive action. The engine of the chopper strained; a last ditch attempt to pull the helicopter clear. The revs had reached breaking point; a futile effort to avoid the inevitable.

A ball of flame. The blades of the chopper cartwheeled into the sea. The tail fin severed from the main body and what remained nosedived before the fuel tank exploded and it was all over. It took just five seconds. Debris scattered on the surface and a few flickering flames of burning oil marked the spot of the crash. But then it was gone. There were no survivors.

The silence returned as the wreckage disappeared and the waves created by the impact subsided. Abdul didn't move. He was in a trance, remembering his daughter, so happy, and then in an instant, she was no more.

275

Only Helford knew that the Sheikh was coming. Whatever the Sheikh had said about him to the CIA, he was in no doubt that his friend had betrayed him. The Sheikh had only agreed to come to Greece because he trusted Helford and believed he was on their side

He could not let this setback change his direction. If he found the scroll, he'd find Helford and shoot him dead.

Mossad safe house Athens. August 3rd 2005, 11 a.m.

The woman stared intently at the satellite images already coming in from the crash site. Her name was Dinah Zevi and today she looked even more severe than when she'd questioned Kleiner in Berlin. Dressed head to toe in leather, Kleiner might have thought she was sexy enough to distract him away from money, but this was far from Dinah's purpose. She was dressed for combat and Kleiner was one of her targets.

A smirk of satisfaction spread across her face and her lips mouthed a word under her breath. 'Yes,' she said to herself. 'Yes.'

Vauxhall Cross, MI6 Headquarters, London. August 3rd 2005 11 a.m.

GCHQ had also picked up the activity as they'd been tracking the *Istanbul Star*'s every move. The satellite pictures appeared on Rowena's computer screen only a few seconds after Dinah had seen them. She didn't look surprised to see the destruction. In fact, quite the opposite, her expression suggesting that she knew all about the missile strike.

Rowena dialled a number. 'It's done,' she said into the phone. Replacing the handset, she wondered whether Richard Helford would ever know what she'd done.

She dialled Brian's number.

'Have you seen the pictures?' she said when he answered.

'Yes, who do you think is involved?'

'GCHQ say it was Israel.'

Brian hooted. 'How the fuck did they know about this?' Brian boomed down the phone. 'Who told them about our operation?'

'The Israelis have a habit of putting their fingers in lots of pies and nobody knows how they do it,' Rowena replied.

'Do you know who was in the chopper they brought down?'

Rowena ignored the question. 'Just don't tell Richard about this.'

'I suppose your silence means you can't tell me what's going on,' said Brian. 'It pisses me off that you don't trust me.'

'Look, Brian, you know how these things work. It's nothing to do with trust.'

'You know what, Rowena?'

'What?'

'Here's me thinking you were crazy to deploy Richard, but now I get it.'

'Get what?'

'You never expected Richard to take out Abdul.'

Rowena sighed. Brian was right of course, but she didn't like the idea of using Richard as a pawn. She certainly didn't want to admit anything to Brian. She hung up and paced the room, staring out of the window towards the river. The wind had got up; wispy white-tipped waves were appearing across its grey surface. A Thames Clipper flashed passed on its way to Putney while another going

277

the opposite way was leaving the quay side at the Tate Britain, fighting for space with other pleasure boats. London was getting back to normal after the bombing. Life had to go on and Five were leading the investigation into 7/7. She was pleased that C had allowed her to focus on this issue rather than the investigation into the bombing, but he didn't know the half of it. Tell me what I need to know, he'd said. She knew she couldn't tell him anything about the double game, with the Americans in one corner and the Israelis in the other. The Americans would go ballistic if they knew Mossad had taken out Sheikh Zabor. He was their man, giving them vital Saudi intelligence. She knew that was bullshit, and so did Mossad who kill first and ask questions later.

Her worry was that Richard would be caught in the crossfire.

Chapter Thirty-Three

Crete, Greece. June 28th 1941

The journey down the mountain was difficult. The descent was steep and there was little light to guide them. They set off after midnight and despite the darkness, Nikos wanted to move fast, convinced that the Germans were going to arrive with reinforcements at first light. He had to reach the village before them, to get as many men as possible to take refuge in the mountains and join the resistance. The women would have to stay to look after the children. Surely the Germans wouldn't kill them, he'd said. Lenny wasn't so sure and he didn't think Nikos was either.

Lenny struggled to keep up, distracted by the pain in his arm, which prevented him using it for balance, or to grab hold of something if his feet slipped. He was relieved when they found the cave where they were going to leave him. It was near a stream, still flowing, not yet dried up by the summer heat. With the sun waiting to rise, the dawn light cast a silvery hue across its surface. Bubbles of water splashed over the rocks and when the water caught some light, it sparkled as it flowed into a freshwater pool, large enough to swim in. The opportunity to bathe his wounds in the clear water was too good to miss. As soon as Nikos and the other men had gone, he stripped off his clothes. The wound hurt like hell and every time he moved his arms, it hurt even more, but the lure of the water was too great to give up. Naked, he lowered himself into the pool, feeling the icy cold rush over his body. It felt wonderful, like an anaesthetic on his arm. Too deep to stand, he allowed himself to sink, letting the water cleanse him and wash away the pain of death. As he surfaced, he floated and allowed his mind to re-live the ambush.

Getting out was much harder than getting in, and it took him some time to find a place where with one arm he could pull himself onto a rock. As the rocks began to warm in the early morning sun he examined his arm. The bandage was blood red, but the bleeding had not got any worse. He found a flat rock and lay down, still naked, allowing the sun's heat to dry him. His clothes were certainly smelling and stained with dried blood. To delay putting them on seemed perfect. It helped him relax and soon he was asleep.

He heard a voice. At first, it came from the middle of a dream; a woman's voice, booming and distinct. His eyes blinked open, squinting in the sunlight, but wide enough to see he wasn't dreaming.

Nikoletta was peering down at him and smiling. 'What do we have here?' she asked, giggling. 'It seems I've stumbled on a glimpse of Arcadia. I think I can see Adam is in his Eden.'

Embarrassed, he covered his genitals and smiled back. 'Sorry,' he said. 'I've been for a swim.'

'Just as well I'm a woman of the world,' she replied. 'That young Callidora would've run a mile, seeing you like that,' she laughed. 'Come on, we need to get you into that cave and smarten you up, just in case the Nazis come knocking.'

He put his good arm round her shoulder and with her help, stepped out of the sunlight into the darkened part of the cave. She'd thought of everything. Some fresh clothes, a bandage for his arm, some candles and, most important of all, some food. Nothing much, but anything was welcome. He'd forgotten how long it had been since he'd last eaten, so this looked like a feast. A large tomato and some cheese and stale bread, not to mention some cooked goat's meat. It was all good.

She spoke, bandaging his arm while he ate with his good hand. Her earlier efforts at humour were fading fast in the darkness of the cave. 'Nikos is taking some of the more able men out of the village into the mountains. Those that are staying put are holding Ikaros.' In the flicker of the candlelight, he could see her face had changed. Her eyes were damp with tears and her expression was far from the earlier smile he'd witnessed in the sunlight. 'They're saying he's the murderer of the German that Callidora met.' The tone of her voice changed to bitterness. 'She's caused so much trouble, just as well she's gone and left the village.'

He looked at her, surprised at the news of Callidora. 'Where's she gone?'

'Nobody knows. She just upped sticks and left. Didn't even wait for Nikos to comeback. She just went.' She stopped and reached for the pocket in the side of her skirt. 'I've got something for you,' she said, handing an envelope to him. 'She's left a letter addressed to you. Yiannis the shepherd gave it to me.'

He took it and stared at the neat writing, amazed she had written to him. He hardly knew her, but somehow there'd been a connection. 'Thank you,' he said. 'I'll read it when you're gone.'

'Yes. I best be going. Only a few are staying to face the Germans. Nikos expects them to be spared. He thinks the Germans won't kill women and children. I don't believe a word of it.'

'What will they do to Ikaros? Will they kill him?' he asked, seeing his comment had struck a chord. She looked shocked by his suggestion. It was an obvious question, but perhaps she'd put it out of her mind. Maybe she just refused to accept the inevitable consequences of German brutality.

She stood up, anxious to leave. 'I'd better go. The Germans will have arrived by now. Seeking revenge. They've already killed Pavlos and Thea and burned their house down, and the houses of some other families I don't know. Nothing is beyond them.'

Lenny didn't know who Pavlos and Thea were, but that didn't mean he wasn't shocked by their deaths. The indiscriminate killing of civilians made him angry, but at the same time a sense of helplessness invaded his spirit. 'Are you sure you'll be all right?' he asked.

'I can't abandon Ikaros. He needs me,' she replied.

Without any more ceremony or any more smiles, she left him alone. The candles were a welcome relief, but he used them sparingly, losing track of the time while he lay there letting the darkness embrace him. Remembering Callidora's letter, he lit another candle and holding it up started to read.

The contents of the letter were no surprise because he already knew about the German soldier's murder.

But that did not stop her words moving him to tears:

Sometimes I think it would be a blessed relief to die in Tirata and end all this suffering, but the Cretan spirit prevails and we know it is our destiny to fight on until we fall dead in the dust.

He'd already seen this Cretan spirit displayed when they ambushed the German convoy, when he saw men fight for their lives against the odds. He may be English, but just like Lord Byron he wanted to be with them in their struggle for freedom. He had to go down to the village and do something.

The heat of the afternoon sun sapped his energy as he walked down the hill, doing his best to stay in the shade of the mountain. His arm still hurt, but at least it had not become infected. It would heal if he was patient. The trouble was he had no time to be patient. He owed it to those people to do something. He owed it to Callidora. But what could he do against the might of the German war machine?

There was no clearly defined path away from the cave, all designed to make the hiding place effective but difficult to find again if he ever had to return. It took him over an hour to reach the border of the village. He was bedraggled and burnt by the sun and dressed in Cretan clothes. His beard was jet black and unruly, perfect for his disguise. The Germans wouldn't be smart enough to notice that his Greek accent was not typical of the Chania locality. The only trouble was that they may notice him from the earlier raid on the convoy. He decided to take that chance.

As he approached, he could hear noises that appeared to be emanating from the square, but everywhere else was deserted. German trucks were parked up and several soldiers milled around smoking, ignoring the noise. As he got near, he drew in gulps of air to calm his nerves, which were on edge as he walked past, trying his best to look nonchalant and unconcerned by the sight of several machine guns pointing in his direction. Reaching the square, he could see Ikaros in front of the crowd. Kohlenz was there this time; loud and in control of the proceedings. Everybody who had remained in the village was standing facing the Nazi. No more than thirty adults and a few children, but enough people to create another atrocity if the Nazi wanted.

Lenny looked around the square and saw Nikoletta, standing at the front, quite close to Ikaros, who was guarded by two armed soldiers. Kohlenz paced the square, glaring at the crowd, making sure they feared for their lives. His interpreter trailed behind, desperate to keep up. Lenny continued to stare in Nikoletta's direction, convinced she would look back at him. Sure enough, she turned, showing no sign in her facial expression, but revealing everything in her eyes. It was as if she didn't want him there because she was embarrassed by his presence, or maybe it was something else. He couldn't put his finger on it.

Kohlenz spoke. 'We have our murderer here before you.' He clicked his heels, turning away from Ikaros to look at the crowd. 'Now that the woman who met Paratrooper Tuebingen has run away, I can only assume that the murderer and the woman were in league with each other. Her leaving is an admission of guilt – she lured my soldier to his death. Rest assured, we will search the mountains for your dear daughter and she'll pay the price for the murder of our son.' Lenny decided that the language was almost religious, manic and crazy. He's a fucking fanatic, just like his leader, he thought.

The German turned back to face Ikaros, waiting for the interpreter to catch up. The accused man stared straight ahead but was unable to hide the hatred in his eyes. Lenny glanced back to Kohlenz, seeing him take pleasure at the sheer scale of the loathing that Ikaros had for him.

Kohlenz seemed to be enjoying himself. A sadistic smirk of pleasure crossed his face. 'He'll be executed immediately,' he shouted, swinging a Nazi salute and clicking his heels in perfect timing. '*Sieg Heil,*' he screamed.

A two-fingered gesture, thought Lenny. Murmurs rippled through the crowd. He wasn't sure if they approved of the execution or were criticising it. Then, as the crowd fell silent, a voice echoed around the square.

'No,' the voice said. It was Nikoletta. One word, powerful in the delivery, crushed the crowd into silence. She moved forward and two soldiers pounced, holding her down.

'Let her go,' shouted Kohlenz, walking up to where she stood. 'We have another spirited woman in our midst. Is this village full of women of passion?' Lenny could see him leer and with his stick run it down her bodice. She stared back, thrusting her bosom towards him in proud defiance. Kohlenz took the bait, like any man with no scruples would do. Nikoletta knows what he wants, Lenny surmised.

'What would you say in this man's defence?' Kohlenz shouted, enjoying the spectacle.

'He is not guilty,' she said, staring straight at Kohlenz.

'Everybody is guilty,' shouted Kohlenz so the crowd could hear, but moving closer to Nikoletta. 'Even if he is not guilty of killing Hans Tuebingen, he is guilty of murdering German paratroopers as they fell from the sky.'

'He is not guilty,' she repeated, more firmly this time.

'I don't agree. I will listen to your plea of innocence, but I want something in return. I want the scroll that this man has promised me and I want the British agent, who I know led a raid on a convoy two days ago.' Kohlenz waved an order and six soldiers positioned themselves in front of Ikaros. They raised their machine guns into a firing position.

'No!' Nikoletta shouted again and again. Lenny felt he should do something, but he was too far away. 'I'll give you the British soldier.'

It didn't sink in straight way. He couldn't believe what he was hearing. How could she betray him? Ikaros was Greek and so was she. It was either him or me, he thought. She chose her own countryman, which made perfect sense.

'It's him,' she shouted. Her hand lifted up slowly, swinging in his direction, reaching out across the square. They were perhaps twenty feet apart, but it seemed like twenty inches. Two of the firing squad broke away and were running towards him. It was a split second decision, which one to take out. He chose the one on his left and charged. Neither soldier was expecting a counter attack. He hit the target hard, plunging his knife into his gut, wincing with pain as his bad arm used force to penetrate the flesh. In the same movement, his good arm was taking hold of his machine gun, as the boy he was killing gave up his grip. He was rolling now, firing on the move, short bursts, making every bullet count, the commando training in Scotland paying off against the odds. The boy on the right was down and he sprayed bullets into the remainder of the firing squad, putting them out of action as they scattered. More soldiers were flooding into the square, shooting in his direction. He saved his bullets, preparing to make the final dash, through a house and out of the back. The rest of the crowd were running in all directions. Some of them were hit, but there was nothing he could do for them. Kohlenz had taken cover. It would have been worth dying just to kill him. But not today. Reaching a cart for cover, he knew that if he delayed he would be killed.

So he ran.

His gun blazed, swinging it from side to side, making sure the soldiers would think twice about getting too close to him, creating mayhem and no more counting of bullets.

A big mistake.

Emerging from the rear of the house, he saw a lone soldier coming around the back. He prepared to fire, but the magazine was empty. He reacted with the speed of someone not ready to die, diving to the ground before the soldier could depress his machine gun's trigger. The chatter of gunfire whistled over his head. A reprieve, but for how long? If he waited, trying to dodge the boy's bullets, he would be dead anyway as the Germans regrouped and got the upper hand. The boy was nervous and slow, but wasn't going to miss this time. Dead meat, he thought, waiting for the bullet to kill him. A suspended second before death. Six feet separated them, a rugby tackle might do it, but he was too far away. It's all over, resigned to his fate, but wanting to relish the last moment as the bullets took him down.

The boy contorted and shrieked, jerked off his feet and thrown forward as a hail of bullets tore into his back. There was no time to wonder about his saviour. He sprinted down the track and off into the woods. Bullets were exploding around him, but somehow he managed to avoid them. Keep off the path, he said to himself as he ran, the smell of pine sharpening his senses, overpowering, but welcome. A way to escape. The Germans had reached the perimeter of the wood and were pressing onward. The woods were providing cover, but he had no way of defending himself. The only thing to do was to keep running. He was looking backwards, when the man grabbed him. Shock quickly turned into joy. It was Ikaros.

'We'll head for the cave,' he said.

'But Nikoletta knows where it is. She might tell the Germans.'

'Nikoletta will say nothing more now I'm free.'

He was sure Kohlenz would come after them. But it was getting dark and Ikaros knew the mountains better than anybody.

Chapter Thirty-Four

London, UK. August 3rd 2005

London didn't feel like home.

Maybe his false identity made him feel alone or maybe it was because he wasn't able to return to his flat off the Holloway Road. The worst thing was not being able to call Becky, because he knew he could never admit that he was in London without seeing her. The safe house they'd given him in Chelsea Harbour didn't help his alienation. It was salubrious without being welcoming. Empty flats owned by foreigners, hoping to make a killing on the London property market, added to his sense of being a stranger in his own city. Richard sat on a chair outside a pub and watched the busy heliport on the other side of the river. He'd managed to book a night charter to Chania from Gatwick but he wanted to leave now. Every minute wasted in London was a minute lost finding his father and Abdul. He regretted allowing the Service to fly him to London under his new identity when it would have been much better going to Chania via Athens. It was too late to worry. He just had to be patient and think how he was going to deal with Abdul when he got there. To kill some time, he decided to buy some shorts and t-shirts to improve his tourist credentials.

The only contact he'd had since arriving back in London was a call to Brian in Athens who'd told him that finding Uma wasn't going to be easy. There wasn't a budget to send someone over to Germany to do a more thorough search, he'd said, apologising while stressing that Vauxhall Cross was out of bounds and Rowena wasn't going to visit for tea and cakes. *You're on your own*, he'd said. The call had been awkward to say the least. Richard detected that Brian seemed uneasy talking to him. More distant and less keen to prolong the call.

He looked at his watch; it was just past midday and his flight didn't leave for another eight hours. Abdul would be nearly there by now. If he didn't get to Crete tomorrow, then the chances that he might find his father and outwit Abdul to recover the scroll were nil. Leaning back in his seat, he took a sip of his beer and looked along the promenade.

He thought he was anonymous, that no one knew him. He was just a face in the crowd, except that the face staring in his direction knew exactly who he was. A woman he recognised, walking towards him. He intensified his gaze, checking he was not mistaken. Someone must have told her where he was. They were only five metres apart when she called out.

'Richard, what a surprise.' Her voice was loud enough to make heads turn. It was fortunate there was no one around but he remained wary, unwilling to reply to his real name when the passport in his pocket said Peter Marchento and not Richard Helford. Rather than say anything, he signalled to her to sit down. She hugged him warmly, kissing him on both cheeks.

'Amira. What are you doing here?' His curt response left her in no doubt that he was suspicious of how she'd turned up uninvited.

She smiled, choosing to ignore his coldness. 'I was worried...I wondered what you were doing in Athens...When I heard nothing, I worried that Abdul had snatched you...to use you to bargain with your father.'

Richard shifted in his seat. Her concern seemed to be genuine but something didn't sound right. How had she worked out that Abdul might try and take him? He just didn't trust her any more – not one iota. 'Last time we spoke, you knew I was in Athens,' he said. 'How did you know I was here?'

'I told you, it was a surprise,' she protested. 'I didn't expect to meet you here.'

'Well you were right about the kidnap,' he said. 'Abdul's men grabbed me, but I escaped.'

Amira's eyes widened; the shock on her face registered disbelief that what she had guessed had actually happened. 'I'm sorry, Richard, I didn't know…I didn't expect to be right.' She touched his hand. 'Are you okay?'

Richard resisted the urge to confront her about her story. She had seemed so innocent when they first met but now things had changed, the way her knowledge of Abdul seemed to be growing. The way she'd found Masood's notebook at such a convenient time.

'I'm fine. But never mind that. As you're here, you can help me. I want to ask you about Masood's icon…how did Masood's family receive it?'

Amira looked shocked that he wanted to talk about the icon. She played nervously with a bracelet of gold beads she was wearing. 'I don't know the full details but Masood's family are from Aleppo…I suppose that's why he took to me. Although he was a Muslim he always liked Christians. About ten per cent of the population of Syria are Christian. There was a story that one of his ancestors received the icon from a Knight of the Crusades during the Siege of Aleppo in the twelve century.'

'Did he know Barnabas was the saint on the icon?'

'Yes, he did, but he had no interest in Christian saints.'

'So he didn't know that there is a Gospel of Barnabas that promotes the idea that Jesus said he was not the Last Messenger of God?'

'He knew about that. He told me about it. I would imagine that his father told him all about it when it was bequeathed to Masood.'

Richard sighed. He was hoping Masood's icon would show a connection with the scroll referred to by Callidora in her letter. 'Is there anything else you want to tell me about the icon?'

'Knowing about the Gospel of Barnabas didn't mean that he believed the story,' said Amira. 'There was no evidence to suggest that the Gospel of Barnabas is authentic. It's true he did become more interested when they discovered a Syriac version of the Gospel which was much older than the sixteenth century forgery that everybody knows.' Amira thought for a minute and then continued, 'I remember him saying that the knight gave it to one of his ancestors because he'd become disillusioned with the Crusades and believed that the Holy Koran should take preference over the Holy Bible. There was a rumour that the rich lord became a Muslim and settled in Aleppo, much to the disgust of his fellow knights.' Amira laughed. 'Of course it's all nonsense.'

'Is it?' said Richard. 'I wonder.'

'But what's this got to do with your father?' she asked.

He didn't have time to answer.

It must have been a glint of sunlight that dazzled him. Something reflected back and distracted his thought process. He blinked in protest before allowing his eyes to scan the apartment block in front of him, searching for the place where he'd seen the flash.

The barrel of the rifle jutted out of one of the windows on the second floor.

This made him react. A second later would have been too late. The weight of his tackle sent Amira flying. Her chair toppled backwards and Richard landed in a heap on top. The first bullet struck a parasol and ricocheted into one of the tables, the second one pounded into the floor.

Rolling over, Richard shouted, 'Get away, Amira. Run.'

The sound of a helicopter drowned out the sound of gunfire and the few people milling about in front of the Wharf were oblivious to the commotion. Richard was on his feet, running to the entrance of the block where he'd seen the gun. He tailgated a woman laden with shopping bags, dashing passed the security guard at the entrance before sprinting up the two flights of stairs to the second floor. There was a corridor of doors side by side in a long landing, but there was no sign of any intruder. The flat he wanted was the last but one along the passage.

'Hey, you.'

Richard swung around and saw the security guard emerging at the top of the stairs, panting for breath and red in the face. There was no point trying to prolong the incident and get into trouble. The gunman was going to get away with it. He needed to find Amira. He ran straight at the security guard who didn't try to stop him. He was down the stairs and out of the building in less than thirty seconds, but when he got there, Amira had vanished.

He tried to call her number but there was no reply. Despite repeated calls there was nothing. Brian called him after his third attempt to reach Amira.

'Who the hell are you trying to call?' he said.

Richard told him about Amira's surprise appearance and the sniper in the apartment.

'Maybe it was just a religious fanatic,' said Brian, sounding unconvinced by his explanation.

'Somebody tipped Amira off as to my location and the shooter knew where Amira was going to be. He was trying to kill her and not me.' said Richard. 'I'm sure of it. I'll talk to Rowena,' he lied. 'We'll get it checked out.' He would say nothing to Rowena. She was hiding the truth. He just didn't understand why and until he did, he would keep silent.

Chapter Thirty-Five

Crete, Greece. June 30th 1941

It was a shame Callidora couldn't be with her goats. It would've been a good way to die. She could pretend she was one of them and climb the dangerous crags, until she slipped down the mountain, smashing her head, killing that wretched bastard that was growing inside her. What if she wasn't pregnant? It was too early to see a bump, or feel it kicking in her belly, but something inside told her she was right. She'd prayed for a sign from God that it was not true but nothing came. God was punishing her for killing the soldier. It wasn't self-defence. She'd been walking the mountains for a day now, surviving on herbal tea made from sage and oregano mixed with water from mountain streams and boiled over an open fire. The bag she'd carried the casket and chalice in contained essentials for survival that she'd always taken to the mountain when tending her goats. A knife, cans of food to cook and a shawl if it got too cold at night, but most important of all, she had her Bible. A precious means of sustenance to make sense of things. It was a relief to still have it for her last few hours alive. After not giving it to Yiannis, she decided to leave it behind, with her bag, when she jumped.

She knew the mountains and knew how to survive, but she didn't want to live a lie. People would judge her. They'd blame her for everything, for seeing Hans, for the death of villagers, for the rape. It was all her fault.

After all the killing and brutality, she felt strangely calm. It was true, as she'd tried to sleep the night before, she'd been haunted by the memory of Kohlenz bearing down on her, thrusting forward, his spit slavering on her face. The nightmare woke her, and she'd sat shivering looking up at the stars, wondering if she could be on one, far away from the suffering. When the dawn broke, she felt at peace with herself. It all made perfect sense. Ending her life was the only way she could find closure. It was inevitable, whether she did it now or waited for them to kill her later. She hoped God would understand and forgive her transgression. She felt like a martyr, sacrificing her life to protect the secret of the scroll and preserve the very essence of her faith. God must surely understand.

As she walked, she revelled in the wild flowers of the mountains, the smell of herbs and bird song. If these were going to be her last moments, she was going to savour them and die happy. Great swathes of lilac campanula covered the hill side and when she moved into forest shrub land, she saw clumps of yellow flowering Jerusalem sage and the occasional orchid standing alone fighting for its life, so delicate, just like her. In these happier moments, she'd thought of Hans, his excitement at seeing the scroll and that first moment in the church. He'd looked so out of place with a machine gun. But how she'd connected to him and that wonderful enthusiasm for the scroll. He'd pleaded with her not to let it fall into Nazi hands. She wouldn't let that happen. To end it now would prevent the possibility of being tortured and forced to confess. If she did it now, the scroll would be safe. Besides, if she was forced to confess, they'd kill her anyway, delaying only until she'd had the child, giving Kohlenz his spoils of war.

She'd always used this crevasse as a landmark to pinpoint her position in the mountains. In the autumn months, grey mists would descend in a matter of seconds, making it easy to get lost. A point of reference like this was essential to keep on track and, over the years, she'd committed hundreds of places to memory so that she could walk around the mountains without fear. It was a huge rock, sheared off, as if God had prised it open with a chisel, leaving a smooth surface sloping at an angle, falling about two hundred feet into a hole at the bottom. The hole was like a cave facing the sky, the end of a sieve, plunging into a huge bottomless pit. Nobody had ever determined how deep the hole was, but she remembered seeing a goat slip and slide down the smooth rock, never to be seen again.

This was the place where she would die.

She climbed onto the ridge and lay down on her back. All she would have to do is let go and gravity would do the rest. A gentle slide down the precipice and into the abyss, lost for ever, returned to the bowels of the earth. There was a small recess in the rock, almost like a shrine, where she could leave her bag, her distinctive red headscarf and her most treasured possession; her Bible.

She was ready. Climbing onto the ridge, she looked once more at the sky, reciting a prayer, exactly as Jesus had done.

'Father, into your hands, I commend my spirit.' Her fingertips were all that stood between her and death. Slowly, she released them one by one, until the last two could not take the weight.

Closing her eyes, she began to slide.

Chapter Thirty-Six

Crete, Greece. August 4th 2005

This is a fine place to die.

Richard stood on the white marbled forecourt of Suda Bay war cemetery, staring across hundreds of gravestones, laid in symmetrical lines in front of him. Where is a better place for a soldier to die, in the land of Achilles, facing the wine dark Aegean Sea and the majestic White Mountains behind? It is a land of heroes, he decided. It is fitting my grandfather is buried here.

The cemetery was perplexing in its simplicity, a symmetry that instilled an aesthetic quality to the landscape. A sense of calm that suited a place of rest. Simple flowers picked out the chalk white colour of the stones. There were red and white geraniums, yellow flowers for the Aussies and Kiwis, and blue thistles to mark the passing of Scotsmen. There was no pattern in the flower arranging, just vivid colour accentuated by the brilliance of the sunlight. That was all you needed, flowers that provided the remembrance, but never taking away the power of the men lying here in front of him.

He walked towards the location of the grave, studying the stones as he went. Although from afar the gravestones looked the same, a closer examination revealed regimental emblems carved into the stone; each carrying a small epitaph of the person lying there, mostly just a name and age. So young, he thought.

Many had no name. Just a simple phrase, with the power to make someone weep:

Known unto God. Three words that said everything.

At last he found his grandfather's gravestone –
*Lieutenant Leonard Helford RN, Royal Marines. 18th
July 1941, aged 24.* There was no mention of his SIS role,
as one of the British organisers of the Cretan resistance,
but did it really matter how he'd died? There was no right
way to die.

Richard knelt down and touched the stone, running his
fingers over the inscription, spelling it out with his finger.
The fierce heat of the sun burned his forehead, but he felt
nothing. Only grief. How could he grieve for someone he
didn't even know? But this stone, he knew, was a symbol
of all his grieving for the people who'd died in London on
July 7th, for Bill Riordan and for Masood.

As he knelt, he became aware that someone was
watching. He glanced up and scanned the horizon, seeing
no one except a gardener, an old man tending a grave.

He smiled and shouted, '*Kalimera.*'

Greetings were exchanged and as Richard returned his
thoughts to the plight of his grandfather, the old man
appeared by his side. An idea flashed across his mind. He
was clutching at straws maybe, but could this man have
known his grandfather? Standing up, he faced him,
offering his hand. The man, gripping it like a vice, making
him wince, stared at him, smiling through broken teeth
and a thick grey beard. His skin, wrinkled by the outdoors,
but still full of the life giving properties of the sun, told its
own story. A good man, Richard thought, a man he could
trust.

'*Xereis afton ton tafo,*' the old man said, pointing at the
stone.

'My grandfather. Did you know him?' Richard replied
in Greek.

'Not me, but I've heard of him. A hero, we were all
told. That's why I work here, to tend the graves of heroes.'

Richard tried another question. 'Do you know where
the village of Tirata is?'

The man didn't look surprised by the mention of the name. 'The village is gone,' he said, betraying his sadness at hearing that name once more. 'You should go and see Ikaros. He'll tell you about Tirata and I think he knew your grandfather.'

Richard could hardly contain his excitement. 'Is that Ikaros Poliakis?' He remembered, his father had written that name down, with the number. Nikoletta had also mentioned Ikaros.

'The very same. He works at the German Cemetery in Maleme. Go to the village on the coast and then follow the signs, you can't miss it.'

It didn't take him long to reach Maleme. The excitement of getting a genuine lead made him feel so much better, relieved to be distracted from thinking about Abdul, Amira and how he felt about his father being alive. On the plane, he'd spent the flight in deep thought, oblivious to his noisy fellow passengers excited about their holiday in Crete. He tried to work out who would want to kill Amira. Abdul would never sanction a hit. But who? And who had told her where he was? Surely not Rowena or someone in the Service. And where had she gone after the murder attempt? But he worried most about his father. How would he react? As he sat on an aisle seat watching young couples trying in vain to get their kids to sleep, he thought about how much he'd missed his father's support in childhood.

Finding his grandfather's headstone had opened his eyes to who he was. Not just his father's son but a grandson of a national hero.

A sign in German pointed to the cemetery. The route to the cemetery went along a track, gently sloping upwards as it wound through fields to a small car park. There were two other cars parked, but he couldn't see anyone about. Locking his car, he walked past a small exhibition of how the cemetery came into being and thought he saw a figure going inside. He hoped it might be Ikaros, but when he followed, there was no one there. On the other side of the path, a collection of war memorabilia had been assembled. Rusty old Jeeps, shell casings, German helmets, all available to be purchased, but he couldn't see someone who might take his money, not that he was interested in buying anything. A stone path led up to the burial ground, through a few small trees that blew in the stifling hot wind. The air shimmered against the leaves and a flash of light dazzled his eyes, as if a mirror was being shone in his face.

The cemetery was a complete contrast to Suda Bay, not by the water's edge, but on a hillside overlooking the airfield with a fine view of the sea below. The gravestones lay flat, like plaques rather than the traditional upright style in Suda Bay. They were lying in the earth, surrounded by beds of short-stemmed red flowers, not the poppies so loved by the British, but something more discreet, giving an impression of blood streaming across the fields. Solitary crosses stood vertical in the midst of all the graves. The crosses were thicker and reminded him of the shape of the German Iron Cross. Maybe that was intentional.

There was nobody around, but he didn't feel alone. He began to read the stones and was surprised to find some of the graves contained two soldiers. At the bottom of the stone was a number, presumably a cross reference to a directory of the soldiers buried in this cemetery. Three numbers, a space and then three more numbers in sequence.

A bell rang in his mind. A sequence. The numbers he'd found with his father's letters were a sequence – 674 675.

For the second time that day, he felt like he'd won the lottery and the ticket was in his father's notebook. He ran up the hill, desperate to find the right sequence, his eyes flicking left and right, until he'd worked out the logic of the grave lay-out. His enthusiasm shut everything out, including an awareness of the man moving up the hill behind him. It didn't take him long to find the stone he was looking for. Sure enough, there were two bodies in this grave, one was unidentified, but the other was who he wanted to see.

Hans Tuebingen 17.11.21–6.6.41.

HT674 675. HT – Hans Tuebingen.

Hans.

Callidora's first letter, telling Lenny about the German shot dead by a jealous suitor. The German was called Hans. A common German name, but too much of a coincidence to be wrong. He had the connection, but why did his father become so obsessed with this that it would be written in his notebook and on that scrap of paper he'd found at his mother's house?

A flicker of light caught Richard's attention. Just as he had in Suda Bay, Richard sensed he was being watched. He caught the glint of the gun's muzzle before he saw the man pointing it directly at his head.

Kleiner,

Richard hadn't expected Kleiner or Abdul this early. The German's hands were shaking. His head was bowed towards the gravestones at his feet and his gun lowered slightly. Richard took a step forward.

'Get back,' Kleiner screamed raising the gun again. 'If you move, I'll kill you.'

Richard froze putting his hands up. 'Okay, okay…I won't move…just tell me what you want.'

The tension in Kleiner's face eased. 'All those soldiers, spread across the field, killed in cold blood by the Greeks, makes me angry,' he said. 'So much more moving than Suda Bay, don't you think?'

'My grandfather is buried in Suda Bay,' Richard snapped.

Kleiner grunted. 'In Suda there is grief and sadness. In this cemetery, there is a sense of the heroism, the glory of death in battle.'

Richard laughed. 'Being killed by a scythe wielded by a peasant woman as the soldiers fell to earth on their parachutes is hardly heroic,' he sneered.

Kleiner raised the gun. 'I should kill you for your insolence,' he shouted.

'Where's Abdul?' said Richard, ignoring the threat.

'He's here, wanting to kill you, but I think I'll save him the pleasure…You know just being here makes me want revenge, to kill someone for all these German deaths.'

'But what about the German reprisals, burning villages to the ground, slaughtering innocent civilians?'

Kleiner sighed. 'It was war. They killed our soldiers, they had to pay with their own lives.'

Richard glared back at Kleiner. 'You said my father is alive. You had his notebook so why would you want to kill me now?'

Kleiner lowered his gun. 'I don't want to kill you,' he muttered.

'But I do.' Although the voice came from behind, Richard knew it was Abdul. Unlike Kleiner, the gun Abdul was holding did not shake. He moved closer, his Glock aimed squarely at Richard's forehead. 'I should have killed you on the boat,' Abdul said. 'I didn't want to kill the son of my friend.'

'What's changed?'

'Now I know for certain your father is my enemy.'

Richard knew he would not miss this time. There was no way out. He was too far away to jump, but not too far away to be killed instantly.

'Why?' Richard's fear could only find that single word, an impassioned desperate whisper. There was a cold logic to what was happening to him. His father had ruined his life and now he was going to be the cause of his accelerated death. He saw Becky walking towards him holding his son. 'At least tell me what I'm dying for. What has my father done?' Richard stared down the hillside towards the sea. His eyes searched the land, hoping for something. 'Where is my father?' he shouted.

Abdul did not reply. His finger tightened on the trigger.

Chapter Thirty-Seven

Crete, Greece. July 1st 1941

Lenny stared at the latest letter from Callidora in disbelief. It was a stroke of luck that Yiannis found him. Since escaping from the village, the mountains had been crawling with German patrols. At times, they were lucky to avoid recapture, being a matter of feet away from the German war machine as it went by. Lenny would never have survived without Ikaros by his side, always knowing what to do. He knew every inch of the mountain paths and was able to melt away from sight, whether it meant hiding down a hole or just lying down in the undergrowth.

Ikaros would understand, he decided. He'd know what to do about her letter. He remembered what Ikaros had said the night before; how he'd wanted to marry Callidora but she didn't love him. Ikaros declared he wouldn't give up because he loved her. He would ask her again when the war was over.

They'd been wandering in the mountains for over five days before they stumbled on Nikos and his men. Yiannis was with them and handed over Callidora's second letter. He'd walked away from the cave, where the men were hiding, and read it over and over. It was curious that the letter mentioned her Bible, but he didn't know where that was. What would Nikos do when he found out she had killed herself? He decided to ask Ikaros to break the news because he'd known Callidora since she was born. Like family, he'd feel the pain of losing her, almost as much as her brother and far more than he himself could ever do.

Ikaros had come to join him and without explanation, Lenny handed him the letter. Ikaros looked at it briefly and then handed it back, an embarrassed look on his face.

'I can't read,' he said.

Lenny sighed, realising that it would be more painful to read Callidora's words aloud. He read them anyway and when he'd finished Ikaros didn't move. He didn't say anything either. It was like he was in a trance. Lenny resisted breaking the silence until Ikaros spoke. At first, he just paced backwards and forwards and Lenny could see he wanted to scream. His face was contorted, staring down at the ground.

'I've got to find her,' he whispered, his voice breaking, trying to hold back the tears. 'I think I know where she is.'

Lenny shot him a glance. 'Do you want me to come?'

'I'll do this on my own.'

Ikaros returned in two hours. He had Callidora's headscarf, her bag and the Bible. His ashen face needed no explanation. 'She's thrown herself down a ravine,' he said, tears in his eyes. 'That bastard Kohlenz is going to pay for this.' His hands were shaking. Turning towards a tree, he hit his head against the trunk, crying with grief. He continued banging the tree again and again. Lenny pulled him away. He kicked and screamed. Blood was seeping from Ikaros' forehead.

'We'll get the bastard, one way or the other,' Lenny shouted.

When Ikaros had calmed down, he sat staring into space. Words could not console him. Lenny didn't know what to say and thumbed nervously through the Bible, trying to hide his shock at what had happened, but equally amazed by the numerous annotations. She wanted me to have it, he thought, and she wants me to find the scroll because she's told me where it is in those letters. The story of the Seven Sleepers made it very clear.

'We must tell Nikos that she's dead,' Lenny said.

Five minutes later, Nikos heard the news. Just like Ikaros, he stood silent, but then began to emit a low groaning sound, which gradually rose into a crescendo of mourning. It lasted for what seemed like an age of agony before he spoke.

'I'm going to kill Kohlenz,' he snarled. 'He can't get away with this. I'm going to make the bastard suffer.' He slumped down onto his knees and began sobbing. The men around him were speechless. They'd never seen Nikos cry before. A Cretan didn't cry, they got even. Nikos looked up towards the men and then to Lenny. 'I'm going to hang Kohlenz by his balls and cut off his penis and let him bleed to death.' The men nodded agreement and several volunteered to go with him, but he only chose two. 'We may never come back, but I'd rather die than let that man stay alive for a second longer.'

'I'm coming with you,' said Ikaros. 'I don't care what you say.'

'We all go,' said Lenny.

It would take three hours to get to the village but they could see it in the distance well before that. They didn't like what they saw.

Smoke rose from every building. An inferno raged in the valley below and they couldn't do anything about it. Machine guns chattered in the air, singing their song of death. A massacre was happening before their eyes and they could only stare with increasing horror. Lenny felt their pain, helpless as the rest of them.

Nikos screamed. 'Oh my God,' he shouted. 'It's being burnt to the ground.' He began running down the hillside. He stumbled, falling headfirst, rolling down the mountain.

Ikaros followed, shouting in a frenzy of hate. 'We must kill the bastards,' he bellowed.

When Lenny reached Nikos, he was lying in the gorse weeping. Taking hold of his hand, he pulled him to his feet. 'You've got to be strong,' said Lenny.

Nikos pushed his hand away. 'You don't understand. That's my family. I've abandoned them to fight this stupid resistance and for all I know they are lying dead in that village. I thought the Germans would not kill women and children, and look what they're doing. It is a crime against humanity.'

'We must go down and see what's happening,' said Lenny. 'We must be cautious, otherwise we'll end up dead and that doesn't help anybody.' He hated himself for his attempt to stay calm. How could he appear to have such a callous disregard for their feelings? 'I'm sorry,' he said. 'I really am sorry.'

His plea had fallen on deaf ears. Nikos and Ikaros were already on their way to the village. The other men followed, distressed and scared, but determined to support the two men. It took them another hour to reach the edge of the village. They wanted to go quicker but the fear of running into the Germans slowed their progress. By the time they arrived, the Germans had gone, leaving a trail of destruction that became more horrifying the nearer they got. Every building was ablaze or had been burned to a state of charred ruins. Walls made of stone stayed standing, but the wooden floors and roofs dissolved into glowing embers.

Blood stained the square but there were no bodies. Lenny wanted to be sick and one of the younger fighters did just that. The immensity of the destruction has been sanitised, he decided. They'd taken the bodies away so as not to leave evidence of the war crimes that had been committed. He cursed them, screaming at the top of his voice, his words echoing in the wind, vowing revenge.

Nikos and Ikaros ran from house to house. Clouds of smoke hampered their search, but they refused to give up. One barn stood alone surrounded by burning buildings, but not yet alight. Screams of terror coming from the barn gave them hope. They forced the door open and one by one they extracted some of the women and children alive. Nikos' mother was there, and little Kosmas. Nikos hugged them both, relieved that he had at least a shred left of his family.

'Where's Father?' he shouted to his mother.

'Dead,' she wailed, hysterical, sobbing with grief. 'They're all dead, except Kostas. They let him go. He's a traitor, a collaborator,' she said, finding the courage to spit in the dust.

Lenny noticed that Ikaros had gone back into the barn, searching for someone else. He caught up with him. 'Who's missing, Ikaros?' he said.

'Nikoletta's gone.'

'She's not vanished,' said Nikos, who had come back into the barn. 'My mother has told me, she's been taken by Kohlenz. Dragged her off to be his whore.'

Ikaros could not contain his anger. He picked up a chair and smashed it into the wall. 'They have to pay for what they've done,' he spoke as a leader. 'We have to get Kohlenz.'

Nikos shouted. 'I'm coming with you.' Lenny watched as the two men set off back into the mountains, determined to make Kohlenz pay.

Lenny ran after them, shouting, 'Wait for me.'

Nikos turned and waited for Lenny to catch them up. Lenny arrived panting for breath. Nikos hugged him. 'You cannot come, my friend. This is for the Cretans. Ikaros would have married Callidora and she is my sister. You help us in the war, but this is not about war. It is about honour. Honour for the Cretans and honour for my family. I cannot allow you to fight my personal battle.'

307

Lenny didn't say anything. He stepped back and let them go. Watching them until they'd vanished in the wilderness.

Chapter Thirty-Eight

Crete, Greece. August 4th 2005

Voices. He could hear voices. Shadows emerging through the smoke. The smell of cordite hanging in the air, burning his nostrils. His eyes stung as he tried to see; splintered trees and blast-damaged cars becoming clearer as the desert wind lifted the black haze. People running towards him, waving their hands. Somebody he knew. The faces he remembered obliterated the identity of the person he'd seen. He could remember Bill Riordan's head lying in the road like a football, a frozen image on his face, like a bad photo snapped at the wrong time. He could remember the face of the mother, hysteria seeping from her terrified eyes, clutching her blood-spattered child. The harder he concentrated on the face, the more he saw Bill Riordan, the more he saw the woman. He wanted to go on sleeping until he remembered but the heat on his eyelids demanded he face reality.

He was not dead. Someone was touching his face.

'*Parakalo*,' the voice said. His eyes were misty, but he could just about open them. Figures seem to be calling him. 'Mister,' it said in English. His eyes edged wider, blinking at the sunlight. A face began to form before him. A Greek face, one he'd never seen before, but knew without asking. 'Ikaros,' he whispered, opening his eyes a little more. The man looked down at him, smiling through broken teeth and a mass of snow white hair, bleached by the sun. His hair framed his face, covering his ears and merging with his beard. All that was left exposed were eyes as blue as the sea and cheeks reddened by the burning air and Ouzo.

Ikaros didn't seem surprised that he might know his name. He nodded and grabbed Richard by the chest, pulling him to his feet. 'Can you walk?' he spoke in

309

Greek. Richard allowed Ikaros to support him while he recovered his balance.

'I'm okay,' Richard replied in Greek, his voice shaking. 'He was going to kill me. The gun was pointing at me.' He remembered the sound of the gun going off. He remembered the smoking barrel. Then there was darkness, like he was floating in the throes of death.

'Who was trying to kill you?

'An Arab...did you see him?' asked Richard, rubbing his eyes and feeling for injuries. There was nothing, not even a bump. He must have been drugged just like when he was snatched in Athens.

'I didn't see anyone but I've found something,' said Ikaros. 'Follow me.'

Richard's mind was still spinning. Could there have been someone else when the gun was fired, somebody who would have been able to drug him?

The body was propped up against a wall. A single bullet hole in the centre of the forehead. A shot fired with ruthless precision.

Kleiner.

Richard staggered, his legs giving way. Ikaros caught hold of Richard's arm, preventing him falling. 'I'm sorry,' Richard said. 'It's a shock seeing him like this. He's German. A minister in the government. There'll be a full murder inquiry if his body is found. It'll cause an international incident.'

'Don't worry about that. Cretans are used to making bodies disappear,' replied Ikaros with a smile. 'We Cretans have never forgiven the Germans for the invasion. Getting rid of this body will be a pleasure.'

Richard glanced back in the direction of the corpse. Abdul killed Kleiner instead of me, he thought. But Kleiner was supposed to help find the scroll so why kill him now, after they've travelled all this way? Why not kill him in Istanbul? Richard leaned closer to the body. Apart from the bullet hole there was nothing to suggest a struggle. The only thing he could see different was that Kleiner no longer wore his jacket. He turned back to Ikaros. 'His name is Klaus Kleiner. He had papers belonging to a Nazi you will have come across during the war...Captain Wolfgang Kohlenz.'

The old man snorted in derision, turning away to spit his disgust onto the floor. 'I never thought I'd hear the name of that bastard again,' Ikaros muttered. 'The only reason I signed up for this cemetery was so I could look out for Kohlenz if he came to visit.'

'Well he won't be coming now...He's dead.'

Ikaros' lips curled allowing a faint smile of approval. 'Burning in hell, if there is any justice. I've wanted him dead for over sixty years. But he never came back.'

'He came back in 1949 to help the fascists in the Civil War but after that we don't know what happened to him.'

'Well I didn't kill him,' said Ikaros. 'Much that it pains me to admit, I didn't do it.'

Richard held out his hand and the old Greek gripped it with the strength of a man half his age. 'I'm Richard Helford.'

'I know who you are,' replied Ikaros. 'I was told you were coming by Stephanos at Suda Bay. He saw you looking at your grandfather's grave. News travels fast in this part of the island. I admired your grandfather very much so it's a great honour to meet his descendant.' Ikaros glanced back at Kleiner's corpse. 'So you saw the Arab pointing the gun at you?'

'Yes...but he must have turned the barrel at the last moment. I remember seeing the smoke but then nothing. Somebody must have come up behind me and applied a drug...I really don't remember.'

'So there was more than one man?'

'Yes. But why didn't they kill me?'

'Maybe...' Ikaros hesitated as if he was going to say something and changed his mind. 'It doesn't matter,' he continued. 'The German bastard is dead, isn't he? And you're alive. That's all that matters.'

A mobile phone rang. Ikaros answered, gabbling away, speaking in a heavy dialect which Richard could barely understand. He worked out they were talking about the body and how to dispose of it.

While Ikaros issued instructions to whoever was on the line, Richard collected his thoughts. There could be only one reason why Abdul spared him. *His father had not betrayed him after all, and Kleiner had.* He scanned the scene. *Someone must have carried Kleiner over to the stone where they'd found him leaning.* He tried to remember exactly where he'd been standing before it all went dark, beginning to retrace his steps, looking for Kleiner's missing jacket. He found it hanging from an olive tree, spread out in a crucifixion pose with each arm hooked on a branch. The lining of the jacket had been slit from top to bottom with a knife. He took the jacket down and walked back to where Ikaros was standing, still shouting into his mobile. He had no idea what the jacket meant. Was it some type of warning? He knew Abdul would be looking for the cave but what about his escape route when he found the scroll? And why had Abdul not killed him when he seemed to regret not doing it in Istanbul?

He called Brian.

Brian as usual didn't linger with pleasantries. 'Where the fuck are you? You're supposed to maintain contact,' he said with his usual anger. Richard smiled to himself while Brian ranted. He's like an overprotective mother, he thought. He knew underneath the bravado, Brian was relieved to hear Richard's voice because he knew just how much danger Richard was in.

'Brian, never mind that. Listen to me. Abdul is on the island already. Can you check whether the *Istanbul Star* has landed, and if so where? We also need a satellite pass of the island to check for any unusual activity. Can you fix that?'

Brian said nothing for several seconds. 'Er…*Istanbul Star* you said…Of course, I'll get on to it straight away.

'Are you okay, Brian?'

'Er…yes. Why do you ask?'

'Oh nothing really…it's just when I ask you to do something you usually protest.'

Brian chuckled. 'You've caught me on a good day.'

Richard didn't believe the nervous laugh. He thought it sounded a little forced. He sighed, wondering what Brian wasn't telling him. He turned back towards Ikaros who'd finished his call.

'He'll be buried at sea,' said Ikaros. 'Tossed overboard. No papers. No missing person. He'll just disappear and good riddance.' He turned away and spat in the dust once more. 'I have men coming to take him away and clean off the blood from the stones.' Ikaros swigged from a bottle, handing it to Richard when he'd finished. 'It's raki, to settle your belly. I wouldn't worry. Nobody cares about a junior defence minister, not even the Germans. If he was up to no good he wouldn't tell anybody where he was going, so he'll vanish without a trace.'

They walked to the car park and Richard knew he could not drive.

'Come and stay with me,' said Ikaros. 'We've got a lot to talk about.'

The journey took nearly an hour and as Ikaros had to concentrate to avoid certain death on the mountain roads, they didn't talk much. As they began to descend a winding road in a deserted valley, Ikaros broke the silence.

313

'I don't come to the cemetery every day,' he said, relaxing a little as the road levelled out for the briefest of moments. 'Living in the mountains is where I find peace, so I try not to leave too often.'

Richard could see why he loved it so much. Situated at the bottom of a deep valley where a stream carved a path through porous rock, palm trees and large tropical plants grew in the dell. Most important of all, it had access to the sea through a narrow slit in the mountain, just wide enough to get a donkey through and let the stream flow. As they approached the house, they descended steeply. Ikaros' car could only go so far, forcing them to walk the remaining distance.

'The walk keeps me fit,' Ikaros said, chuckling to himself. 'During the war years, I knew every inch of the mountains, but now I just stay here, enclosed in my lost valley.'

'Doesn't the winter weather cause your house to flood?' Richard enquired.

'A little, but we improvise. I have generators which give me electricity and help to pump the water out when the rains get too heavy.'

They arrived as the sun went down. Darkness fell quickly making the valley seem remarkably cool. The house was a simple affair; a ground floor made of stone and a slanted wooden roof to fend off the rain. Not that there would be any rain for months. A small sheltered veranda at the front with a table, two easy chairs and what looked like a wood-burning stove, provided the outdoor living space in the hot summer months. Cultivated land surrounded the house and Richard could see that Ikaros had gone to great effort to grow vegetables.

Richard sat down on the veranda and waited while Ikaros went inside. After a few minutes, he brought out a salad bowl and a large stewing pan full of meatballs in tomato sauce, which Richard decided he must have been living on for days. He put it on the stove and poured out a jug of wine from a barrel.

'I should tell you something about your grandfather,' he said as they sat down on the veranda.

'Yes, please,' he replied, full of anticipation that there might be an answer to the mystery.

'I'm sorry to have to tell you this,' said Ikaros. He paused and walked over to the stove to give the meatballs a stir, as the sauce was beginning to bubble. 'Your grandfather is not buried in the grave at Suda Bay.' He waited for his statement to sink in before continuing. 'He disappeared and we wanted him to be remembered, but we had no body. We assumed he had to be dead because he vanished and was never seen again, so we buried a sheep wrapped in a blanket. Nobody was suspicious.'

Richard's jaw dropped. He didn't know what to say. The pain in his head came back, a hangover from whatever they'd drugged him with. He struggled for words. 'You've brought me all this way to tell me that? Why didn't you tell me earlier?' He tried not to be angry, but his frustration got the better of him. 'So even after all these years, you have no idea where my grandfather died?'

'I'm sorry to say that's true, but I've brought you here because I knew your grandfather very well. I can tell you about him, surely that must help? Besides, I can't just sit here alone knowing that Kohlenz is dead and gone to Hell. I need someone to celebrate with. Who better than you, the grandson of one of my greatest war comrades?'

'Kohlenz may have been dead for years but nobody knows for certain. No one saw his body so he might still be alive. I doubt it…but it's a possibility.'

Ikaros nodded, looking dismayed that there was still a small chance that Kohlenz might not be dead.

Richard mellowed a little, seeing the benefit of talking to somebody who knew his grandfather. 'Please go on,' he said. 'I'm sorry to be so rude.'

'Not at all,' said Ikaros. 'You're understandably upset that nobody knows where your grandfather lies or what happened to him.' He stirred the meatballs once more. 'Your grandfather and I escaped from a German firing squad and spent time in the mountains together. After Kohlenz destroyed the village, I was spitting blood, wanting to kill him. Nikos wanted it too, he's Callidora's brother, you see.' He stopped again to swig the red wine and sighed. 'Callidora committed suicide after Kohlenz raped her,' he said angrily.

'I know. I've seen her suicide letter to Lenny,' said Richard.

'So you have them. I've often wondered what happened to those letters. Do you have them with you?'

'I'm afraid not. The Arab I told you about stole them, but I can tell you what they said.'

'There's no need. I remember. They made me weep,' replied Ikaros. 'I just wanted to see her handwriting on the page. You see, I loved Callidora, but I was angry with her for seeing the German.'

'Hans.'

'Yes. His grave is in the cemetery. Shot by a jealous Greek. They thought it was me.'

The mention of Hans' grave reminded Richard of the references in the notebook. 'Did you ever meet my father?' he said.

Ikaros evaded Richard's eyes. 'Er…not directly…'

'What do you mean…not directly?' said Richard.

Ikaros stood up and stepped off the veranda. As the light faded from the setting sun, Richard watched as the old man filled a bucket from the stream and began watering his geraniums. 'I promised not to say anything,' he said.

'I'm his son, for Christ's sake,' Richard shouted, his anger building in his gut. He dashed over to where the old man continued to water his plants; his eyes fixed on the flowers. Richard took hold of Ikaros' arm. 'I have a right to know. Have you seen him?'

Ikaros continued to ignore Richard's pleas. 'You know, in one of Callidora's letters, she relates the story of the Cave of the Seven Sleepers. In those days, I couldn't read, so your grandfather read to me, which is why the detail doesn't stick in my mind.'

'Why don't you answer my question? Have you seen my father?' Richard repeated.

'There's something about that story, but I'm damned if I can remember what it is.'

Richard stared at Ikaros with increasing incredulity. 'Why won't you answer my question?' he said again, exasperation carved into his face.

'Because I can't,' Ikaros whispered. The old man appeared lost, trapped in his memories of the war, as if they'd happened a few weeks ago. 'I promised I'd say nothing.' The old man's face looked fatigued. 'Please don't make me say anything.'

Richard decided to change tack. 'Go on with your story,' he said.

'We set off for the German camp at Maleme, leaving your grandfather behind, hoping that we might get a chance to kill Kohlenz by sniper fire. Our guns were hopeless for a long-distance assassination attempt, but we each had a machine gun, stolen from a dead German. The only way we were going to kill him was to commit suicide by running at them, all guns blazing, in the hope that we could cut him down before they did the same to us.'

The meatballs were ready. He carried the pan over to the table and doled out portions for them both, covering the meat with liberal amounts of tomato sauce. He took

317

some salad leaves from the bowl before continuing. 'I realised that it was futile trying to get close to Kohlenz but Nikos had other ideas. We'd waited for two days and then one morning we saw Kohlenz leaving the camp in a car with Nikoletta.'

Richard looked up from his food, his eyes widening at the mention of the familiar name. 'I met Nikoletta in Athens. She told me about Kohlenz,' he said, noticing how the expression on Ikaros face changed. He seemed angry.

'I was really shocked to see her.' said Ikaros. 'Kohlenz had ruined another life. Nikos was in a seething rage. Without warning, he leapt out of the ditch and ran in towards the German car, firing wildly as he went. It was a death wish. He hit one of Kohlenz' escorts, but got nowhere near him. I can still see the bullets tearing Nikos apart. He was crazy and I'm ashamed that I never had the guts to die by his side. But what good would it do?'

Richard was silent, seeing that Ikaros was getting emotional, with tears running down the old man's face.

'I watched as Nikoletta ran to where Nikos fell and, picking up his limp body in her arms, hugging him. I could hear her crying even though I was one hundred metres away. Kohlenz just sat in his car, unmoved by what had happened; that a man hated Kohlenz so much he'd lose his life in a futile effort to kill him. Nikoletta went back to the car and started hitting Kohlenz with her fists. The Nazi just pushed her off and signalled to his driver to leave.' Ikaros stopped talking and wiped his eyes on his shirt. Taking another large glass of wine, he drank it straight down. 'Alcohol loosens the tongue,' he said, trying to counter the distress he felt.

'Why have you not kept in touch with Nikoletta?' enquired Richard.

Ikaros looked sad. 'Because she let me down.'

'What do you mean? She let you down?'

'I took pity on her and we married after the war. We had to move away to this valley to escape the persecution because she'd collaborated with the Nazis. One day she was attacked and nearly died. They cut off all her hair and beat her up. It took her months to recover. She stayed with me for almost six years in total isolation and then one day she left without warning.' Ikaros took another large gulp of his wine and lit a cigarette. 'I don't normally smoke,' he said, apologetically. 'All this talk of the past has made me miserable. The tobacco will cheer me up.' He exhaled the rough thick smoke of his Greek cigarettes and coughed. He sighed, weary; the years of pain taking their toll on his memory. 'It wasn't as if she didn't give it a try. Six years is a long time, but Nikoletta was a restless woman and didn't take kindly to living a lonely life. I could see she was unhappy even though she thought she loved me. I think her time with Kohlenz had affected her ability to react to kindness and she felt unworthy of me.' His voice was breaking with emotion. 'Besides, I suppose she knew that I never really loved her. Callidora was the only woman for me and she was dead.'

Richard wondered how Ikaros would react to the news that Nikoletta was also dead. 'I'm sorry to have to tell you this,' he said, a grave expression on his face.

'She's dead. Isn't she?'

'Yes. I'm afraid so.'

Ikaros was silent. He stood up and reached for a switch on one of the veranda pillars. Lights flickered to life, strung on a cable all-round the garden from tree to tree. Ikaros filled his bucket again and began watering his tomatoes, picking the odd fruit and using a fork to pull up a few weeds. A forlorn figure in a lonely valley, Richard thought. He decided not to tell him that Nikoletta was murdered.

After a few minutes, Ikaros returned to the table. 'You know I should have contacted Nikoletta and forgiven her for leaving me. At the time, anger and betrayal was all I could think about, but after all these years I can see the problem. At least that bastard Kohlenz is dead.'

'Yes,' said Richard. 'Did you ever tell this story to anyone else? It's very upsetting.'

'Yes, I did,' said Ikaros. 'A German woman, would you believe?'

'Was she a professor?'

'Yes, she was. It was a long time ago. In 1949. She told me she was researching the issue of German war crimes,' Ikaros said, taken aback by the question. 'She wanted to bring to the attention of the German people that it wasn't just Jews that were murdered by their countrymen. She asked me about the scroll and of course I said nothing other than I'd heard the arguments about giving it to the Germans...Why are you asking this?'

'I think she knows what happened to my father after 9/11 when he was declared dead,' Richard replied looking directly into Ikaros' eyes. 'I think you do to.'

'I'm sorry.'

Richard could see Ikaros was wavering. 'My father didn't die, did he?' He looked into Ikaros' eyes, which gave away the truth. 'I'm right, aren't I. He is in grave danger. I know he's here on this island. I've got to warn him.'

'Your father wants you left out of this. That's his wish not mine...I'll honour his wishes.'

'Do you know where he is now?'

'I don't.' Ikaros appeared relieved.

Maybe he's telling the truth, thought Richard. 'Do you know where he might be or why he's on the island?'

'He phoned me, said he needed somewhere quiet to stay for a few days. In the mountains near where Tirata used to be. I found a deserted farmhouse belonging to a friend who intended to renovate it for the tourists but never got round to it.'

'But he's not there now?'

'No. Never was. He never turned up…As I told you, I don't know where he is.'

Richard stopped and thought for a minute. He had to be near Abdul. Find Abdul and he was sure his father would appear. 'Please continue. I shouldn't have interrupted you.'

'I'm sorry I can't answer your question about your father,' Ikaros said. He pushed the meatball around the plate and then pushed his plate aside, unable to eat.

'So what happened to you after Nikos had been killed?' said Richard.

'Fortunately, the Germans didn't mount any kind of search, so it was easy for me to disappear back into the mountains. They must have thought that Nikos was a lone gunman. The death of Nikos affected me greatly and as I trudged back to the hideout, I was falling into a deeper despair. Imagine my increasing sadness when I discovered that Lenny had gone and so had all the other men that made up our resistance cell. I stayed the night in the cave, but when morning came, the daylight revealed something that I should tell you about. Especially as I told the German professor.'

'What was that?' said Richard.

'Inside the cave, someone had drawn a pattern on the walls, like points on a map.'

Richard's mind began to race. 'Can you remember anything about the points on the drawing?'

'It's been a long time since I saw it, scrawled on the wall. They must have used charcoal from a stick taken from a fire. It was difficult to read. It was really a list of places joined by lines.' He thought for a moment, recalling what he's seen all those years ago. 'At one point, the lines crossed. Let me see if I can remember the names.' He thought for a moment. 'They were Ephesus and Patmos…Aleppo and Chania,' he said. 'And one other…begins with an L…' Ikaros stood up and paced the veranda, his head down trying to recall. 'I know,' he said, excited, 'it's Lapithos…that's it…Lapithos. I don't suppose it is still there now. I saw it only a few days after it was written so it hadn't faded. Is it significant?'

Richard jumped out of his chair and hugged the old man. 'This is fantastic,' he shouted. 'I suddenly feel incredibly hungry.' He sat back down at the table and began swallowing the meatballs at a furious pace. Ikaros laughed, pleased that he'd given something to Richard that he could use.

'What is it?' he asked, mirroring Richard's excitement.

'This is the lead I've been looking for. It means something, I'm sure of it, if only I could work out what it is. These names were written in Callidora's Bible, but not in Lenny's hand. They were written by Callidora. This must hold the secret of where the scroll is hidden.'

'I thought it was something to do with the Cave of the Seven Sleepers.'

'There is no Cave of the Seven Sleepers. That was in Ephesus.'

Ikaros looked puzzled. 'Are you sure?'

Richard could not sleep. His brain worked overtime; the adrenalin rush overriding his intense fatigue. He'd known all along that there was no Cave of the Seven Sleepers in Crete, pretending it existed to throw Abdul off the scent. The scroll was in a cave near Tirata. That much he was sure, but which cave? And why had Callidora written about the cave in her letter if there was no such cave in Crete? There must be hundreds in the area and if there had been a landfall, it would make the job of finding it that much harder, if not impossible. The only chance was to find a link between the cave in Crete and the Cave of the Seven Sleepers in Turkey. The writing on the cave wall was all he had, but in truth, how was he going to make the association of these names with a cave somewhere in Crete? Ephesus was named in the list and so was Chania. So a link did exist. He'd learned somewhere that in ancient Islamic civilisations lines dissecting holy places had been used to pinpoint the location of Mecca. Maybe this same method could be used to identify the cave. But he had no time to pursue such a tenuous link. His earlier optimism he'd shown Ikaros was turning to despair. He tossed over and over in his makeshift bed and groaned at the sheer discomfort of the wood boards he was lying on.

At least Abdul was no further forward, so it was not too late. If only he could find his father. He dreaded seeing his father again but was sure his father would have the answer.

Fifty miles away, Abdul had already worked out where the scroll was hidden. He had one advantage over Richard. Richard's father had told Abdul where to look.

Chapter Thirty-Nine

Crete, Greece. June 30th 1941

She decided to live in the moment she struck the water. It was an instinctive reaction to stay alive, something she never expected.

Until that second, she'd waited for the impact, knowing there was no going back. She'd closed her eyes, sliding down the mountain, praying in her last seconds of life that it would be quick. She'd wondered what the pain would be like, her brains smashed against rock, where there was no resistance to death. But here, there was no pain. When the water overwhelmed her, the sensation of the end of life did not materialise. Down she went, dazed by the impact and unsure why she was still alive.

The water gave her an option; she could drown or live. She chose to live.

Breaking through the surface, gasping for air, she swam to the edge of the pool and dragged herself onto some stone that stood by the side of what looked like a small underground lake. Light shone down at her in sharply defined beams from where the crevasse opened. It was a hundred feet at least to the break in the roof. Climbing was out of the question. Maybe she was going to die after all, as everybody would assume that falling down the crevasse meant certain death. Nobody, least of all her, realised what was below.

No taste of salt lingered on her lips, suggesting an underground reservoir filled by a river. As she watched the light flickering, causing ripples of stars across the lake, she thought she noticed the current. She sank back onto the rock contemplating why she now wanted to survive. Her suicide was meant to be quick, but dying at the bottom of this hole would prolong her agony. She had to try and escape. Her faith in God had to mean something. Had her times with the monks and all those books been wasted?

It was all becoming clear now. Everything she'd ever done had led her to the moment she'd discovered the scroll. Without her education, she would not have realised its significance, and to find it with Hans, a theology student, could only be destiny and the will of God. To understand the significance of the scroll and to save it from the Germans was what God wanted. Kohlenz had raped her because she refused to give up the secret and now she was sure she was carrying his seed. A sign from God? The fog in her mind lifted. She had found her reason to live.

Without further thought, she lowered herself gently into the water again and followed the ripples on the surface. It took her only two minutes to reach where the current seemed to disappear at the edge of the lake, but there was no way through. The river must flow under the rock, she decided.

'You can't give up now,' she shouted, her voice echoing around the cavern.

Taking a deep breath, she went under, allowing her hand to touch the edge of the rock as she got deeper. About five feet down, she found a curve. There was a way out. But how long was it? Turning, she resurfaced and swam back to the edge. Out of the water, once more, she removed some clothes to reduce drag. For another moment, she sat shivering by the water's edge, thinking again about what she had to do and decided it was her only chance. If she couldn't get through she'd drown and be dead like she always intended. The decision was simple. If it had to be, she was ready to die. She'd leave it to God to decide, like she'd always done. Without warning, a warm breeze wafted over her face, coming from nowhere. She smiled, a wave of emotion flooding her senses. She knew God was protecting her. The smile had not left her face when she sank back into the pool. She would survive.

Reaching the edge once more, she filled her lungs with as much air as she could hold and without further hesitation went under. Finding the channel was easy, she turned and began to swim along the river, keeping as near to the roof as she could so she could feel the surface where she might find air. Swimming against the current wasn't easy, but she made progress. The further she moved down the channel, the more desperate she got. The point of no return passed by, but still no space to breathe. Further into the hole she went, her lungs beginning to burst, her cheeks bulging and only darkness before her.

It was no use. There was no air. Her lungs were about to burst. She was about to give in and let the water fill her lungs; drowning would be quick. As a final act of desperation, she turned on her back and allowed her face to float up to the roof of the river. Her lips touched the stone and she spluttered. Bubbles of air exploded from her lungs, a comforting sound in her ears, as the last vestiges of life were leaving. There was no alternative, but to allow her lungs to fill with water.

Some water did enter, but there was also air. There must have been less than two inches of space between the roof and the water line.

Enough to breathe.

She stopped and tried to fill her lungs. Water lapped around her face, hampering her attempts to take on air, but a chance to survive had to be taken. The current was light and she managed to ease herself along the hole, taking what little air she could.

Without warning, her hand slipped upwards. She needed no second prompt. Her head shattered the surface like a whale coming up to breathe after hours at the bottom of the ocean. Fresh air almost hurt, as her lungs fought to absorb as much oxygen as they could find. It was the same air she breathed barely an hour ago when she'd jumped, but somehow it tasted sweeter.

The pool must be at the bottom of a waterfall, she decided, as she climbed out onto dry land. It would rage in the winter, but it had long since dried up for the summer. It was secluded, she thought, giving her safety while she dried out her clothes without the threat of German patrols.

She began to remove her clothing, placing it on a branch where it might dry best in the sun. Her nerves frayed, her heartbeat quickened as she struggled with the fastenings. Steep woods grew down towards the water; the trees rustling in the warm summer wind. She peered warily towards the undergrowth, sure that Germans would emerge from behind the trees at any minute. She'd seen so much these last few days and with her clothes off, her nakedness made her feel even more vulnerable.

Her caution was justified.

Three soldiers appeared out of nowhere, rushing down towards her, waving their guns and laughing. They were younger than her and enjoying their sport.

Callidora, screamed, but the soldiers were having none of it. She stood on one side of the pool, the water separating them, but not for long. One of them jumped in and dashed across the pool, splashing and shouting. She backed away, trying to swing at the man with her foot, but he took hold of her ankle and pulled her into the water. She thrashed out screaming and kicking as the soldier carried her.

Reaching the other side, he laid her on the ground, but she stood up, defiant, deciding it would do no good to scream and no good to be exposed to his advances. She tried to be brave, fighting back tears, but the thought that she might be raped again made her collapse into a fit of sobbing. The other two were losing interest, shouting to go. But the one who'd grabbed her continued to leer. She could see the lust in his eyes. He had blond hair, like Hans, but his eyes were narrow and troubled, capable of bad things, scanning her body, which left little to his imagination. She cursed herself for trying to dry her clothes, because now she stood before him in nothing but a corset. She could see that the others were leaving and that she'd be on her own with this man. Just as she'd refused to die in the hole, she would not let him have her.

Alone, he began to edge forward towards her. She stepped back again, her eyes darting from left to right. *What could she do?* His gun was near.

She forced herself to smile and then allowed her fingers to trail over her bosom. She could see him relaxing, sensing an easier time than he'd expected. He lowered his hands to his flies and began to loosen the buttons. She waited, smiling, moving closer to him and then lying down, as if she was preparing herself for him. His trousers fell to his ankles. He was helpless, waddling forward.

The gun was in her hands and in one movement, she pulled the trigger. The kick of the machine gun surprised her and it sprayed several bullets in his direction. At least two found their mark, splattering blood onto the trees around him, killing him instantly, with his trousers down and shock etched on his face. She revelled in the sense of revenge, but knew she only had seconds to disappear.

The other soldiers had heard the shots. She could hear their voices, but instead of running back, they must have taken cover, waiting for reinforcements. This was going to give her vital minutes to get away.

She was thankful she still had her shoes, but only wore a corset. To get away there was only one way out and that was upwards. A narrow gap in the rock would provide cover but she needed to be on the flat where she could move quickly. The climbing slowed her down, but she knew how the rocks would be formed. Looking down, she could see the soldiers assembling below. Machine-gun fire ricocheted off the rocks around her, but she kept climbing. Callidora had a different attitude now. If a bullet hit her, she would die, but somehow she felt invincible and had no fear of dying. Up she went in full view of their guns.

The Germans did not follow and for the first time, as the security of darkness began to fall, she felt safe.

But she'd killed another German soldier. There was no going back to the village. She'd be hunted now, not just by the soldiers but also the collaborators helping the Germans. There was nowhere to hide and nowhere to go. As the sun set she had to take her bearings and try and get to a position where she knew where she was. At first she walked with the instinct of someone who knows the mountains, but when the stars came out, she took a fix on the North Star and begin to plot her direction of travel.

Hunger sapped any drops of energy she still retained. She was wandering aimlessly in an easterly direction in the vain hope that she might find someone who'd help her, stumbling as she walked, getting weaker and weaker, footsteps slower and slower. Her legs gave way. Sinking to her knees, she could go no further. She crouched in a foetal position and warm air blew over her face once more, just as it had done in the cavern. If she didn't find food, she'd die on these mountains. It was getting desperate.

Chapter Forty

Crete, Greece. July 2nd 1941

The haunting shadows disrupted any attempt at sleep in the cave. If Lenny closed his eyes, nightmares plagued his mind, forcing him to wake up. He didn't know whether it was fear or the cold, but he couldn't stop shivering, however close he crawled to the smouldering fire. He missed the comradeship of his fellow resistance fighters. After Nikos and Ikaros had left, he couldn't keep the others by his side. It was Nikos they followed, not him. They wanted to return to the villages and fight to the death, if that is what it would take to defeat the Germans. And who could blame them? What good were they doing here with him?

Before darkness had fallen, he'd spent what was left of the day trying to fix the wireless that had been smashed after an airdrop from Cairo. Being alone played tricks with his senses and any optimism he still retained began to evaporate. A black cloud of despair descended over him, and he knew that he'd have to find other SOE men if he was to lift himself out of the misery that was enveloping him. Without a wireless, finding these men would be difficult, but he knew he had to try. If he stayed waiting for Nikos and Ikaros to return, he'd go mad with nightmares. Images of the dead bodies in the village streets rising like spirits, blood on their faces, pointing at him with accusing stares. Innocent people, he'd been unable to help. He had to make amends and began to curse himself for not joining Nikos and Ikaros in their mission to kill Kohlenz. He should have ignored their heroic rhetoric that killing Kohlenz should be carried out by a Cretan.

July 3rd 1941

The night passed slowly, but as dawn came and faint beams of light began to pierce the cave entrance, he succumbed to sleep. If he'd stayed awake just a few minutes longer, he'd have seen the man enter the cave and creep towards him.

When he awoke, it was too late. He heard the clicking sound of a gun being cocked and opened his eyes.

'Get up,' shouted the man with the gun; his voice sounded uneasy, even nervous.

'Kostas,' said Lenny, trying not to sound or look surprised. 'Kind of you to drop by when all the fighting's been done.' He spat in the dust, a clear insult that Greeks understood only too well. 'Isn't it strange how you're still alive when everybody else is dead?' He didn't wait for an answer but piled on the pressure. 'And wasn't it nice of you to set up Ikaros for the murder of the German?' Distain oozed out of Lenny, like he was lancing a boil and he didn't know when to stop and bandage the wound. 'Do you realise what you've done by aggravating the Germans?' He looked at him and sneered. 'Yes, you do, don't you? What's more, you've saved your own skin.' There was no use pretending to be scared in circumstances like this, he decided, Kostas was a coward and if he felt vulnerable, he was more likely to make a mistake.

'Get up, get up,' Kostas shouted in a staccato fashion as if he'd learned something from the Germans way of issuing orders. Lenny could see he was far from relaxed about the situation. 'Put your hands up. Go out of the cave. Now.' He gripped the gun in two hands, finger on the trigger, but he was shaking so much his aim wasn't sharp.

331

Lenny calculated that if he moved quickly, he could take him out with one swift kick.

'Tell me something, Kostas,' he said. 'How did you manage to keep your rifle straight when you shot the German paratrooper?' Lenny knew he was pushing his luck by goading him so much, but for now, it seemed like the right thing to do. He saw Kostas trying to bring his shaking wrist under control, but he wasn't having much success. Lenny put his hands up and continued to face Kostas. He walked backwards slowly, never losing eye contact, making Kostas nervous until he reached daylight outside the cave.

'Over there,' said Kostas, pointing at a straight tree. He picked up some rope and moved closer to tie him up.

Lenny swung his foot upwards into Kostas' groin. The Greek screamed, bending double with pain. A follow through and he had his hand on Kostas' wrist, swinging the gun out of harm's way, but unable to stop it firing. The gun fired, echoing around the mountains. Disarming Kostas was easy, having taken a firm hold of his wrist, Lenny twisted it until he dropped the weapon.

'You really shouldn't have fired that gun,' he shouted at Kostas. 'We've got to move.'

Lenny shoved Kostas forward, prodding him with his gun, a German Luger, he noticed, arousing his suspicions that there might be more trouble nearby. He picked up the only machine gun he had, with four magazines of bullets as an extra precaution. 'Move,' he shouted.

They didn't get far.

Bullets ricocheted off the trees. A German patrol must have heard the gunshot and started to investigate. The first bullets missed, pinning them down.

Kostas shouted. 'I've a British soldier holding me here.'

The Germans in the patrol didn't understand the Greek and kept firing. They'd be calling for reinforcements.

He'd have to act quickly while there were only four of them. He watched as Kostas stood up, moving forward with his hands up, thinking they'd understood him that they wouldn't fire.

He was only partly right. A bullet caught him in his ribs, blasting him sideways, wounded and out of action. He'd been right that the Germans wouldn't fire, but the bullet hadn't come from the Germans. It had come from the shrubland to his left. Somebody out there was providing protection.

Someone else was firing.

Lenny didn't need to wait. He moved forward drawing fire, sparing with his bullets, knowing he was short of ammo. But as he took cover, one of the soldiers screamed. Lenny saw bullets cutting into the German's body.

Not from his gun.

He wasn't going to ask questions. His machine gun cracked back into action as he began rushing forward. A grenade was coming his way; a missile, floating through the air and for a tantalising moment hanging there before it began to fall. Exposed to fire, determined to stop the explosion, he dived forward, arms stretched, reaching out. In his mind it seemed an age.

Catching it by the handle, he tossed it back in one sweet movement, relieved to see the explosion twenty feet from him. When the smoke cleared, he could still hear gunfire, not his own, but on his side.

In three minutes, all four were dead, but he'd killed only two of them.

Silence resumed in the forest. 'Whoever you are, show yourself,' he shouted to the trees, trying to rouse his benefactor. 'Thank you for your help,' he spoke with a reassuring voice. 'Come forward, I owe you my life.' There was barely a sound except from the moaning of Kostas, who was losing blood. 'The Germans will send reinforcements. We've got to go,' he shouted again, his voice echoing back at him. But still nothing could be heard.

'Don't leave me,' pleaded the Greek. 'I'm losing blood.' He was clearly in agony and dying. If he was still alive when the Germans arrived, he'd betray Lenny's position without protest.

Lenny didn't need to think twice. 'Consider it a mercy killing.' He lifted his gun. 'For all those people you sent to death with your stupid act of petty jealousy,' his voice was faltering, his hand shaking as he lifted the gun, levelling it at Kostas' head. A brief silence hung over the air and then he fired. He turned away, slightly disgusted with himself for the execution.

'He was a traitor,' a voice spoke from behind him.

Chapter Forty-One

Crete, Greece. August 4th 2005

Abdul stood at the foot of the gorge, staring at the cave's entrance. This is the place, he thought, but what he saw before him confirmed his worst fears. A rock fall had tipped down the gorge, engulfing the entrance to the cave. Huge boulders stood between him and the secret he craved.

He clenched his fist, crumpling the letter in his hand: the letter that told him where to find the cave and why he should kill Kleiner. A boy handed it to him when they docked in Gavdos. That was the problem. If he had nothing to hide, then why would David Helford write to him? If they were friends, why wouldn't he show his face?

He had no regrets about killing Kleiner, who he'd detested since he first saw him in Afghanistan. The letter told him that Kleiner was responsible for the death of Sheikh Zabor. He could still see the image of the helicopter in his mind, carrying his great mentor, exploding into thousands of pieces before disappearing into the sea in a matter of seconds. The note told him that a GPS tracker guided the pilot in to its target from the lining of the Nazi's jacket. At first Abdul thought it unlikely that a neo-Nazi would work for Mossad but his anger inclined him to action. He killed Kleiner and enjoyed the moment. There was no need to ask further questions, except one which had nothing to do with the German.

How did David Helford know all this?

The question nagged him, demanding an answer during every second of his long trek into the depths of the gorge. He wanted to believe that his friend was on his side because he'd given him the secret of the Cave of the Seven Sleepers. Abdul knew all about the original story, which is told in the Holy Koran. He also knew that it originated in Ephesus, where John of Patmos had been bishop and where he'd met Barnabas. It was almost as if the name of the cave had been ordained to keep the scroll. But this cave had a different story. Helford's letter completed the mystery. The cave he faced had been named after seven families who'd hidden in it, only to be slaughtered by the Turks while sleeping. Perhaps there were more than seven families, but whoever named the cave wanted to draw this parallel with the holy story. It all made perfect sense. In the holy story, the sleepers had been trapped and suspended in a supernatural timeless sleep, just as the scroll was now, trapped behind immoveable rocks.

Abdul laid his prayer mat down on a clean piece of rock and took out a compass to confirm the direction of Mecca. Kneeling he prayed to Allah for guidance in how he should avenge the death of the Sheikh. He prayed for a just and holy jihad.

After prayer, he stood up and gazed at his surroundings. Just standing there at the foot of the gorge, in front of the cave's entrance, filled him with an overwhelming desire not to be beaten. He felt so small against the might of the landscape, but with strong faith, Allah would allow him to move these very mountains. The beauty of the gorge stretched before him. He allowed his eyes to drift up the sheer face of the rock on both sides, marvelling at the wonders of nature. Cypress trees found the most unlikely places to take root, acting as a stark contrast to the white rock. He looked at his map to pinpoint his position and to retrace his steps back up to the top. The gorge floor opened out at this point, providing plenty of space to move the rock away. The path he'd followed was wide enough to bring in equipment to assist with the opening of the entrance. Earth-moving equipment was one way it could be done, but that would take too long. Money and dynamite would answer the question.

Within three hours, he'd set up an account with the Greco Zeus Private Bank. He would use the bank only for the transfer of funds and therefore not in breach of Sharia law. The bank was known to him as being relaxed about money-laundering procedures, requiring just an assurance that the account would be credited with three hundred thousand euros the very next day. A text to a special number belonging to the Bin Alim Saudi construction company, owned by Sheikh Zabor Bin Hitani, and the funds were in his account before close of play. That somebody wanted to bring money into Greece, when most of the rich were moving it out, raised a few eyebrows, but nothing more. The Greeks are used to deceiving the authorities, he thought. A transaction like this was normal. He had become Doctor Zayan Bashir, an archaeologist, prepared to spend lots of money to excavate the cave. He never ceased to be surprised at how easily his American accent and passport opened doors. They impressed more than his credentials at Harvard, which had been entirely fabricated. Next, he established that the government owned the land the cave stood on and when Abdul paid twenty-five thousand euros to a bank account in Cyprus, crediting an official responsible for such things, mountains were indeed moved and he had his permit.

Finding a mining company in Crete with expertise to plant sticks of dynamite in the right place was not as easy as opening a bank account. If you ask around somebody will know, he'd been told at the bank when he'd enquired. Sure enough while drinking a coffee, a man directed him to talk to Theo Georgakis. He'll be having lunch in George's Taverna, he was told.

Dressed in an ill-fitting suit with a figure gained by eating kebab rather than smashing rocks, Theo did not look like a miner, but Abdul knew he had no time to be choosy. There was no doubt that Theo wanted the work, gushing with enthusiasm at the sight of wads of Euros waved in front of his face. His little company was more used to mining gypsum that could be sold for fertiliser than moving rocks weighing hundreds of tons.

'We will learn,' Theo said in broken English.

'I have no time,' said Abdul. 'I need the entrance cleared in a day. Do it and there will be a bonus for you.' Abdul could see Theo didn't understand, but every time Abdul produced more money, the language barrier fell away in an instant.

August 5th 2005

True to his word, Theo arrived as daylight began to pierce the gorge's narrow opening. Abdul had spent the night dozing by a fire, waiting for morning to come. He watched through his binoculars as a caravan of donkeys wound their way along the track. More light found its way down the side of the gorge. Silhouettes of rock with an almost shadowy existence became solid masses, changing colour as more light penetrated the air. A cart carrying a mini digger led the procession, while Theo and his men walked alongside other donkeys, weighed down with enough dynamite to blow up the whole of the White Mountains.

It was the start of his third day on Crete. He wanted to alert his leaders in North Waziristan about the killing of the Sheikh, but he knew it was too risky. The only thing he could do was carry out the wishes of his murdered leader. He had to find the scroll and read it to the world. Whatever he did, he must carry out the Sheikh's wishes to the letter.

Pleased that the men were working hard to achieve his objective, he sat on a rock and waited. Logistically, operating at the bottom of a gorge presented all sorts of problems. While the men laid the dynamite, others began moving the smaller rocks. They tried various methods, but the donkeys came to the rescue. Once harnessed, their amazing strength was used to pull the rocks free. Theo was a good leader, organising his men with precision, and while the gorge was still cool, pushing them to keep working.

With all his men hard at work, Theo lit a cigarette and, leaving it drooping from his mouth, walked over to where Abdul was sitting. 'Do you see the way the rock is inverted, forming a natural groove?' He spoke in Greek and then laughed at Abdul's blank look. He took a piece of chalk out of his pocket and began to draw a diagram on a stone, showing Abdul where the dynamite was going. He superimposed an arch where he imagined the entrance to the cave would be and then a large arrow pointed at it. Turning away, he gesticulated towards the mountainside, trying to explain how his picture fitted into the geography of the mountain.

It took nearly three hours to prepare the mountainside for the explosion. At last, the fuse for the dynamite was being unwound off an enormous reel. Abdul and the rest of the men began to walk away, following Theo as he placed the fuse where the chances of it blowing out before it reached its destination were minimised. Sweat soaked Theo's shirt as he worked on the final connection with great care. He'd inspected each piece of dynamite, making sure they were all in the right place. Abdul was impressed by his attention to detail. They'd walked about two hundred metres back before Theo signalled that they should all stop. He waved at them to take cover behind the rocks and then, with the end of his cigarette, ignited the fuse.

The silence before the explosion took an age. Abdul thought it had failed, but looking across towards Theo he could see he remained calm, confident that it would go off.

He was right.

It wasn't just one big blast, but repeated small explosions, like a firework display, but much louder. The noise echoed around the rock and bounced the blast off the walls, accentuating the sound with a deafening pitch, forcing Abdul to cover his ears. He'd heard explosions in Afghanistan before and these were tame by comparison, but protecting his ears had always been a priority. Looking out in the direction of the cave, a great plume of dust was rushing towards them. He covered his mouth and buried his head in his hands, waiting for it to pass. Memories of that day on September 11th 2001 when the cloud of dust he'd witnessed had been a thousand times larger, flooded into his mind.

A few more moments went by before Theo shouted and the rest of his crew stepped out from the shelter of the rocks, moving back towards the cave where they hoped it would be open to the world. Abdul felt a rushing sense of gloom that they hadn't done enough to forge a way in. His premonition looked justified. The rocks had parted and were in piles on either side, but there was no evidence that an entrance had been found. Abdul clambered onto the rocks and began climbing over to where they'd thought that the entrance was hidden. It seemed hopeless.

Theo came to join him and barked orders off to his team. A harness was lashed around a rock and a donkey began to walk while the men pushed to budge the boulder he'd focused on. A sudden surge forward by the donkey showed some movement and gravity took over. The rock was free. Theo bent down and shone a flashlight down a crack, no more than a few inches wide and certainly not wide enough to get in a human.

But wide enough for a stick of dynamite.

A small detonation this time, which didn't need them to stand quite so far away, but the results were more spectacular. When the dust cleared once more, there was a wider gap, this time a hole with a diameter no more than four feet. Small, but wide enough to get a man through.

Abdul took the flash light from Theo and crawled into the cave, almost bent double to avoid hitting his head on the roof. After a few feet, the cave opened out into a large chamber. He shone his torch up onto the roof. A huge natural cavern towered above him like the dome of a great mosque, the floor and ceiling decorated by nature with stalactites and stalagmites creating a wondrous sense of the greatness of Allah. He'd spent a lot of time in Afghanistan hiding in caves, dodging American bombers, so the cave seemed like home and not a place to fear.

But there was something else.

It was like breaking into a crypt; bones littered the floor, not laid down in reverent poses that befitted the dead, but prostrate where their bodies fell. His torch caught a skull first and then as he slowed his movement, more skeletons came into view. There were several children, huddled together, as if they'd laid down and died in the arms of their loved ones. Even with a torch, the darkness was unnerving, such that if his hand veered even slightly, he lost his bearings and struggled to find his sense of direction. He stumbled blindly, searching for something, but the darkness made his task impossible. The torch barely provided any depth of vision and he knew that if he went any further into the cave he'd be lost. He turned, and for an agonising moment, he couldn't see where he'd come in. He called out and Theo appeared with a candle to guide his path back to the entrance.

The sight of the light quickened his pace and, moving forward across damp rock, he slipped. As he fell, the torch spun out of his hand and crashed out of reach, its light useless. His instinct to reach out could not stop him falling. He winced as his hand grazed some stone, jagged like glass, and his palms hit strewn debris of all shapes, digging into his skin. The pain rippled through his body

341

and in the darkness, he couldn't assimilate what he'd hit. He ran his hand over his knee, which felt tender but not broken. But there was something else intruding into the pain of his fall. Something softer and more welcoming.

He was touching cloth.

Theo had seen him fall. Climbing into the cave, with a brighter paraffin light, he reached Abdul in a few minutes. The larger light was all Abdul needed. Theo helped him onto his feet, while he groaned with pain when his weight rested on his ankle. Standing up at last, he looked around.

'Shine your light down there,' he gestured to Theo, pointing down to the ground. Theo obliged and moved his light along the ground. 'I'm looking for something soft,' he said.

It was a blanket, lying at his feet where he fell, threadbare, but still intact, tied in a parcel, secured by a rope. He picked it up and pointed to the entrance.

Outside, he handed the money over to Theo and said thank you. Theo was overjoyed, chuckling to himself as he counted the notes twice, still unable to believe he'd just had the biggest payday in his life.

'We help you some more...yes,' he said in his broken English, pocketing the rolls of notes.

Abdul touched his nose. 'Tell nobody I'm here.'

Theo touched his own nose in unison. Assuring Abdul that he'd say nothing.

'There is something I need,' said Abdul.

'We bring you food. Yes?'

'Food, light, a tent. Lots of light,' said Abdul. 'I'll work on my own in the cave.'

'Doctor, we'll bring you a generator, big light.' He smiled and shook his hand firmly.

'Good,' said Abdul. 'I'll pay well.'

Theo shouted orders to his men to pick up their equipment and load their donkeys, ready to move out. After thirty minutes, Abdul was alone again, turning his attention to the blanket wrapped in rope. He could not contain his excitement, but didn't want Theo to see. As far as he was concerned it was just a mouldy blanket that was no use to anyone. As Abdul unfolded the blanket, he discovered a muslin bag at the centre of the parcel, tied with leather cord. His heart pounded with excitement. Could this be the scroll? His hand shook as he lowered it into the bag. There was something there. His hand quivered, he was nervous that he was about to see something profoundly important to the conflict between the Crusaders and the Muslim world.

Chapter Forty-Two

Crete, Greece. August 5th 2005

It was past 6 a.m. when Richard opened his eyes. Ikaros didn't have a spare bed so Richard had curled up on the veranda with a pillow and a blanket and made do. His head still hurt and the hard-wooden boards he'd been sleeping on only added to his aches and pains, but his exhaustion had got the better of him and he'd slept soundly. His brain switched on as he lay there, playing out all the probabilities over and over in his head. He needed a map of the Mediterranean and the Middle East to see if he could establish some links with the names that Ikaros had found on the wall. Would they link with the clues he'd found in the Bible? He felt there was a pattern emerging, but he didn't have time to figure it out for himself. Finding Abdul was more pressing. He fumbled for his mobile, swearing when he saw no signal. Maybe if he called Brian, the guys at Vauxhall Cross would crack it more quickly than he ever could.

Ikaros was already up, making some coffee.

'Why didn't you wake me?' Richard said as he stood up. He'd slept in his clothes and felt dirty without a shave or a shower, but being smelly was preferable to Ikaros' wash facilities. He ran his hand through his hair in a half-hearted attempt to smarten up. 'I've got to get to a phone, Ikaros.' he said impatiently. 'Can we take your car? There's no signal here.'

'Take it, my friend. I know you'll return it, but I won't come with you.'

Richard sipped the black coffee that Ikaros had made. The heat stung his lips, forcing him to spit it out. 'I'm sorry, Ikaros. I can't wait for this to cool. Please can I have your keys? I'll fill the tank for you.'

Ikaros handed him the keys and he sprinted to the car. He got in and fired up the engine. As he reversed, he glanced back towards the house, seeing Ikaros jumping up and down, waving his hands.

'Shit,' he cursed, cutting the engine. He wound down the window.

'Come back, Richard,' Ikaros cried, continuing to wave his hands. 'I've remembered something. It must be significant.'

Richard got out of the car and trotted back down the hill. 'What is it?' he said, a note of irritation in his voice.

Ikaros was cautious with his reply. 'The Cave of the Seven Sleepers, there's one here on Crete. It's not the real cave, but its story is similar, which is where it gets its name.'

Richard's eyes widened. 'That's great news. Where is this cave?' he said, feeling his excitement grow.

'There's nothing left now.'

'What?' exclaimed Richard, exasperated at having his hopes raised and dashed in the space of a few seconds.

'The cave's gone...no more. A landslide buried it, don't know when it happened.'

'Show me.' Richard raised his voice, finding it hard to stay calm. 'Do you have a map of Crete?'

Ikaros went inside and produced a rather torn tourist map. It was not very detailed. 'It's somewhere near where our old village was,' he said, pointing at the area on the map. 'You know, where we lived in Tirata, before the Germans burnt it to the ground.' He folded the map up, recognising it hadn't been much help. 'I've never been to where the cave was supposed to be. I can't tell you the exact location. Try the curator at the Archaeological Museum in Chania, he'll know. Can't think what they call him.'

Richard turned back towards the car.

'By the way, Richard, you'll need this.'

He swung back to face him and saw the old man standing with a double barrel shotgun and a box of cartridges. It was a shock to see it and to think he might need it. 'Thank you,' he said softly, taking hold of the gun. He'd held a gun like this before, but only to shoot pheasant. This was going to be different.

Ten minutes later, he stopped the car and looked at his mobile once more. He smiled, seeing the bars to confirm he had a signal from Vodafone. He punched out the special number Brian had given him, breathing a sigh of relief when he heard the ringing tone.

'Brian. I've had no signal on my phone for ages. Did you manage to get the details of the ship?'

'Do you know what time it is?

'I know, Brian. I'm sorry. Can you talk?'

'Hang on. I need to get out of bed before I wake Mrs Soper.'

'I'm sorry, Brian. Apologise to her for me.'

He waited, listening to sounds of Brian stumbling about, doing his best not to wake up his wife who he could hear snoring in the background.

After a few more minutes, a crashing noise came from the mobile, telling him Brian had dropped the phone onto the floor. 'Shit,' he heard Brian say. More noise as he picked the phone up 'Right, I'm in my study. The ship has not docked in Heraklion. It's moored up on the island of Gavdos.'

'Where's Gavdos?'

'Just off the south cost of Crete. Near Hora Sphakion.'

'What about the satellite pass over Crete?'

Brian didn't reply.

'What are you keeping from me, Brian?'

'I'm sorry, Richard, Rowena wouldn't authorise. Too costly and would require too much explanation. We can't tell people what we're up to.'

Richard sighed. 'Okay. I'm not surprised. I'll just have to find him on my own. Abdul is on Crete. I believe he's somewhere in the White Mountains searching for the scroll. Trouble is, it will be impossible to find him as the area is so remote.'

'And what about your father?'

'Nothing.'

Brian was silent. Richard noticed Brian's breathing into the phone had become quicker.

'What's going on, Brian? You know something.'

Brian hesitated again. 'I shouldn't tell you this but you need to know. We are getting intelligence that they're planning a terrorist spectacular.'

'On Crete?'

'Yes. I'm sure it's connected…Abdul is behind it…it's…'

'Spit it out, Brian?'

'We believe your father is involved.'

Richard's heart pounded. His mouth was dry. 'You still think my father is a terrorist. Is that it, Brian?

'Yes, we do.'

Richard sighed. 'Whatever my father is, he's not a terrorist.'

Brian said nothing for several seconds. 'We've got to take Abdul out but not until we can be sure where the target is.'

Richard decided to say nothing more on his father being a terrorist. In the recess of his brain, he wondered if he could kill his father for king and country. He doubted that he could even kill Abdul. How was he going to neutralise Abdul? He had no idea. 'Look, Brian, take these place names down for me. I need you to get some of the boffins in Vauxhall Cross to look at it for me. There is a connection that leads to a location. It's the location I'm trying to pinpoint.'

'What names?'

'Ephesus, Patmos, Lapithos, Aleppo, Chania and the Cave of Machpelah in Hebron.'

Brian, repeated the names one by one as he wrote them down. 'Okay, got that. Where's Lapithos?'

'I was hoping you could tell me.'

'The name rings a bell. I think it's in Cyprus.'

'There are some other clues that are connected in some way to the names I've given you. These are, *Foot of the Mountain,* which was underlined from a Bible phrase in Exodus about Moses. The *Cave of the Seven Sleepers*, which is both a Christian apocryphal story and in the Holy Koran. Finally, there is this extract of poetry from Byron.'

'Hang on, let me write that down.' There was a pause while Brian caught up.

'Are you ready?'

'Yes.'

'It's taken from Byron's poem 'The Isles of Greece':
'In vain – in vain: strike other chords;
'Fill high the cup of Samian wine
'Leave battles to the Turkish hordes
'And shed the blood of Scio's vine!'

'Okay, I've got that,' said Brian. 'No idea what it all means.'

'Nor have I, Brian, I just think the boffins might find an answer.'

'This may take some time. What are you going to do while you wait?'

'I'm going after Abdul.'

'Richard. We know sweet FA about this guy, but we know he's dangerous.'

'He's not a suicide bomber,' Richard said. 'He's an educated man.'

'An educated man who kills people.'

Richard knew Brian was right. He'd seen Abdul kill Kleiner for starters. As he spoke, he looked at the gun on the seat and wondered whether he'd use it. 'I know, Brian, but I'm the only person who can get to him in time.'

'You're on your own, chum,' said Brian. 'Cock up and you're toast.'

'Cock up and I'm a dead man.'

'Whatever you do…just stay alive. Fuck the career.'

Richard forced a chuckle. 'Thanks for the advice, Brian. I've no intention of getting myself killed. Just get the guys in London to work out what all this means. I'll call you again to check on progress.'

He hung up. Finding Abdul would be difficult unless he had the answer to the clues. He decided that he must head to Chania and visit the museum.

An hour later, Richard arrived in Chania, a bustling city with traffic to match. With the heat of the day still building, the city was a hive of activity, everyone trying to do their day's work in the early morning before it became too hot. He cursed the slow-moving traffic wending its way through the narrow streets to the port. At last, he found a space to leave his car and continued on foot. The old city clustered around the harbour; a maze of shops and cafés geared to the tourist market. Racks of leather bags and fake football shirts stacked up on hangers overhung the street, blocking out what little light reached the narrow alleys of the old city.

He bought a map of Crete from a tourist shop and a torch. The shop keeper gave him directions to Halidhon, where the museum was situated in a converted Venetian church. It had only just opened and there were few tourists about. A man, looking studiously intellectual, a tanned bald head with what was left of his hair running loosely over his ears, sat at a desk hunched in front of a computer

349

screen, reading Greek newspapers on the internet, a Marlboro smoking in an ashtray by his side.

'Excuse me,' Richard said. 'I'm looking for the curator.'

The man grunted, looking disinterested. 'I'm the curator.'

'Good morning, sir,' he said, holding out his hand. 'My name is Richard Helford. I'm a British diplomat based in Athens. I'm here to investigate reports that some remains of British soldiers who died here in Crete during the war have been discovered. I've heard that British soldiers perished in a landslip at the Cave of the Seven Sleepers and have been buried there until now.'

The man's face transformed from a state of boredom to a look of fear in a few seconds. Richard knew he had the curator's attention. He watched him stand up abruptly, picking up the burning ember of his cigarette and inhaling deeply.

'You have the wrong island, my friend,' the man chuckled. 'You even have the wrong country.'

Richard stared back in disbelief that the man could change his tune so rapidly, when he looked scared to death a few moments earlier. The curator looked shifty and troubled by his lie.

'Are you sure? British soldiers died on Crete, that is certain,' replied Richard. 'I was told that you'd know the cave I'm talking about.'

'Your friend must be mistaken.' The man was stuttering and his face was turning red as he fought back his embarrassment at his deception.

'I don't think you're being helpful, Mr...' Richard read the nameplate on his desk. 'Mr Dionedes. Should we start again? Do you have an old geological map of Crete that we can look at to confirm that this cave doesn't exist? Or something that shows the gorges and caves? We can see if I'm mistaken.'

Mr Dionedes turned reluctantly and pulled out a map from a filing cabinet by his desk, handing it to Richard with a grimace that said, I know I've been found out.

Richard opened the map onto the table and pored over it. In a couple of minutes, he'd found what he was looking for.

'Ah. The Cave of the Severn Sleepers. What a stroke of luck you were wrong,' Richard said sarcastically, glaring back at the man in disgust. 'Mr Dionedes, why have you been lying to me? I know you Greeks want the Elgin Marbles back, but that's no reason to start a diplomatic incident over our war dead.'

Mr Dionedes sat back down in his chair, relaxing a little now that his secret was out. 'There's a man down there already. An American. I sold him a licence to excavate. He wants to keep his actions secret. That's why I didn't want to tell you.'

Richard didn't need a description. He turned and left the building. Abdul was already at the cave. There wasn't much time, but before finding Abdul, he needed to check something. There was an international bookstore down at the port. Twenty minutes later, he emerged from the shop with a book about the travels of Barnabas and Paul throughout the Mediterranean. Barnabas was in Callidora's Bible and also on the icon that Masood had given him. It was only a hunch, but he felt there had to be a connection.

The book was in Greek, so his reading was erratic, but he quickly established that Barnabas had been to Lapithos, which he discovered was in Cyprus, and that he'd fallen out with Paul.

Why?

His theory was making sense. He just needed Brian to confirm a few of the details.

Chapter Forty-Three

Crete, Greece. July 3rd 1941

The shock on Lenny's face made Callidora smile. He stood, still panting from the skirmish with the Germans, transfixed, unable to believe he was seeing the woman he thought was dead.

'Yes, it's me,' said Callidora calmly, but she appeared tired and distressed. 'You look like you've seen a ghost.'

She saw him come alive when she spoke, her words releasing him from his trance. His strong arms wrapped around her, lifting her off the ground.

'I can't believe you're alive,' he said, his voice breaking with emotion. 'We found your clothes. We thought you'd killed yourself.'

'It's a long story, Lenny,' she said. 'But I'm glad I've found you. I've been starving, running around the forest without my clothes like some mad peasant woman.'

'And killing German soldiers?' he said, eying the German machine gun slung over her shoulder.

'Yes. The first time I did that it scared me to death. I've changed. I know God is with me and if he says I'm to die then I'll die. But that hasn't happened.'

He put her down and, taking hold of her hands, he led her back to the cave.

'I'm starving and cold, even in the summer heat,' she said.

'There are some blankets in the cave, but we can't stay here for long with all these dead Germans lying around. We've got to head south and get you off the island.'

Back at the cave, he made her a makeshift cloak, slitting the blanket and creating a hole for her head and securing it with a gun belt wrapped around her waist. He collected some wood and lit a fire. As the flames crackled into life, he noticed the golden light shining on her face as she moved closer to warm herself. She looked so different from the young woman he'd first seen. Her black hair was straggly and knotted, her face dirty and scratched and the blanket made her look like a street urchin, but she was hardened by war and mature for it. He decided she was ready to hear what he had to say. Trying to soften the blow he said. 'Your mother and little Kosmas have survived, but...' He paused, trying to discern her reaction. 'I'm sorry to have to tell you this...the Germans have burned Tirata to the ground. Everything has gone.'

Even in the firelight he could see her face turn white, her eyes widened and her mouth opened with shock. 'Nikos and Ikaros think you're dead. They've gone after Kohlenz for revenge because your brother has seen your letter to me.'

Callidora covered her face and started sobbing. 'They'll be killed, all because of me,' she cried. 'And they know about the rape...I can't deal with the shame.'

'You've got nothing to be ashamed about,' Lenny said, putting his arms around her. He could feel her whole body shake as she wept.

She buried her head into his chest, all the trials of the last few days getting the better of her. 'I've been a fool from the moment I met Hans to my stupid attempts to kill myself. I couldn't even kill myself properly,' she wailed.

'No, no, no' said Lenny, emphasising each word more strongly than the last. 'You did what you thought was right at that time. You survived and believe in saving the scroll. I respect that.'

'But what matters are people, not a piece of paper,' said Callidora, freeing herself from Lenny's embrace and wiping her eyes.

They sat in silence warming themselves by the fire.

After several minutes, when he was sure she'd stopped crying, Lenny spoke. 'Why is the scroll so dangerous that you'd risk your life to save it?'

'If the Nazis get hold of it, it will give them an excuse to exterminate even more people, especially the Jews. We have to stop them getting their hands on the scroll.'

'So why don't we just destroy it? Problem solved,' said Lenny.

Callidora looked straight at Lenny; her expression changed. The tears had gone and her face had become animated. 'It's stupid really, but every time I hold that box, I feel miraculous, like a great surge of energy. I know it's real for no other reason than the way it makes me feel.'

'I can see you're passionate about it,' said Lenny. 'But is it worth dying for?'

Callidora hesitated, contemplating the question. 'It's hard to explain, but yes, it is. The Germans are destroying our island and this little box gives me hope that we'll come through this. It's a reason to survive. When I nearly killed myself I felt that God wouldn't let me die.'

Lenny noticed her smiling.

'When I found the scroll, I also found a beautiful chalice and a casket. In the casket was more papyrus; a letter from the student of John of Patmos who was called Prochorus and a new Gospel by Thomas, the apostle who doubted Jesus had been resurrected. Prochorus explained why the scroll was hidden where it might never be found. In his letter, he says that he travelled to places to find answers.' She took out a piece of wood from the fire and began to write on the cave wall using the wood's charcoal to make a mark, writing each word underneath the next.

Ephesus
Patmos
Lapithos
Chania

'There's a pattern here,' said Lenny. 'St John was the Bishop of Ephesus. He wrote the Revelations on Patmos. We're here in Chania, where the scroll was found. But the other two, I don't understand.'

'The scroll talks about Barnabas,' said Callidora. 'It must be something to do with him but I don't know what.'

'So where does this get us?' said Lenny.

Callidora didn't reply. She was scratching lines on the wall. 'Lapithos is here.' She drew a line. 'And Ephesus is here, and Patmos is here.' She drew another line from Ephesus to Patmos and then another line joining Lapithos and Chania.

'I still don't see.'

'Well, it gave me an idea. If I continue to draw the lines until they cross, they meet in the White Mountains near Tirata. It gave me the idea to hide the scroll in the cave where the children were slaughtered by the Turks. The one that Father Agathangelos renamed the Cave of the Seven Sleepers.'

They set off, at first climbing through thick undergrowth, ascending higher into the mountains. After an hour, tiredness found its way into every part of her body. She felt her legs give way, staggering on for a few more steps, before collapsing under the shade of a carob tree. She could go no further.

'I need to rest and eat,' she said.

He encouraged her to keep going, but she felt sick. 'We're nearly at the top,' he said. 'Then we'll be heading down the other side to Preveli.'

Callidora perked up at the mention of the name. 'Do you mean the Monastery of Preveli?'

'Yes. We're getting a boat into the beach there. People are being taken off the island.'

'Do you know, the monks educated me when I was twelve? They are holy men, but I've betrayed their goodness,' she sighed, nervous at the thought that she might meet them again.

'They'll help you off the island so Kohlenz can't touch you.'

'He'll touch me, all right,' her voice raised, laced with bitterness as the memory of the rape, forced its way into her mind. She trembled, ashen faced. 'He raped me.'

Lenny looked embarrassed that he'd forgotten. 'I'm sorry,' he said. 'I should've realised.' They'd reached a small clearing in a forest of Cypress trees. With access to sunlight, grasses had grown forming a soft carpet. 'This is a good place to rest,' said Lenny. 'You look exhausted. We'll stay here for the night.'

Callidora flopped onto the ground while Lenny surveyed the area checking for escape routes. He was only gone a few minutes but when he returned Callidora was already asleep. He settled down himself and tried to sleep. Time seemed to pass but Lenny could only doze alert that a German patrol might find them even though they were a long way from the road.

Callidora's voice made him jump. 'Did you hear that?' she said quietly.

'No,' said Lenny, looking concerned.

'It's not Germans, its goats. Quite close.' He watched as she jumped to her feet. Her senses seemed sharper, driven by the greater need to eat.

'It's a goat,' she whispered. 'I'd know that sound anywhere.'

Nightfall. A fire burned in a clearing. Her nostrils inhaled hungrily the sweet aroma of roasting goat drifting from its burning embers. The warmth of the night did not detract from the welcome comfort and security of the fire. She felt safe in the mountains, a long way from the Germans and the trail of death. Sleep had renewed her aching body and, with Lenny beside her, she felt able to go on.

She looked across the flames as he poked the meat with a stick.

'I think it's ready to eat,' he smiled. 'I expect you're ready for this.' Using his knife, which he'd disinfected in the flames, he'd expertly cut up the carcass before putting it on the fire to cook. Now, with two sticks, he removed a couple of the pieces, leaving the rest to continue cooking. 'We'll cut this up and take it with us,' he said. 'Food is scarce and there'll be people on the south coast desperate and hungry.'

Despite her hunger, her mind was on other things. 'If I leave the island, we've got to recover the scroll,' she mused.

Lenny cut off a piece of meat and slipped it into his mouth, chewing with a glow of satisfaction spreading across his face. 'Delicious,' he said. 'I'll get it for you,' said Lenny. 'You need to leave Crete before the Germans find you.'

'I don't want to leave,' said Callidora. 'I want to fight.'

Lenny looked up from the meat he was carving and stared into Callidora's eyes. 'How different you are since you I first saw you.' He could see her eyes were fiery with hatred for what had happened to her. 'You deserve to escape. Crete is proud of what you have done,' he said.

He put the meat in a billy can and proceeded to carve it up into smaller pieces. She watched him at work, devouring the meat with her eyes, savouring the smell. At last, he handed her a fork skewered with meat. She tore at it with her teeth, ripping it away from the fork and filling her mouth in a greedy display of hunger, chewing it relentlessly, eking out the benefits of nutrition, which might have to carry her for a long time until her next meal. Swallowing the last bits, she cleared her mouth, sipping the weak coffee Lenny had made from his last remaining rations.

'Don't worry, Callidora. I'll get the scroll for you, but not until I've got you off this island. Kohlenz must not find you.'

July 4th 1941

It was still dark when he woke her. 'It's going to take us all day to reach Preveli,' he whispered. 'We need to leave before daybreak.'

They set off in the dark and soon stopped climbing, which was a relief. They began walking across the mountain range, finding their way through a pass, which was almost at the top. She was pleased he had a map and a compass, but as the sun began to rise, only one reference was necessary; the vast expanse of the Libyan Sea glistening in the early morning twilight. They continued to walk for hours, seeing only the odd German plane in the sky, but not much else. It was dusk when they finally saw the monastery on the hill. It had an amazing position, close to another steep gorge carved out by a river that flowed even in the summer.

The monastery was a series of buildings surrounding a small square in front of a church. She remembered the fountain in the centre and reminded herself of the inscription – *Wash your sins not only your face.* She read the words out aloud before lowering her face into the water, washing away the grime and sweat of the hike across the mountains. The water was cold but she decided not to risk disapproval by trying to wash her feet, which were blistered and cut where the leather of her shoes had completely worn away.

Several years had passed since she'd been to the monastery, but Father Agathangelos remembered her immediately.

'My child, Callidora. It's been such a long time.' He took a few steps back. 'Let me look at you. Ah yes...I can see you have grown into a beautiful woman. I suppose your studies have not continued with this wretched war.' He embraced her warmly.

'I'm afraid not, Father, but they will.' She loved to see his beaming eyes, so much alive and not the least bit scary, despite his sweeping long and straggly, unkempt beard. He wore a long black cassock and flat-topped hat that stood high on his head, attached to a black veil that hung down on his shoulders, which she knew signified his seniority. A large cross was draped around his neck on a long impressive silver chain. She linked her arms with him. 'Come, Father, show me the icons again so I can appreciate them through the eyes of a woman. The last time I was too young to understand their meaning.' She thought about the scroll and remembered it was dedicated to St John the Theologian. Was he the same person as John of Patmos?

'Of course, my child, I would love to show you them again, but first I must meet your friend,' said the priest, looking in Lenny's direction.

Lenny didn't wait to be introduced. 'I'm Lenny Helford of the British Army. We need to get Callidora off the island on the next available ship. She's wanted by the Germans.'

'There's a boat tonight. Is that quick enough for you?' said the priest, smiling.

Inside the church, Callidora marvelled at the paintings and one in particular caught her eye. 'Is that St John the Theologian, writer of the book of Revelations?' she asked Father Agathangelos.

'Of course it is, my child, the church is dedicated to St John of Patmos, known to all as the Theologian.'

'Who is that young man by his side, Father?'

'That's Prochorus, his faithful student. Rumour is that he once came here to Preveli. Long before the monastery was established but it established a connection to St John.'

Callidora stepped back. She began to feel giddy. The letter she'd found was from Prochorus. He had been here. It all made sense.

'Are you all right?' said Father Agathangelos. 'You looked a little flushed.'

'I just need to sit down,' she replied. 'We've walked miles to get here. I'm tired.'

For a moment, she thought about telling the Father what she'd found. Her mind buzzed with the possibilities. The monastery was dedicated to the man whose prophecy she'd hidden in the cave. And the student Prochorus had been right there in this church, or at least an earlier version of it. She felt his presence like a warm glow covering her body, but something inside made her say nothing. The Germans must not know. She couldn't tell the monks until the war was over.

A few hours later, Callidora looked at the moonlight and wondered when she'd ever return to Greece. They had indeed timed their arrival to perfection, as the news had only just come in that the British submarine, *HMS Thrasher*, was going to attempt to land at Preveli Beach. Crowds of men, and the odd woman, were already assembling outside the church. She reckoned that there must have been over fifty soldiers who were going to attempt to escape. She only knew they were soldiers because they spoke English with a varied range of accents. She concluded that there must have been Australians and New Zealanders in the group of escapees. None of the soldiers could be identified by their uniforms, which were long gone. Their clean-shaven army discipline had disappeared and they sported beards just like the monks who were helping them. Their fingers were blackened and their faces cut, dirty and tanned. More monks had appeared in the square, dressed more for war than for God. She decided 'warriors' was a more appropriate description as most wore a black beret and dungarees tucked into leather riding boots. Slung around their shoulders were rifles and of course they all had a bushy unruly beard, just like Father Agathangelos, which would have looked terrifying to a young German paratrooper unversed in the art of killing. She looked across the square to where Lenny was standing in animated conversation with a group of soldiers. It was the first time she'd heard him speak English. Their eyes met and, apologising to the men he was talking to, he came over.

'It's all sorted, you are on the boat. You're going to Cairo.'

The signal to descend the steep path down to the beach came through from the front of the crowd. Being one of the last ones to file down the narrow path, she listened intently for the sound of Germans, but all she could hear were the crickets.

Two monks guided the way and everybody was silent. The only sound was the rushing water below as the river carved its winding path to the sea. It took over thirty minutes to descend to the bottom of the gorge, and gradually the sound of the river was replaced by the sound of waves gently lapping against the pebbles of the beach. In the moonlight, she could see a small lake formed at the point where the river met the beach and was blocked by the rising pebble dune, creating a reef. One of the Australians climbed onto a rock and flashed a light into the darkness. It seemed to her longer than thirty minutes, and she felt so exposed on the beach, Lenny holding her hand, waiting for something to happen.

It was worth the wait. About one hundred metres out, a strange beast emerged from the sea. There was very little sound except the parting of the waves as they washed over the metal hulk of the submarine. Callidora turned and embraced Lenny.

'Thank you,' she said softly. Tears filled her eyes and she wondered whether it was leaving Lenny or Greece which meant the most to her. With one last look in Lenny's direction, she waded into the water and swam towards the submarine.

Chapter Forty-Four

Crete, Greece. August 5th 2005

It was about fifty kilometres to the start of the gorge and then Richard would have to walk the remainder by foot. He filled up the car and set off along the road out of Chania following it west along the coast. At the first opportunity, he took a road that tracked away from the sea and into the mountains. This appeared to be the only way to the gorge. At a reasonable height, he checked he had a powerful signal and, after stopping the car, called Brian.

'What have they come up with?' said Richard when Brian answered.

'Interesting stuff. As you said, it didn't take them long to crack the mystery. One of the guys got his degree in Cambridge on the history of religion. He knew everything.'

'Hope you've covered the reasons for asking. I'm sure Rowena doesn't want these questions coming back to me,' Richard joked, his excitement building. 'Go on. Tell me, Brian, don't fuck about.'

'All right. All right. Give the old boy a chance.' He paused and sneezed before continuing. 'Looking at the names, our boffin decided to use an ancient technique for pinpointing holy places. They even used it to find Mecca before they had compasses.'

'I already know that, Brian. Cut to the chase,' said Richard, impatiently.

'First, if you run a straight line on a map from Ephesus, through the North of Patmos and keep going until you hit Crete, you begin to cross land just West of Chania and very near Tirata. Next, if you follow a line on the exact same latitude as Lapithos, which, by the way, I was right, is in Cyprus, and carry it straight in the direction of Crete, noting down where the two lines dissect each other. Where do you think the lines cross?'

'The Cave of the Seven Sleepers,' said Richard excitedly.

'Congratulations, you win the car.'

Elation was his first reaction and then panic, because Abdul was already at the cave. He gripped the steering wheel, trying to stay calm. 'What about everything else I gave you?'

'Easy,' said Brian. 'We've mentioned all the places except Aleppo and the Cave of Machpelah. *Foot of the Mountain* can be explained by the Cave of the Seven Sleepers as it lies at the foot of a gorge. Second, Byron is referring to the Turkish Civil War in his poem. Greeks hid from the Turks in this very cave but were found when a child cried. All of the people in the cave were murdered. Byron's poem provides a message about a Turkish atrocity.'

'Okay. So what can you tell me about the Cave of Machpelah and Aleppo?'

'I was coming to that. These places are the link to everything. The Cave of Machpelah is where Abraham was buried by his sons, Isaac and Ismael. It's where the faith of Islam, Christianity and Judaism merge into one. Isn't this what Abdul is looking for? The scroll will answer the religious million-dollar question. It will prove the supremacy of Islam. The cave of Machpelah is where it all starts.'

Richard had worked this out already, but to hear it come from Brian made it sound even more real. 'And Aleppo?' he said.

'Nothing much, except to say that these were staging posts for Barnabas and Paul to spread the Gospel. They went to all these places, Ephesus, Lapithos, and Aleppo.'

Richard couldn't hang up quick enough. He could feel a tension in his stomach as his mind buzzed with the realisation of what all this meant. He drove on with great care and it was lucky that there were few cars on the road as he drove slowly up the mountain, immersed in his theory that Barnabas was the key to the mystery. Versions of his Gospel were considered to be forgeries, but that was only because all the authentic versions had been destroyed to protect the word of Jesus Christ. The scroll would prove the word of Barnabas to be the Gospel truth. It all fitted.

Richard stopped the car so he could think. He went over the theory in his mind. He needed to try it out on Brian, so he called him again.

'Twice in the space of an hour,' said Brian. 'I'm beginning to think I matter.'

'Look, Brian, we haven't got time to joke about this. Abdul is already at the cave. If he's allowed to get away with the scroll, it will undermine the whole Western strategy in the Middle East.'

'Okay,' said Brian. 'I hear you.'

'Listen, I'm going after Abdul, but if something happens to me I want you to know my theory about what all this means.'

'All right, I'm all ears,' said Brian.

Richard started before Brian had finished talking. 'Barnabas travels to Lapithos, Aleppo and Ephesus with Paul. They meet John of Patmos in Ephesus while he is Bishop. Barnabas and John argue about the future of Christianity, writing in his Gospel that Jesus acknowledged that he was not the last prophet and that somebody greater than him was still to come. They discuss his Gospel with Paul who does not agree that Jesus was not the Son of God. Barnabas is discredited and his Gospel destroyed. Years later, John is in Patmos, writing his Book of the Apocalypse, when he receives a vision from God. He cannot not refer to it in his Book because it destroys his view of Jesus as being the son of God, but he cannot ignore it. He makes a passing reference to the prophecy of the little scroll in Chapter 10 of the Book of Revelations and then writes the prophecy down, where it is hidden for thousands of years until a German bomb reveals its secret. The prophecy supports the words of Barnabas. Christianity was just a staging post to prepare for the ultimate voice of God – the voice of Islam.'

'Shit,' said Brian. 'This is big stuff. We need to report this to the Joint Security Committee.'

'I've got no proof because I haven't seen the scroll, but if I'm right the consequences will be devastating. Up until now, the Gospel of Barnabas has been proven to be a forgery dating back to the Middle Ages and is riddled with errors. There is even a reference to Dante's *Inferno*, which of course was written in the sixteenth century, not the first.'

'So what you are saying is that the scroll gives this forgery credibility?'

'Yes, but there is also something else.'

'Go on.'

'In 2000 the Turks discovered a much earlier version, dating back to the 1st century. It was written on animal hide, in Syriac, which the Internet tells me is a dialect of Aramaic. The Vatican have even asked to see this new version but have made no comment. The Iranians are saying it will bring down Christianity as we know it. Of course none of this will be believed unless there is new evidence. The scroll could give the world the evidence it needs. Of course, Christians would never accept the Holy Koran, but Islam will have the moral high ground to the detriment of Christian and Jewish faiths. It is going to turn people against one another and lead to a war between the religions.'

'All this stuff is on the Internet then?'

'Yes. But now there is intelligence about a terrorist spectacular. Maybe it is to announce the scroll to the world. It needs to be dramatic to make the world listen and get them to take it seriously.'

'What are you saying?'.

'I don't think it will be like 9/11 or 7/7. I think it'll be more theatrical.'

'Why do you think that?'

'Crete is not New York or London. This is about where the scroll has come from. It's about the scroll's message.'

'I'm going to call Rowena. You need back up?'

Richard sighed. 'I think it's too late for that.'

Richard waited for nightfall before descending into the gorge. Abdul was down there somewhere. He quickened his pace as the light began to fade; an involuntary reaction to nerves playing tunes on his spine. The warm night air squeezed perspiration from his pores, but as the black rocks sucked the heat away from the dying sun, he knew it was fear that made him sweat. His hands fidgeted with his rifle holster, slung across his shoulder, wondering whether he could use it. The darkness of the gorge reflected his mood. No blaze of glory as the sun spread its mantle of colour across the sea in a final act of resistance against the onset of the night. No dramatic sunset. He knew, in a matter of minutes, he would be swallowed up by the shadow of the mountain's embrace and facing up to Abdul.

Looking up, he could see a thin strip of blue sky turning grey as the cliffs of stone closed in around him and the sun sought refuge behind the mountain. At least the path is defined by the rocks on both sides and wide enough, he thought. He would still be able to find his way in the fading light. As he continued, the chasm of forbidding rock formations became more severe and overpowering. A sense of alienation swept over him, taking his mind in other directions. The tall towers of rock became the twin towers, collapsing in on him as the night crushed his spirit.

The rocks dissolved into dark haunting shapes. They were no longer defined. Soon it would be pitch black, making it impossible to see his own fingers, let alone a rock. Earthquakes proliferated in the area and with every new tremor another large boulder would fall down the mountain. It would be easy to lose the path in the pitch darkness. Frustrated, he switched on his torch, not something he wanted to do, in case Abdul saw him, but unavoidable because he couldn't see enough. The track started to descend more steeply and he found it difficult to retain his hold on the crumbling path. He let the beam track the ground in front of him, hoping that nobody would see him, least of all Abdul. The light picked out animal hoof prints embossed in dried mud. As he continued to go down, he felt his pulse quicken, wondering where Abdul might be and what might happen when they met.

The path began to level out, opening up into a large clearing with the mountains on all sides. For a moment he couldn't resist shining his torch upwards, observing an overhang, defying gravity about one hundred feet above. A flat plateau of rock was immediately below and he guessed that millions of years ago it would have been joined before being severed by an almighty earthquake. It felt like an oasis in the darkness. There was a bed of mossy grass beneath his feet and oleander trees peeking through the cracks. The silence was broken by the trickle of a stream nearby, although he couldn't be sure where.

Then he saw a tent. It could only belong to Abdul. There was a fire burning next to it, but no sign of the man he wanted to kill.

The knife against his throat told him why.

He gasped for breath, feeling the grip of an arm round his neck, catching the glint of the blade as his feet sliced from under him. He screamed with pain as he hit the ground, staring down the barrel of a gun.

'Hello, Richard,' said Abdul.

Chapter Forty-Five

Crete, Greece. July 5th 1941

The thought of the long hike back across the mountains, trying to avoid the Germans, filled Lenny with dread. Finding colleagues from the SOE lifted his spirits because he knew he wouldn't be lonely on the march. After a day walking through rough terrain, fit only for goats, he worried that he might slip and break an ankle, which would be hell, trapped on such a barren upland. His feet were aching, making the risk of injury even greater, and the soles of his boots had become so thin he could feel the stones on the ground digging into his feet. Wearily he trudged on, enjoying the conversation with the officers, but becoming more disillusioned with the benefits of being on the island.

'The Cretans never say a word about our whereabouts so the Germans burn their villages. If we weren't here, then maybe they'd leave them alone,' said Peter McCloud, a burly Scotsman, dressed in traditional Cretan clothing and hiding behind a curling moustache that the Greeks admired. Unfortunately, the disguise was spoiled when he spoke Greek with a Scottish accent.

After a day hiking through the wilderness of mountain peaks, Lenny said his goodbyes and left the group to head toward Tirata, agreeing to meet up again in the village of Galatas near Chania as soon as he'd completed his mission. He didn't tell them what he was doing because of the explanation that would be required. How would he explain the scroll? He was also not sure how long it would take because, after recovering the scroll, he'd need to take it to Preveli for safe keeping. The monks would be amazed and would guard it with their lives, he thought, just as they'd hidden all those soldiers who had escaped from Preveli beach. As he walked alone, he thought of Callidora and hoped she would soon be safe in Cairo. It was a brave thing to have Kohlenz' child, but he decided she'd taken the right decision to survive.

As night began to fall, he reckoned he still had about ten miles to go and needed somewhere to rest. A village came into view and he decided to seek some shelter. He didn't know what the village was called and nor did it matter. Villagers always made him welcome as soon as he spoke in English.

After questions at the *kafenion*, a man pointed to a house. Conditioned to expect a man, he couldn't hide his surprised look when a woman came to the door. She smiled, enjoying his discomfort at asking for a bed for the night.

'Of course you may sleep in my house,' she replied. 'My name is Eleni,' she spoke in Greek, having satisfied herself that he was English. 'This is my daughter, Diana. We are alone as my husband fights in the mountains in the resistance.'

'You must tell me his name in case I meet him,' he said.

'Stavros Klestakis,' Eleni replied.

Diana looked to be in her teens; her beauty reflecting a youthful sense of innocence not yet tainted by the war. She was unlike Callidora who spoke her mind, had fierce eyes and raven black hair. Diana smiled, soft and demure, saying little, her curls floating around her delicate shoulders as she moved.

July 6th 1941

The next day Lenny felt completely refreshed. They'd fed him with a bean stew and some tomatoes and he'd slept better than he had done for days. They even packed some cold mutton and bread for him to take on his journey. He tried to decline, not wishing to take food while it was in such short supply, but Eleni insisted.

As he got closer to Tirata, he decided that the best way to approach the gorge would be to take the path that Callidora had taken from the village. Seeing the remains of Tirata once more made him weep. Although he'd already walked through the smouldering remains of German destruction, he couldn't bring himself to go there again. He'd seen it before they'd burnt it to the ground and memories of such a vibrant, happy place left him in despair. He took the path that skirted the village and headed onto the trail that led to the gorge.

Callidora had given him landmarks to distinguish where the cave was and they worked with ease. The entrance was tall and narrow, where two boulders had been forced apart by earthquakes. He had a whole box of candles and a British Army issue torch, which was down to its last hour. He decided to waste no time and go straight to where Callidora had told him the scroll would be.

He lit candles as he worked his way into the cave, melting wax into the stone to support them. Edging forward, trying to ignore the skeletons Callidora had warned him about, he moved nearer to the spot where she'd hidden the scroll. It was unmistakable and exactly as Callidora had described. A mound of rocks, carefully constructed, but it didn't seem like a great hiding place. She had so little time, he thought, and yet the rocks had been assembled with great care. Her prime concern must have been to protect the box from damp rather than hiding it in a place impossible to find. He decided to get the box first, before looking for the chalice and casket, which Callidora had told was nearby, but deeper in the cavern. The rocks weren't heavy and one by one he removed them with great care, trying to remember the order in case he had to reassemble them.

Then he saw it, his torch illuminating the masterpiece. The paintings had no perspective and the figures were expressionless but seemed better for it, expressing an aesthetic quality like no other he'd ever seen, better than Duccio or Giotto he'd seen in Italy. Placing two hands on the box he eased it out of its hiding place.

Without warning the ground began moving under his feet in great waving shudders; everything was shaking and an enormous grinding sound echoed around the chamber, throwing him off balance. He toppled backwards, clutching the box for dear life, unable to use his hands to halt his fall. A searing pain ripped its way through his body as he crashed against a sharp rock. Rolling over, he smothered the box, a great compulsion to protect it, as rocks began falling around him. He screamed in agony as one boulder hit his back; he felt a crack, sure it had smashed his ribs.

Less than five seconds and his world shattered before him. He might have been dead already, as a complete stultifying darkness engulfed him. The candles he'd lit had all blown out and for a moment he lay there, feeling only the pain in his chest. He still held on to the box and with great effort, wincing because his ribs hurt like hell, he managed to pull himself up. One hand let go of the box and fumbled in his pocket for his torch. Mercifully, it still worked. Switching it on, he placed the box on a ledge and began to trace his way back to the entrance, picking up candles as he went. At first, he thought he'd lost his way, doubling back, retracing his steps, but no, he hadn't got it wrong.

The entrance was blocked.

He knelt down in the dust and began to claw at the boulders in a helpless frenzy as the realisation of his predicament began to sink in. None of the boulders would shift and he had no means of moving them. He was buried alive.

The moment he touched the scroll, an act of God had refused the world access to the secret. He didn't believe in God, but the timing seemed more than just a coincidence. He felt calm, accepting that the end had come in this darkness. A German bullet may have ended his life, but now he would have to do it himself. He felt the pistol in his pocket and, reassured, found his way back to where he'd left the scroll. Finding it, he lit a candle and switched off his torch to preserve what little light he had left. Next, he removed the nails that secured the box and removed the papyrus text. Unrolling it, he gasped at how clear and legible the Greek appeared to be. He would read and understand what others did not. After all, he had all the time in the world.

The rest of his life.

Chapter Forty-Six

Crete, Greece. August 5th 2005

'Get up,' Abdul snarled, kicking him in the stomach.

Richard could barely see Abdul's face as he climbed to his feet, the pain of the kick stabbing his ribs. He sighed, feeling foolish at how easily he had capitulated.

As he stood, the gun prodded him hard between his shoulder blades, urging him forwards.

'Walk,' Abdul shouted.

With his hands up, he walked towards the fire. Reaching it, Abdul ordered him to kneel.

'Put your hands behind your back,' came the next instruction. He felt some plastic ties wrap around his wrists and pulled tight. He gritted his teeth, suppressing the urge to scream, feeling the plastic bite into his skin. In front of him he could see the narrow entrance of the cave, illuminated by paraffin lamps. More lamps lit up the area around the fire.

'Stand up,' Abdul's voice was softer.

He could see a look of satisfaction spreading across Abdul's face. He even rested the gun against a rock, displaying his confidence that Richard was no longer a threat. 'Have you found the scroll?' Richard asked nervously, staring at Abdul's eyes.

The Arab's face changed in an instant, contorting with anger. 'No,' he snapped. 'And I want you to tell me why.'

The news disturbed him. 'It must be here,' Richard said, shocked that he'd found nothing. He watched as Abdul disappeared into his tent, returning a minute later carrying a sack. For a moment, while he was gone, Richard considered running, but decided against it. 'I've found this,' Abdul said, holding up what appeared to be a book bound in a rough animal hide. 'I found it wrapped in a blanket, lying on the floor in the cave, as if someone had intended to take it away but forgotten. I may not be able to read Greek but I'm certain it's not the scroll.'

'Show me the first page,' said Richard, moving closer to see the book.

Abdul turned over the page so he could see the writing. It was written in Greek and Richard began to read the words out loud.

'And he said: Whoever finds the correct interpretation of these sayings will never die.'

'What does it mean?' asked Abdul.

'It's the Gospel of Thomas,' Richard replied, pleased that he had got something over Abdul, despite the plastic ties cutting his skin. 'That's a find even without the scroll. There's only one other version of the Gospel in existence, found in Egypt in 1945. This one, in Greek, is unique as the other one was written in Copt. It's priceless.'

'I don't care about money,' Abdul replied. 'I care about what's in the scroll. It's what your father told me that I'm interested in.'

'Don't you see what this means? Somebody got here before us and left the Gospel by mistake. They only realised when it was too late and they'd closed the entrance.'

'Your father said to me that he didn't have the scroll but knew what it said. He was researching its message when I met him in New York. He told me about the Cave of the Seven Sleepers, but I always assumed that was in Ephesus. He never said it was in Crete.'

'It was only Kleiner and the story of my grandfather that brought us here,' said Richard, surprised that he was helping Abdul figure out why the scroll had to be in the cave.

'It wasn't you. Your father sent me a note when I landed in Crete. He told me to come here.'

'Are you saying he's on the island?' said Richard, pretending that he didn't know this already.

'He's here. He must have known that the scroll was missing from the cave. He'll appear and when he does, I'll kill you both.'

Richard could hear his stomach churn. He tried to breathe slowly, closing his eyes to think of something calming. Becky flashed into his mind. He had to survive for her sake.

'I know nothing more than you,' Richard replied. 'My relationship with my father was poor. I never saw him. It was only after the London bomb that my mother told me of his search for the truth surrounding my grandfather's death. But she knew nothing about the scroll.'

'I've scoured the cave from top to bottom, but have found nothing.'

'You could untie me and let me look,' said Richard hopefully.

Abdul thought for a moment and then picked up the rifle, flicking off the safety catch. 'You were going to kill me with this,' he said calmly.

'No,' Richard lied.

Abdul smiled, and Richard knew by that look he didn't believe him. 'Killing the first person is always the hardest, but after that it gets easier.' He took out his knife and while still holding the gun, cut open the ties. Stepping back, he cocked the rifle in his direction.

'Go,' he said. There was an air of concern in his voice, as if he might be regretting his decision.

Richard knelt and began to crawl through the narrow tunnel. As it opened out into a huge cavern, he saw skeletons staring back at him. He gasped, feeling his heart pumping in a frenzy of adrenalin-fuelled fear. For a moment, he stepped back, unsure whether to go any further. He took deep breaths, slowing down his pulse, until he could move forward again. Abdul had placed several more lanterns in the cave, casting eerie shadows across the surface of the rock. He picked one of the lanterns up and walked further from the entrance.

Averting his eyes from the bones, he looked upwards, seeing the whole area hanging above him, like some vast cathedral defying gravity. His eyes had to come back down to the skeletons and, less fearful, he forced himself to confront their ugliness. The seven sleepers are an underestimate, he thought. There must be over thirty in here, including many children. He felt strangely calm and the more he looked, the less perturbed he became. One skeleton caught his eye. It was apart from the main group and seemed to peer back at him, propped against the rock, hands wide apart, beckoning him to stay. He didn't feel scared any more, however forbidding this cave appeared, something reassured him and he didn't understand why. He swung the light away and tried to focus on what he was looking for. An unseen force led him deeper into the cave. He sniffed the air, trying to find an explanation for what he might be following. A faint breeze brushed his cheeks and he noticed the lamp light quivering, making the walls appear to move. He shone the lamp on both walls and saw them converge into a tunnel. Turning back, he checked his position, realising that the other lamps were barely visible and the only light was that coming from the lamp he held.

It didn't matter how far he was from the exit because he sensed a need to keep going. There was a spirit driving him on, deeper into the hole. The tunnel must have curved because all light guiding him to the entrance had gone. He was at ease in the darkness and the breeze had disappeared. Slowly, he lowered the light to the floor, placing it on the ground. Kneeling down, he rubbed his hands along the damp gritty ground. Sediment stuck to his fingers.

Then he saw it.

Two round disks lay part covered by fragments of rock and sand. He spat on them cleaning away the sand caked to their surface, holding them closer to the light. One of the disks seemed to be red and the other green, not metal, but some sort of fibre. They were stamped with lettering. He held them close to the lamp and began to read:

Helford

2567456

L

M

He called out loud with joy in the darkness, his voice echoing around the walls, bouncing around the tunnel in a fearsome cacophony of deafening sound. *His grandfather's spirit had drawn him to this spot, but why here?* He swung the lamp around the walls of the tunnel, running his hand over the rock, tracing every imperfection.

The light did not move as fast as his hand and he felt the cleft in the rock before he saw it. It was about three inches wide and big enough to reach into. He positioned the light on the ground so it would give him just enough visibility to be able to poke his hand into the fissure. He noticed more signs of his grandfather's presence; candle wax had solidified down the walls. Wary at what he might find, he put his hand into the hole and began to explore. He'd almost got as far as his elbow, when he realised he couldn't go any further without becoming trapped. 'Shit,' he whispered to himself.

But there was something there.

As he withdrew his hand, he brushed against a soft object. Instinct made him jerk away, thinking he might have touched a dead animal. Retracing where his hands had been, he moved his arm back into the hole and discovered a ledge he'd missed on the first attempt. His fingers explored the area and immediately found the object he was looking for. With great care, he prodded it and decided it was some sort of package wrapped in material. Lifting it out, his hands shaking with excitement, he examined what he'd discovered. It was no more than two inches by three and wrapped in several layers of what felt like a piece of clothing. Unwrapping it, his excitement turned to joy. It was a small leather-bound diary, with close writing using every inch of the paper, as dry as a bone with the ink clearly still legible.

Tears rolled down his face. For a moment, he stared at the book, not taking in the words on the page. For the first time in his life he had a tangible link with his past. His grandfather had led him to this place.

His hands shook, turning the pages, wanting to know everything. He read the first lines and felt a tingle of excitement running down his spine. He'd forgotten Abdul. He'd forgotten the darkness of this cave. He just wanted to know.

July 4th 1941. *C is free.*

July 6th 1941. *I came to this cave to recover the scroll for C and get it out of Crete. It was easy to find because C had told me where she'd hidden it. Guarded by the skeletons of the Seven Sleepers, she had carefully hidden the box behind a mound of small rocks. I quickly moved the rocks and fished out the wonderful painted box. Holding it in my hands, my candle seemed to flicker more brightly in its presence, but then the ground began to shake. An earthquake. Rocks were falling all around me and I knew if I didn't escape I would be buried alive or crushed to death. The earthquake must have lasted only a few seconds, but it had done enough. My way out was blocked and nobody would ever discover me. I'm buried alive.*

I don't believe in God but the timing of this earthquake is too much of a coincidence. If there is a God, he doesn't want the scroll to see the light of day. I have some candles and a small bit of food and my torch, which will soon run out. I'm going to read the scroll and write down my thoughts here. The Greek is clear and my classics degree will support me well in this quest. When the last candle is burned out, I have my pistol to finally snuff out my life.

Richard closed the book, experiencing the terror his grandfather must have felt when he knew he was going to die. How calm and accepting his grandfather had been. The thought made Richard shiver. He felt stifled by the cave and wanted to escape. Maybe the scroll was still here after all, but he was in no mood to find it now. A sound of footsteps echoed behind him, shattering his hope that there might be a way out. He swung round and saw the danger.

Abdul was staring at him, gun in his hand.

Chapter Forty-Seven

Cairo, Egypt. May 1942

How could she love him? The little boy looked so innocent, staring back with slightly bemused eyes. Perhaps he suspected that his mother was struggling to return the unconditional love that any baby would impart without question. Callidora tried so hard to love him, but every time she saw his face, she thought of his father, the sadistic brute who she'd watched murder her friends in cold blood. She could still recall the putrid smell of his stale sweat as he forced himself upon her. But no mother can ignore the tears of her child, crying to be fed. Picking him up, she pressed his mouth to her nipple, smelling him; a distinctive baby smell that might erase the memory of his father. As he suckled, his little fingers rested on her breast as if seeking reassurance that she was there and, despite everything, she smiled.

But maybe he was all she had left; her only family. She remembered Lenny had said that her mother and little Kosmas had survived the destruction of Tirata, but were they still alive? The thought of Kosmas, with no one to look after him, brought tears to her eyes. But should she grieve when she didn't know whether her family was dead or alive? Would she ever know?

Her mind drifted over the visions and memories that she couldn't shut out. It always happened when she fed baby Andreas, as if the relaxing process of breastfeeding made her meditate. She knew the war had changed her outlook on life and her faith in God. The scroll had played its part in her disillusionment. Now she feared the damage it could do if the world saw its contents.

She looked down at Andreas and wondered whether he sensed his mother's grief. Seeing his eyes closed in a vision of contentment, she gently freed herself and put him in the basket next to her bed. Sinking back in the chair, her mind turned once again to Lenny. It had been ten months since they'd parted and she felt certain he'd been killed. In the final days of her pregnancy, she'd wept bitterly that he might be gone and, whenever she thought about him, she cried again. With Andreas no longer in her arms, the brief happy moment had been extinguished by sadness that she might never see Lenny again.

She'd been to the SOE office in Cairo, trying to find out whether they'd received a radio message from him. They were a cavalier bunch who seemed uninterested that one of their men might be missing. She'd spoken to a Captain Blyton, who'd initially shown concern and then immediately invited her to dinner at Shepheard's Hotel, the centre of the universe as far as the British were concerned. At first she'd been glad to go, naively thinking that he'd taken pity on her situation, but nothing could have been further from the truth. She enjoyed the cool ambience of the hotel with its wicker chairs and octagonal tables but when he started flirting with her, like she was a whore he'd picked up in Giza, she quickly became uneasy. She told him she was pregnant and his mood changed. They didn't even get to dinner. He paid the bill and suggested they left.

At the time she didn't mention the scroll because the priority was to find Lenny but, if he was dead, maybe the Germans had got it and were using it to promote their distorted view of the world. It would justify their extermination of the Greek people and most of all, she felt sure that if they had the document, they'd kill more Jews. She had to tell the British.

Maybe Ari would help her. She'd met him on the submarine on the way to Cairo. He'd told her he was a Greek resistance leader with a German death warrant on his head, which was why they were getting him out of Crete. The journey had been horrendous, with so many people on board she could hardly breathe. Unlike Captain Blyton, Ari had protected her, using his influence to get her rooms in the army quarters when they finally arrived in Cairo.

He'd told her that he'd call on her this afternoon, so she looked out of the window to see if she could see him. A thick veil of dust almost obliterated any view she had from the window and this reminded her of how much she hated Cairo. In Greece, she loved the mountains; the smell of oregano in the air. In Cairo, everything was dirty and dilapidated and overflowing with people living on top of each other. There was no space to breathe. When the wind blew, sand storms covered all the buildings with a thick layer of dust which choked her. Windows became opaque with dirt and nobody could be bothered to clean them. Her window was no exception and she gave up in disgust.

Ari arrived, as he'd promised, on time, which was so unusual for a Greek. She let him in and they embraced. She noticed how he hugged her with more feeling than before, now that he knew the circumstances behind the birth of her baby. For a Greek, he'd been sympathetic when she knew many would have disowned her as damaged goods. She welcomed his interest, not just because of his kindness, but because she felt safe in his arms, sure that he would sweep away the horrors in her head and make everything good again. 'Come and sit down,' she said. 'I need to speak to you.'

Ari looked concerned, his blue eyes narrowed and his swarthy face tightened as he heard her story.

'You remember I told you about the man who gave up his place on the submarine for me?'

'Yes, of course.'

'Well, he seems to have gone missing and maybe he's dead.'

Ari nodded in agreement. 'Yes, that seems likely. I'm sorry,' he said.

'He was going to recover something for me.' She told him the full story and he became more and more fascinated, never once interrupting. There was a whimper from Andreas and she stood up to check on him. Seeing he was all right, she sat down again and continued. 'Do you remember your Bible and what it says in the last book about the end of the world?'

Ari looked embarrassed and shook his head.

Callidora smiled and continued. 'Well, Chapter 10 of the Book of the Apocalypse refers to the little scroll. It is the scroll that tastes sweet in the mouth and bitter in the stomach.'

'Yes,' said Ari. 'Go on.'

'The scroll I found tells us what that means.' She paused and took hold of his hand. 'It seems that *sweet in the mouth* refers to fornication, to sex.' Ari's eyes widened and seemed a little shocked that she'd actually said the word. 'Bitter in the stomach is the aftermath of sex,' she continued, looking nervously across to Andreas sleeping. 'Population explosion and not enough food to feed the world is what the pain is. The pain of starvation. It says that population must be reduced; calling for the reduction of the Jewish race because of its failure to accept the words of Jesus, and any prophet that follows as being the word of God.' She stopped and allowed Ari to take her words in. 'This is what the Nazis want.'

'Okay, so what do you want me to do?'

'Speak to the British. Somebody must go back into Crete and recover the scroll if Lenny failed...and if it's not there, find out whether the Germans have got it.'

Ari looked back at her and smiled. 'I'm going back anyway,' he said. 'I'll get the scroll for you. The British are dropping me by parachute tonight so let's go and see the British officer in charge of the resistance in Crete and you can tell him about the scroll.'

It was a short walk to the SOE office but Ari was seen immediately by the head of station, who invited them both in, offering them tea.

The head of station did not introduce himself by name and needed a translator to hear Callidora's story in Greek and, as luck would have it, only Captain Blyton was available. She scowled at him as he entered the room but continued with the story.

'We know that Leonard Helford is missing and we've told his wife,' he said when she was finished.

'Wife?' said Callidora, completely taken aback. 'He never mentioned any wife.'

'They married a couple of weeks before he went to Crete. Probably there wasn't much to tell.' He leaned over his desk and looked at Callidora. 'Does that change anything?'

'No, of course not,' she replied, with Captain Blyton rattling on behind her, putting her shock into words that could be easily understood.

The older officer put his hand over his mouth and stroked it, considering what to do before speaking. 'The discovery of this scroll is interesting. Intelligence reports suggest that the Nazis are already embarking on incarcerating Jews in all the countries it has conquered. I need to speak to London and get back to you, but my view is that we should recover it.' He stood up, signifying an abrupt end to the conversation.

'Aristotle, you are flying out tonight. If we don't hear back from London, you should go ahead and get that scroll and bring it off Crete before the Germans get their grubby little fingers on it.'

'Yes, sir.' Ari replied in English.

An hour later and Callidora was called back into the SOE office, this time without Ari, which surprised her. The head of station looked very worried when she walked into the office. He wasted no time with pleasantries. Blyton was already there, sitting ready to translate.

'We've spoken to London,' he said, 'and the Prime Minister has been informed. He has demanded a fuller report on what the scroll says and has ordered a covert operation to be mounted to recover the scroll. How much can you tell us about it, other than what you've already told us?'

Callidora looked at him and realised that once she spoke about what she knew, the secret of the scroll would no longer be safe. She'd promised Hans that she'd say nothing but felt she had no alternative if the British Prime Minister wanted to know. Clearing her throat, she swallowed hard and began to speak.

'It says many things which I can't remember but the main point sticks in my mind. He said that when St John of Patmos wrote the Book of Revelations, he was doing so with the belief that Jesus was the Son of God. But something was troubling him. He inserted a clue to a more devastating secret in Chapter 10. The secret of the little scroll.'

'Go on,' said the head of station.

'It says that Jesus himself predicted the coming of the Prophet Muhammad, a prophet greater than himself, and that his word will be the last word of God and therefore the true word of God. It proves the supremacy of Islam. If true, it could trigger the collapse of Christianity.'

The older officer sighed. 'We need to find the scroll and find it quick.'

Chapter Forty-Eight

Crete, Greece. August 5th 2005

'What have you found?' Abdul shouted.

'Let's go back outside and I'll show you,' said Richard. Walking towards Abdul, he knew his fear had gone. What he had in his hands gave him strength; the way his grandfather had faced death with dignity was how he would. He glared at Abdul. 'I wouldn't fire that thing in here if I were you,' he said. 'It's likely to bring the roof down and we'll all be buried alive.'

'Get out of here,' snarled Abdul. 'You go first.'

Richard moved past, feeling the gun digging into his ribs once more. This action was almost the final straw. Barely able to suppress his anger, he pushed the barrel away and for a moment there was a standoff. For the first time, Richard began to calculate how he might disarm him. He was younger than Abdul. If he moved quickly, he could succeed.

But he didn't do anything and, when he stepped out of the cave in front of Abdul, he knew he'd made the right decision.

A face greeted him, discernible by the orange glow of the fire. A face pointing a Kalashnikov.

'Run,' it screamed.

Richard didn't need a second prompt, lurching to the right as the bullets began to fly.

He had a window of no more than two seconds to get away.

Abdul emerged from the cave, spotting the danger and diving to the ground. The man with the Kalashnikov was too slow. Bullets drilled into the dust, too late to catch

Abdul who fired a single bullet, throwing the man backwards, loosening his grip on the gun; it fell with a clatter to the ground. Richard saw it first and took his chance, rushing out from his cover, his hand almost reaching it, when Abdul's second bullet exploded from the rifle. The impact took him by surprise, a searing pain spread through his body as the bullet pierced his flesh. In the semi darkness, broken only by the fire and the lamplight, he had no idea where he'd been hit. The pain made him dizzy and he knew he couldn't hold on to the gun. Abdul pounced, ripping the Kalashnikov from his grasp.

He wanted to retaliate, but once again Abdul had the upper hand, kicking him hard in the stomach in the same place as he had done before, causing pain worse than his gunshot wound. Richard could only watch, his anger reaching boiling point, while Abdul crouching in a combat pose, checking there were no others to deal with, continued to exercise total control. Richard could see Abdul's face had changed; the threat had been neutralised with clinical efficiency. Shadows from the fire threw sinister shapes across Abdul's body. He looked like a terrorist. No fear, only a single-minded desire to win at whatever cost.

Satisfied that the man had no accomplices, Abdul advanced, his finger twitching on the trigger. 'Who are you?' he shouted.

The man clutched his shoulder, trying to stem the blood that stained his shirt. 'I'm Callidora's son, Andreas,' he replied slowly and calmly. 'I know where the scroll is.'

The shock extinguished the pain in Richard's own shoulder. He stared at Andreas, wondering how old he might be. He seemed the right age to be Callidora's child. 'I thought she died in 1941,' said Richard. 'In her letter to my grandfather, she said she was going to kill herself and the baby.'

'She didn't do it. She survived and your grandfather helped her escape to Cairo where she gave birth to me,' said Andreas.

'Why is the scroll not here in the cave?' Abdul shouted.

'Because my mother took it,' said Andreas.

'And where is your mother?'

Andreas was silent. Abdul repeated the question.

'In New York,' came back the reply.

'So that's where my father heard about the scroll,' said Richard. 'But how did he know that you and your mother were in New York?'

'I don't know how that happened. He just turned up one day out of the blue,' Andreas said.

Looking back at Abdul, Richard could see the conversation annoyed him. Abdul moved closer, hitting Andreas with the butt of the gun. 'Are you telling me that the scroll's in New York?' he said, venting his anger by hitting Andreas again. He turned back to Richard. 'Your father told me it was here. Why did he lie?'

'To get you to come here,' shouted Richard.

Andreas pulled himself back up, blood was running down his face, but he looked defiant and in remarkable shape for a man in his sixties. 'It was in New York but no longer. If you kill me, you'll never find it,' he said sneering. 'I'm too valuable to kill.'

'Try me,' said Abdul, hitting Andreas again.

Richard could stand it no longer. He stood up and staggered towards Abdul, his hand felt light as if all his blood was draining out of him, drop by drop. 'Stop this now.' He held out Lenny's diary, trying to catch Abdul's attention. Anything to stop him hitting Andreas. 'I found something in the cave.'

Abdul didn't even look up. All his attention was devoted to Andreas, whose swollen face with eyes only just opened, stared back at Abdul. 'I can take you to the scroll,' Andreas muttered, wincing as he spoke.

'You know where David Helford is?'

'Yes. He has the scroll.'

Abdul turned back towards Richard, unperturbed that he had his back to Andreas, no longer seeing him as dangerous. He pointed at Richard. 'Why do you want to help this man?'

'Because his grandfather saved my mother's life, and lost his own trying to save the scroll.' He hesitated, pulling a face as the pain in his arm continued to bother him. 'I need treatment for my arm,' he said, changing the subject.

Abdul stood up, a smirk seemed to cross his lips, something had occurred to him and Richard didn't know what it was. He waved the gun at Richard.

'Sit down next to him and don't move.'

Still carrying the gun, he disappeared into his tent, before returning with bandages, pain killers and antiseptic. He threw them over.

'It's just as well I'm a good shot. These are only scratches,' he said. There was a noticeable change in mood again, which worried Richard even more.

He soon knew why.

Abdul watched, still pointing the Kalashnikov at them both as they dressed their injuries. For Richard, the bullet had torn the flesh, causing a deep gash in two places but not lodging into the bone. It had caught the soft bit of his belly before grazing past his arm. He took off his shirt and began cleaning the wound with antiseptic, gritting his teeth as the liquid stung its way into his flesh. Andreas had a hole in his shoulder, but didn't have any bullet to remove. They helped each other bind the bandages and secure them as the painkiller began to take effect.

When it was done, Abdul spoke looking directly at Andreas. 'We're going for a walk, until we get a signal on my phone and then you're going to make a call.'

'Who am I going to call?'

'David Helford.'

'Tell him to come here to the gorge and bring the scroll to me. If he doesn't come within four hours, then I'll kill you both.'

Chapter Forty-Nine

Crete, Greece. February 16th 1950

After an arduous journey, Chania didn't seem welcoming. Rain sprayed the harbour front whipped up by fierce winds blowing in across the bay. Waves swirled at the entrance and surged through the defences, drifting at great pace, gathering momentum, rocking moored fishing boats huddled together, before the sea poured over the wall and splashed against the boarded up tavernas. Callidora hadn't seen him for over nine years, but recognised Kosmas immediately. He stood under an awning, sheltering from the rain, almost a man, but not quite. Seeing him, she dashed across the curved promenade as the rain drenched her in a matter of seconds. She didn't care. Kosmas was all that mattered. Her brother, the last link to her family ravaged by war.

'Kosmas,' she shouted, her voice only just audible above the thrashing of the rain on the awning. Holding out her arms to hug him, she smothered him in kisses. But Kosmas didn't respond in kind. She felt his reticence, holding back a part of him that refused to be hurt.

'Come on,' he said in a matter-of-fact way. 'We need to get out of the rain. There's a hotel just down the street. They've plenty of rooms. It's a miracle they're not closed during winter.' He didn't smile.

Thirty minutes later, they sat in the hotel bar supping Greek coffee. There were no other guests and the owner grumbled about serving them. 'It's not as if he got any better offers.' Callidora joked, trying to lighten the mood.

Kosmas appeared preoccupied, as if he was going through the motions. 'It's great to be back,' Callidora said smiling, hoping to get some response from her brother.

'Is it?' said Kosmas abruptly. 'What's good about it?'

Callidora stared directly into Kosmas's eyes. She could see he'd matured way beyond his years. All the pain and killing, not just fighting the Germans, but also in the civil war. No way for a boy to spend his childhood. 'What's the matter?' she said softly. 'You don't seem pleased to see me.'

Kosmas stared at her, his young eyes welling with tears. 'You can't just come back after all this time and expect everything to be okay. It's nine bloody years and for most of that time I didn't even know you were alive.'

'I've wanted to come back...but the journey's so long and the civil war...'

Kosmas let out a cynical laugh. 'The civil war.' He sneered. 'A disaster for Greece...worse than the war with the Nazis. It's been a nightmare.' His voice was breaking. 'You know, I lived in the ruins of Tirata, but fighting around our village made it impossible to stay. They even had a battle in the Seven Sleepers gorge. You know where the cave is, where there are all those skeletons.'

Callidora raised her eyebrows. 'Is the cave safe?' she enquired, trying not to make too much of her concern. 'Has anyone plundered it?'

'Why would anyone do that?' said Kosmas. 'It's full of bones and not much else.'

'Yes. I know,' she replied. 'I ask out of respect for the dead in the cave.'

Kosmas clearly thought she was mad asking such a stupid question. 'It's okay...never been better. A rock fall saw to that. Blocked the entrance.'

Callidora frowned. It can't be, she thought. 'Do you know when the fall happened?' she asked.

'Sometime during the war, I think.'

Callidora felt a shiver run down her spine. Lenny must have been in the cave recovering the scroll, but God had stopped him revealing the secret. The second mission must have also failed.

The scroll must still be in the cave.

She glanced back towards her brother. His lips were trembling and his anguish marked his troubled demeanour. Everything became too much. He burst into tears and Callidora reached out to hug him. This time he was more responsive, resting his head on her chest. She stroked his hair and let him cry. 'I've missed you,' he said. 'Everybody's gone...I'm on my own. Even Ikaros has gone. And you know about our brother, Nikos?'

'Yes...I know, I still blame myself for his death, but I didn't know about Ikaros being dead. It can't be?' she replied.

Kosmas shook his head. 'No, he's not dead,' he said, suppressing a thin smile. 'It'll take more than that to kill Ikaros.'

'So where is he now?' said Callidora.

'He left and ran off into the mountains with Nikoletta, to protect her from all the people who wanted to kill her because of her time with the Nazi. I've not seen him for years. He never comes back to Chania.' He hesitated. 'Did you know they married each other?'

'What?' said Callidora, incredulous. 'Nikoletta was with Kohlenz and then married Ikaros? It can't be.'

'He took her after you left,' Kosmas replied. 'The villagers didn't like it after she betrayed the Englishman.' Kosmas's demeanour changed again. 'They're hypocrites the lot of them... Bastards,' he snapped.

'Don't talk like that, Kosmas,' she scolded. The disappointment surprised Callidora. She hadn't expected to be jealous that Ikaros had married Nikoletta. She looked again at Kosmas. At sixteen years old, her little brother could not just be concerned about Ikaros leaving.

395

There was something else. 'What else has happened, Kosmas? You must tell me,' she pleaded.

Kosmas looked distraught. 'That Nazi who was with Nikoletta...you must remember him, the bastard who burnt down our village. He came back to Greece to help the fight against the Communists.' His voice was getting louder. 'After what he'd done, how could those bastards accept him? I hate them.'

Callidora's jaw dropped; her eyes rolled back; her gut tightened. She tried to stand, but her legs were like jelly. She staggered forward grasping Kosmas' shoulders.

'He's here.' Her voice barely made a sound. She wanted to scream. She wanted to groan but nothing came out. 'Kohlenz is here.' She swallowed hard, gulping down water that had come with the coffee. The anger and hatred festered. Eventually she found her voice. 'Where is he?' she shouted.

'I don't know,' replied Kosmas tersely. 'He was living in one of the villages...in the mountains...I can find out.'

Callidora's hand shook. Her desire for revenge was seething in her veins. She was silent and then she spoke. 'I want you to do something for me.'

'What?' said Kosmas.

Callidora lowered her voice. 'I want you to get a message to the Nazi. Tell him Callidora is back on Crete and wants to see him. At the sight of where Tirata burned. The day after tomorrow. Have you got that?'

Kosmas looked around, a look of shock on his face. 'You're not seeing him,' he whispered. 'He's a sadistic bastard.'

'Exactly, that's why I have to kill him. For Nikos' sake. He must die.' Callidora took hold of Kosmas' hand. 'Do this for me Kosmas. For the honour of Nikos. For our family...for Crete.'

Chapter Fifty

Crete, Greece. August 6th 2005

'Okay. Okay. You win,' Andreas stepped backwards, focusing on the gun.

The fire, reduced to embers, struggled to stay alight and one of the lamps, starved of paraffin, had gone out. Abdul just stared, saying nothing, continuing to stroke the trigger of the Kalashnikov.

Dawn was beginning to break. The twilight illuminated the edge of the gorge with a line of white light; the day beginning to squeeze out the night, while the sky remained dark and full of stars..

Abdul grabbed Andreas by the shirt. 'Get me the vest, in the tent over there,' he yelled. Andreas did as he was told, bringing out a suicide vest, explosives bulging from its many pockets.

'Put it on him,' said Abdul, gesticulating at Richard with the barrel of his gun.

Andreas obliged, carefully handing Richard the phone, which he decided must be the detonator. Andreas' hand shook as he pulled the straps tight. Richard caught his glance.

'I'm sorry,' said Andreas.

'Tape the phone to his back so he can't reach it and then tie his legs and hands.' Abdul continued to issue instructions.

When it was done, Abdul looked pleased. 'Come on,' he said to Andreas. 'You're going to call his father.' He turned back, looking at Richard. 'Don't move an inch. One false move and you're history. The trigger is very sensitive.'

They set off walking up the track but didn't get far.

Chapter Fifty-One

The ruined village of Tirata, Crete, Greece. February 18th 1950

The sounds echoed in her conscience. Voices from the past. Music at Easter. Dancing and laughter. Bouzouki; its flat metallic twang accompanying the wailing stories that her brother told. The men dancing; Ikaros, Pavlos and even Kostas, the traitor, the man who killed Hans. Firecrackers. Father Manousos preaching in the church.

Echoes of the past ringing through her memory.

Sweat ran down the palm of Callidora's hand, hidden under the folds of her smock, tightly gripping the butt of a Luger.

A gun to kill Kohlenz. A German gun; a gift from the soldier she'd killed by the waterfall. She'd hidden it in the cave where she'd met Lenny and now after all these years, she had it in her hand. A link to the past, taking her back to the dark days of 1941.

The wind blew across the square, rattling shutters on the barn, which still stood – whistling through the skeleton buildings, devoid of wood except a few blackened charred window frames.

Only the cold stone remained.

Her eyes scanned the square; the evidence of the terror laid out before her; drinkers in the *kafenion* disturbed by bullets riddling the walls. Cups broken on the floor. Coffee never drunk. Conversations never had. The stone walls splattered with the blood of the dead, never washed in the rains, stained for eternity.

Callidora wept. The sight of the family home was too much to bear. Wild herbs were growing around the table, the place where the family met to eat and talk. She could see the sorry remnants of their possessions still strewn among the rubble.

Entering the ruins, desperate to find an outlet for her grief, she knelt among the debris, raking through it with her hands.

'Callidora.'

She swung round to see the man she'd come to kill; a gun pointing directly at her head. She knew Kohlenz would not miss and would kill her if she attempted to draw her own gun. The odds were against her, but she no longer feared dying.

With her one free hand, she tore at her dress, ripping away the material covering her chest, thrusting it in the German's direction. 'You killed me the moment you raped me, so finish the job,' she screamed, in English; the language she'd learned in New York. The language she knew Kohlenz would understand. 'Is that clear enough for you?'

Kohlenz smiled. An evil smirk that fed the hate she had for him.

'Kill me,' she screamed. Her tears were hysterical. She bowed her head waiting for the bullet; her hand on the concealed Luger.

'Stand up,' Kohlenz said. His voice quiet, conciliatory. 'I didn't kill you during the war and I don't want to kill you now. The war is over.'

'My war is not over,' she bellowed, standing up. 'It will never be over until one of us is dead.'

'I want the scroll.' said Kohlenz. 'That's all I want. It's still in the mountains, in one of these caves, isn't it?' He sounded desperate. 'Put your hands up.'

Callidora walked towards Kohlenz. A determined stride, no concern that the nearer she got, the nearer she came to death. Her hand still clutching the gun, refusing to follow Kohlenz order. 'Never. You'll have to kill me first,' she said, continuing to stare directly at the Nazi. He looked less terrifying without his uniform to hide behind.

Kohlenz looked worried, something she'd never seen during the war. He stepped backwards. 'Put your hands up or I'll shoot,' he cried, panic sounding in his voice. She had the upper hand.

She was less than five feet from him. *How could she miss?* In one swift movement, she pulled her gun and squeezed the trigger. The surprise on Kohlenz face registered on her brain, but only for a second. There was no kick back, no recoil. The gun had jammed.

Kohlenz burst out laughing. An evil laugh. His confidence returning when the odds of survival swung back in his favour.

But Callidora was unperturbed. She ran at him screaming. He turned quickly and sent her flying. He was on her again. On top, just like before; she turned her face away and closed her eyes. He had his hands round her neck, forcing the butt of the gun against her windpipe.

'Where is the scroll?' he shouted again.

'Never,' Callidora whispered, struggling to breathe, opening her eyes defiantly before closing them again.

The wind blew harder, kicking up dust, blurring her vision, but in that split second between opening and closing her eyes, she noticed a movement behind the Nazi.

She was right.

'*Stoppen,*' a voice shouted. A woman's voice. '*Lass sie gehen.*'

The sound of German being spoken made Kohlenz jump, releasing his grip on Callidora's throat. He put his hands in the air, still holding the gun. Callidora opened her eyes and looked at the woman. Tall, wearing a long black coat, her blonde hair was tied back in a severe fashion, but she had no gun.

Kohlenz with his back to the woman must have assumed the worst.

'*Wer bist du*?' said Kohlenz.

'*Lass die waffe fallen*,' said the woman.

Kohlenz obeyed and dropped the gun. Callidora moved quickly, picking it up, pointing it at Kohlenz. This time the gun would not jam. Her hand tightened on the trigger. Tears streamed down her face.

'No,' shouted the woman, firmly, this time in English. 'This is not the way. He must go to a court of law and be tried.'

'He has no right to justice. He's a murderer.'

'No,' said the woman again. 'You'll be arrcstcd.'

Callidora continued pointing the gun. Her hands shook and it took all her effort to keep its barrel upright. She thought of Andreas. Her little boy, who'd never seen his father, the man she was about to kill. Her mind raced. There was no need for a court of law. He was guilty. She'd seen his murders with her own eyes.

'No,' said the woman, shouting louder. 'Please don't kill him.'

Callidora sank down on to her knees; the little innocent face of Andreas still in her mind. All the hate had been translated into something good: her son. God would decide the fate of the Nazi and she was sure that one day he would rot in hell. The moment when she might have pulled the trigger had past. Weeping, she lowered the gun to the ground.

Kohlenz stared down at Callidora, smirking with gleeful contempt. Slowly, he turned round to face the woman, laughing out loud when he saw she had no gun. He lunged forward, picking up his gun and pushing the woman to the ground.

'Who are you?' he snarled.

The woman crawled backwards, trying to get away. It was too much for Callidora. Regretting her decision not to kill Kohlenz, she ran at him, rage overtaking her common sense, her attack certain to fail. He hit her hard sending her rolling into the dust. Dazed, her head spun, her eyes blurred, but she could hear the woman speaking.

'I'm from the Nazi war crimes investigation unit in Dortmund...I've been tracking you for months. A force of investigators is already in Crete. If you kill me they'll find you and punish you even harder than the war crimes tribunal.' Callidora was surprised by the tone of her voice, which sounded strangely authoritarian, but not scared, as if she knew Kohlenz would not kill her.

The news stopped Kohlenz in his tracks. Swinging the gun from right to left, aiming at them both, he backed away.

'Don't try to follow,' he shouted. With that, Kohlenz turned and ran.

Callidora could not see Kohlenz when she heard the gun go off. She picked herself up and crouching down ran towards the sound of the gunfire.

Kohlenz lay in a heap. As she moved closer she saw two bullets had ripped gaping holes in his back. Blood was flooding the wounds. The sound of groaning confirmed he was still alive.

'I heard everything.' The voice came from behind and she recognised it before turning. Kosmas was standing, frozen with fear. A double-barrelled rifle in his hand. 'I learned to shoot in the Civil War,' he said. Tears filled his eyes. 'I couldn't let him live...I couldn't...not after what he did to you.'

Callidora hugged her little brother and wiped away his tears with the edge of her shirt. 'Thank you,' she said softly. Letting go of Kosmas, she walked back to where she'd left the German woman.

'What's happened?' said the woman.

Callidora ignored her pleas and picked up the Luger. 'This time it won't jam,' she said to herself.

Reaching Kohlenz, she pushed him over onto his back. Kohlenz screamed in pain and that pleased her.

She looked down at Kohlenz. His eyes were open. 'I want to see your eyes when you die,' she said. The Luger was less than a foot from Kohlenz's face.

It was too close when Callidora fired. Blood splattered her face.

It tasted sweet.

The German woman saw everything. Callidora turned to face her. 'I suppose you want to arrest me for murder,' she said.

Before the woman could answer, Callidora raced into one of the ruined houses. 'You see this house...' she shouted back through the space where their window had been. 'This is my home.' She hurled two chairs into the square. 'I used to sit on these chairs and eat with my family. Kohlenz did this.'

'I'm sorry,' said the woman.

'Sorry,' Callidora shouted. 'That bastard killed thirty-five people in our village. Cut them down in cold blood. In this very place. How many he killed elsewhere, I don't know. I just know it was indiscriminate slaughter and you talk about sorry.'

Callidora came back into the square and faced the woman again. 'Who are you?' she said.

'My name's Uma Kastner. I'm a Theology professor at the University of Heidelberg. I taught Hans Tuebingen and discovered one of his letters in the University archive. It was sent from Crete and mentions the finding of an ancient manuscript by a Greek woman. You're that woman, aren't you, Callidora?'

'What if I am?' Callidora replied tersely.

'I want to study the document for Hans' sake, for his memory.'

'So all this prosecutor stuff is nonsense. There's just you?'

'Yes. It is just me, I'm afraid.'

'So you won't say anything about Kohlenz.?'

'No.'

Kosmas spoke. 'We'll get rid of the body. Nobody will know what happened. There will be the briefest of investigations but without a body they'll never prove its murder. I'll answer to God over this, not the police.'

For the next two weeks, the two women, with the help of Kosmas, struggled to remove the few rocks that blocked the entrance to the cave. The rock fall had been relatively modest and one by one, with the assistance of a couple of donkeys, the stones were taken away and a space cleared, allowing a narrow path back into the cave.

Callidora squeezed through the gap, feeling relieved to be entering the cave on her own. Uma had said she wouldn't try to follow and Callidora didn't argue. She tasted the earth on her lips as she wiggled on her belly, shivering; terrified that she might get stuck in this claustrophobic space. Sweat dripped out of every part of her body and she fought a battle to stay calm. She remembered the time when she'd swum along the water-filled tunnel. Her fears had been kept in check because she didn't care whether she lived or died. Now she had a cause to live again and all the fears returned.

The first thing she saw was Lenny's body; identifiable by the clothes still wrapped round his decomposed corpse. She'd seen the skeletons before, but this was different. A man she might have loved. A man who'd given up his own place on a boat to give her the chance to stay alive. She began to cry; an almost hysterical grief made more intense by the darkness of the cave. She'd always known he'd be dead. Seeing the remains of his body gave her closure but also filled her with guilt. It was her fault he was lying here.

'A skeleton is just a pile of bones,' said Callidora out loud to herself, tears pouring down her face. 'Until you know the person who occupied the bones. The real person is what makes this hard to bear.' Lenny's fingers were wrapped around the scroll, a final gesture to her that he'd done what she'd asked. She cried as she lifted the scroll clear of his fingers and realised that she loved him. The realisation made her determined to remove his body and bury it where it belonged, with his comrades at Suda Bay.

She could not get out of the cave quickly enough. She'd come back later to get the chalice and casket and bring out Lenny's body. Something was unnerving her, driving her out into the sunshine.

Outside, Uma poured over the document, frustrated that she did not read Greek. 'What does it say?' she said waiving the papyrus in Callidora's direction.

'I'll not tell you until the monks of Preveli have seen it,' replied Callidora. 'It's what Hans wanted.'

Uma looked angry. 'The monks will keep it for themselves,' she snapped.

'I don't care what you think. The monks will see it first. That's final.'

Callidora started to untie the donkeys. They were getting restless, shaking their heads and stamping their feet. One of them launched into a repeating bout of braying, something she'd not seen before.

A rumble and then the floor turned to jelly. She stared at the ground and could barely see the moving earth. 'Run,' she shouted. Great boulders began to shudder, breaking loose. A boom like thunder echoing from the top of the gorge. She could see the fear on Uma's face as the rocks began to tumble down the mountain. Uma seemed frozen to the spot. 'Run,' Callidora shouted again.

It was over in seconds. As the dust began to clear, the first thing she noticed was the number of boulders covering the entrance of the cave. This time her bare hands would not be able to clear an entrance.

Dear Lenny was trapped for ever.

She found Uma lying on the floor, suffocating under a pile of grit and debris. A miracle stopped her dying, just like the miracle that made Callidora sense she should escape.

Chapter Fifty-Two

Crete, Greece. August 6th 2005

A single shot whistled past, striking a rock and bouncing back towards the fire, but doing no damage. Scary, but not intended to kill. It made Abdul jump, but he reacted, rolling over and over until he had cover.

'It's him,' Andreas shouted.

The man who fired stepped into the open. He was about one hundred metres away.

At this distance, he had his chance with what looked like a high velocity rifle. Richard could just make out the telescopic sights. Straining his eyes, he watched the man move closer. He could see him clearly as the sun rose above the mountains, driving a shaft of brilliant light into the gorge.

But he didn't recognise his father.

The beard didn't help. Attention to detail was what he remembered, always clean shaven and smelling of Dior's Eau Sauvage. A Brookes Brothers suit and Thomas Pink shirt and silk tie with Windsor knot, clean finger nails never sullied on their farm, and a wedding ring always displayed. He wasn't the man to run away, his mother had said. But what did she know about her husband? Along with the beard, which hadn't seen a pair of scissors in months, straggly long curly brown hair, shades and a scruffy bomber jacket completed the picture.

Abdul kept his head down and watched, flicking the safety catch of his rifle.

Within shouting distance but still out of range, the man stopped. 'Abdul,' he shouted. 'I have the scroll.' He held up a cylinder in one hand while still clutching his rifle. 'I could've killed you then but chose not to. I don't want to kill you, Abdul.'

Abdul laughed. 'Because if you had, your son would've been blown to kingdom come.'

'Let him go, Abdul, and we can talk.'

The voice sounded like his father's clipped accent from Harrow, all the vowels clearly spoken. It felt strange and surprising to hear his voice. Strange, because he didn't know whether he felt anger or relief that his father was here. Surprising, because he recognised the voice immediately even though it was over four years since he'd last heard him speak. It was as if his father's voice had been indelibly engrained in his memory. Something that could not be erased, however hard he tried. Richard strained his ears to listen to hear every word that his father spoke. He tried to move a little but the ties were grazing his skin and the gunshot wound had started bleeding again through the bandage.

'You betrayed me in New York, so how can I trust you now?' Abdul yelled, climbing to his feet, he began walking forward with his gun cocked, ready to fire.

David Helford remained unmoved by any sign of danger. 'It's true I was working for them, but I never lied to you about my reasons for studying Islam. I never lied to you about the existence of the scroll.' David moved his gun upwards in response to Abdul's aggressive stance. 'I know they're hypocrites, I told them about the attack and they did nothing,' he shouted back. 'The Americans need to be taught a lesson and we can do that, Abdul. If you'll only let me.'

Richard felt his stomach churn. *What was his father saying?*

'You said that to me before,' screamed Abdul. They were both standing still now, within range, waiting for one of them to fire. 'We were going to release the scroll to the world.'

'We still can, Abdul. I have the scroll and there's something else I need to tell you.'

'What?'

'I've got a tape of the conversation I had with the CIA.'

Abdul had stopped walking. 'What are you saying?'

'That's why they are hunting me. They want me dead in case I tell the world about their incompetence. We'll release the scroll together when you carry out the action you are planning here on Crete. We'll silence these hypocrites. It's what Sheikh Zabor would have wanted.'

Abdul lifted his gun again. 'What about Kleiner? How did you know it was Kleiner who betrayed us and tipped off the Israelis?'

'I guessed.'

'What? How?'

'Well I knew it wasn't me so it had to be Kleiner.'

'I don't believe you.'

'Look, I'm here now…with the scroll. Why would I be risking my life if I didn't believe in this cause? Sheikh Zabor trusted me so, why don't you?'

Richard almost screamed at what he was hearing. It was as if he didn't exist. His father didn't seem to notice him, which made him sick.

'If you trusted Sheik Zabor then why didn't you tell him where you were hiding?'

'I didn't even tell my family.' Richard looked in his father's direction expecting at least an acknowledgement that he was family, but there was nothing. The CIA would have found out. I had to stay secret.'

The two men continued to stare at each other. Richard looked first at his father and then at Abdul. Both were laying down their weapons. Both were beginning to trust again. They were still apart, within firing range, but their guns were on the ground. Richard could not believe what he was hearing. His father had to be bluffing. He could not endorse that future.

Slowly, they walked forward to face each other. They embraced like long lost brothers. Richard noticed Andreas move forward. He was gritting his teeth. Anger bled from his face like the blood he was still losing. The two men had forgotten about him, so focused on their own reunion. Without warning, Andreas rushed forward, running towards the two men. 'Bastard,' he shouted, directing his abuse towards Richard's father. 'You know my mother didn't want it revealed. After all I've done to help you hide from the CIA.'

David swung around, grabbing Andreas by the arm. 'Your mother supported the pursuit of truth. Denying Muslims the right to truth is a sin in her eyes. She'd support what I'm doing.'

Andreas glared back at him. He hesitated, as if he might agree with David's point. 'Besides,' he shouted. 'You don't have the scroll. It was destroyed in 9/11. '

Abdul looked shocked. He turned on David. 'Is this true?' he bellowed.

'No. It's not true,' said David angrily. 'It's here.' He waved the cylinder in the air, triumphant, the spoils of war, and this made Richard hate him more. 'I had the combination to your mother's safe deposit box. HT 674 675 and used my influence in financial circles to gain access to it. I took the scroll to protect it. I was worried your mother would destroy it.'

So that's what the number means, Richard thought. He felt so helpless, still tied with explosive. He wanted to kill his own father, but could only watch the scene unfold before him.

Andreas flew into a violent rage, striking David across the face. 'There's something else you don't know,' Andreas snarled. 'My mother's dead and it's your fault she died.'

410

Chapter Fifty-Three

New York City, USA. September 11th 2001

Callidora could never bring herself to burn it. But now it would be burned. The moment she heard the explosion, she knew that this was the day that she'd die. She could hear the building groan, feeling it move from side to side. Huge girders of metal grinding together. Like another earthquake, just like the one that killed Lenny.

It would now kill her.

She could hear the shouting and screams but could see nothing. Nobody would look in the room. Why should they? It was windowless, a vast array of filing cabinets and safe deposit boxes. Just papers, she'd said to her lawyers, nothing of any value.

Except to God.

Why now? She'd not seen the scroll for several years and the moment she decided to remove it, this happened. She didn't know what *this* was and nor did she need to know.

She knew it was the end.

Her cell phone rang, making her jump. A connection with the outside world, someone to say her goodbyes to. She looked at the number on the screen for several seconds, wondering whether she would share her last moments with this caller.

It was Andreas. Her son. The only person she cared about.

'Hello,' she said.

'Mum, for God's sake, where are you? I'm watching it on television, two planes have hit the twin towers. Are you in there?'

'Is that what it is?' she replied calmly.

411

'You're in the North Tower?'

'Yes. I am. I said I would get the scroll.'

'Shit, Mum. You've gotta get out!'

'No.'

'What do you mean, no? You'll die if you don't. Have you got the scroll?'

'Don't you see?' She spoke slowly. 'This is how it's got to be.'

'What? I'm telling you, Mum, just get out now,' he pleaded.

Another crash. The floor moved under her feet, knocking her to the ground, sending her phone skidding across the floor. It felt as if the floor was no longer level. She crawled upwards to retrieve it and spoke into the mouthpiece. 'God doesn't want the world to know the secret.'

'That's ridiculous. What do you mean?'

'I've told you the story. Father Agathangelos was right. When I showed him the scroll, he told me to destroy it. I could not bring myself to do it and now God is making me pay the price. He'll destroy it for me.' She coughed, the heat was getting intense and smoke was seeping under the door. 'You should understand,' she whispered. The building was moving again. It wouldn't be long now. 'Hans was killed when I shared the secret with him. Lenny died while trying to recover it. I must also die for failing to destroy it.'

Tears filled her eyes, mixing with the drops of perspiration rolling off her forehead. 'I'm going to die,' she felt her voice breaking. 'I'll tell you a few more things,' she said.

'Anything you want, Mum.' The tone of his voice had changed, as if he had become resigned to his mother's fate. 'What do you want to tell me?'

She thought for a moment about whether she should tell him after all. The room was getting hotter and, looking up, she could see smoke beginning to trickle through the air conditioning vents. Sitting down felt better, she'd tell him one last thing, whether he cared about her or not, it no longer mattered.

'I didn't tell you that I told the British about the scroll when I was in Cairo,' she said. 'Winston Churchill heard about it and demanded the scroll's recovery. They sent a Cretan, a man named Ari, who helped me when I escaped from the island, but he was shot dead by the Germans before he could reach the gorge.'

'So how did you get the scroll out of Greece?'

'It was 1950 when I went back. The Civil War had finished so things were easier. There'd been gunfights in the gorge but nobody knew what was in the cave because the entrance was still blocked. Knowing where the cave was helped me find it. There were only a few rocks blocking the entrance, which were easily removed with the help of mules. I found Lenny's body in the cave.'

The noise outside became deafening, much louder than before, like a huge, powerful surge of an enormous waterfall. The building was swaying even more violently, so strong that one of the filing cabinets tipped on to the floor.

'Oh my God,' shouted the voice on the line. 'Oh fuck!' he was screaming. 'The fucking tower's coming down.'

She continued to be calm, ready to face death, convinced that it would end here.

'Father, please forgive my sins,' she prayed.

'But…' he hesitated, 'don't do it.'

'I can and I will. I'm eighty years old. If I'd tried to reveal the secret before, God would have destroyed me earlier. The moment I agree to share it, look what happens. This is God's will.'

Andreas no longer spoke. All she could hear were cries and *Oh my God* repeated over and over again. The television images were more real to him than her own

413

voice. After several seconds his voice came on the line again.

'Goodbye, Mum.'

'Goodbye, Andreas. I've always loved you.' She pressed the red button on her phone and threw the mobile across the floor. She turned the scroll in her hand. Something felt different, but she couldn't decide what. Maybe her memory was fading, it was so long since she'd last seen it. She coughed, thick smoke irritating her throat, desperately trying to find some pockets of uncontaminated air. An incredible thirst, just like Jesus on the cross. Her last moments sucking in the hot air of a hairdryer, clinging to life. She'd read the scroll one last time.

'I John of Patmos, who shared with you the Revelations of God, bring you witness to the last word of God who gave me visions of the end of the world. There is one other prophecy that I was forbidden to write down. It is the prophecy of the little scroll, the scroll that tastes sweet in the mouth and bitter in the stomach, referred to in my book of Revelations, but never revealed. Something compelled me to write the words down, against the wishes of the angel who appeared to me in my dreams. I had to write it down in order to be released from the pain of the great lie, burning a hole into my soul.

'Before I relate the words of the prophecy, I must explain how the words of God came to me. When I wrote the Book of Revelations, I could not forget the arguments I had years earlier with the disciple Barnabas. I met Barnabas when he travelled with Paul to Ephesus, where I was Bishop. Paul had fallen out with Barnabas because Paul would not allow the inclusion of his Gospel in the Holy Bible. Paul shared my view about Jesus being the Son of God. The Gospels he wanted to include supported that premise whereas the Gospel of Barnabas did not. Barnabas had written that when Abraham was

414

willing to sacrifice his son before God, it was his only begotten son Ishmael who was chosen and that it is the word of his descendants who will the rightful heirs to the word of God. Jesus was a descendant from Isaac, Abraham's second son. The Gospel of Barnabas stated that Jesus had said he was not the Messiah and he was not worthy to untie the shoes of the Messenger of God, whom you should call the Messiah, who was made before me and will come after me and shall bring the words of truth, so that faith will have no end. Barnabas told me he was there when Jesus spoke these words and swore to me that they were true. So I asked God for one last vision and this is what my dream revealed.

'A mighty angel came to me from heaven, wrapped in a cloud, with a rainbow over its head and said, the revelation of Jesus Christ is the testament of God and should be adhered to, but it is not the only word of God. God will reveal his message in many ways and has done so through Abraham, Elijah, Jeremiah and Jesus Christ. And I tell you this, Jesus is not the last messenger of God. One will come after him with a message stronger than the last, whose word will prevail until the Day of Judgement. He will be a descendant from Ismael and will represent a break from the tradition of Isaac.

'Before the Day of Judgement, the seven churches of Asia will plunge into the valley of despair. It will not be only Babylon that becomes a dwelling place for demons. The pursuit of fornication will taste sweet to many, but when babies are plucked from wombs, their stomachs will be bitter and ache with hunger.

'Those that refuse to accept the word of the prophets, whether here, now or in the future, will be punishable by God and will perish in everlasting damnation.'

415

The building gave its final gasp. With popping sounds and grinding steel snapping like matchsticks, it buckled outwards and then down it came, collapsing into oblivion.

Chapter Fifty-Four

Crete, Greece. August 6th 2005

The first thing Richard noticed was horror etched onto his father's face. He seemed genuinely distressed that Callidora was dead. 'What happened?' he said quietly.

'9/11 happened,' snapped Andreas. 'She was in the towers trying to get back the scroll that you stole.'

'I didn't know she was going there, Andreas. If I'd known I would have contacted her. I didn't want your mother to die, I swear.' David looked sad. To Richard, his father appeared sincere, but that didn't stop the disgust he felt at his father's betrayal.

Abdul was getting impatient. 'Give me the scroll.' he said.

David handed it to him. 'It's written in Greek, but I've included an English translation.' Abdul sat down and began to read, his gun still in his hand; his finger still on the trigger. Richard kept his eyes on Andreas, refusing to look his father straight between the eyes. Andreas was getting more and more agitated. 'You can't let him have it. It's not what my mother would have wanted,' he shouted. 'It will lead to more war and suffering. More tyrants like Kohlenz. More good people like your father, Lenny, being killed. Can't you see that?' he pleaded with David.

David looked at Andreas and then at Richard, addressing them both. He seemed concerned that he couldn't make either of them understand. 'That's precisely why we're doing this.' He pointed over to where Abdul was sitting. 'This man had no issue with America, until his daughter and wife were killed by an American bomb. He retaliated and took part in 9/11. Has the war in Iraq or Afghanistan improved the lot of those countries?

Have the thousands of civilians died in vain?' Seeing his father staring at Andreas, Richard stole a glance, trying to believe in the stirring words, but all he saw was a troubled man, who'd been running for too long. He didn't avert his eyes quickly enough and found himself locked onto his father's piercing stare. Richard could not pull his eyes away as his father continued to speak. 'The scroll will bring an end to the conflict by unifying religions. Christians will no longer be non-believers. Islam will no longer be the enemy of Christianity. They will be allies.'

'Untie me,' Richard screamed.

Abdul raised his head from the document. 'No,' he said abruptly.

David didn't even protest. 'Don't you see,' David said. 'The origins of Islam are grounded in the religions that went before. Allah is the god of all religions. There is only one God. There is no reason to fight each other. All I want is peace between our peoples,' said David.

Richard was speechless, shocked by his father's naivety. 'Do you honestly think this is what Al Qaeda want?' shouted Richard.

David looked back in Richard's direction. Their eyes met and Richard saw the gulf between them and yet the blankness of his father's expression did not tell the whole story. Richard could barely speak. 'Crazy,' he whispered.

'You're both mad,' shouted Andreas. 'A fucking sick misguided scheme that'll achieve nothing but more killing.'

Abdul glared, not amused by Andreas' rants. He put the document down carefully and standing up, without warning, charged, swinging his rifle butt. He struck Andreas on the jaw, shattering the bone and breaking his teeth. Andreas staggered backwards, holding his mouth, his hand covered in blood.

Abdul stared at Andreas. 'If you want to stay alive, do not say another word.'

The sight of blood on his hand threw Andreas into a frenzy. He screamed, grabbing the muzzle of Abdul's gun. Falling backwards, he pulled Abdul down, both hands on the barrel, but Abdul still had the trigger. Abdul was younger than Andreas and fitter. They rolled over and over and his father just watched. Richard could do nothing, nailed to the spot. One false move by him and they'd all be dead.

The bullets shattered the early morning silence, an explosion at point blank range. A flock of birds perched above them took off, squawking, terrified of the sound. Big shells blasted into Andreas' stomach and cascades of blood erupted. Richard felt his body shake. He saw Abdul's gun smoking, spent with the instruments of death.

'No,' Richard screamed.

Abdul rolled away, his tunic covered with blood and guts. He seemed unmoved by what he'd done. Richard wanted to retch. He was dumbstruck, appalled at his father staring impassively at the body and back to Abdul.

'You shouldn't have done that,' David said calmly.

'You shouldn't have fucking allowed it,' Richard screamed. 'Are you satisfied?'

Richard watched his father's indifference to the death of Andreas. The anger Richard felt inside was overpowering.

Chapter Fifty-Five

Crete, Greece. August 6th 2005

The heat of the sun burned Richard's face, forcing him to open his eyes. He pulled himself up and tried to remember. The suicide vest had gone and he could move his wrists, red raw from the rubbing of the plastic ties no longer restraining him. His legs were stiff and painful from being crouched in the same position, but he could move. Staggering to his feet, he felt queasy, even dizzy as blood pumped around his veins. His head hurt and his shoulder looked a mess. Congealed dried blood caked around the bandage, but at least the bleeding had stopped. He remembered his father coming towards him and then nothing. A blank page until he woke.

The body lay a few feet in front of him, a red stain on the stone floor, emphasising the memory of the night when he'd found his father and lost him again in a few short minutes. He closed his eyes, struggling to recall what his father had said.

And Abdul, how he'd wanted to bring him down but every step of the way, he'd been out fought and out manoeuvred. If he ever got out of this, he'd leave MI6. All he was good for was a quiet life in academia, reading books and thinking. Maybe he'd teach, be a good husband who comes home every evening and reads a bedtime story to his son. Killing people was not something he was ever going to be good at.

But he could not let go now.

He looked again at Andreas' body and thought of the suffering of his mother – Callidora. He thought of his grandfather dying trapped in the cave only a few feet from where he was standing. He owed it to them to find the scroll and stop its secret being revealed.

But he had no idea where Abdul and David had gone? They'd left in a hurry, as the tent and all the equipment had been abandoned. He looked at his watch and calculated that they must have been gone for four hours. They could be anywhere by now.

His brain ticked over the options. They'd leave by boat, he decided. The same boat that landed Abdul on the island. The ship was docked in the island of Gavdos, so they'd need another boat to take them there. He looked at his map and saw the route of a ferry that went from Hora Sphakion. He wondered whether his father would know that it was where the defeated Allies escaped from in 1941. If he did, it might appeal to his sense of irony. He switched on his mobile phone, relieved to see his battery was nearly full, half expecting a signal to pop up, but knowing it wouldn't. It would take him at least an hour to get back to where he'd left the car and where he could make a call. They'd be at sea before he even reached it. GCHQ would have to track the ship to give them time to decide what to do.

Without thinking, he started running along the path, determined to get to the car as soon as possible. Twenty metres down the track, he remembered Andreas' body lying face up in the dirt, staring at the sky.

The falcons were already circling on the thermals immediately above him, waiting for their chance to pounce on the corpse. He couldn't leave him to be ripped apart.

'Move him into the cave,' he said out loud to himself, panting for breath, conscious that he needed to get away, but knowing he should do the right thing. Thoughts rushed through his mind. The Cave of the Seven Sleepers is the right place to be laid to rest, he thought. It's where Andreas' mother had been and is already a crypt for the

421

dead. He'd close the entrance and leave them all to rest in peace.

Andreas was lying about fifteen feet from the entrance to the cave. His face didn't look calm in death, suspended in a moment of anger. Gripping him under the arms, Richard pulled the body towards the cave. He strained in the heat, sweat running down his face, parched with no water to drink. Reaching the entrance, he sat down and eased himself backwards, pulling the body as he edged towards the cavern. The confined space made him retch as the scent of death pervaded the air around him. The lamps had gone out and, with little daylight penetrating the entrance, he was in almost total darkness. He switched on his torch and, pleased he could now stand up, pulled Andreas the final few feet. Laying him down, he crossed his arms and thought he should say something. Words failed him in the darkness.

'Goodbye,' he said. 'You did your mum proud.' He flashed the torch and noticed something reflecting back at him. It sparkled high up on a ledge, about fifteen feet above him. He stopped and picked it out with his torch. Lying on its side and looking dented, he could see what looked like a chalice or goblet. Despite it being covered in dirt, it still managed to sparkle in his torchlight. He wanted to leave it there and get out of the cave. Every second he delayed, Abdul and his father would be further away.

But he couldn't leave the chalice. It was too important. He flashed his torch up the cave wall looking for a way to climb and saw there were a few foot holes. It took him over thirty minutes to reach the ledge. His first attempt failed, and he slipped, falling all of six feet back to the cave floor. Sheer exhaustion was getting the better of him. He cursed his decision to try and retrieve it, knowing he was losing valuable time to find Abdul and his father. But when he reached the ledge, he knew his climb had been worthwhile. He also found a casket, not visible from the cave floor, Catching his breath, he shone his torch downwards wondering how it had got there in the first place. Then he realised: earthquakes had rearranged the rocks in the cave, raising the ledge several feet in the air.

Something else caught his eye. Another skeleton, but this one seemed different. He flashed his torch and studied the shape. One hand was pointing to the sky. He shone the light more closely and noticed a ring, exactly like his father's; a ring joined by a distinctive V shape. Not all the clothing had disintegrated, unlike the other skeletons.

It had to be Lenny. *How did he miss his grandfather's body when he first came into the cave, just a few hours ago? It was as if his grandfather's soul had prevented him seeing his body until he had found his notebook.* A decision to leave him in this spot was the only thing to do, but one day he'd come and see him buried in Suda Bay.

Back outside, he looked at the objects. Their beauty was astonishing and, although he could not be certain, he felt that they must be connected to the scroll. Loading the treasure into a haversack found in one of the abandoned tents, he strapped it to his back and prepared to leave the gorge.

Before he left he found some more dynamite in the tent. Lack of time prevented him doing something sophisticated. Instead, he ignited the fuses attached to the sticks and tossed them one by one into the entrance. One of them missed the intended target and rolled down the rock towards him.

He turned and ran. The blast threw him off his feet and, exposed, he covered his head as debris peppered the floor around him. The haversack protected his back from injury and once again he felt a mystical force; a protection from danger. A cloud of dust filled the air, shielding the cave entrance. Covering his mouth, he pulled himself to his feet and waited for the curtain to lift. His efforts had paid off.

423

The narrow cave entrance had collapsed, blocking the opening from the world once more.

The Cave of the Seven Sleepers could return to its slumber.

When he finally reached the car, lack of water had taken its toll. His throat felt like sandpaper and his forehead stung with the effects of sunburn. The drugs he'd been given hadn't completely worn off, draining his reserves of energy. Abdul and his father would be halfway to Turkey by now and he could do nothing about it.

He telephoned Brian. The phone seemed to ring for ages before anybody picked up. At last, a voice answered and he breathed a sigh of relief.

'Brian, listen to me,' he said 'Abdul's got the scroll and escaped. He's with my father. I think they're going to leave Crete on the boat they arrived on.'

'Sorry to disappoint you but they're not leaving that way,' Brian's voice seemed subdued. There was none of his usual brash enthusiasm laced with expletives. 'The boat left last night about twelve hours ago, it's heading in the direction of southern Turkey.'

'Shit,' said Richard. 'So how are they going to get off Crete?'

Brian sighed. 'I don't know. but we don't think Abdul knows either.'

'What do you mean?'

'He's on a suicide mission. The intelligence is strong.' He sighed again and added, 'Or at least I'm told it's strong. Something is going to happen on Crete.'

'But why Crete?'

'This is not like 9/11. It's something to do with the scroll.'

'So where's the intelligence coming from?'

'I don't know. All I know is that it's come from Rowena and she won't say who her source is.'

'What *do* you know, Brian? For Christ's sake, why do I get the feeling you're not being straight with me? Get Rowena on the line.'

'No.' Brian sounded irritated. 'She won't speak with you. You're on your own. You'll never stop Abdul. I'd get off the island and come home.'

Richard knew Brian was right. Why else did he want to leave the Service? 'If I come home, I might as well hand my resignation in.'

'Maybe, maybe not. Whatever happens it's better than being dead. Abdul's too good for you.'

'I can't just leave it, knowing my father is out there with some deluded idea that he's doing the right thing.'

'I don't know, Richard. The whole thing is full of shit. Maybe your father is the only way we are going to stop this happening…So what's the story on your father?'

'He's a fucking terrorist, that's his story,' Richard snapped, his eyes were filled with tears. He was embarrassed by his breaking voice. Exhaustion was taking over. He took deep gulps of air but the heat made it hard to breathe. His father's situation was unfathomable. He tried to speak but his mouth was parched. He supped at the last remnants of water he'd found in the car. The water was warm and unrefreshing. At last he managed to get some words out.

'I think he's been seduced by the moral side of Islam. A stand against Western materialism and imperialism. A stand against globalisation. All that shit. After 9/11, he went to ground. Running from Abdul and the CIA. Both wanted him dead.'

'But how could he lie low for four years without a whisper?' asked Brian.

'Somebody must have helped him,' Richard replied. 'I mean, how did he get out of the US? The country was in lock down after 9/11.'

'You're right,' said Brian. 'He must have been helped.'

'Look, it's true what Rowena said. My father was working for the CIA just before 9/11, following Abdul. He became interested in the scroll and Islam while searching for the reasons for my grandfather's death.'

'And what happened?'

'He met Abdul and they became friends. The CIA were watching Abdul and recruited my father to do their dirty work.'

'So you're telling me that's why the CIA wanted us off the case?'

'Yes. That's correct. Abdul was working with the terrorists, a sort of logistics man on the ground. My father managed to get Abdul to let down his guard. He let slip details of the 9/11 attacks two days before it happened. My father reported it to the CIA who told the President.'

'They knew 9/11 was going down, and they didn't do anything about it?' Brian bellowed down the phone.

'Yes. My father was pissed off that they did nothing.'

'Not as pissed off as all the dead in the twin towers.'

'I know, but it gets worse. My father has a tape, proving he warned them about 9/11. He wants to help the Islamists...He's gone over to them.'

'Holy shit.' said Brian. 'No wonder the CIA want your father dead.'

'But where are the CIA *now*?' said Richard. 'I mean, if they wanted Abdul that much why the fuck aren't they on his tail like I am?'

Brian didn't reply.

'Are you still there, Brian?' Richard shouted.

'Yes...I'm here...Look, Richard, I'm in the dark about this as much as you...I'm sorry I haven't been straight with you. That's because I don't know what's going on and Rowena won't tell me or talk to you.'

The reality of his situation hit Richard hard. 'She's stitching me up, isn't she? Using me to get close to my father and flush out Abdul. That's what all this is about, isn't it?'

It was Brian's turn to be angry. 'Look, Richard, spying is a dirty game and you better believe it. You've done your bit. Get on the plane and come back to London.'

Richard cut the phone connection and put his head in his hands trying hard to think. It was tempting to do what Brian suggested and run. Go back to Becky and his child and live out his life as a good father. But there were too many unanswered questions that would plague him for the rest of his life.

He decided to drive for Hora Sphakion anyway. The ship may have left Gavdos but that didn't mean Abdul and his father weren't going to join it using another boat. The one that got them onto the mainland. Abdul must have landed in Hora Sphakion and so somebody might know where he was heading. Brian seemed convinced that Abdul was going to do something. A last act. They could be anywhere on Crete by now. He knew he was clutching at straws but that was all he had.

Driving was nearly impossible, but somehow he managed to stay on the road, annoying Greek drivers at how slowly he moved. It was still early but he'd had nothing to eat or drink for hours except for a few drops from the bottle he'd found in the car. His thirst had reached crisis point and his eyelids were like swing doors, determined to shut, no matter how hard he resisted. The drugs hadn't completely worn off. Reaching the village of Kares, he cried out with relief at the sight of a roadside taverna. Like all Greek restaurants, they had plenty of bottled water. He bought six bottles, not because he needed six, but he felt more secure having them in the car.

Replenished, he tried to drive on, but his eyes fell shut almost immediately. The car began snaking from side to side. He was on the wrong side of the road when he woke up, a pick-up truck, blaring its horn, coming towards him.

427

Swinging the wheel was an impulse reaction, avoiding the truck but sending the car into a wild under steer. Too tired to contemplate getting the car under control, he took his foot off the accelerator and, gripping the wheel, refusing to brake, he drove into the skid and waited for the impact.

Nothing happened. It was fortunate he'd entered a plateau, surrounded by the mountains. The road levelled off and he began to lose speed. Sighing, he touched the brake and came to a stop. It took less than five seconds for him to fall asleep.

His mobile phone rang.

His eyes opened immediately, he sat up with a start, unable to work out where he was. He looked at his watch. He'd been asleep less than fifteen minutes, but felt refreshed and relieved he was awake. God knows how long he would have slept for. Still fighting off sleep, he fumbled for his phone.

'Hello,' he said.

'The ship has moved to a position about ten nautical miles off the coast of Gavdos. It has stopped moving.' said Brian. 'We're trying to get satellite pictures.'

Richard thought for a moment. His mind kept going back to the conversation between his father and Abdul. 'Who is Sheikh Zabor?'

'What's he got to do with all this?' said Brian.

'It was something Abdul said about Kleiner tipping off the Israelis.'

'What did you say?' Brian shouted.

'It's probably nothing. Abdul asked my father how he knew that Kleiner had tipped off the Israelis.'

Oh shit…that's it.' Brian exclaimed.

'What?'

'Sheikh Zabor is an American Saudi billionaire beloved by the Americans. The Israeli's have assassinated him and the Yanks aren't best pleased.'

'They didn't say they'd killed him.'

Brian laughed. 'The Israelis don't do things by halves. Take it from me, they've killed him.'

'So, how did my father know about this?'

'The Israelis.'

'But we know my father worked for the CIA?'

'Unless it was the Israelis who got him out of America when he became persona non-grata with the Yanks.'

'So what happens now?'

'Rowena's spoken to the Americans.' He paused changing his tone. 'The CIA want the ship sunk.'

'What?' Richard said, raising his voice. 'You're joking, aren't you?'

'The Prime Minister's been told and he's speaking to the President.'

'But nobody is talking to the Israelis?'

'No, of course not. They haven't even told the Americans they were responsible for the death of Sheikh Zabor.'

'But we know Abdul and my father aren't on the ship…well not yet, anyway.'

'We'll monitor the situation and hit them when they are. It's just a contingency plan in case they make it back to the ship. It may never happen.'

'But if it does…' Richard hesitated. 'You're going to kill my father?' Richard didn't know why he said that. It just came out. Something inside of him wanted to be loyal to his own flesh and blood. God knows why, he thought. His father was a traitor. 'You can't just bomb the ship in Greek waters,' he shouted.

'We can and we will. The Greeks won't be told. They're a member of NATO. It's time they earned their fucking dues.' Brian's tone changed. 'Look, Richard, I'm sorry about your father. I'm afraid he's a danger to the West. He's going to have to be eliminated.'

'But what if my father was working for the Israelis?'

'We don't know that.'

429

Richard heard his phone bleep. His battery was running down and he was unable to charge it. It made no sense that his father might be working for the Israelis. It was improbable that they helped him escape from the US. Why would they want to help him and go against their allies?'

'So all this is to keep quiet about 9/11?' Richard said. He felt his anger growing at the idea.

'Listen to me, Richard. 9/11 happened. Get over it. It's a done deal. Raking over things doesn't help the dead.'

'You mean Blair will protect the President.'

'They've cocked up in Iraq and Afghanistan. Not to mention the balls up over the London bombings. They can't afford another major scandal if this gets out. These wars were a direct result of 9/11. What if the public find out they could've been stopped? There'd be riots in the streets.'

'But what about truth?'

'Fuck truth.' Brian was getting angry now. 'You're a fucking spy, Richard.'

'You know, Brian…' Richard spoke quietly. 'You know I'm not so sure I'm a spy any more or even want to be.' At that moment, Richard began to understand where his father was coming from. He was fighting for truth. He respected the Muslim faith and wanted to do his bit for them. To win jihad with the truth. The Gospel of Barnabas was suppressed. The truth was suppressed about the religions and about 9/11.

'And another thing,' Brian said.

'What?'

'The fucking scroll. Look what the Muslim world will say when they find this out. That Mohammad was the last prophet. How are the American people with all their Bible bashing, happy clappy Christians going to take it if someone tells them they need to start reading the Koran? Remember when Bush used the word "crusade".

Everybody said it was an accident. He didn't mean to say those words, they said. It's bullshit. Plenty of Americans see this war as a battle between Christians and Muslims.'

'The American people won't believe the scroll,' Richard replied.

'Course they won't, but how will they disprove it? The Yanks will've lost the argument.'

'So what are you going to do?'

'We need to destroy the scroll. If they board the ship, they'll be heading to Southern Turkey. We'll scramble Tornados from Cyprus. A night bombing raid. The *Istanbul Star* will be at the bottom of the Med and the Greeks won't even know until it's too late.'

'You're not serious.'

'Course I'm fucking serious. You got a better idea?'

'You don't honestly think they would be fool enough to get on the ship? That's a decoy, he'll escape some other way.'

'You may well be right but we have to cover all the options.'

'Options...I don't see you looking for any other options.'

Ending the call, Richard started the engine and began to descend the final stretch of road towards Hora Sphakion. Pumped up by what Brian had said, he no longer felt tired. The more he thought about it, the more Richard began to sympathise with his father's point of view. If he knew about 9/11, why didn't he do more, even if the CIA didn't listen? Brian was right, there had to be a bigger picture and his father was being naïve thinking he could change the world.

But something still worried him. Where were the CIA? What game was Rowena playing? What had the Israelis got to do with all this?

He drove on in a daze, thinking less about the road he was on and more about what he would do when he got to his destination. The road seemed to go on for ever as a series of incredible hairpin bends slowed his descent, forcing him to meander down the hillside as if there was all the time in the world. Time, he didn't have.

The road wound its way through sand coloured rock, peppered with Cypress trees; a stark contrast to the sea below, which appeared more intensely blue and translucent. At last he reached the outskirts of the port, parking his car where he could see the jetty. A ferry came in, crowded with tourists.

The harbour was lined with tavernas, bustling with the tourists who'd just got off the ferry. The village nestled in a cove, surrounded by steep mountains falling into the sea. A curved harbour wall provided shelter for a few yachts and motorboats moored away from the ferry. He found a seat in one of the tavernas that had a view of the harbour, ordering a Greek salad and a beer. The ferry sounded its horn and began pulling away from the quayside. The waiter brought his salad and beer and he handed over a twenty euro note.

'*Epharistou*,' he said. 'When's the next ferry to Gavdos?'

'You've just missed it,' the waiter replied. 'No more until tomorrow.'

'Can I hire a boat?'

'Ask for Stravros, where the fishing boats are.' He pointed down to the quay. 'He'll take you.'

Richard poured olive oil onto his salad and took a mouthful of feta and a chunk of tomato. He chewed the food slowly and surveyed the people walking along the harbour front. His eyes darted around, desperately looking for some sign that Abdul and his father might be here.

Then he saw someone.

A woman.

The woman wore a veil and was dressed head to toe in black. She looked out of place, surrounded by scantily clad tourists, walking along the quayside heading towards the jetty where the yachts were moored. Although she stood out, nobody gave her a second glance.

Richard left his half-eaten salad and followed the woman. She was about fifty metres in front of him. He held back, hiding amongst a group of tourists sauntering past the tavernas, pretending to look at the menus as he went. He almost lost her. She turned abruptly and began walking away from the harbour. Richard broke into a trot but the woman slowed down without warning, turning down a narrow alley. He stopped and peered around the corner.

He was staring straight into the barrel of a gun.

His hunch was right. The woman holding the gun was somebody he knew.

'Amira,' he shouted, putting his hands up.

Amira pulled him into the alley. 'Richard.' She looked shocked but also relieved to see him. 'I thought you might be dead,' she said.

Richard gazed at her, thrown once more by her intoxicating beauty. But there was a hardness which he hadn't experienced before. The weak vulnerable woman he'd met at her house in Dagenham had vanished. The men who accosted them in London would not have had it so easy now. Despite the veil, her face was made-up, but there was no sparkle in her eyes. She acted with ruthless assurance. A woman who knew how to handle a gun and wasn't afraid of using it.

'I know I owe you an explanation,' she said at last. 'I've been helping Abdul but it's not what you think.'

'So who tried to kill you when I saw you in London?'

'I'm not sure but I think it was Mossad.'

Richard's jaw dropped. 'What have the Israeli's got to do with this?'

'I'm working on the theory that they're protecting your father.' Richard stared at Amira unable to hide his shock

433

at what she was saying. 'You're working on a theory. What are you saying, Amira? I thought this was all about finding the killers of your family...All about Masood?'

Amira dropped her head, averting her eyes from Richard's gaze. 'Because I want to kill your father.'

Richard surprised himself by how shocked he was at Amira's statement. After seeing his father last night, the way he callously dealt with Andreas' death, his feelings were hostile but something inside made him instinctively resist Amira's intentions.

He could see she was concerned by his reaction. 'Why?' he said angrily.

Amira paused before speaking. 'It's difficult for me to say this,' she said, quietly. 'I work for the CIA. When I told them of Masood's contact with Abdul, they told me to feed them any information about Abdul. I tipped the CIA off about Abdul's exact location in Afghanistan. I thought they were going to send in a drone but they did nothing as if they didn't want to kill him. When the connections between Abdul and your father emerged, they told me to find him as well and kill him. I knew if I supported you, then maybe your father would come out of hiding.'

Richard felt his blood drain. He had never understood why the CIA were nowhere to be seen. Now he had his answer. He tried to collect his thoughts. 'So all this stuff about discovering Masood's notebook – all made up?'

'Yes. I'm afraid so.'

'And all this time, I thought you were a grieving widow...I knew there was something not quite right about you, but working for the CIA, that's not you.' Richard stared at Amira, unable to hide his feelings. He still didn't know whether she was telling the truth. 'I never took you to be a contract killer,' he said, accusingly. 'You seemed so gentle, so vulnerable.'

Amira could no longer hold his stare. She looked embarrassed by her admission.

'I thought you loved Masood,' Richard continued. 'Masood would never have gone anywhere near you if he knew you were so devious.' Richard sounded disappointed and his voice was laced with bitterness.

'Do you think I don't know that?' Amira retaliated. 'You know nothing about my relationship with Masood…I was grieving for him. He was a good man…I…' She hesitated, contemplating what she was about to say. 'Yes…I loved him.'

'Not enough to tell him the truth,' Richard sneered. He turned and banged his hand on the wall. 'Tell me something. The day we met on the Southbank, how did you know I was in London and where I was?'

Amira bowed her head again. 'I was tipped off.'

'What?' Richard struggled to contain his anger. 'The only people who knew where I was were in MI6.'

'Yes, that's right,' she replied calmly.

Richard stared at Amira. A terrible thought struck him. *It was why Brian was so evasive. Who could he trust? Not the woman standing facing him now, not Rowena or Brian?*

Amira continued speaking unperturbed by Richard's shocked expression. 'I wanted to ask you about your father but then the gun went off. You saved my life, Richard. I'm grateful.'

'Not grateful enough to stop trying to kill my father.'

'Your father is a danger to the West. He has to be eliminated.' Her voice was low and hard and he knew she had a point.

Richard decided to let the Rowena question slide. Brian had already indicated that there was something going on that he didn't understand. 'So when did you come to Crete?' he said.

435

'I flew out the same day as you and waited for Abdul to arrive. I helped him get what he needed to carry out his excavations at the cave.'

'So, apart from your logistical help, what does Abdul get out of your friendship?'

'He's an honourable man. He made a promise to Masood to protect me …I think he likes me…maybe as a wife for him.'

Richard looked at her and wondered whether any man would not find Amira attractive.

'Ha bloody ha. What a gullible man he is,' he replied. 'Just like me.'

'How…?'

'We're all stupid bastards, taken in by you.'

Amira pushed the gun back into his face. 'We've got to work together, don't you see, Richard?'

'Even when you're trying to kill my father?'

'Yes…he's betrayed you…you hate him…'

Richard turned and grabbed Amira by the wrists. 'Whatever I think about my father is my business, so don't assume I'll let you kill him.'

Amira's eyes were hard. 'I care about you, Richard, I really do. I've no argument with you, but if you stop me eliminating your father, I'll kill you as well.'

Richard stared at Amira in disbelief. 'I saved your life.'

'It's a dirty game you're in, Richard. We can't afford to have morals.'

'But you said you believe in God. *Don't you?*'

Amira was silent. Richard could see he'd struck a nerve.

'Yes. I do,' she said at last. 'But I can't let your father change my view of the world.'

There was a lack of conviction in her voice. *A contract killer couldn't possibly believe in God.* Richard sighed. 'I just don't understand you, Amira, any more than I understand my father. But he is my father,' he said quietly. 'Don't make me choose.'

He decided to drop it and watch his back. He needed Amira, for now at least. 'So where are we going?' he said. 'Do you know where my father is?'

'Let's get in your car and I'll tell you,' Amira replied.

11.00 a.m. Road to Chania from Hora Sphakion

Ikaros' car was not built to withstand the way Richard was driving around the winding roads across the mountains back to Chania. Every time he went around one of the hairpin bends, his wheels screeched. He was still angry with Amira and that reflected in the way he was driving. Amira said nothing until he was well clear of Hora Sphakion.

'I found this on Abdul's boat,' she said.

Richard slowed the car down and glanced at what Amira was holding and recognised it immediately. 'It's Callidora's Bible,' he said. 'Stolen from me. She was the Greek girl who found the scroll during the war.'

'There's a bookmark in it and some notations that Abdul must have written as they are in Arabic. The bookmark opens the Bible at Chapter 19 of the Book of Revelations. Abdul's underlined this section. I don't understand the Greek.'

Richard braked sharply, bringing the car to a standstill.

He took the Bible from Amira and read the words.

'*These two were cast alive into the lake of fire, burning with brimstone*. Oh my God,' said Richard. 'Is that what he's going to do…burn people to death?' Richard remembered what Brian had said about a terrorist incident, not like 9/11 but connected to the scroll. 'They're going to read the scroll out to the world and then throw some innocent people into a lake of fire.' Richard looked at Amira. 'Okay, so you think they are going to pull something off by a lake. There can't be many lakes in Crete, and how will they get the gasoline to burn the lake?'

'There's an oil tanker which docked in Heraklion yesterday. We think one of Abdul's men has got at least a truck load of gasoline…we think its heading to Lake Sikonas.'

'Who's we?'

'The CIA. We've tracked the arrival of a known Al Qaeda terrorist who has landed on the island. He's a Libyan called Mohammed Zorakuni. He's assisting Abdul.'

'Should we be telling the Greek authorities?'

'No. We don't want them knowing anything about this until it's all over and we've got Abdul and your father.'

'Okay, so let's suppose you're right, how are we going to stop them? There is just the two of us and I haven't got a gun.'

'That's where you're wrong.'

She removed her veil first, allowing her long black hair to fall loosely around her shoulders. The confines of the veil made the hair look unkempt but, as she ran her fingers through it. The long black dress was the next to go. Underneath she wore jeans and a long-sleeved t-shirt. The shape of her body was not what caught Richard's eye. The long black smock she'd been wearing concealed an arsenal of weapons. Two Glock 18 machine pistols and two ammunition belts full of bullet magazines. 'One of these is for you,' she said.

Chapter Fifty-Six

Crete, Greece. August 6th 2005

11 a.m. Suda Bay Harbour

Dinah Zevi was worried.

She stood on the bridge of Abel B Multzeimer's yacht, *Achilles*, and surveyed the scene, fixing her binoculars on every inch of the harbour, looking for anything that was out of place or might suggest an ambush. The yacht was enormous, so big that it had to dock in Suda Bay, which was normally used by cruise liners and cargo ships. There were two rusty container vessels sharing the harbour so the battleship grey of the yacht with jet black tinted glass and helicopter perched on the ship's helipad could not fail to attract attention. It had an almost military presence, deliberately austere to hide the secrets of its billionaire owner. Today, it needed to hide more secrets than usual.

Dinah didn't want to deceive David. They'd worked well together as a team. She remembered his lovemaking with appreciation but the age difference was always going to be a barrier to their relationship. He had become too reliant on her support. Now was a good time to dispense with his services. Maybe Mohammed Abdul Alim would do her job and make the goodbye that much easier. The thought that David might die this way brought a tear to her eye. Embarrassed by this sign of weakness, she wiped her face as if she was wiping away sweat rather than tears. Mossad had no time for human frailty and certainly didn't do sentimentality. Dinah looked around to see if anybody had noticed. She breathed a sigh of relief when she realised that she'd got away with it. Shedding a tear for a lost comrade was never tolerated. Being sentimental about David was not part of the brief.

A large door opened at the side of the vessel. Released slowly, the door swung downwards supported by heavy-duty chains, until it rested on the quayside. Two grey Mercedes vans came out of the exit and drove away at speed and without ceremony. The yacht's door began closing as soon as the vehicles had cleared the gangway.

Dinah's radio crackled into life, demanding attention.

'Z1 preparing to approach the target. Permission to proceed.' The man speaking on the radio spoke in Hebrew.

'Permission to proceed is granted, Z1,' said Dinah. 'Do not engage until authorised. Wait for orders...Z2, please confirm, over.'

'Roger. Z2 confirmed,' answered another voice.

Dinah was standing only ten feet from the helicopter. The pilot was already seated at the controls. She checked the safety on her AK-47 and swung the leather strap over her head. As the rotor blades of the Bell 429 chopper began spinning, she ran across the deck and climbed aboard. She was wearing combat fatigues and Randolph Aviator sunglasses. Her long blonde hair was tied back, preventing it being blown by the wind from the helicopter. She was ready for action. The pilot took off, even before she had secured her seatbelts. Dinah put on her headphones and spoke to the pilot. 'How long to Lake Sikonas?'

'Ten minutes,' the pilot responded.

'I want you to put down on the hillside that overlooks the lake. I want to be close enough to view what's happening down by the lake's beach. Approach from the back of the hill and keep low so they can't see you land from the lakeside. Is that understood?'

The pilot nodded and put his thumbs up.

11.35 a.m. Lake Sikonas

Abdul reckoned that there were over three hundred people already on the beach. Most were sunbathing near the clusters of tavernas at the end of the access road. On the lake, he could see pedalos and kayaks spread across the water. Before sunrise, Abdul had moved a tanker of gasoline into a quiet position at the end of the beach and no one noticed. His team of twelve Libyans were also in place, hiding in the undergrowth that fringed the beach. They'd arrived in Crete by boat the night before, docking in a quiet cove, ten miles east of Hora Sphakion. Mohammed Zorakuni had picked them up just as Sheikh Zabor had instructed. When the men arrived as planned Mohammed arranged for three Suzuki 4-wheel drive Jeeps to bring them to the lake. The men hid their AKs and grenades and proceeded as if they were tourists and had all the time in the world to perfect their suntans. Mohammed had done a good job so far. It was only a matter of time.

Abdul relaxed, knowing he could rely on the men. They were Al Qaeda operatives, armed to the teeth and ready to fight for the cause. Colonel Gadaffi was losing his grip on power, making it easier to train fighters at a secret base, out in the desert south of Benghazi. These men were true jihadists who would never hesitate to greet Death when it came knocking. They would embrace it. Abdul stared in the direction where the men were hiding but could see nothing. That was good, he thought.

Everything was ready. The camera he'd rigged up on a tripod only needed a button to be pressed. It would record the whole wonderful event. The world would soon know the secret of the scroll and how it proved the supremacy of Islam.

Abdul glanced at David who was standing next to the tanker beside the camera. David's face betrayed nothing that suggested he might not go through with what Abdul wanted. And yet Abdul still had his doubts. He

441

contemplated killing David, but for now that wasn't possible. He needed David's appearance on camera to give the scroll some credibility. A Westerner, a British subject no less, previously lost in the twin towers, resurrected by the grace of Allah. David Helford commanded a profile to make people sit up and listen. He was the one to read the scroll and declare the supremacy of Islam over all other religions.

Abdul let his eyes wander over the beach, staring in the direction of the tavernas which were filling up with people trying to get out of the sun if only for a few minutes. He congratulated himself at how perfect the location was. It would be easy to round up some of the sunbathers just as soon as he gave the word. His men had learned rudimentary orders in Greek so they could marshal the members of the crowd who were not singled out for special treatment.

He just had to give the order.

11.35 a.m. Hillside overlooking Lake Sikonas

Dinah lay flat on her stomach and looked down on the lake. From her vantage point, she could see an almost perfect oval shape, within sight of the sea. Being the middle of summer, the freshwater had begun to evaporate, forming a beach, perfect for sunbathing away from the salty breeze. An idyllic scene. Normal, except for one thing.

A petrol tanker was parked on the edge of the beach at the furthest point from the tavernas.

At first, she thought it was abandoned but then she saw two men standing beside it. She refocused her binoculars and tried to see who they were. A smile crept across her face. She had them.

Abdul and David.

Dinah looked down at the tracking device she was holding. The signal was strong. The GPS coordinates

442

popped up on her screen. She took out her mobile and started typing in the numbers that revealed David's position. Dinah's fingers hovered on the send button as she wrestled with her conscience by going over the details of why she was doing this.

David's tracking device had been concealed in the back of his watch. It was David who brought her here. Her orders were to kill David to appease the Americans who by now had learned about Sheikh Zabor's demise. The evidence Mossad would produce would prove once and for all that the Sheikh was funding terrorism and that Abdul Alim was not a double agent, despite what the Americans might think. Putting Abdul on the Kill List, to disguise his true intentions must have seemed like a clever idea to the CIA, but Dinah knew that the terrorist act they were about to disrupt would be the proof that Abdul Alim had other ideas.

Dinah sighed. She convinced herself that it was the right thing to do but it didn't seem right to betray the man she'd loved. The man she'd promised to rescue.

Calling in the F15 to deal with David and Abdul would mean the tanker would also be destroyed; a fireball would kill many more and start a wild fire in the forest surrounding the lake. They'd probably end up killing more civilians and causing more damage than the terrorists could do on their own. She looked again at the coordinates on her mobile. Her finger hesitated and then she hit the delete button.

She'd have to do this herself, without help.

A voice came over the radio. 'Z1 calling. We'll be in place in fifteen minutes. Over.'

'Don't break cover until I give the all clear,' barked Dinah. 'You must stay hidden until the men assisting the target show themselves. You need to get in position now so you are ready to engage with the enemy as soon as I give the okay. Is that clear? Over.'

443

'Roger, Leader. Over.'

'Z2, acknowledge. Over.'

'Roger, Leader, Z2 confirmed. Over.'

Dinah put her radio down and stared back in the direction of the tanker. What was Abdul going to do? What was the tanker for? What was David going to do when she did not come for him?

Chapter Fifty-Seven

Lake Sikonas, Crete, Greece. August 6th 2005

11.55 a.m.

Richard and Amira didn't speak as they drove down the road leading to the lake. Everything was normal, like any other beach on a hot day. People carrying canoes, others laden with beach umbrellas and sun mats, mothers holding children's hands. Richard wanted to warn them to get out, but of course that was impossible. He sensed Amira was thinking the same, which is why they were both silent. There was nothing they could say.

He parked the car as far away from the main road as possible where there was no one about. Amira got out before he'd killed the engine, running forward, Glock in hand, a determination he hadn't seen before etched on her face. She didn't stop until she'd reached the cover of the trees on the edge of the beach. Richard followed, pushing through a dense thicket of shrubs, thorns and weeds.

They were less than ten metres from the beach when they first heard the screams.

Amira reacted, hitting the ground and continuing to crawl using her elbows to lever herself forward. Richard was slower, he kept running until a sudden burst of gunfire stopped him in his tracks. He tasted the dirt as he hit the forest floor. Looking through the grass he could see the water and people running.

He crawled the final few feet and peered across the beach. About twenty metres to his left Richard counted six men, all armed with machine guns. He could see that the men had driven a wedge through the crowd. The beech was narrow so easy to cover. Three of them pointed their guns in the direction of a petrol tanker parked on the beach.

Twenty or more people were trapped between the tanker and the cordon. Richard feared that two cast alive into the burning lake would become twenty. The other three men in the line of six were pointing their guns towards the larger throng of people running away. Richard stood up, feeling protected by the terrified crowd, and tried to see what was going on. There were at least six more terrorists forming an arc near the tavernas, firing into the air to halt a mass escape.

One man had other ideas, making a break through the second line, he raced along the water's edge. Strafes of bullets bounced like jumping pebbles, ricocheting across the water, causing fountains of spray, tracking a line to the man. He crumpled face first into the water as the bullets pounded into his back. A woman ran screaming to the man's aid and she too received a hail of fire. The crowd was transfixed with fear.

But there was another distraction.

The lake was burning.

12.02 p.m. Hillside overlooking Lake Sikonas

Dinah saw the men move into place before the crowd and before the firing and screaming started. Her men were split into two groups. The first group which she called Z1 had taken a wide berth around the lake, trying to get through to the tanker. The other group – Z2 – had hung back so as not to attract attention, stationed in their vehicles fifty metres from the beach. They heard the guns before they received the message from Dinah.

'Engage the enemy now…six men…a lot of innocents around. Make every bullet count.'

Chapter Fifty-Eight

Lake Sikonas, Crete, Greece. August 6th 2005

12.03 p.m.

David spoke into the camera. His face appeared unmoved by the screams and gunshots in the background. Abdul stood beside him holding a man he'd grabbed from the crowd. The man was struggling but Abdul had him in an a head lock gripped around his neck. The barrel of Abdul's Glock dug into the man's ear. One shot would blow his brains out.

'My name is David Helford. I'm a British citizen who was pronounced dead in the attack on the World Trade Center on September 11th 2001. I have been hiding for the last four years from the CIA who want to kill me because I warned them about the pending attack and they failed to act. I have tried to give evidence to the 9/11 Commission, but my attempts to come out of hiding have been blocked by those who are trying to silence me. My information regarding the attack was obtained from this man…' David stopped and pointed to Abdul before continuing. 'His name is Mohammed Abdul Alim, a peace-loving Afghan whose family were destroyed in 1998 by an American missile. Before that date he had no interest in Western imperialism. He came to America in 1999 where he was granted asylum with the support of Sheikh Zabor Bin Hitani, a Saudi billionaire resident in the United States. The US government placed Abdul Alim on their Kill List when he fled back to Afghanistan after 9/11…'

David stopped abruptly and swung round to see the flames leaping across the surface of the lake. He stared at

448

Abdul and then towards the crowd. Their screams were louder, more terrified, the gunfire more prevalent.

It was Abdul's turn to speak to camera. Still holding the man, he shouted in his crisp American accent, 'Chapter 19 of The Book of Revelations says two were cast alive into the lake of fire, burning with brimstone. Why am I choosing that extract?' He paused and turned to face the burning lake. 'There are many reasons, not least that Americans revere the last book of the Bible – The Book of the Apocalypse. Here in Crete we have discovered the little scroll that is referred to in Chapter 10 of the same book. It is the scroll that tastes sweet in the mouth and bitter in the stomach. The little scroll, never intended to be read because John of Patmos did not want to admit that Barnabas was right. His Gospel was discredited as a forgery. This scroll written by John will prove that there was a conspiracy to suppress the Gospel of Barnabas. It will prove that Ismael not Isaac was Abraham's first born. It admits that Jesus said that he was not the Last Messenger.'

Abdul stopped speaking as the man he was holding became more desperate. A struggle ensued which Abdul was never going to lose. He dragged the man to the edge of the lake, pulling him into the water. Dense pillars of flame and plumes of black smoke leapt into the sky. Undeterred, Abdul kept wading closer to the fire, his arms still gripped firmly around the man's neck. They were waist deep when he let go, levelling his gun as the man ran, splashing through the water. Abdul fired two shots. The bullets zipped into the lake, missing the target but fired to create fear. They had the desired effect. Instinct drove the man away from the gun but nearer to the fire. He panicked and tripped, tumbling head first into the water. The flames seemed to engulf him like a tiger finding its prey. For a moment, the man was out of sight and then emerged like a flaming torch lifting out of the lake, rushing to where the lake was free of fire. Reaching a clear spot, he submerged himself in the water, extinguishing his burning body.

The camera recorded everything but David and Abdul were no longer watching. The sounds of machine guns were becoming impossible to ignore. The bullets were flying both ways and the crowds were caught in the crossfire; hysterical men, women and children.

They were under attack.

The Mossad agents acted with ruthless efficiency. Z1 attacked the front row nearest to the tanker at precisely the same time that Z2 engaged with the back line. The element of surprise gave them an advantage, which they put to good use. Z2 killed three of the jihadists in quick succession allowing the crowd to surge forward in a desperate attempt to escape. But the crowd also gave cover to the terrorists still alive. They turned their guns on the crowd. A child fell but was picked up by a screaming mother. Another man toppled in a hailstorm of bullets. Some others were driven into the burning lake by two of the jihadists. The sight of the carnage may have made some lesser fighters hang back to save the civilians, but not the Mossad fighters. In their minds, terrorism would never pay whatever the cost, there was no room for compromise.

They charged through the crowd. In a second they faced the jihadists who stood their ground; AK-47s blazing death from both sides. It was a question of who was the best shot. One of the Mossad men was hit but as he went down he continued firing. His bullets found their mark, sweeping across the beach in an ark. He managed to hit two of the terrorists before he hit the ground. His comrades made sure the jihadists were dead.

Z1 group had an easier task. There were no crowds acting as human shields as they were running towards their only means of escape. The jihadists were good but the Mossad fighters were better, maintaining accurate fire while running. This was the difference between life and death. The terrorists stood still, refusing to move, ready to die for Allah, their machine guns pumping bullets but with no clear target. That was their downfall. If they hit someone, it would be luck. The Z1 one group advanced at speed, running in an erratic and unpredictable line. Mossad didn't do luck and there was nothing erratic about their aim.

The whole attack lasted three minutes but Abdul had already escaped. There was a path behind the tanker that led through the forest. David was distracted by the shoot out and staring at the sky. He didn't notice Abdul leave.

Chapter Fifty-Nine

Lake Sikonas, Crete, Greece. August 6th 2005

Richard had noticed Abdul leave.

He'd watched the way Abdul had dealt with the man in the burning lake. He'd watched him calmly talking to the camera while innocent people were being shot dead. Any sympathy Richard had due to the tragic death of Abdul's daughter had gone. There was no excuse for brutality. He could not allow him to get away with what he'd done. Not this time. He'd watched the unexpected arrival of what looked like Special Forces killing Abdul's men and had no idea who they were. One thing was certain. They were good. It was time to show that he was also good and worthy of his grandfather's memory.

As Abdul disappeared into the undergrowth, Richard followed. Abdul advanced as any soldier would do, holding his AK-47 in a firing position while running along the forest path. Richard moved with stealth, using the trees as cover. He knew it would take just one sound for Abdul to be on the ground firing, unlikely to miss. He still felt the pain from the wound he'd received the previous night. He didn't need reminding of Abdul's effectiveness. Richard gripped his Glock 18 machine pistol, tighter than before, his finger hovering over the trigger. It was as if he needed the weapon to reassure himself that it would not let him down.

Abdul reached a clearing and stopped. He was standing fifty metres away looking impatiently at his watch, as if he was expecting something to happen. Richard knew this was his chance. His heart pounded and his sweating hands shook as he tried to flick the gun's safety catch. *If I fire the gun like this, I'm going to miss,* he thought. He forced himself to relax, pushing his back hard against the tree, sure that Abdul would spot him. He breathed in large gulps of air, closing his eyes to focus his mind on what he needed to do. There was no sign of Amira. He had to do this on his own.

Richard peered around the tree. He half expected Abdul to be looking back at him but there was nothing. His back was exposed to the Glock. All Richard had to do was squeeze the trigger. Stepping out, he adjusted his aim and fired.

At the crucial moment, Abdul moved. It may have been deliberate, a sixth sense that smelled danger. The bullet fell short, ploughing up the earth a few feet in front of where Abdul was standing. The immediate response took Richard by surprise. In a split-second Abdul hit the ground while returning fire in a sweeping movement, forcing Richard to take cover behind the tree. The stream of bullets splintered the bark of the trees and Richard knew he was pinned down. Adrenalin pumped into his veins. He was scared that if he stayed put Abdul would kill him. He decided to try to move forward again but only when Abdul reloaded his gun.

He didn't need to wait that long. The unmistakable sound of a helicopter gave him his second chance. Abdul was distracted, only for a few seconds, but it was enough time for Richard to get into a firing position. He ran no more than three paces and let off four rapid-fire rounds. Abdul saw him coming and fired again. But there was only one bullet left in his magazine. He had to reload. The momentary advantage allowed Richard to keep firing before he dived to the left and rolled behind a fallen tree. The bullet hit Abdul in the leg throwing him off his feet only metres from the landing helicopter. But Abdul kept going, reloading his AK, and limping with his back to the chopper, spraying the trees where Richard was lying in a frenzy of gunfire. The firing stopped for a second. The noise of the chopper had reached a pitch that told Richard it had landed. He raised his head and saw Abdul climb onto the helicopter. Seated, Abdul fired again but the pain in his leg and the movement of the chopper affected his aim. Richard was moving fast, completely exposed. There was no way he could let Abdul escape. He ran forward, screaming, firing repeatedly until his magazine was empty. A sharp pain made him stumble; a bullet had grazed his thigh but he kept going. It was that close. Two of Richard's bullets shattered the glass of the helicopter and another hit Abdul once more. This time it was more serious. The helicopter began rising into the air.

Richard sank down onto his knees, exhausted and frustrated that Abdul was going to escape. But the helicopter wasn't rising quickly enough. The rattle of gunfire continued, aimed at the chopper. It was not from his gun. Richard looked around and saw the guns of their Special Forces' rescuers finishing off the job he'd started. It was not long before shells pierced the fuel tank and it ignited. Another helicopter was circling the stricken craft, watching it go down in a ball of flame. It went into a spin first, less than one hundred feet up and burning out of control. The rear rotor was out of action, which rendered the main blades useless. It began to spin wildly. When it hit the ground the other helicopter moved swiftly away.

Richard slotted a new magazine into his Glock and ran to where Abdul's helicopter had landed. It was less than fifty metres away and took Richard only a minute to reach it. The other helicopter was still circling and Richard didn't want to trust it. He kept out of sight and stared towards the machine, still burning. He could see the charred remains of what looked like the pilot but there was no sign of Abdul.

A voice from behind gave him his answer.

'Turn around slowly and drop the gun. Put your hands high into the sky.'

Richard recognised the voice. He did as he was told and turned to face Abdul. There was no gun in Abdul's hand. No reason why Richard should have dropped his own weapon. Abdul was losing blood from a gaping stomach wound. His clothes were in shreds barely covering his blackened blistering body. His black hair was smouldering and his face was like a living skull. There was no skin left. His eyes were closing.

Richard stayed calm and left his weapon on the ground. 'You need treatment, Abdul, or you'll die.'

'Allah will treat me in Paradise. There is no need here on Earth. I will soon be with him.'

'But what of the scroll?'

Abdul said nothing. Two bullets stuck what was left of his head. The back of his head was blown away.

Richard turned slowly to see where the bullets had come from.

Amira's gun was still cocked, but this time it was facing him. Richard was calm.

'He was dead anyway,' Richard said quietly. 'So, now are you going to shoot me, are you?'

'Where is your father?' said Amira. 'I went after him but he's vanished.'

Richard ignored the question. 'The other helicopter's landed.' He was already running.

Chapter Sixty

Lake Sikonas, Crete, Greece. August 6th 2005

Dinah's helicopter approached the landing site at speed, hitting the ground with a bump. The engines remained switched on and ready to be airborne in seconds.

Dinah knew she had only minutes to find David.

Her two assassination squads had done well. No deaths and only two wounded. The civilian body count was more of a concern, which is why it was essential to get herself and all her men away from Crete before the Greek authorities realised what had hit them.

But it was David who found her.

The sound of the spinning chopper blades made conversation impossible. They were separated by ten feet as she walked towards him holding her AK-47 with the safety off. He was smiling, clearly pleased to see her. She could see he was unarmed.

She had to kill him. Her finger tightened on the trigger. Her eyes focused on his eyes. She wanted to hug him, just one last time…for old times' sake. She wanted to shout in his ear and tell him she was sorry.

Dinah didn't see the blade until it was too late and sticking out of her abdomen. The pain came when David pulled the knife out and stabbed again. This time higher, finding her heart. He pulled the knife out for the second time and watched her staggering backwards, her mouth locked open, holding her stomach, trying to do something to stem the blood even though she knew she was dying. She stared at him, feeling a strange sense of satisfaction that he wasn't enjoying killing her. She saw the horror on his face at the sight of her blood on his knife. He rushed forward and caught her before she hit the ground, as if he was trying to make amends. It was her fault he reacted like that. The Mossad way.

'You bastard,' she groaned. Her last coherent memory cursed her own weakness. She'd broken rule number one and paid the price.

Mossad doesn't do emotion.

Richard and Amira got to the clearing moments after David killed Dinah. They didn't know who she was but the shock of the woman lying in a pool of blood was still devastating. Amira drew her gun and prepared to fire but Richard pushed the gun away. He twisted Amira's arm roughly, forcing her to drop the weapon.

'I'll do this,' he shouted, not sure whether Amira had heard him over the noise of the chopper. He didn't care. All his anger was channelled towards his father. For a moment, he watched as David dropped the body and jumped into the chopper, hitting the pilot and pushing him out of the cockpit before he could react. David sat down at the controls and stared back at Richard. It was a look of resignation, even sadness at what he'd done. The eyes of his father were probing Richard's brain, trying to unravel a memory. Richard found himself running, unable to stop. He wanted to be closer to that memory. A memory of Iraq.

But he also wanted to kill his father. He fired once but the next bullet didn't come. He'd forgotten to reload, but he kept on running.

The helicopter was already a few feet off the ground when Richard jumped catching hold of the skid landing gear. The door was open, making it easy to pull himself into the cockpit.

David looked in his direction, shocked to see his son at such close quarters. Richard flew at him, trying to grab the joystick his father was holding. The helicopter tilted forwards but Richard held on.

'Get away,' David shouted.

457

The noise of the rotor blades drowned out his father's voice but somehow Richard heard the words. They were engrained in his consciousness. Words he'd heard before. A simple phrase but one remembered from the past. The shock made Richard drop his guard. He relaxed his hold just enough to let David punch him in the face. Richard fell backwards, his head dangling over the side of the doorway, his body jolting sharply as the helicopter bumped onto the ground. He could feel his father's hands grab him by the ankles and bundle him backwards out of the chopper. He winced as his head hit the landing gear. Dazed, Richard struggled to open his eyes, staring upwards at the blades of the chopper spinning faster, cranking up the noise until the machine lifted into the air. He was confused and unsure where he was. The words his father had spoken rung like a bell in his head taking him back to Iraq. He could hear Bill shouting from the past. Did he say, *Get away*? Bill was waving his hands and shooting.

'Get away!'

The sound of gunshots made him open his eyes. Amira was firing at the undercarriage of the helicopter as it rose rapidly upwards. He half expected an explosion when the fuel tank was hit but there was nothing. In just a few seconds, it was already at two hundred feet and moving up to towards the White Mountains.

Amira ran towards Richard. 'Are you all right?' she said, looking concerned.

Richard rubbed his head. 'Oh shit. I'm sorry.' He blinked his eyes, watery with tears. 'He's got away and it's all my fault. I should have let you kill him when you had the chance...I'm sorry, Amira. I really am. It's just that seeing my father flicked a switch in my head.'

Amira stared at him and said nothing for a few seconds. She looked up to the sky towards the chopper, barely visible as it climbed towards the mountains. 'I could have killed you both, you know,' she said. He could see anger in her eyes. 'I couldn't kill you, Richard, despite what I said…You were blocking a clear shot at your father.'

Richard sighed. He heard his own voice say, 'Thanks,' but in his head he wondered whether it would have been better for them both to die. He looked across at Dinah's body. 'Who is she?'

'My guess is she's Mossad,' Amira replied.

'But Mossad were helping my father. Why would he want to kill her?'

'Because she was going to kill him herself.'

'What?'

'For the same reasons as I was. He's a terrorist.'

Chapter Sixty-One

Suda Bay, Crete, Greece. August 6th 2005

The *Achilles* yacht had already set sail when the helicopter landed. A man was standing on the deck smoking a large cigar and wearing a towelling dressing gown. He looked like he'd just been for an early morning swim. He was older than the pilot of the helicopter and overweight. His face was tanned, his hair short and silvery, greased back with oil applied to protect it from the ravages of the sun. His dark glasses were sinister. A deep tint so black that it turned his eyes into impenetrable black holes.

David Helford cut the engines and stepped out of the helicopter. He ducked below the spinning rotor blades and ran over to where the man in the dressing gown was standing.

'Did you have to kill her?' said Abel Multzeimer.

'I had no choice. She was going to kill me,' David replied.

Multzeimer chuckled. 'You're right of course. You would be a peace offering. Your head on a plate to the Americans in compensation for the killing of the Sheikh.' Multzeimer's thin lips allowed a small smile to creep out into the open. 'But that's Mossad for you. I may have a dozen Mossad agents hiding in my yacht but that doesn't mean I work for their organisation.'

'Of course not. You're a billionaire. You work for no one except yourself,' David said.

'Exactly,' said Multzeimer, pointing in the direction of the yacht's lounge. 'Come with me.'

The complementary smells of mahogany and leather greeted them as they entered the room. Polished wood panelling covered the walls and creamy coffee sofas provided the luxury that only comes with wealth. In the centre of the room was a dining table and a desk with a computer terminal with several screens. Some displayed stock market information but the TV screen, broadcasting pictures from the lake, caught David's eye. It was clear that the police had only just arrived at the scene. They were struggling to keep control of the hysterical crowds. The reporter and cameraman were also having difficulty filming. His Greek was just about good enough to recognise the phrase *many dead*, which he saw flashing across the bottom of the screen.

Multzeimer saw David looking at the TV pictures. 'It's not good that we have an Israeli Mosaad agent lying dead among all those innocent Greeks. If she is identified it will cause a big problem for the Israeli government. I hope it will be worth it...' Multzeimer turned away from the TV and looked at David. 'Have you got the scroll?' the billionaire said.

'Have you got the money?' replied David.

Multzeimer sighed and turned back to the computer terminal. He punched the keys and a previously blank screen burst into life. David peered at it and soon realised he was looking at an image of an international bank transfer between two Swiss bank accounts.

'I have the transaction ready. As you can see,' said Multzeimer. '$500,000 to be paid into your Swiss bank account when I press this button. Show me the scroll first.'

David lifted his shirt to reveal a leather pouch taped around his chest. He unzipped the pocket and produced the document. Multzeimer laid it out on the table and pored over it. 'It looks real enough but of course it's in Greek. Have you got the translation?'

David put his hand into the pouch and said. 'Yes, I have it here. Send the money and I'll give it to you.'

461

Multzeimer hesitated, his finger hovering over the send button. 'If I produce the scroll in public, the government will know that I was involved in Dinah's death.'

'You should have thought about that,' said David. 'Press the button.'

'No,' Multzeimer said abruptly. 'I don't think I will.' He pressed escape on the keyboard and the screen vanished. He looked slowly up at David. 'You are in no position to negotiate.'

When David's hand emerged from the pouch, he wasn't holding the translation. A small Beretta with silencer was all he needed. He fired twice, hitting Multzeimer between the eyes. He seated the billionaire carefully in a chair with his back to the door and left the room.

David cursed, one of the Z squad was running up the stairs to the helipad. 'I saw Dinah's helicopter. Where is she?' he shouted.

'Dead, I'm afraid,' said David, his face grave and upset. David knew he wasn't pretending. The kill or be killed argument didn't make it any easier. Inside, he was hurting.

'How did it happen?' said the Mossad agent, looking suspicious.

'Dinah landed to pick me up. One of the jihadists was still alive. Shot up the chopper…Dinah was unlucky. They killed the pilot as well. I managed to shoot the jihadist.'

'I don't understand it,' said the agent, angrily.

'Look at the bullet holes in the chopper,' David shouted pointing out the damage to the choppers undercarriage.

The Mossad agent bent down to examine the damage. 'I'm going back to the lake.'

'No, you can't go back,' said David. He'd seen the man wasn't armed. He shot him twice in an identical fashion to Multzeimer, ensuring instant death. David climbed back into the helicopter and checked the fuel. Barely enough for another sixty miles, if he was lucky.

Chapter Sixty-Two

London, UK. Three days later

His father was still running. Richard remembered his father running in Iraq, shouting, 'Get away.'

The suicide bomber was young, no more than fifteen. Why should he run from him? Bill Riordan saw the danger when it was too late. He tried to kill the boy but, when he kept coming, he rugby tackled him to the ground, lying over the boy's body until the bomb exploded, cushioning the blast. That was real bravery.

It was why he is alive. He remembered it all now.

It was nothing to do with his father. If his father was trying to save him then why did he know about the bomber? He must have known about the terrorists? Why was he in Iraq when he should have been lying under the rubble of the twin towers?

His father was in his sixties and a terrorist. Why would any man of his age do such a thing?

The telephone rang at Richard's desk. It must have rung half a dozen times before he picked up. Engrossed in his thoughts, wondering what he was going to do with his father, where he was now, the real world seemed to be far away. He picked up the handset and waited for someone to speak.

It was Rowena. 'I'll see you now,' she said quietly.

Richard walked down the corridor as slowly as he could, trying to calm his anger, nervous that he might explode. Reaching the door, he knocked and entered before she could look up from her papers and signal through the glass partition that he should enter.

'Hello, Richard. It's good to see you,' she said, without looking up from her papers.

'Is it?' said Richard. He sat down and waited for her to speak. A couple of minutes passed while Rowena continued to read. Richard stared into space, breathing slowly, continuing to resist the urge to talk even though he had a thousand words to say. The standoff was not something he was going to rise to.

At last Rowena spoke. 'I don't know how to put this.' She shifted awkwardly in her chair and Richard enjoyed her discomfort. 'I apologise if I wasn't entirely frank with you,' she continued, looking him directly in the eye.

'I think that's an understatement,' he said, curtly.

Rowena ignored the comment and continued. 'The only thing I can say in mitigation is that it was for reasons of national security that I acted the way I did.'

'Go on.'

'MI6 has been concerned for a long time about Sheikh Zabor Al Hitani, a Saudi billionaire living permanently in the US and with connections to the Saudi royal family. We had evidence, as did Mosaad, that he was actively funding terrorism, including providing cash to one of the 9/11 hijackers. MI6 were concerned that he was also providing money to jihadist cells operating out of London who were preparing for attacks in the UK. We were also aware of his links with Mohammed Abdul Alim, who you are aware of.'

Richard nodded. 'You could say that. I've got the scars to prove it, but what's all this got to do with me?'

Rowena stood up and went over to a table where there was a jug of coffee. She poured two cups and passed one of the cups to Richard, placing a jug of milk in front of him on her desk. Returning to pick up her own cup, she stopped and stared out of the window across the Thames. 'When you were out of contact, I stared out of this window, just like I'm doing now, and tried to reconcile

465

putting you in danger with our overall mission to keep this country safe. I felt you were taking those risks willingly and therefore were prepared to die if necessary. You had personal reasons for this, things about your father which we shamelessly used for our own ends.' She turned back to Richard. 'I can only say I'm sorry.'

Richard could see that Rowena's determination under stress had taken a battering. She didn't like to admit to him her underhand approach. He remained stern, refusing to show that inwardly he was moved by her apology. 'I'm listening,' he said.

'When we discussed this with the CIA they refused to countenance the arrest of either the Sheikh or Abdul saying that they were both moles in the Al Qaeda network and were working for them. The Sheikh was regarded as an important link to the Saudis which the CIA would not compromise. We knew that was not to be the case but the special relationship tied our hands. C would not countenance going against American policy and eliminating the Sheikh.'

'But Mossad would.'

'Yes, I have worked with Mossad over many years and particularly Dinah Zavi, a female agent. In Iraq, Mossad operated a clandestine hit squad who would assassinate known Al Qaeda operatives who had infiltrated Iraq while it was in so much chaos. It was Dinah who asked me to remove you from Iraq in 2004 after you were attacked by a suicide bomber.'

Richard's jaw dropped. 'Since when do you take your orders from an Israeli agent?' he shouted.

'They were doing us a favour getting rid of people who were giving us problems, but in no way did the trail lead back to us. Dinah told me that you were compromising the operation with your interrogations of captured terrorists. The boy who tried to kill you, I have subsequently discovered, was the brother of Masood who was being held by British forces. He was seeking revenge for his brother's capture. The irony was that Masood was released without charge six weeks after the bomb attack on you and that you had never personally been involved in Masood's interrogation. Bill Riordan and Masood's brother died in vain. All we knew was that Masood was an Egyptian who had turned up in Iraq and was in the Muslim Brotherhood. Any non-Iraqis found in Iraq were deemed to be terrorists. It seems that nobody really checked his background in the Egyptian GIS.'

Richard leapt out of the chair and began pacing the room. 'So why did we not know this when Masood's body was found after the Piccadilly Line bomb?'

Rowena looked away again from Richard's accusing eyes. 'We did know,' she said softly. 'But we couldn't tell you about his wife.'

'Amira?'

'Yes. She's been trailing your father because of his links to Abdul.'

'Why? You know you should not knowingly allow another intelligence agency to go after a British citizen.'

Rowena nodded but did not comment. Instead she continued with her main explanation. 'I had to support the CIA because I was going against them with respect to the assassination of Sheikh Zabor. The CIA wanted your father badly enough to overlook us going behind their back with the assassination of the Sheikh. We also think that Amira was commissioned to go after Abdul to provide some cover for the fact that he was on the CIA Kill List. Whenever Amira tracked him down they never acted.'

Richard remembered what Amira had said about Abdul. How the Americans never sent a drone despite her intelligence. 'I see,' he said.

'Because of Abdul's status with the CIA, we had to prove that Abdul was a terrorist working against

America's interests with the full support of the Sheikh. Of course, we could have picked up Abdul at any time but the lake attack gave us the proof we needed to get the Americans back on side.'

'And his body,' said Richard.

'Yes. That's true. I know you killed him.'

'But there are loose ends,' said Richard.

'Mossad had their own agenda and decided that David must be killed to pay back the Americans for the murder of the Sheikh. Mossad have no wish to fall out with the Americans but will always do their own thing. Dinah was tasked to kill him even though we know they had been lovers and that she'd trained him in the Mossad ways.'

'It seemed that they trained my father too well. He killed Dinah and escaped with the scroll.'

'Yes, that's correct. The Greek authorities found the chopper he escaped in abandoned on a plateau near the top of the mountains. It had been torched. Your father disappeared into thin air.'

'I don't suppose the Greeks have conducted a search.'

'No...They're a bit scared of Cretans and I suspect they want to concentrate on investigating the killings by the lake. They have limited resources.'

'I know all this. I was there, I saw Dinah's body.'

Rowena said. 'There is something, you don't know which the Israelis are hopping mad about.'

'What don't I know?'

'Your father not only killed Dinah, he also killed another Mossad agent and Abel B Multzeimer, Jewish billionaire and arms trader. It seems he wanted to level the score for the Sheikh.'

Richard sat back down on his chair. 'Shit,' he said. There was nothing more he could say.

Rowena looked back at Richard and her countenance changed 'He is now one of the most wanted men in the world,' she said. 'If he releases the scroll to the world, he'll do untold damage. He's a lone wolf, Richard. After the 9/11 setback, and then being let down by Dinah, who was his lover for Christ's sake, he is now on a single man vendetta. He's hiding somewhere. I want you to find him and eliminate him before he does any more damage.'

Chapter Sixty-Three

London, UK. Three days later.

Richard walked out of Vauxhall Cross and headed to the river turning right along the Southbank walk way. He never tired of the view along the river. Despite the growing list of tower blocks in the City, St Paul's never looked underwhelming. Like Tower Bridge or the Tower of London, it was a landmark that told him he was home. He walked close to the water's edge enjoying the atmosphere of the river, letting the breeze wash over his face. Pleasure boats packed with tourists having afternoon tea were speeding up stream, avoiding barges and the huge clipper ferries favoured by workers which zigzagged down the river. It's so much more civilised than the Tube, he thought. There was space to breathe and bombs would not do the damage they did on the underground. He allowed himself a brief memory of July 7th but was pleased it no longer made his hands shake with fear. Iraq, on the other hand, still troubled him. His memory had returned, triggered by his father's words of warning, but that was the problem. His father remained an enigma to him. A terrorist who wanted to show some compassion towards his son but refused to let him into his world. The sun was moving lower in the sky, changing the reflective light on the surface of the water. Photographers were bustling for vantage spots where they could capture their moment against the iconic landscape of the world's capital city as the sun began to set.

Amira was sitting on a bench in front of the Tate Modern, a few feet from where they met after Masood's funeral. Richard had not arranged to meet but somehow expected her to be there.

'Have you been waiting long?' he said.

Amira turned and gestured to him to sit down. 'Rowena contacted me and said you were walking.'

'Oh…you're friends now, are you?'

Amira smiled, looking a little embarrassed by her admission. 'I wouldn't go as far as saying that.'

Richard sat down and turned to face Amira. 'You know, I still don't understand who you are. You are a contradiction. A gentle woman, beautiful, with a certain holy quality that I can't put my finger on. Something that makes me want to believe in God. But you claim to be a trained CIA appointed killer. The idea you would kill my father in cold blood like some ruthless hitman just doesn't wash with me.'

Amira looked down to the floor and closed her eyes, as if she was trying to remember something from her past. After a few moments of contemplation, she opened her eyes again and began to speak. 'When I first meet Masood in Cairo, I was a low-key CIA agent. I wasn't spying on my country so my conscience was clear. My job was to infiltrate organisations that might have links to terrorism. Masood was at one of those meetings and we talked briefly. When I met him again at the time my family were blown up, I told my station chief who encouraged me to cultivate the friendship. It was only later that I fell in love with him. The contract on your father was something I thought I could do but, you're right, I'm not a killer. I had the opportunity but didn't take it. There is a reason for that.'

'Tell me.' said Richard.

'Masood and myself met your father in 1999. We were visiting Cyprus and wanted to find out more about St Barnabas who appears on Masood's icon. We went to the St Barnabas Monastery and Museum in Famagusta. We saw your father studying documents in the museum. He was very interested in the rift that was known to have developed between Paul and Barnabas. Masood showed him the icon and he was fascinated that it might date back to the first century. It was further proof that the sixteenth-century forgery of St Barnabas' Gospel is a red herring. Barnabas *really* did write a Gospel, which is proven by Masood's icon. The discovery of the scroll in Crete provides further evidence.' Amira stopped talking and took hold of Richard's hand. 'When Masood entrusted the icon to you, Richard, he was respecting your father's interest. I think Masood kept in touch with your father. They became friends. How could I kill a man who was the friend of my husband?'

'But my father is still out there and has the scroll and seems intent on causing damage.'

'It's true, he killed people to survive. He needs help, Richard. And you are the only person to provide that help.'

'And what about you? Where will you go?'

'Now that Abdul is dead my family can rest in peace and I can leave the CIA and try and rebuild my life without Masood.' Amira stood up and kissed Richard on the cheek. 'Take care, Richard. Find your father.'

'I've been instructed to eliminate him and destroy the scroll. I don't want to do either.'

Amira looked once more into Richard's eyes. 'That is a question only you can answer.' She turned and walked away from him.

He wanted to follow but he knew that this time he could not.

Chapter Sixty-Four

London, UK. Four days later

A torrential shower washed the streets of Clapham where Becky had her flat. He had less than a mile to go, but his clothes were drenched, forcing him to shelter under a bus stop canopy on Lavender Hill. He watched his face reflected, like some smudged watercolour, as the rain lashed against the glass. The thunder grew louder until it reached a crescendo overhead, then leaving the minute it arrived, the sound getting fainter as the storm moved away. The pavements glistened as the rain began to ease and the sun emerged from behind the clearing clouds. A new beginning, pavements wiped clean along the polluted streets. Richard wondered whether he could ever start again while his father remained a wanted man. He'd put off seeing Becky for too long, worried that he could not look her in the eye and tell her his demons had been slain.

Rowena had answered questions, but the doubt remained. A doubt which melted, at least on the surface, when he saw Becky's face. She'd been crying, mascara streaks were running down her cheeks. Becky stared at Richard, who was soaked to the skin, a palpable sense of surprise frozen on her face. He felt pathetic in his wet clothes, like some recalcitrant dog returning with his tail between his legs.

'Oh my God…Richard,' she screamed. 'Where have you been?' She threw her arms round him and sobbed. 'I've been so worried that you might never come back.'

Richard smiled, hugging her tightly, enjoying the warmth of her body and the familiar scent of her perfume. 'I've missed you.'

Becky stepped back, laughing. 'Come in and get warm. You looked like a drowned rat.'

They stood in the hallway and continued to look at each other. Richard allowed his eyes to drift down towards Becky's belly. 'Is everything okay?' Richard said, emitting a sheepish smile.

Becky noticed him looking and smiled back. 'I'm fine,' she said. 'My baby's fine. It's you I'm worried about.'

'Me,' Richard exclaimed. 'Why should you worry about me?'

'It's not over, Richard, is it?'

'What's not over? I don't know what you're talking about?'

'Get out of those wet clothes and we'll talk about it. Your dressing gown is still hanging up behind the bedroom door. Put the wet clothes in the airing cupboard.'

Richard found the cosy domesticity of Becky's instructions to be comforting. Normal life seemed more desirable than it had done before all this had started. He found the dressing gown and joined Becky in her sitting room.

'So what's all this about? What do you mean, it's not over?' Richard said.

Becky shook her head, wagging her index finger. 'Don't lie to me Richard…I know your father is alive.'

It was Richard's turn to be surprised. 'You what…how do you know?'

'He telephoned me about six days ago. He said you were in great danger.'

Richard said nothing at first. In his mind, he balked at the idea that his father could speak to his girlfriend but instinct told him it was true. 'How could you be sure it was him? You've never heard his voice.'

Becky glared at Richard. 'Of course I thought about that…I told him he was dead, killed in New York…Then he said something that made me sure he wasn't lying.'

'What did he say?'

'He said he was pleased that I was carrying your baby. No one knows this except the doctor who confirmed my pregnancy and you.'

Richard's jaw muscles clenched. Initial astonishment turned to anger. 'How could he know that?'

'That wasn't all. He said you had a heart-shaped birthmark about two inches to the right of your belly button.'

So, it was him, Richard thought. He felt a part of him had been taken away. His inner most secrets were supposed to be something he could keep from his father but now even that privacy had gone. 'Okay, so he knows everything about me but refuses to be part of my life,' he replied, unable to hide his anger. 'What does he want from me?'

Becky's face turned serious. She stared at him and took hold of his hands. Richard remembered Amira doing the same thing and wondered which felt better, more secure, more loving. He didn't know. His emotional intelligence had been locked away since the killing of Abdul. He waited for her to speak.

'He told me to tell you to leave the spying game, to marry me and be a father to our baby unlike he was to you. He told me he regretted the way he treated you, but now he is in a mire that he can't escape until he is dead.'

'I can't do that.' Richard spoke quietly. 'I love you, Becky, but I've got to find my father.'

Becky stood up immediately and pointed to the door. 'Get dressed and go.'

He tried to protest but Becky was too upset to listen. Tears were streaming down her face. 'I can't go through my life wondering whether you are alive or not,' she said.

475

'Your father's advice should be heeded. You need to put the past behind you and do something else. Leave the service and be a father and a husband. Is that too much to ask?'

Richard said nothing. He went upstairs and slipped into his damp clothes. He knew Becky was right but he couldn't make what had happened between him and his father go away. Before he left, he looked in at Becky once more. She was standing, staring at the rain splashing against the windows. He approached her and put his arms round her waist. She swung round and reciprocated, hugging him close. It was as if she understood but could not bring herself to sanction what he was doing.

'I will always love you Becky and maybe one day I'll be able to follow my father's advice,' he said, his voice faltering with emotion. 'If you will still have me,' he added. She said nothing and for several minutes they just held each other in silence. He didn't want it to end but when she let go and turned back to the window, Richard knew it was time.

He had to find his father, not because of his MI6 orders, but for the good reputation of his family. He had to do this for his grandfather and for his child. He had to do it for his mother. What would his mother say if he told her that his father was alive and the world's most wanted man? His father was an aberration. A tumour in his soul that he needed to cut out.

Only then would he be free.

THE END

The story continues:

THE BARNABAS LEGACY is coming soon.

If you want to know when the second book in the series will be out. Please sign up to my mailing list on jonathanmarkwriter.com. My website also carries background discussions on the various themes and historical context of *The Last Messenger*. I am also happy to answer any questions if you wish to contact me through my website.

If you enjoyed the book and feel inclined to write a positive review on Amazon, please contact me and I will send you a free copy of *The Barnabas Legacy* as soon as it is available.

Jonathanmarkwriter.com
@jonmark1956